Fletcher and the Great Raid

Also by John Drake

Fletcher

and the Great Raid

JOHN DRAKE

LUME BOOKS

LUME BOOKS

This edition published in 2021 by Lume Books
30 Great Guildford Street,
Borough, SE1 0HS

ISBN 978-1-83901-372-0

Typeset using Atomik ePublisher from Easypress Technologies

www.lumebooks.co.uk

In fond memory of
David Burkhill Howarth

----------- DBH -----------

1946 – 2009

PATRIFAMILIAS AMATISSIMO
MAGISTRO DOCTISSIMO
INGENIOSISSIMO TECHNITAE
OPTIMO AMICO

Introduction

Fletcher and the Great Raid is the fourth book of Jacob Fletcher's memoirs, following Fletcher's Fortune, Fletcher's Glorious 1st of June and Fletcher and the Mutineers. Readers may therefore be familiar with the notorious Admiral Sir Jacob Fletcher (1777-1877) who differs from all other heroes of Nelson's Navy in that he was press-ganged into it, struggled to get out of it, and never wanted to be a naval officer at all because his heart's desire was to go ashore and make his fortune in trade, being the illegitimate son of billionaire industrialist, the late Sir Henry Coignwood, who left Fletcher his entire fortune which Fletcher lost to Lady Sarah Coignwood, Sir Henry's evil wife.

Also, on his arrival on board of the brig-sloop *Serpant* in January 1796 – when this book begins - Fletcher was under the domination King George III's cousin, Lord Richard Howe, Admiral of The Fleet, who in Naval matters walked on water, raised the dead and made the blind to see. Lord Howe could never, never forgive Fletcher for sinking HMS *Calipheme* with a submarine mine (See Fletcher and the Mutineers) but Howe admired Fletcher as a seaman and wanted him for the Navy whether Fletcher liked it or not.

As regards the format of this work, it is mainly Fletcher's own words as dictated in the 1870s to his reluctant clerk Samuel (later the Rev. Dr) Petit, celebrated author of Darwin's *Errors Revealed*, Scripture's *Triumph Over Simianism* and other works now enjoyed for their unintentional hilarity.

Petit was forced to record Fletcher's words in Pitman shorthand, bellowed into his face by the old Admiral who famously promised to gut *and* fillet Petit if he did not record every word and syllable. This Petit did, transcribing the result into twenty-five, leather-bound volumes, the first twelve in beautiful handwriting and the rest via a Sholes and Giddon typewriter imported from America. Then, after Fletcher's death, Petit found courage to insert chastising footnotes into the volumes and these I have represented:

[inside square brackets, signed by Petit's initials, S.P.]

Also, based on my archive of Fletcher papers I have extemporised a prologue, plus chapters describing other relevant events, occasionally including entire transcripts of letters where these give such viewpoints in words better than mine.

Finally, readers of the magnificent, heroic, incomparable and splendid C.S. Forester will recognise an astonishing similarity between Fletcher's examination for Lieutenant as reported by Fletcher, and Mr Midshipman Hornblower's examination for Lieutenant as reported by Forester, but I am quite unable to explain this.

John Drake, Cheshire, England, 2016

Prologue

'It is proven fact that many British intellectuals are seduced by the ideals of the French revolution. A hundred thousand of them met recently in Islington Fields, London, and it is just such traitors as these that have burned down our West Block.'
(From a letter of Friday 14th September, 1795 from James Watt, engineer, to his business partner Matthew Boulton at 48 Thames Road, Westminster, London.)

*

The heavy, open-top farm waggon was packed with men. Some had crowbars and axes, but most had guns and pistols. Its two big horses were hauling at the gallop, straight towards the watchman standing in the entrance to Boulton and Watt's Soho foundry, who raised a feeble hand to stop the onrush.

'Go*on! Go* on!' yelled the cart's driver. He laid on hard with the whip, and iron-shod hooves struck sparks off the cobbles while iron tyres roared as the vehicle charged straight between the pillars and pediment of the foundry gates, and the watchman dived aside, and the men aboard cheered, while their leader – on the box beside the driver – yelled into his ear, telling him where to go.

The watchman got up, brushing dust, and saw the waggon go tearing down the main yard, skid shrieking around a sharp bend and disappear into the depths of the biggest and most modern manufactory of steam engines in the entire world.

At the same moment, in his personal sanctuary as he called it, up on the fourth floor of the West Block, James Watt: inventor, engineer, multi-millionaire and half-owner of this enormous enterprise, looked up from his papers at the sound of hoof-beats and rumbling cart wheels somewhere below, coming on at inordinate speed. He frowned. How could that be? Traffic within the foundry moved at a steady pace. And why not? There was no cause for speed. He blinked and looked round to reassure himself that all was as it should be, and a dozen of his men looked back and smiled.

Watt smiled too, and why not? This was his favourite place in the foundry: a roof-top office and experimental work-shop all in one, running side-to-side and back-to-front of the entire block: a rectangle sixty yards by thirty, lit by glazed lights in the roof to give an illumination that an artist would envy for his studio. There were tables and easels for draftsmen, with papers, ink, pencils, rulers, and water-colour sets. There were dividing engines, precision-lathes, vernier scales, micrometers, rivets, nails, screws, anvils and hearths. All that, plus cast iron stoves against the winter, and a ready store of steel, copper and brass, waiting to be translated into whatever next wonder of mechanism came out of the combined genius of James Watt and his men. Because this was the team that had turned the steam engine from a cranky novelty to the pounding heart of the coal-and-iron industries now transforming Britain from agriculture into something utterly new.

But then Watt heard the waggon grinding to a halt and men shouting: actually shouting! Watt frowned. There was never a need for shouting. Things were done decently at Soho, with proper respect between master and man. But then there was a crashing from below, and a rumble of feet on stairs, and frighteningly soon the doors to this top-floor office were thrown open, and a crowd of young men poured in: well-dressed and seemingly respectable but each one bearing a weapon. They charged in, grim and silent, behind a leader who was far from silent.

'You there!' he cried to Watt's draftsmen and machinists, 'all of you over there, by that back wall! All of you over there and you'll come to no harm!' then he turned to his own men: 'See to it! Get 'em moving!' and Watt gasped and raised hand to mouth, and stood up out of his chair as his men were driven like sheep under the deadly threat of firearms. He soon had more to worry about, because the leader of the intruders came straight up to him.

'Mr Watt!' he said, 'I've things to say and things to show!'

'McCloud!' said Watt, 'Donald McCloud! What are you doing here? Why are you not in Cornwall in my service?'

'Traitor!' said the other, 'Deceiver and thief!' and Watt said nothing because he guessed the meaning of these insults and was stabbed with guilt. So he kept quiet, knowing that he'd been found out in a sin he'd thought buried. He knew this because the two men shared much history, and for his part McCloud saw the guilt on Watt's face. 'Oh yes,' said McCloud, stepping forward, 'I know you now, sir, I know you indeed.'

They looked at each other. Both were Scots, both were engineers. Watt was in his fifties, with grey hair combed back off his brow, and worked into side curls. But his eyebrows were black, and he had a worried expression on his face. McCloud was younger and taller: aged thirty-five, muscular and fierce with a large chin and heavy fists.

'Huh!' said McCloud, 'Now, see what I've got here, Mr James Watt,' and he turned to one of his followers, a man remarkably like himself with two others beside him whose features said that they were brothers. 'Jamie!' said McCloud, 'Give me the satchel!' The brother came forward and handed over a leather document bag. Donald McCloud took it and swept all the papers off James Watt's desk with deliberate contempt. Watt gasped. McCloud sneered, dived a hand into the satchel and pulled out a document lavishly illustrated with coloured diagrams. He laid it flat on Watt's empty desk

'Here, sir!' said McCloud, 'Look here!' Watt cringed but McCloud grabbed him and pulled him forward then pushed his head down so that Watt was compelled to study the document. With his free hand McCloud stabbed a finger.

'D'you see, sir?' he said. 'This is a copy of your patent of August twenty-fourth, 1784, and here is Item Seven, sneaked in at the end, where you specify a claim on,' he quoted by heart, 'steam engines which are applied to give motion to wheeled carriages.' He glared at Watt, 'You villain, sir! Do you not recall how we wrote to you with our proposal for road engines, having drawn detailed plans and made actual working models? And how you sent your partner Mr Boulton to dissuade us from taking patent on the idea?' McCloud paused, stepped close to Watt and – to growls of anger from Watt's people – shoved the flat of his hand into Watt's chest, causing him to stagger back. 'And so,' said McCloud, 'trusting you, we took no patent. But you did, sir! You treacherously took out your own patent on our idea!'

'Now, now, Donald McCloud,' said Watt, stumbling with his words, 'I…I… took out…ah..many patents in those…ah…years. Many ideas I was playing with…and… and, you were most generously employed, and at excellent wages in compensation. You were, and are, the finest team of engine-builders in the kingdom. My own team in my own employ!' But Jamie McCloud stepped forward.

'Donald. He betrayed us. He stopped us building the road engines which would have made our fortunes! He did it by falsehood and kept his patent secret to be held against us, and we've only just found out, and found out only by chance.'

'No!' said Watt, 'You misunderstand! I warned you off the road engine because the whole idea is dangerous, needing strong steam – high-pressure steam – in the cylinders which could burst and kill all aboard the machine.'

'Then why did you patent the idea of strong steam?' said Donald McCloud and grabbed Watt again, forcing him to stare at the patent document, 'See here?' said McCloud, 'It says: strong*steam* to*drive* the pistons. So why take patent if you weren't going to use the idea?'

'Ah! Ah!' said Watt, 'That is…I mean…That is…,'

'Show him the other one, Donald,' said Jamie McCloud, 'The Declaration!'

'Bring it!' said Donald McCloud, 'Put it here!'

Jamie McCloud took a large, coloured print from the satchel and laid it on top of the patent papers. Watt stared at it. it was a parody of the ten commandments showing gold letters on black stone, with an angel figure on one side and a woman breaking chains on the other. It was in French and was obviously some product of the enormous struggle now taking place across the Channel. Watt knew enough French to translate the words over the stone slabs. They said: Declaration of the Rights of Man and of the Citizen. But what first caught Watt's eye was a certain symbol at the very top of the document.

'Ahhh!' said McCloud noting where Watt was looking, 'We'll come to that later. But first, Mr James Watt, are you aware of the golden age that is dawning over France?' Watt said nothing. McCloud continued. 'The liberty, equality and brotherhood? It is a revolution of thought! It changes everything!' he paused. 'So what do those ideals remind you of, brother Watt of The Glasgow Lodge? Or did you not notice this?'

McCloud's finger moved to the symbol of a human eye in a triangle radiating beams of light. It was a key emblem of Freemasonary, and James Watt was a Freemason as were McCloud and his men. But Watt shook his head.

'I don't know,' he said, 'I've not been in The Craft for years.'

'Well we have, brother Watt!' said McCloud, and our lodge is also a Revolutionary Corresponding Society in contact with friends in the new France.' McCloud turned to everyone in the room. He was intoxicated with an idea: one of those mighty ideas which persuade decent men that inhuman actions are justified for the greater good of humanity.

'Let us be brothers!' said McCloud to Watt, 'I appeal to you in the name of the Masonic Craft. I ask that you should make right your theft of our ideas, by bringing myself into full partnership, and entirely devoting the profits of this enterprise to the uplifting of mankind according to the new world order that is coming forward!'

'Aye!' said McCloud's brothers.

'Aye!' said all the rest that had come with them, and who were standing with their guns, hammers and axes.

'Conversely, if you will not do this,' said McCloud, 'then you become the enemy of mankind and a traitor to The Craft, causing me to take my ideas to another place, and God's curse on your patents because I shall ignore them!' he shook Watt forcibly and ranted on, enwrapped in the righteousness of his cause, 'But first,' he yelled, 'I shall smash this place, and make fire of all your machines and plans!'

This brought a roar from Watt's men. They were not members of any damned Corresponding Society! They despised revolutionary claptrap! They were patriotic Englishmen and the elite of James Watt's service: loyal to him, proud of their work, and contemptuous of allegations made against him – shamefully and outrageously – here on his own home ground by violent intruders. So they surged forward cursing and yelling, and were cursed and shoved in return by McCloud's men. Then punches were thrown, collars seized and shins kicked, until a Watt machinist – stung by a blow – retaliated with a heavy spanner, smashing a rival's skull with lethal force.

Watt did his utmost to prevent anything worse. He called on his people to fall back. But it was too late and there was total combat with gunfire and powder smoke, and men struck down and trampled.

And that was only the beginning.

Chapter 1

I'd not been aboard the brig-sloop *Serpant* a month before I was summoned for my examination for Lieutenant, and though it was mid-winter it was a splendid day for a splendid event which I was greatly looking forward to, as my best chance to get myself out of King George's bloody navy.

The sky was clear, the sea was kind and the busy seagulls ducked and squawked as they fought over all the shite and corruption that a fleet-full of jolly sailormen heaves over the side each day by the bucket-load, as tribute to Father Neptune. Thus *Serpant* was safe anchored off Spithead, between Portsmouth and the Isle of Wight, as was the entire Channel Fleet in great, black-and white rows of monster line-of-battleships, with masts like a forest and a spider-web of tarred rigging against the sky.

Aboard *Serpant* all was sharp and proper with white decks, neat-coiled lines and gleaming brass where once slackness and filth had prevailed, and I was merry as could be while Mr Douglas the Bosun and his crew stood to attention, awaiting my orders. So I let them stand a while, and I scowled for the fun of it, to make the lubbers cringe as I paced up and down with heavy tread, for I was a very big man in those days and all my weight was muscle. Unfortunately that meant I was a quart in a pint pot as far as clothing was concerned. Thanks to his almighty-ness, Lord 'Black Dick' Howe, Admiral of the Fleet, I did actually have a uniform coat, with cocked hat, and a miserable little toy of a midshipman's dirk at my side, but it was all too small, and all the cloth was old and worn: Black Dick's further punishment, I suppose. In addition I had a bundle of papers under my arm, likewise provided by Black Dick for his own black purposes.

'Mr Douglas!' says I, at last.

'Aye-Aye, Mr Fletcher, Sir!' says he and didn't he just jump? Him and all the rest of them, because I'd had them three weeks now and they knew me well. By George they did an' all! They jumped when I said jump and strained to be the one who jumped highest.

'Sway out the launch, and be damned quick about it!' says I and the hands set to at the double, heaving mightily to rouse *Serpant's* launch out of its midships berth, with a tackle and block made fast to the main-stay.

'Heave-ho! Heave-ho!' they cried like good boys under the schoolmaster, and up shot the launch, and out she swung over the side, and 'Heave-ho!' they cried again, all eager and keen, and why indeed should they not be keen, because they knew what they'd get if they weren't.

*

Here, I pause to take opportunity to give you youngsters the benefit of your Uncle Jacob's experience, just as I have done before in these memoirs. Thus I exhort you most emphatically that if ever you take command of a ship of war, or a merchantman or anything else that floats, then be sure on first coming aboard to seek out the ship's bully boys and give them a hearty thrashing on the spot. It's the kind thing to do and the gentle thing since it avoids the use of the cat, or stopped grog, or any other kind of punishment, none of which in all my career have I ever needed to use. You just ask any man that served under me.

*

Soon I was going down into the launch, and the Bosun piping the side, and six men sat with tossed oars, straight backs and staring rigidly astern. The coxswain was at the tiller, and all of them wore the boat's-crew costume that I'd insisted upon for smartness: tarred hats, red neckers, blue jackets, clean slops, and shoes and striped stockings, all delivered up by *Serpant's* purser at no cost to the men, out of the Purser's Christian charity and my hand twisting the scruff of his neck.

'Oh, yes!' says I, to myself, for they looked smart and all hands were proud of them, and the slovenly tub that *Serpant* had once been had never dreamed of such a boat's crew. This, because her captain was one Captain Cuthbert Percival-Clive, who I'd served alongside of in *Phiandra*, frigate, when he was a midshipman and myself a foremast hand. Poxy-Percy, as he was known, was a blockhead, no-seaman but his father was a West India sugar-millionaire and his mother was William Pitt's sister: that's Billy Pitt the Prime Minister. Thus young Percy, who was only two years older than me, had been hauled up the greasy pole of promotion and given command of a ship he had neither the interest nor competence to master, and was now wallowing ashore in a hotel, and don't tell me it's an hotel, because it bloody-well ain't!

[Note Fletcher's intemperate and ignorant response to any attempt of mine to correct his grammar, let alone his gross profanity and obscenity. S.P.]

So: there were no officers in *Serpant* when I came aboard, despite the fact that a Brig-Sloop like her, was a substantial vessel embarking one hundred and twenty men. Thus *Serpant* should have been under the hand of two Lieutenants and a sailing master. But Poxy-Percy had brought along his own nest of creepy-crawlies who were snug ashore like himself, doubtless warming their backsides to a roaring fire, while swilling brandy and damning the French in manly voices for the benefit of the chamber maids in the hope of getting them into bed. So that left me: Mr Midshipman Fletcher, nineteen years old and driven by circumstances into a Sea-Service I'd done every conceivable thing to get out of.

But now I smiled as my boat's crew pulled for His Majesty's Ship *Neptune* of one hundred guns, where a board of three post-captains would convene this Monday, February 1st 1796 at two bells of the Forenoon Watch, in order that postulant midshipmen might be put to the torture of an oral examination for the rank of Lieutenant. This process would either send them back in shame to seek greater wisdom, or gloriously enter them among the select who would receive His Majesty's commission: the first step up the ladder and - exceeding all else - the King's own formal recognition that the fortunate ones were GENTLEMEN. They were no longer such lowly wretches as the vulgar herd of mankind, which is all very nice and proper. But unfortunately, neither could a gentleman officer be a trading, enterprising, manufacturing men of business such as I longed to become. So it was Black Dick Howe's punishment upon me for my wicked sins that I was facing the examination for Lieutenant.

So: he thought he'd got me in his fist, did Black Dick, but I smiled as we closed on Neptune because I'd found a way out, and that was why I was so happy. That and the fact that for weeks I'd been my own man, in charge of my own ship, and free to make the world run just as I wanted: my own little world aboard *Serpant*. So as far as I was concerned, Lord Howe could hold his nose and take a running jump down the privy, because I'd found the way out of the Navy. It wasn't a neat way or a sure way, but it was a way, and that was enough for me.

But then I was out of my thoughts because there was a lot of bumping and creaking as our launch came alongside of *Neptune*, with boats from other ships bringing mids in full dress with their papers under their arms.

'Aye-aye!' yelled most of the coxwains, looking up at the officer of the watch who peered upon us miserable minnows from the companionway at the top

16

of a neat-rigged set of steps, and he sneered because the coxswains' Aye-ayes signalled that nobody of any importance was seeking to come aboard. So there was a bit of scrambling, and skinny young mids made their way up on thin legs, with hands to their hats, and I was about to go aboard myself when another boat came clanking up and its coxswain gave a mighty roar.

'Actimodes!' he cried, and I turned to see a boat's crew fabulously kitted out in scarlet jackets, and white wigs and gloves, for in those days a boat's crew wore whatever the captain fancied, and you saw everything from clowns to harlequins at the oars. At once, all else fell back, since the giving of a ship's name - in this case that of another first-rate - signalled that one of the mighty ones was in the boat, and Bosun's calls screeched as the man himself, an admiral in fact, went up the steps glittering in gold lace, with bullions on his shoulders and the star of the Bath on his breast. I soon learned that he was Lord Illingworth, an inner member of Lord Howe's circle.

Soon after it was my turn up the steps, and I lifted my hat to the quarterdeck, and the officer of the watch waved me on into the hands of a tall, sharp-faced civilian in beautiful clothes, fitted like a fine woollen skin by one of Saville Row's finest. He leaned heavily on a stick, he behaved as if he owned the ship, and he looked me up and down like a farmer buying a pig and I got the feeling that he knew me without being told.

He was quite a man: something special. It hit you as you looked at him. He was old and shrivelled, with scars on his face, a painful look about him, and the finger-tips gone from his right hand. But I wager he'd been a handsome fellow when young: something near my own height, but not so heavy. I'd go further and say he'd been one for the ladies to flutter their pretty eyes at. And as for the gentlemen they'd have given him respect because he had the charisma that great actors have, and great commanders, too. Nelson had it by the ship-load, but he was a mystic. So I'd put this particular beauty alongside the Duke of Wellington, as a more practical, damn-your-eyes man who got things done by booting the laggards right up where they needed it: a man like myself, in fact.

['Vanity of vanities, all is vanity.' Ecclesiastes, 1: 2. S.P.]

'Huh!' says he, and I do believe he was guessing my thoughts, because he nodded as if accepting a salute, and then he waved me on to where a group of little mids were gulping and attempting last-minute revision out of crib-sheets, and being told by a Captain of Marines to take station outside the Master's day cabin at the break of the quarterdeck, while the tall, elderly civilian strolled at his ease, even on the quarterdeck of a King's ship, and all the world deferred to him.

And there I stood and waited, as the ship's bell sounded the half hours, and the ship's routine went on, and not a minute of it was boring, not with so much to see on this giant ship, with drills and exercises to keep the men active even at anchor, and the whole busy life of a crew near eight hundred strong which was so many men that if you sailed with them, there were many you'd never even meet.

Meanwhile, great guns were secured in rows on the maindeck, and masts and yards rose thick and tremendous, and the rails were lined with rolled hammocks in nettings, and marines drilled on the quarterdeck. Then, one by one, the little mids were called below, and some came out in tears and others sprang forth in joy, and boasted of their experience:

'Rhumb lines!' said the first of the beaming faces. 'They began by asking me to define a rhumb line!' and all the rest dived into their notes to find out what that might mean. They were mostly boys and they were all tiny beside me, so I looked down on the little squirts, because a rhumb line runs straight out from any point of a naval chart compass except from the four cardinal points. Anyone knows that, or ought to know it, but some of these cherubs didn't. Not that that would stand in the way if their daddies wielded influence. That's why Poxy-Percy was a Captain at twenty while James Cook of Australia - the finest seaman God ever made - didn't make Captain until he was forty-seven because Cook joined from the merchant service and his daddy was a farmer.

But then the civilian came and took my eye. He stared at me like, with eyes like cannon mouths.

'Fletcher,' he said, 'Jacob Fletcher of Polmouth in Cornwall.' It was a statement not a question. 'You will follow me.' So off we went, down a companionway to the great cabins at the stern, past marine sentries with muskets and red coats and black hats and polished boots. These made pretence of challenging the civilian who dismissed them with a wave of the hand, and then we were inside the cabin, with three officers sitting at a huge table with chairs all around it and the light behind them from the stern windows, and elaborate furnishings of carpets and candelabras, and pictures and side-tables and vases with fresh flowers. It was more like a lady's salon than a cabin. But that's how some captains liked things in those days.

Meanwhile my eyes had to adjust to the light, before I could properly see the men behind the table. The one in the centre was the admiral who'd come aboard just before me.

'Gentlemen, I bring you Fletcher,' said the civilian and sat himself down beside the three officers, clearly perceiving himself as their equal and accepted as such by them.

'You will sit there, Fletcher,' said the admiral, and pointed to a chair on my side of the table, before turning to the civilian. 'Might I ask you to make the introductions, Mr Rowland?' So that was his name: Rowland.

'Yes my lord,' said Rowland, and turned to me. 'Fletcher,' he said, 'You are to be examined by Admiral of the Blue, Sir Daniel, Lord Illingworth, of Actimodes.' And that was it. Neither of the of two captains were introduced, or even spoke as far as I remember, nor was any explanation given as to why a Rowland – a civilian- sat beside sea officers during an examination for naval rank.

But never mind them, because Admiral Lord Illingworth was speaking, and he was a typical specimen of the went-to-sea-as-a-baby, Sea Service officer who knew his craft inside out, was laden with mighty prejudice, and was entirely without patience of any kind.

'Fletcher?' says he, 'Your certificates!'

So I shoved him the bundle of papers I'd brought with me, as provided by Black Dick's minions. These were the certificates that proved I had served the minimum legal requirement for promotion to Lieutenant, which is to say that I had served six years at sea (which indeed I had not) and had served two years as a midshipman (which indeed I had not) and that furthermore I was a man of sobriety, diligence, and proven ability as a seaman (which indeed I was, although the ships' captains who'd signed these certificates had never even met me). Any midshipman up for the Lieutenant's exam had to produce such certificates, and usually they were genuine, though in some cases they were not, and certainly not when someone like Poxy-Percy was being greased through the process. Indeed, it was common to certify a candidate as having had sea time before he was even born, if his father was a prestigious officer.

Illingworth took the documents, untied the ribbon that bound them, and studied them carefully, though he must have known they were rot because his every breath and gesture proclaimed that he'd been fed the whole iniquitous story of my life, as that story was understood by Lord Howe. So he didn't like me, didn't Illingworth. Not him nor neither of the other two captains sat there in judgement upon me: not them, my jolly boys: not one bit! And then Illingworth- who clearly looked down on me as a villain - nodded and pushed the papers back to me, conniving that their lies were truth: or so I thought. Then he leaned forward and lifted his voice in fierce aggression.

'You are close hauled on the port tack, Mr Fletcher, beating up channel with a north-easterly wind blowing hard, with Dover bearing north two miles. Is that clear?'

'Aye-aye, m'Lord,' says I.

'Now the wind veers four points and takes you flat aback! What do you do, sir? What do you do?'

The technique is to strike terror, you see, and if ever it's done to you youngsters, just remember that any answer at all is better than none. What they're trying to do is frighten you into silence. They want to make you quake and show you're unfit for command, and there's good sense in it too, because if ever you are in command of a ship then you really will have to deal with terror and hideous surprises. So that's what his Lordship was at, but it didn't work. Not on me it didn't. Not for a second. It didn't work because I was waiting for it, and my moment had come. It was the moment when I was going to turn the game upside down. I'd rehearsed some answers in advance and I knew exactly the sort of thing I was going to say. But I paused too long, relishing the moment.

'Come, sir!' cried Illingworth, slamming his hand on the table, 'What do you do, sir? Before you're dis-masted? What do you do?' And in my mind I answered him.

'Why, m'Lord, I'd piss my britches and call for Mamma to save me. And if that failed I'd summon the chaplain and call the hands to prayer or I'd order abandon ship and lead the rush. Or better still, I'd issue double grog so's we'd all die happy!' It was a seminal moment in my life because I could easily have said it. Indeed I very nearly did, and yet I didn't, because this is what I said instead:

'I'd wear ship, m'Lord. If I was in *Serpant* with head-sails set, I'd strike all other canvas and put up the helm to heave her bow through the wind. Then I'd bring her fully about on to a safe course, under easy sail, and always wary of the Goodwin sands to the north.'

'Well stap my precious liver!' said Illingworth, 'Well enough, Mr Fletcher. Well enough!' and he actually laughed. But then he asked a lot more seafaring questions and every time I answered him back, and it wasn't even hard because I wasn't a fluffy duckling like the mids outside. I'd faced death and disaster, shot and shell, and the sea coming solid green over the bow to sweep the decks and snap the masts. So I answered like a seaman when I could have acted the fool and got myself out of the Navy. After all, Black Dick wanted me as a officer for the good of his precious Service, did he not? So maybe he'd have given up if I proved a fool? But I didn't prove the fool, and who knows why? Because I certainly don't.

[Fletcher's words in this passage are an insight into the profound dichotomy of his personality, because despite his constant affectation of disdain for his own seamanship, he was proud of it and in all truth he loved the Navy dearly, though never in his entire life would he admit it. As in much else, he was a fraud in this matter. S.P.]

Then finally Illingworth was done. He leaned back, nodded to himself, and looked left and right.

'Gentlemen?' says he, and the two post captains nodded curtly. Neither of them smiled or even looked at me. They were Lord Howe's creatures, the pair of them, and determined not to like me. But they nodded. 'And Mr Rowland?' said Illingworth.

'I am satisfied if you are, my Lord,' says he, 'since, in seafaring matters, I have no opinion worthy of bringing to your Lordship's notice.'

'But are you satisfied, Mr Rowland?'

'I am satisfied, my Lord.'

'So!' says Illingworth, 'Then I shall leave you to complete your business, Mr Rowland.' So I stood as Illingworth did, and then he shook my hand as he passed, and the captains did too, though they all seemed to have a bad smell under their noses and out they went and the cabin door closed after them.

'Sit down, Fletcher,' says Rowland, and waved a hand at my chair, 'We're not done, you and I.' So down we sat, and he stared hard at me and spoke, and never a word of explanation of what he had to do with seafaring matters, but straight to practicalities. 'Mr Fletcher,' says he, 'you are as good as Gazetted Lieutenant, and will be provided with all such uniforms, instruments, books, charts and small-arms whatsoever, as are befitting to your rank, plus a sum of money to cover any incidental expenses.'

'Oh,' says I, taken aback.

'Don't gape like a fish!' says he. 'Is that all you've got to say? Just 'Oh'?'

'Oh,' says I, utterly confounded and not knowing what to think, let alone what to say.

'Bah!' says he, 'I am informed that you are a tremendous fine seaman, sir, and that every man says so as has ever sailed with you, and that you are a first class gunner and navigator and a natural leader of men!'

'Oh,' says I.

'God bugger me backwards!' says he, 'If you say oh just once more, Mr Fletcher, I'll break you before ever you're made! So: if you've no better words, just hold your tongue.' Which indeed I did for want of better words. 'Now listen here, Lieutenant Jacob Fletcher,' says he.

'Aye-aye, sir!' says I.

'That's better,' says he and smiled. The first time he'd done that, and as he did, a little oddity prickled at the back of my mind. 'The case is, Mr Fletcher, that I am likewise informed that you are an unprincipled, lying deceiver with a long history of self-serving cunning and the fixed determination not to serve your King and Country in their hour of desperate need. So what do you say to that, sir?' He paused and stared at me, but I'd had time to think by then. So I sat up straight, like Jolly Jack Trueheart outrageously defamed.

'I say that you have been grossly miss-informed, sir,' says I, 'most likely by the deliberate conspiracy of malicious persons acting for hidden reasons!' which wasn't a bad effort in that moment, and this time he laughed out loud.

'Bloody rogue,' says he and the oddity prickled again and this time I knew what it was. I liked him. He had style. He laughed at life. He wasn't one to be deceived with such a bucket of old cod's wallop as I'd just tried to feed him. So I liked him and what's more, I had the strong feeling that he liked me right back.

'Now this time listen carefully, Mr Fletcher,' says he. 'There are certain preparations under way across the Channel,' says he, 'preparations that threaten the safety of England. It is my duty to be expert in such preparations, and to contrive,' he paused for effect, and resumed with emphasis 'to contrive counter-preparations to deal with them.'

With that, any comfort that I'd taken from his friendship went right down the plug-hole with all the merry happiness that had been mine these past weeks: down and down and down. Because never mind the small matter of my failing to get out of the Navy - never mind that - I was about to be dragged in uttermost deep. I could see it coming like the enemy's mastheads over the horizon. I knew it. I feared it. I felt it in my bowels. They weren't going to allow me even the relative peace of being an ordinary sea office: no, not them! My guess was Lord Howe and Mr Rowland – whoever and whatever he was - had picked me out as someone particular, to do something particular, which meant something particularly dangerous. Oh burn and sink me! Oh skin and salt me! Oh damned bloody hell! That was my guess and I was right too, except that it turned out far worse.

Chapter 2

'McCloud and his followers are indispensable and we are lucky to have any of them in France, and if some will not leave home and family then that is no misfortune, because much that McCloud needs can only be made in England by those of his followers who remain there.'
(Translated from a letter of Tuesday 5th January 1796, from Citizen Inspector Claude Bernard, at the Frangnal-sur-Longue Barracks, to Citizen General of Division Napoleon Bonaparte, Hotel D'Echange, Paris.)

*

Citizen Inspector Bernard wore a cloak over well-made civilian clothes artfully contrived to appear proletarian, together with politically-correct long hair and a red cap of liberty bearing the Republican blue-white-red rosette. Citizen Colonel Sauvage wore a greatcoat over his Artillery Blue uniform, with a red-plumed bicorne hat and top-boots. The two men got on well, having met that morning, and spent some hours over an excellent lunch, giving each the opportunity to talk very cautiously, and to listen even more cautiously in these times when the wrong opinion could be fatal. Then finally and with great relief, each had recognised a kindred spirit in the other.

Both were senior men of confident bearing: men in their fifties, who enjoyed their comforts and whose bellies strained at their waistcoats. But more than that, they were both military engineers who'd learned their craft under King Louis (God rest his soul) at the Douai Academy of the Royal Corps of Engineers and Artillery. So they shared a dangerous past, did Bernard and Sauvage, and a dangerous present too, in constant fear of being denounced as counter-revolutionaries. But fortunately they had skills the Revolution needed, and they'd learned to keep their mouths shut and their eyes open.

So now they stood in the cold afternoon in the cobbled square of the walled, Barracks-block, peering at Mr Donald McCloud, who was walking back to his followers. They peered at him, and at the massive complexity nearing completion in the Barracks yard. It was a monster of the future, made of iron and rivets, bricks and mortar, bolts and rods, and beams in massive timber. It gleamed and shone and was a great wonder to the engineering souls of Bernard and Sauvage, who longed to see the monster breathing and heaving.

'Huh!' said Bernard, and nudged Sauvage and grinned. The two shook their heads at the monster in a shared moment of satisfaction, because already they thought of it as their monster. They thought so even though it was the foreigners who'd built it. But they consoled themselves that most of the less specialised parts were French: pillaged from across the Republic, and brought here for this special purpose.

'Watch McCloud!' said Sauvage, 'He'll be back in moment,' and he pointed at the tall man in his thick clothes and a muffler round his neck. He was standing by the train of wagons that had arrived this morning, and were being unloaded by a small group of his countrymen. Of these, three were McCloud's brothers and the rest were men who admired him enough to follow him into France. They had a block and tackle up for the heavy loads, and they worked very well together. They'd been busy all day and Bernard and Sauvage had smiled as they barked in their ugly language, hauling on lines and swaying out the loads. The dragoons had smiled too: those who'd ridden along with the wagons to guard them, and so did the sentries of the 134th Regiment, whose Barracks this was, as they paced their beats, muskets clasped across their breasts in French style.

Now the foreigners were shouting and gabbling again, as foreigners do, and Bernard wondered how it would feel to be so cursed by God as to be unable to speak French? He shook his head in pity. How could anyone bear it?

'What the Mary and Moses are these Englishmen talking about?' said Bernard, and gestured at the tall man, now pointing and chattering at the highly-specialised, imported ironmongery laid out so very neatly on the courtyard cobbles. As an engineer Bernard looked on their works in approval. They were very smart, these English, very proper and precise. But who knew what the Holy Virgin they were saying?'

'Not Englishmen!' said Sauvage, 'Not all of them. The McCloud brothers are Scotsmen, and the Scots fought the English at Culloden in '46, remember? For their Bonnie Prince Charley?'

'Huh!' said Bernard, and gave a French shrug. 'That's nothing to what we're doing to one another in the Vendée!' Then he sniffed, and looked round for eavesdroppers. The civil war in the Vendée was in its third year: Royalist against Revolutionary...a hundred thousand dead...massacres...atrocities...a bad subject, a dangerous subject and he wished he'd never mentioned it. So did Sauvage who instantly changed the subject.

'McCloud is saying what he always says. He says he'll need more special parts from England, because they can't be got here in France!'

'Oof!' said Bernard, his pride struck in a painful spot. 'Aren't these enough?' he pointed at the stacks of newly-arrived metal.

'No,' said Sauvage, and listened again to Donald McCloud, and nodded and turned to Bernard. 'He's saying they need a Ramsden dividing engine, a Watt steam-lathe, some gears and valves, and he says they'll need the best coal that France can provide, to feed the monster when it's working.'

'French coal?' said Bernard, 'I'm surprised he didn't ask for English Newcastle coal!'

'Oh but he did!' said Sauvage. 'He asked for that yesterday!'

'Did he though?' said Bernard and laughed.

'Yes! So I told him there was a limit to what we can bring in by the smugglers.'

'Is there?'

'Yes. The English collier fleet won't trade with us. Not in wartime.'

'Who does then?'

'The fisherman. Theirs and ours, and the Dutch fishermen too, and all the people in the English Channel Islands,' Sauvage spread hands in exasperation, 'These people – these sea-people - they recognise neither frontiers nor laws nor wars. They never have and never will! It's ancient tradition with them. They are fine seamen, they know all the coasts and bays, and they're smugglers as much as they're fisherman. They carry brandy and lace from France to England, cloth and machinery from England to France, and ...,'

'Wait!' said Bernard. 'He's coming!'

Donald McCloud hurried back to the two Frenchmen. He had a question. He stopped and bowed politely to Bernard and Sauvage, and gabbled off words, smiling a bit, trying to be friendly and pointing at the empty wing of the Barracks. Sauvage nodded, but Bernard caught only the first two words.

'Citizen Sauvage...,' said McCloud, then 'gabble-gabble-gabble...' When he was done, he nodded politely and Sauvage gabbled right back at him in an impressive display of English, fortified with Gallic shrugs and expressive hands.

Then the three men went into the empty wing of the Barracks block, which was not empty at all, only empty of soldiers. They stood in the doorway and looked round in the excellent light provided by the excellent windows of this first class piece of French military architecture. Everything was fresh and clean - a high, bright space with a smell of paint and plaster, because the diligent engineers of the 29th Sapeur-Brigade had done a fine job of knocking out walls, putting in props, and building work-benches according to McCloud's design. The 29th had even pierced an outside wall and plugged it with a precise ring of stone, to admit a drive shaft from the engine being built outside, such that belt-driven machine-tools within would be powered by steam according to the very latest English practise. Nor had the efforts of the 29th stopped at builder's work. There were anvils, vices, drills, lathes, tools of every imaginable description, together with a ready store of metals, awaiting the attentions of the craftsman.

But McCloud was speaking again: gabble-gabble-gabble. Sauvage replied with many words, all the time smiling and resting a friendly hand on McCloud's arm, and McCloud beamed in delight. The conversation went on for some time. Finally McCloud grabbed Sauvage's hand and pumped it up and down in the manner of the English.

'Citizen Colonel!' he said to Sauvage, then, 'Citizen!' he said to Bernard, with a faintly blank look, not knowing Bernard or what he represented, but he seized his hand too and shook it. Then a few more words to Sauvage, and he was off, nearly running to get back to his brothers and followers, and Bernard and Sauvage watched him go.

'What the Holy Ghost was that all that about?' said Bernard.

'He said the workshop is ideal, though there is still a need for precision equipment from England. Only the English foundries can make these things. He says he needs more model machines, too.'

'More?' said Bernard, 'And would he like Champagne and a plump young virgin every night?' Sauvage laughed.

'He wants the models to show to our people,' said Sauvage, 'Those he's training, so they can see how the machines function,' Bernard nodded. It made sense, 'And he says that provided we get the dividing engine and the lathe and the rest, then once his men have copied and built the English machine-tools, they will be able to make, here, anything that the English can make!' Bernard frowned.

'But doesn't he realise – this McCloud - that he'll be a traitor to his own people?'

'No, no, no!' said Sauvage, emphatically. 'We're dealing with a true believer! He's swallowed everything. Him and all the rest of them.'

'What do you mean?'

'The revolution, rights of man, equality, liberty, brotherhood: the whole parcel! They really believe it. That's why they're here.'

'True believers?' said Bernard, sadly, 'Are they indeed?' he shook his head, 'God bless my soul!' he said, in all sincerity, and he dared to cross himself in the pious rite now forbidden under the Revolutionary Enlightenment, 'Then may sweet Jesus protect their innocence,' he said, 'and keep them out of the Place de la Révolution when Madame la Guillotine is busy. She's chopped three thousand in Paris alone. Thirty a day sometimes, and tens of thousands if you count the whole of France.' Bernard waved a hand to send away the image, 'Bah!' he said, and came out of his mood and looked at Sauvage, 'So: what do I tell my master in Paris? Him that walks a tightrope over the crocodiles.'

'Is it that bad in Paris?' said Sauvage.

'Yes,' said Bernard, and could not help but look around.

'There's nobody here,' said Sauvage, 'Only us old servants of a dead King.' But he whispered very low as he said that.

'Then listen,' said Bernard. 'It's bad. You never know from one day to the next who's in power.' Bernard looked round again, 'But it's all going to change. The future is Bonaparte.'

'The young general?'

'Yes. I'm his man now. I'm his engineering inspector. I speak in his name on these matters,' he looked round the quiet workshop, 'That's why I'm here. He's a genius, and it's his influence that's caused all this.'

'Is it?' said Sauvage.

'Yes!' Bernard moved closer and looked around yet again. He couldn't help it, because he was used to a world of back-stabbers and informers. 'Did you tell that English-Scottish exactly what we agreed?'

'Yes,' said Sauvage, 'I told him that he and his brothers can make their steam road carriages and be given every support that France can provide, and all profits to go to the public good.'

'You told him that and nothing more?'

'Indeed not!'

'Good!' said Bernard, 'Bonaparte wants McCloud busy making his high pressure steam engines, and teaching us how to make more. So let him put his engines into road carriages if that keeps him happy … because we don't want him upset by knowing what we're really going to do with them.'

Chapter 3

If you've never been aboard a first rate of my young day, then you should understand that there are numerous decks at the stern, which part of the ship you poor unfortunate landmen can easily find by the fact of its being the blunt end. Having found the stern, note that the uppermost deck is the poop deck which is given over to the ship's gentlemen and navigators. Beneath that is the quarterdeck, at the after end of which are the cabins of the captain, the master and the captain's secretary. Proceeding below to the main deck you will find the large and various cabins of his mightiness the Admiral since first rates were typically built as flagships, and it was in one of those cabins where I had been examined for Lieutenant and was about to be treated to the most amazing technical demonstration of my life so far.

But first Rowland got up and looked around, because although we were in the Admiral's day cabin, which spanned the full width of the ship, it wasn't good enough for Illingworth. I could see that in his face as he looked around, passing over all its gaudy decoration, and frowned.

'No room!' says he, of one of the biggest cabins to be found aboard, 'We'll go for'ard.' He looked at me, 'Make shift: Lieutenant!' says he, and I stood up and followed him into the Admiral's dining cabin which was the biggest cabin in that ship or anywhere afloat in those days, being over thirty feet wide and twenty feet long. But even that weren't big enough, as all those within it soon learned.

There were plenty of them too, because while the dining cabin could indeed be rigged for entertaining, with table, chairs and sideboard, just now it was a counting house where the ship's business was done, and it was full of clerks, papers, inkwells, purser's mates, Lieutenants and the marine sentries who guarded the various doors, plus middies to run errands for their masters. All these instantly shot to their feet in respect. But one among them was already standing. He was one of the captains who'd sat beside Illingworth. He turned out to be Neptune's commanding office, Sir James Bancroft, and Rowland addressed him.

'Sir James,' says he, 'I'd be most greatly obliged if you'd strike the bulkheads and clear for action.' He said that to a Post Captain, aboard the ship under his command, and the ship a First Rate! It was unbelievable.

'Clear, Mr Rowland?'

'Clear!' says Rowland. Bancroft was profoundly mystified, profoundly annoyed… and yet…and yet…understanding that he must obey. Obviously he knew more about Mr Rowland than I did, and I wondered profoundly what it might be? Meanwhile:

'As you wish, Mr Rowland,' says Bancroft, finally. 'Both bulkheads?

'No,' says Rowland, 'Strike only those between the cabins.' Bancroft puffed out his cheeks, looked round to assure himself that all present had heard these bizarre orders, then he shrugged and raised his voice.

'Clear!' says he, 'Strike 'tween bulkheads! Stand fast for'ard bulkheads!'

Then there was a great roaring and stamping, and dozens of hands appearing at the double, and papers hauled in and furniture hauled out, and carpets up and pictures down and everything rushed below, and tackles heaved and guns rumbled, and not a vase dropped or a flower bruised, and not a man getting in the way of any other, because that's how it was done in those days, when ships cleared for action against the stopwatch. So in very deed the bulkheads were struck, and all furnishings disappeared, leaving a huge, great, naked space of deck with nothing in it aside from the massive thirty-two pounders, which lived there all the time, three on each side, now run out through the hinged-up gun ports which let in the wet winter breeze and daylight all over the panting gun-teams standing ready to load and fire. For the clerks were long gone with their clutter, and only seamen remained.

'Very creditable, Sir James,' says Rowland, 'Smartly done, Sir!'

'You are most kind, sir,' says Bancroft.

'And now I would be most excessively obliged, Sir James,' says Rowland, 'if you and your people would permit me the private use of these cabins for a brief while.' Captain Bancroft's face was a study in perplexity. But orders were orders and he was bred up to obey them.

'Aye-aye, Mr Rowland,' says he, and he bowed, and turned to his men. 'All hands for'ard!' he cried. So off they all went, and the bulkhead doors closed, and there was I together with Rowland, and nothing else than the bare decks, the guns and tackles, and the miserable grey seascape beyond the gun ports.

'So!' says Rowland, 'Follow me, Mr Fletcher, and give such assistance as your famous strength may permit,' and he led me to the side of the stern windows, where a small door led into one of the privies to be found on either side: a privilege of rank, enabling senior officers to do in private what common hands must do upon the seats of ease wide open to wind and weather in the bows of the ship. Rowland produced a key, unlocked the door, swung it open and stood back.

'You'll find a chest in there,' says he and yes, there was a big, round-topped chest inside; the sort that the gentry carry on their travels, strapped to the stern end of their expensive carriages. 'Set to, Lieutenant!' says Rowland, sharply, 'set to, now!' So I took hold of the chest and hauled it out, and in all fairness to Rowland, he'd never have budged it by himself, because it was damned heavy.

'Over here, Sir!' says he, 'Bring it here!' So I hauled the chest across the deck and dumped it in the middle beside him. Rowland produced another key and unlocked the chest. In fact, he unlocked it three times, there being three locks with three different keys, because somebody didn't want just anybody getting into the chest and it was a big, strong, iron-bound chest at that. By now I was becoming seriously interested. Just what had Rowland got in there? What was it that could only be brought out and displayed in secret? He saw my expression and laughed.

'Why don't you open it, Lieutenant,' says he, 'and take out what's in there, and we'll have a good look.' So I swung the lid and found the chest full of nothing: just sawdust. It was sawdust packed tight by the flat underside of the lid that squeezed it flat. 'Dig, Sir!' says he. 'Dig and you shall find what you shall find!' Good enough: I dived in with my hands and found such a thing of wonder as I'd never believed possible, and I would point out that I knew something of mechanical matters.

[For once Fletcher is uncharacteristically modest, because in earlier adventures he became expert in the manufacture and repair of metallic pumps and other mechanisms, such as were used in the Jamaica rum distilleries, and he later helped install these complex equipments into a submarine boat, where they caused the vessel to rise or sink in the waters. S.P.]

So I pulled out what I'd found, in a cascading shower of sawdust. Up it came, and round and out, and down with a heavy bump. The thing was wrapped in flannel to keep the sawdust from its works but I could tell there was something wonderful inside, and it was just like the delightful instant before you haul the drawers off a juicy trollop. Then away with the flannel and all was revealed.

'Good God almighty!' says I.

It was a wheeled machine, an engine, about four feet long, a foot and half

30

wide, and near three feet high from the bottom of its wheels to the top of the tube that rose up from its front and which looked like a smoke stack. It was entirely made of metal and made to the exquisite perfection of chronometer by Harrison or a gun by Manton. It had pistons, valves and gears, a furnace at the back on a steel plate over the rear axle, and it had push-rods to turn the rear wheels, which were a foot in diameter, while the front wheels were half that size, on a swivel axle, with hauling chains at the outermost ends leading to a device like a ship's wheel, whereby the machine might be steered.

It was a steam carriage, or rather the model of one. I'd heard of such things, even in those days, because they were the stuff of fantasy, the flight of dreams, the nonsensical speculation of philosophers. But this was no dream. This was real. And by George it looked fit for purpose, and made by genius craftsmen. I stared and stared and you must understand that I was transported into wonder because the thing before me was not of that age. You youngsters must note that in that moment, as I looked around me, I saw the innards of a ship such as Francis Drake had known two hundred years ago, and the Greeks and Romans too, if you left out the guns, because it was entirely made out of wood, with canvas sails and hemp rigging, and depended entirely upon the wind. Likewise, any ship of those days was based on the scale of a man's body. Planks were an inch thick: the breadth of a man's thumb. Rope came in fathoms: the stretch of a man's outspread arms, and all else was hand-hewed and hand-sawn to the feet and yards deriving from a man's walking pace.

But Franky Drake would never have understood the little beast before me now, because it was made of steel, brass and copper, and machined so fine that there wasn't a hair's breadth between the joints, and most of all, and before all else, if this really was a steam carriage, then it didn't depend on the wind, nor on beast or man to pull it, because it was driven by fire and steam…and that, my boys, my very jolly boys, was a new thing upon the face of the Earth.

So I stared and stared and eventually noticed that somebody was shaking my shoulder who'd been talking and ignored by me for some while. It was Rowland.

'Fletcher!' says he, with a smile, 'Will you come back and join me, sir? Or are you gone away for ever?' So I looked up at him from where I was crouched beside the machine. 'Well, Sir?' says he, 'What do you think of it?'

'Marvellous!' says I, 'Truly marvellous. But will it run? Can it be got under way?'

'Ah!' says he, 'I told them you'd recognise it for what it is!'

'Told who?' says I, but he ignored the question.

'We've made inquiry of you,' says he. 'You and your submarine adventures with pipes and pumps,' and he pointed at the machine. 'So let's get it going,' and he smiled, 'We shouldn't want to disappoint Mr Pitt, now, should we?'

'Pitt?' says I.

'Yes,' says he, and pulled a sheet of notes out from the inside of his expensive, tailored coat, and with much effort, he put aside his walking stick, and got down on his expensive tailored knees and spread out the notes on the deck, while the two of us fished in the trunk and got everything out, of which there was a lot more than just the engine itself. We got it all out, shoved the sawdust out of the way and lined it all out in a row. There was a two-wheeled carriage to hook behind the machine carrying fuel and water – a tender we called such things in later years – then a four wheeled carriage to be towed for cargo, plus spare parts, a tank of pure water for the boiler, a tin box of neat-cut charcoal blocks for the furnace, a flask of spirit to help get the charcoal alight, and funnels and spanners and gauges of all kinds, plus a small shovel for the fire-box, and a most elegant tinder-lighter in the form of a pistol lock that made fire instantly at the pull of the trigger.

The notes explained what everything was for, and how the machine should be got under way. Thus a fire had to be made in the furnace and water poured into the boiler, then steam raised, and various valves turned in sequence to let steam into the pistons. After that, the steering wheel would have to be set to make the machine run in a circle, which circle was the reason why Rowland had cleared so large an open space for his demonstration. But Rowland would never have got it going on his own. He'd obviously studied the machine and he understand its principles, but he was no mechanic while I suppose that I was, even in those days, and I soon took over and he beamed to see me do so, and heaved himself up on his legs again, and stood back, satisfied that his pet ape – myself – was performing just the sort of tricks that he'd hoped.

So, once there was a bright fire in the furnace, and steam was coming from the escape valve, I set the machine off and it puffed and smoked, and ran in a great circle, and we stood back and damned ourselves if it wasn't just amazing. Amazing and beautiful too because the various metals, fine polished as they were, all gleamed in their own colours, the wheels whizzed and twinkled, and the pistons hissed in the most smooth and pleasing manner. And later it was even better when I had the idea to catch the machine and I hooked up the cargo carriage behind the tender, and tested the engine by setting it off with a thirty-two pound shot on board! The engine didn't like that. It huffed and shuddered and wheezed. But once it got going, why, the little rascal went round as fast as before, because such was the strength of steam in its belly.

Much later when we'd had a good look, Rowland chose a moment when the fire was running down and the machine slowing.

'Clap hold of it, Fletcher,' says he, 'Douse the fire, make all safe, and load everything back into the box.'

'Aye-aye, sir,' says I, 'But shouldn't we wait till all parts be cold? Otherwise we'll have a fire in the sawdust.'

'Quite so,' says he, 'but that is no impediment since we have much else to discuss.'

'Throw the coals away, Mr Fletcher,' says Rowland. 'It'll cool all the quicker.' So I took up the machine, squeezed past one of the guns, opened the furnace door, and shook out the hot contents through a port, while Illingworth gathered his thoughts. By the time I put the engine back on the deck, he was ready, having got himself half-seated on one of the gun carriages to take the weight off his feet, since we'd been standing some while and he was weary, and his breath was coming in gasps. He looked at me as I looked at him, and gave a short laugh, 'Breathless,' says he in explanation, 'I suffer pains down my left arm, when the emotions stir. The afflictions of old men, Lieutenant Fletcher.' Then he beckoned me over, and I stood before him with hands clasped behind me as if I were on watch beside the binnacle.

'You will have noted, Fletcher,' says he, 'that I am indeed quite old.' He paused and I nodded, thinking that some reaction was in order. 'Huh!' says he, and continued. 'So I have served many…' he sought for the right word, 'Many…*great* and*superior* beings,' says he, and recited a melancholy list, 'Henry Pelham, Tom Pelham-Holles, Billy Cavendish, George Grenville,' he went on and on, with me wondering who these men were, though later I learned that they'd all been prime minsters in the distant past. Illingworth waved a hand dismissively, 'All of them so proud and mighty, and all of them gone.' He looked at me, looked right into my face, and gave a laugh. 'All gone, Fletcher.' Then he paused, and cocked his head on one side, and measured carefully my reaction to his next words, 'Just as Black Dick Howe will soon be gone because their Lordships of the Admiralty are, even now, measuring up Sir Peter Parker to put in his place as Admiral of the Fleet.'

'Oh!' says I.

'Fletcher,' says he, 'You're gaping again.'

'Aye-aye, sir,' says I.

'Huh!' says he, staring even harder, 'Then understand, Mr Fletcher, that once Lord Howe is gone, then the doom that he has pronounced upon yourself, goes with him.'

'Oh? I mean Aye-aye, sir!'

'Oh indeed, Mr Fletcher. And then, with the right patron behind you, you might find yourself allowed out of the Navy with a substantial gratuity to set you up in business!'

'Oh!' says I, I couldn't help it.

'Oh!' says he in the same instant, and laughed. But then he stopped laughing, took hold of his stick and got himself on to his feet, and stepped towards me quite close. 'So,' says he, 'I can give you freedom. 'But are you fit for it? Do you want it enough?' and I felt the power of him. The little engine wasn't the only creature here with fire inside of it. Old and shrivelled he might be, but he was the Big Man and no mistake, and one hell of a leader. I do believe that if we'd been in the face of the enemy, and he'd said 'fix bayonets and follow me!' then I'd have gone with him, and there weren't many men who could do that to your Uncle Jacob.

'I'm with you, Mr Rowland,' says I, 'You may bet your soul on it, if it leaves me free to follow my dreams.'

'Bet his soul?' says he, 'His soul, indeed?' and then he got very confidential and introspective, almost talking to himself. 'Then are you the man to do as I did, before I grew old? I'm nearly eighty, Mr Fletcher. Sixty years in my country's service, and I've picked you out, wondering if you can act like me,' he took my arm and shook it hard, 'Can you do what must be done, and never an order written down, and knowing that you will be denied and abandoned if things go wrong?' I said nothing. I just blinked as another page of his personality turned over. By George but he was more ruthless than me! Me, who'd done murder and mutiny, broke sacred vows, slain men in hand-to-hand battle, and blown the bottom out of a British ship and drowned all aboard. But he was still talking. 'Listen to me, Fletcher,' says he, 'because here is the contract that I offer. I shall see you given your heart's desire, if you can contrive that certain devices similar to that one,' he pointed to the steam carriage, 'if you can contrive that these devices, which are presently in the hands of the French, are broken, smashed and destroyed, and the workshops laid low and burned where these machines are being made.'

Well, there was an offer indeed. The prize was enormous and I never did like the French, so I was swept on the flood of the moment.

'Aye-aye, sir,' says I, 'I'll do that for you,' and I meant it too.

'Aye-aye, sir,' says he, mockingly, and shoved his nose forward till it almost touched mine and lowered his voice almost to silence. 'But that is not all, Mr Jacob Fletcher of Polmouth in Cornwall. Because the machines themselves are small things. We turn now to the Englishmen who make them, and whose treacherous cunning has given them to the French. Those men could rebuild what you destroy. So they must not be left alive. They must - each one - be cracked like a louse. So! You say that you desire above all things to follow a life in trade?' I nodded. 'But to grasp this most noble aspiration,' says he, 'you must become a man who follows orders. I therefore ask you most seriously, as once and long ago it was asked of me, by a man who was then what I am now,' and he smiled like Satan beckoning a sinner into Hell, 'Are you prepared, Mr Fletcher, to kill in cold blood, all those men who are pointed out to you as being in need of the swift knife, or of quiet strangulation?'

Chapter 4

'You will accelerate the recruitment of young men to be trained as machinists in the English manner. You will accelerate the production of high pressure engines at Fragnal. You will proceed irrespective of cost and you will state that you act in my name.'
(Translated from a personal commission for Citizen Claude Bernard, late Colonel of the 22nd Artillery Regiment, and dated 12th February1796, and signed by Citizen General Napoleon Bonaparte.)

*

Bernard felt tired. His joints ached and his breath condensed like smoke in the cold. He wondered if he was fit for all this: the responsibility of command and the finding and bringing together of everything needed? That and the bone-pounding, twenty-hour carriage journey from Fragnal, and everything done to the sharp timetables of the new superman. Bernard sighed. At least he didn't have to carry anything.

He looked back at the small group of Sapeur-Engineers of the 29th brigade following after him, and after them came a dozen men of the 134th Line Infantry in two groups of six with a sergeant and corporal, and a spot-faced young Lieutenant in charge of the lot of them. The sergeant had them shuffling along at quick-march speed: teeth clenched, knuckles white, gripping stretcher poles with lashings supporting two heavy trunks. They were all under his command, now. Them and a troupe of dragoons, and the promise of a staff of clerks and book-keepers, and as many more men as the job might need.

'Mother of God,' thought Bernard, 'Am I too old for this?'

'Halt!' cried a loud voice, and Bernard turned to face two magnificent grena-diers of the National Guard.

'National Guard?' thought Bernard, because the name changed every time the political tide turned, 'French Guard? Republican Guard? Little Cabbage Guard? Whatever in Holy Mary's name they called themselves now? Bernard shrugged. They'd been a real regiment once and loyal to the King. But not now. Bernard looked at the two young men - tall and straight, chosen for height - splendid uniforms, red-plumed bearskin caps, black moustaches, black gaiters, fiercely-polished muskets with fixed bayonets.

'Who goes there?' said the one who'd given the challenge, and the two of them levelled at Bernard, who nodded in approval, because that's what sentries ought to do. But then he let them have it in a big voice.

'Friend!' cried Bernard, 'I am Citizen Inspector Claude Bernard, here on the service of General Bonaparte,' he frowned and advanced a pace towards these huge boys in uniform. He might be tired and aching, but he was a veteran of thirty-five years service and could grow a better moustache than them just by not shaving in the morning. 'So if I were you, my lovely lads,' he said, 'my bonny citizens, I'd run fetch your officer pretty damn quick and tell him I'm here, because,' Bernard yelled, 'he *damn* well *ought* to *be* expecting me!' Bernard heard the sniggers from his men behind him, and saw the two grenadiers blink, and fall back and look at one another.

'You go!' said the one who'd spoken, 'I'll keep guard.'

'That's better,' said Bernard, as one scuttled off, 'and you lads can ease your loads while we wait,' he said to the men carrying the trunks.

'Ahhhh …,' they said and lowered away.

Bernard looked around. These were the famous *Jardins Saint David*, most exclusive of all the Parisian pleasure gardens. It was where the bright and the beautiful had strolled and played in the summer evenings in past times, though not any more. The Revolution disapproved of pleasure. So the famous arch of bright-painted wooden flowers, over the entrance gate, was chipped and broken by the stones thrown at it by the Paris mob, ever eager to show what good boys they were and true believers in The Enlightenment. But the close-shaved hedges that surrounded the gardens were still there, so none of the busy traffic of people now passing by could see into the interior of the gardens.

Soon the grenadier was back with not one, but several officers who saluted Bernard, and bowed to Bernard, and abased themselves before Bernard, and welcomed him and his men inside the gates.

'This way, Citizen Bernard!'

'Of course, Citizen Bernard!'

'Do you need more men, Citizen Bernard?'

Bernard swelled in self esteem as any man would under such treatment, but he knew only too well whose enormous name it was, that was causing everyone to throw rose petals before his feet. So off he went with his heavy trunks and his men behind him, deep inside Les Jardins, which even in winter were beautified with elegant cafes, floral booths, Chinese pagodas, exotic topiary and neat little private corners decorated with lusciously-naked nymphs in fine white marble. Bernard was impressed. He was equally impressed to see the National Guard sentries everywhere, because France was at war, and something vital to that war – vital and secret – was about to be demonstrated.

'He'll be here at eleven, Citizen Bernard,' said the most senior Guards officer, and leaned forward to impart a confidence, 'He's got the job as Commander of our Army of Italy! Biggest army in the Republic. They'll go through Italy like a dose of salts, and there's not enough hours in the day for him to organise it and…Ah!' he said, 'This is it: The Elysian Bathing Pool,' two more sentries stood aside, as Bernard was ushered through the gates into yet another private place, this time a particularly private place, enclosed within plastered white walls, covered in paintings of classical mythology: mermaids, tritons and water-sprites that cavorted in merry profusion.

Bernard looked round. Yes, this would do. It would do very nicely even though it was intended for another purpose entirely. This was the place where the rich brought their tarts for naked bathing. Bernard recalled the assurance of friends who'd tried it, that there was no better way to perform the carnal act, than standing in chest-high water when all weight disappeared and the girl could ride easy on the man's shaft… provided only that the weather be warm of course! In any case, there was a row of changing cubicles like miniature Greek temples, and a level spread of marble flag stones, and a rectangular pool, thirty yards by ten, with steps leading down into the water. There was even a combined band-stand and café, so cleverly designed so that the musicians and servants could entertain, but see nothing of what was going on in the pool. Bernard was impressed. He gave a little laugh, and shook his head at the cleverness of it. What fun it must have been in those days! And wouldn't he just love to take a girl into that pool…Hmmm.

But there was work to be done.

'Right!' said Bernard and drew out his pocket watch by Guillemin of Paris, a present from his wife, all neatly enamelled with an image of the Virgin and Child. He turned to his men. 'The General should be here in an hour,' he said, 'and we've just got time to get everything working. So! Get to it!'

They did. The Sapeur-Engineers did the important work, but the rest joined in where needed, and the National Guard officers and men stood back and stared and pointed and puffed out their cheeks in amazement.

Then, at eleven sharp, there was a rumble of cavalry along the avenue outside Les Jardins and shouted orders, and guard challenges and much stamping and yelling, as The Man Himself, burst into the enclosed bathing area with sentries straining to utmost attention, and some two dozen of his innermost staff coming after him. There were shakos, busbies, pellises, sabres, swords, gold lace, sashes, uniforms of every imaginable colour and boots polished like mirrors. These together with a small corps of clerkish civilians with note-pads, pencils and spectacles. All clung close to the remarkably small, thin and energetic young man who led them, wearing remarkably plain clothes: just white breeches and waistcoat, blue uniform, grey greatcoat, and long, wild hair streaming out from a plain bicorne with a small cockade. His face was pale, his nose was thin, and he had blue-grey eyes that stared at everything.

Bernard stood to attention with all the rest, because this was Napoleon Bonaparte: military genius, master gunner, saviour of the Revolution and the man who rumour said would soon displace all politicians to become supreme ruler of France. And this at just twenty-six years of age!

'Bernard!' said Bonaparte, and marched up to him, seized him by both shoulders and grinned, 'My boy!' he cried, 'My friend! How's your family? Madame Aveline Bernard? Your daughter Amelie? Your sons Maxime and Perceval?' Later, Bernard wondered if Bonaparte had done some research? Either that or his memory for names was phenomenal, because Bonaparte had indeed met Bernard before, and talked of family. But in that moment, when Bonaparte greeted him before all others, as a friend and comrade, and using the proper title of Madame for a man's wife, not the crass Citizeness…well…Bernard was Bonaparte's man to the death. He beamed with pleasure, even though Bonaparte, who was younger than either of Bernard's sons, had addressed him as my boy. But what did that matter? This was the man who was going to crush the Revolution and sweep it away.

'My General,' said Bernard and mumbled something, in happy embarrassment, with Bonaparte's men looking on, and his own men too, in awestruck amazement.

'So!' said Bonaparte, 'Are these the machines? Which is French and which is English?' He laughed and everyone laughed, because of course he already knew everything, but everyone looked where he was looking.

Standing together beside the bathing pool were two wonders of mechanical science. One stood on four wheels, and one was a small boat mounted on a wooden stand. Both were hot and shimmering in the cold air, giving off quiet little clouds of vapour, and the wheeled device had a fitting that spun round constantly, occasionally emitting a small blast of steam. Each machine was over three feet long, and was constructed from exotically crafted metals like steel, copper and brass, apart from the wooden hull of the boat. Each had a small furnace and a funnel that emitted lazy wisps of smoke.

'Now then, you English steam carriage,' said Bonaparte going up to the wheeled machine and staring closely at it. 'What a little devil you are!', he said, and leaned forward for a closer look. He shook his head, 'So finely made!' he said. 'How clever these English are.' Then he pointed at the spinning device, 'Bernard?' he asked, 'What's this?'

'It's a regulator, my General,' said Bernard, 'It prevents the steam in the machine gaining too much pressure. As the pressure rises, it causes the regulator to spin, and lift a plug which voids steam. Then it sinks again, and the plug goes home, and stops further emission until the pressure rises too high again.'

'Wonderful!' said Bonaparte, 'But let's look at our French machine. Let's see why France can't do what England can!' he made a joke of this and everyone laughed. But Bonaparte was a trained gunner and an engineer in his own right. So he knew very well that he wasn't really joking. He went to the wood-and-metal boat and stared at it, beckoning Bernard to follow. 'Well?' he said, and his face became serious. Bernard stood beside him and explained.

'This is the Marquis de Jouffroy's model boat, made twelve years ago, for the Academy of Sciences,'

'Yes, I know,' said Bonaparte, 'The Royal Academy of Sciences.' He stressed the word Royal and grinned at everyone's reaction to the politically incorrect word. 'Pah!' he said. 'Come on, Bernard, tell me what's wrong with our French machine.'

'In the first place, my General, the steam engine is an inferior copy of the Englishman, James Watt's atmospheric engines.'

'Atmospheric engine,' repeated Bonaparte, 'which means that the motive power depends on condensing the steam in a cylinder, to make a vacuum that sucks the piston inward for the power stroke.'

'Yes, my General,' said Bernard, 'Whereas the engine of the English steam carriage is powered by the explosive force of high-pressure steam which expands in the cylinder to drive the piston forward.'

'With more force than the suction machine?'

'Much more, my General, very much more!'

'And what else?' said Bonaparte. 'I can see it in your eyes.' He laughed. Everyone laughed. Bernard continued.

'The English machine is better made than ours. It is made to greater precision and is very reliable. De Jouffroy built a full-sized boat that ran on the Saône river, but it was always breaking down, and there were dangerous accidents. That's why the Academy of Sciences never supported him.'

'I see,' said Bonaparte, 'Now let's watch them run...and swim!' everyone laughed again, and Bernard's men soon had the steam carriage running round in a circle towing a little cart behind it for fuel and water, and a big cart for loads. Then a couple of the Sapeur-engineers took off their boots, rolled up their breeches, picked up the steam boat and took it down the steps into the pool, and set it going, its pistons driving a pair of paddle wheels that sent it steadily down the pool to much delight from the assembled, uniformed Frenchmen who walked merrily alongside the puffing boat, waving and cheering it on, because nobody had enjoyed Bernard's comparison of English and French machines.

Some of them would have played all day with the delightful machines, but not Bonaparte. He proved to himself - by watching - that the steam carriage really would run, and that the steam boat really would go forward without sails or oars. But that was enough. After a few circular runs of the carriage, and a few transits of the bathing pool, he told Bernard to stop the machines, and took Bernard's elbow, and walked off to one side, away from everyone else, bringing just one secretary with him, who took notes of what he said.

'Bernard,' he said quietly, 'The Revolution has made a great mistake. Just one but catastrophic.' Bernard blinked. Such talk was really, truly dangerous. He didn't know how to respond, or even why Bonaparte had said such a thing. But Bonaparte smiled, reading Bernard's thoughts with ease.

'Trust me, my friend,' he said, and gripped Bernard's hands in both of his own, 'can you guess what this mistake was?'

'No, my General,' said Bernard, because he couldn't.

'They ruined our navy,' said Bonaparte. 'They killed, imprisoned or exiled the entire corps of professional, sea-service officers that ran the navy. They did so because they were Royalist.'

'Oh!' said Bernard, understanding. The navy couldn't work without long-service, professional experts. He understood easily because it was the same for the artillery.

'That's right,' said Bonaparte, reading thoughts again, 'They saw the need for artillerymen. That much was obvious, with the enemies of France advancing upon us by land. So they kept the Royalist gunners,' Bonaparte grinned. 'Men like you, Bernard!' Bernard gasped.

'Pah!' said Bonaparte, 'D'you think I care who you followed in the past?' he let go Bernard's hands and stood back. 'They kept the gunners, but they thought they could do without the navy, so they purged the sea-service officer corps, and we won't have another for a generation! But England still has its sea service officers, which means we can't beat their navy, which means we can't invade England, which means that England will be forever at my back, with its eternal desire to damn everything French!' he paused, 'Or rather, they will unless we do something about it.'

Bonaparte looked to where the Sapeur-Engineers were taking the steamboat out of the water, and emptying the coals out of the furnace of the steam carriage.

'This English machine, the steam carriage…,'

'Yes, my General?'

'You say it was made by the McCloud brothers?'

'Yes. Made in England before they came to France.'

'Are there any others like it?'

'Yes, my General. More are being made in England by McCloud's followers there, because McCloud can't yet make them at Fragnal. They will be used to train up our own French machinists and they're being smuggled across to France,' he shrugged, 'One's been lost in transit. We don't know how.'

'Perhaps the English navy caught the smugglers?' said Bonaparte.

'Perhaps,' said Bernard. 'We only know that it was delivered to the smugglers but never arrived in France.'

'Never mind,' said Bonaparte, and beckoned his clerk to come close with his notebook. 'Here's what we are going to do – what you are going to do, Bernard – because I shall be busy in Italy. This is what you will do to deal with the English navy …'

Chapter 5

It was Monday when I was examined for Lieutenant and only Thursday when Poxy Percy came aboard with his followers. I remember that for the incredibly short time it took for Rowland to make water flow uphill in terms of getting everything done, that ought to have been done already. So here's a further word about Rowland:

He was far more than he seemed and even that was heavy enough. Thus I never learned the full truth of him though it's blindingly obvious that he was political: deeply political with connections in Parliament, the Army, the Admiralty, and wherever else there was power. But never a hint of this appeared on paper. Years later I tried to look him up in libraries and not a word did I find, and never an honour or title was given him. So my best guess is that all those great and superior beings who employed him, liked to pretend that he didn't exist, and most especially they liked to pretend that the things he did were never done, even though they'd told him to do them. Or perhaps they were like that king who didn't precisely tell his knights to murder the Archbishop - not quite he didn't - but just asked a greasy question in that direction.

['Who will rid me of this turbulent priest?' Henry II speaking of Thomas A'Becket in 1170. S.P.]

And there's more. I've lived an adventurous life and occasionally met other men -not many but some - who recalled the name of Rowland and who tapped their noses confidentially, and grinned and said no more. They were all like me - big, bold and bad - and they'd all been caught in the end and sentenced to hang. But none of them danced the Newgate Jig because they all got Royal Pardons, except one who miraculously escaped the condemned cell and ended up in Australia living rich on secret loot, and if you can't see politics in that then you're blind.

So when I got back aboard *Serpant*, I had a long ponder about what he'd said, and even more about what I'd said concerning cold blooded murder because faced with his direct question regarding what I must do to get out of the Navy, I'd said:

'Aye-aye, sir, I'll do it.'

But would I? I didn't know, and it got all the harder when less than an hour after I'd said goodbye to Rowland, a boat came out to *Serpant* with a number of oilskin packages for me, and mark well the speed of that delivery, which proves that everything in those packages had already been brought together by Rowland in confidant expectation that I'd be wanting them.

As the boat came alongside I was doing my thinking at the stern rail of *Serpant*, wrapped up against the cold in a mouldy old greatcoat, sea-boots, mittens and a thick woollen cap - something else for you youngsters to take note of, because seamen at sea don't dress like you see in the picture: not short jackets, thin slops and a loose shirt. Not in winter! So I was standing there when the boat came up, with tars at the oars and a middy in charge.

'Delivery for Lieutenant Fletcher!' says he, and the boat's cargo was made fast to lines run down from our main-deck, and the parcels hauled aboard, then off went the middy and his boat.

'For you, Mr Fletcher, Sir!' says Douglas the Bosun, with a smart salute and men behind him carrying parcels, while more of them were doubling up from below and grinning all over their faces. I was surprised to see that the ship's company was turning out, and when all were on deck, Douglas saluted again, 'And might I say, Mr Fletcher, sir, in behalf of all hands aboard,' he turned to face the rest, 'here's three cheers for Lieutenant Fletcher!' He led them hip-hip-hip, and hats were in the air and cheers on all sides, and there was more than cheers because it was the first time I heard the hands shout Jacky Flash: their nickname for me based on their trimming down of Jacob, together with the west-country sounding of Fletcher as Flasher. The name followed me ever after, as far as the lower deck was concerned, though I never could decide whether I liked it or not.

[No. Fletcher relished the nickname and would boast of it, believing that it conferred roguish charm upon him, which indeed it did as far as the ladies were concerned. S.P.]

All this display surprised me. It really did. I never wanted to be a sailor in the first place, so I never cared whether the lower deck liked me or not and I kept discipline by knocking down all those who misbehaved. But British seamen would chose a Tartar for a captain any time because they knew that unrelenting discipline was the only way to run a wooden warship in northern waters, where it was constant battle against wind, tide, rocks, rot, breakage, disease, bugs, fleas, wet and cold. Even the enemy sometimes gave trouble, though he was the least of it because you could fire cannon into him, and you couldn't do that the wind or tide. So even if Jacky Flash was ever-ready with the boot aboard ship, I suppose the tars understood because they'd have done it themselves had they been me.

But then I realised what this was all about. It was because I'd had so much to think about, coming back from the Examination, that I'd not spoken to anyone and my glum face had persuaded them that I'd been failed the examination. But then they'd heard the middy call me Lieutenant, and they knew I was promoted, and now they were giving honour. Well, my jolly boys, the Service has its traditions where such courtesies are concerned, and they have to be honoured in return. So I gave my reply

'Thank you, lads,' says I, and turned to the Boatswain, 'Mr Douglas! You may pipe Up-Spirits and issue a good tot for all hands!' This time the cheering shivered the topmasts, and I had my tot with the rest, but then I went below to see what had come aboard, and spread it all out on the table in the Captain's cabin. It was everything Rowland had promised, including a full dress uniform and two undress uniforms all made to my fit! So think on that. How did they know my measurements? Rowland's work, I'd guess, the clever bastard. And it wasn't just uniform coats but hats, small-clothes, shirts, stockings and shoes. It was everything to make me look a gentleman. Then there was a three-draw Dolland telescope, a Hadley's Quadrant, a pile of charts, a large sum of money in golden guineas, plus a first-rate pair of Nock's sea-service barkers fitted with belt hooks, and finally a blue-and-gilt fighting sword by Henry Tatham, sword maker to the King. It had a heavy knuckle guard, and a two-inch wide, curved blade fit to take off heads with a flick of the wrist. That alone must have cost the price of a decent cottage.

But with all this came something else, in a fitted case and a note folded up inside it. It was another piece by Henry Tatham: a dagger with small, straight quillons and a sharply pointed blade eight inches long, hollow ground on both sides like razors. It was more of a surgeons knife than a weapon, but it sat beautifully in the hand and I made passes with it, as any fool does who gets hold of such a thing. Then I looked at the note:

'Keep this safe. Remember what I said. I will send word.' That was all: just that, signed with the single letter 'R'. So I did remember what he'd said as we parted. 'You'll be summoned in due course, Mr Fletcher,' he'd said, 'because other matters must intervene before we send you into France.' Then he shook my hand.

So I looked at the dagger and I didn't like it. It didn't suit me at all. So I turned away from Rowland and towards something better. I turned to *Serpant*. Doing that was safe, it was secure, and it was something I knew. It was what they called an anaesthetic fifty years later: something for the pain that was festering in my mind as I asked myself over and over: just what had I agreed to? What would I have to do for Rowland, against whatever it was that was brewing across the Channel? And what of these treacherous Englishmen making steam-machines for the French? Was I supposed to use the dagger on them?

A pox on it. A bloody damned French pox at that. I pushed the dagger aside and turned to the ship, which was easy because she was a fine ship. *Serpant* was an experiment. She was the direct ancestor of the Cruiser Class brig sloops that the Navy built in such profusion during the French wars. She was just under four hundred tons burthen, a hundred feet long, thirty feet in beam, and far cheaper than a frigate. Flush-decked, with only two masts, and carronade guns on technically-advanced carriages, *Serpant* needed only a half of a frigate's crew. But she mounted a pair of six-pounder bow chasers and sixteen thirty-two pounder carronades, so she could fight a frigate at close range, having more weigh of broadside per ton of burthen than any other vessel in the navy. And she was fast, too, and seaworthy. A fine craft and just the thing to blow away the African blues.

So I gave all hands aboard *Serpant* two and a half days opportunity to think again about their beloved Jacky Flash, because I left Rowland's clutter where it lay, and went up on deck.

'Mr Douglas!' says I.

'Aye-Aye, Mr Fletcher, Sir,' says he with a boozy grin, and I could see from the look on the faces all round, that more than one tot had gone down their merry throats.

'Clear for action,' says I, and out came another of my new toys: a fine gold watch by Spencer and Perkins of Whitehall, complete with a sweeping second hand. 'I'll see it done less than two minutes or know the reason why!' And then, in that moment, I was just a little proud of Mr Bosun Douglas: him and myself too, because he'd been an idle rogue when I first came aboard, and the first of all of them that I knocked own. But now he knew what must happen when I give an order, and he barely gulped and barely blinked, before lifting back his head and bellowing.

'Beat to quarters! Clear for action!' and the Bosun's mates came up along-side of Douglas, and stamped about the deck, and kicked backsides just as I'd have done myself, and roused the laggards as if the French Fleet was coming into range. So the marine drummer boy hammered away, all hands ran in all direction, cartridges were fetched up from the magazine, sand strewed on deck for sure footing…etc…etc…etc.

And after that, by George, didn't we just have a jolly time? I couldn't burn powder at anchor, nor could I take us to sea. Not without permission from above. But in those two-and-a-half days we damn near took *Serpant* apart and put her back together again.

'Send down all yards and spars above the tops!'

'Aye-Aye, Sir!'

'Now send 'em up again!'

'Aye-Aye, Sir!'

'All hands to fire drill! Fire in the orlop!'

'Aye-Aye, Sir!'

'All larboard guns re-secured to starboard, and starboard to larboard!'

'Aye-Aye, Sir!'

'Watches to race - by messes - to the main-truck!'

'Aye-Aye, Sir!'

'Fo'csle crew to race waisters in getting up anchor!'

'Aye-Aye, Sir!'

'Marines to race larboard watch, kedging ship!'

It was everything and anything I could think of. I made them race each other and race against the watch. I think they actually liked it. They certainly turned out their fiddler and piper whenever it made sense, and sang their shanties with a will. I leave it to wiser heads to fathom the working of seamen's minds, but it worked for me, and probably saved me in the long run, and in any case our games came to an end on the Thursday, when a boat came out with two letters for me, as senior officer aboard. The first was from Rowland, terse as ever, saying:

'Your captain will come aboard this morning. You will obey his orders as if they were my own, which in large part they are.' The other was much longer, written by a skilled pen-wallah, probably a clerk, but signed in a scrawl by 'Cuthbert Percival-Clive, Master and Commander.' It advised me that the ship must proceed at once to sea, on sealed orders, as soon as extra stores were taken aboard, which they would be with utmost despatch, and then it grumbled on, complaining of 'the iniquities of arbitrary orders which take no account of what reasonable men may achieve in reasonable time.' It was a warning of what was to come.

It started as a procession of boats came out from the shore, and the coxwain of the foremost yelled aloud.

'*Serpant!*' says he, indicating that our new sea-monarch, Cuthbert Percival-Clive, was aboard, and indeed he was. So I stood to attention, in my full dress beside the companionway rigged on the lee side, for the newcomers to climb aboard out of their boats, of which the first man up, and over the side, was Poxy Percy himself, to the long-drawn, up-and-down whistle-blasts of the Bosun and his mates giving formal salute.

I'd not seen Percy for years but recognised him instantly. He was now in his twenties, gangling, thin and stooped-over, with a remarkably white face for a seaman, but he'd spent more time ashore than afloat, hadn't he? He was exceedingly smart, with his hair done fancy-style like the Prince of Wales's, and everything about him bright and clean thanks to fresh-water laundering and servants to press his linen, and brush and clean and tidy. But two things spoiled him. First, his face was disfigured after adventures we'd shared, when my half-brother Alexander Coignwood shot Percy just before I ran a cutlass through Alexander's chest and sent him to hell. The ball had knocked out some of Percy's teeth, left a dark-stained shrivelling in his cheek, and damaged his tongue so that he spoke as if with his mouth full. That, of course, was none of his fault. He wasn't to blame for his scars any more than Nelson was.

But the second failing was entirely Percy's own. It was a self-satisfied belief in his own wisdom that came from being constantly surrounded by a company of arse-kissers, who greeted his every pronouncement with the words:

'By Jove, sir, how clever!'

So he had no idea how dim he really was, and he was prone to explaining the bloody obvious at great length, and he couldn't bear to be interrupted or contradicted. That much I learned later, but what annoyed me at first sight, was the expression on his face: half-frown, half smile, all sad and suffering like the governess of idiot children who pities them as hopeless yet carries on out of duty.

Now…If you youngsters have read this far in my memoirs, then you'll know that such an expression as that, don't please your Uncle Jacob one little bit. God's boots, but it don't! So I freely admit that I detested Poxy Percy from the instant he came aboard, such that it was only the fear of hanging that stopped me wringing his neck there and then, which thin as it was would have gone round nice and easy, and snapped with a crack, and saved much trouble later on.

But having said that, please note that if I've rambled on about Poxy Percy, then I insist that I didn't – nor did any man aboard – pay more than a second's interest in him as he clambered over the side, because all our attention was taken by the creature that followed him. She was a woman, and a lovely woman at that, and Percy turned and took her in his arms, and lifted her down from the bulwark so close and intimate as to announce that she was his woman, though never a glint of a wedding ring was on her finger.

48

She was later introduced as Miss Maitland. She was tall and very slim, dressed in a close-fitted greatcoat - a redingote they called them in those days – with fur trim at collar and cuffs and a neat little fur hat, and a neat little nose and pointed chin, and creamy-smooth complexion and big brown eyes. She was older than him – about thirty - and stared straight at the world with complete composure. I took her for an intelligent woman, as indeed she proved to be.

But she was a woman aboard a King's ship in wartime and she shouldn't have been there. Not when the ship was about to set sail. Not under King George's regulations. So I glanced round the deck, where the crew were paraded in their best for the new Captain, and I saw knowing grins, because the Navy had always damned the Regulations and smuggled aboard a few women. Even folk ashore knew that - until Queen Victoria's time, of course, when they all pretended they didn't - and women included a captain's pampered princess just as much as the lower deck's Dolls and Molls.

[Lamentably true. Note just one example: Admiral Sir William Dillon's famous 'Narrative' reports Captain John Bowen of HMS Camilla, as disgracefully keeping his mistress aboard ship in 1809. S.P.]

Once we'd had our look at Miss Maitland, we turned to the rest of our new shipmates as they came aboard. They were all Percival Clive's placemen, and in order of climbing over the side, they were:

Mr O'Flaherty, the Sailing Master, who was in his fifties and balding. He was an exception to everything else that followed Poxy Percy because he looked every inch a seaman and stared at *Serpant* from keel to main truck with obvious professional interest. Thank God for him at least, because the Master, though not a commissioned officer, held senior responsibility for all matters of seamanship and navigation. Thus no man aboard had a greater opportunity of drowning the entire crew of us should he prove to be a wrong 'un, but contrariwise, and many times over, I blessed the fact that O'Flaherty was the veteran seafarer that he was.

Next came a puffed up gnome, who unlike most of the rest wore no cloak, having need to display his rank, with scarlet tunic, epaulette on the right shoulder, and shiny gorgette hanging round his neck. This miserable grub was a Lieutenant of marines, with the King God-bless-Him's commission, which was a travesty because a brig sloop like *Serpant* had only fifteen marines plus a sergeant and corporal, and did not rate an officer. Yet here he was, as further proof of what money and influence can achieve. He was an undersized little runt who stood stiff as some small men do, to make best of what height they have, and he threw out his chest like a cock-pigeon courting a hen. Once aboard, he stamped and strutted in shiny top-boots, pretending to knock the cold out of his feet, but really affecting a manly posture to prove what a bold fellow he was. This was Mr Lieutenant Chancellor, a boyhood school-fellow of Poxy Percy and as fathomlessly stupid as him.

Then there was Dr Sir Richard Rogers - Sir Richard mark you – Percy's own personal physician. The swab was a penniless baronet, deep in Percy's father's debt. He'd been put out to work as a younger son having no expectation of the title, but two elder brothers drank away the father's cash, then died, so he inherited after all. He was young, pink, fat-necked and growing a belly, but he'd graduated out of Cambridge University, and was no mere butcher who'd learned his trade with rolled up sleeves. This erudite scholar did his utmost to copy Poxy Percy's facial expressions, manoeuvring to catch his eye in order to share a moment of disdain for everything around them. I marked down Sir Richard as a nasty piece of work: cunning and sly.

Both O'Flaherty and Sir Richard wore cocked hats and long blue coats beneath their cloaks, with shiny buttons bearing fouled-anchor insignia. These uniforms officially marked them out as gentlemen fit to mess in the Wardroom with the ships officers, despite their not having commissions. Even the Purser was entitled to that dignity, but next came Mr Myers: Percy's secretary who was a clever-cunning, middle-aged, pen-driver dressed in a gold-laced version of domestic servant's livery. He proved to be the most incredible crawler I ever met in my life, even among the fiercely competed field of Percy's followers. He bowed low whenever the master's eye came his way, and delivered a mincing, grovelling, smile with tiny-tight lips that said:

'Oh, sir, you are so wonderful! It's an honour to carry your piss pot.'

In my view he was very much not fit for the Wardroom and should have been an actor instead, which of course he was in a way.

Finally there was a pair of immaculate little midshipmen, in uniforms fresh out of the tailor's hands. They were twelve and thirteen years old respectively, and were round-eyed and skinny: Mr Copeland and Mr Barkley, both at sea for the first time and both younger sons of West India millionaires like Percy's father, who wanted some officer-class lustre for their rich but vulgar families. Vulgar because they were in trade, you see? Just as I dreamed of being: me that already had the King's Commission but didn't want it. What games fortune plays with us, don't it just indeed?

As well as these, there were two boat-loads wallowing alongside which contained Percy's chums, every one of them a Knight Companion of the Ancient Order of the Brown Nose. They were all in the latest London fashions, and were come out to see him off, a-waving of their handkerchiefs, and a-weeping of real tears and calling out their fond goodbyes to the dear one who'd been signing off their expenses these many months past. So Percy got up on a carronade slide, the better to see them, and waved over the side, palm turned inward like royalty, and bade farewell as if he were going forth to save the nation at cost of his precious life.

Only when that was done did the last dregs came aboard: half a dozen of Percy's servants: his cooks, lackeys, valets and the like who were no-seamen and never would be because they were in Percy's service, not the King's.

Then once this circus was aboard, Percy stood before the assembled crew and performed the formality – without which he was not truly our Captain - of reading aloud his commission from their Lordships of the Admiralty, appointing him Master and Commander into the brig-sloop *Serpant*. That was all perfectly proper as was his next action, in turning to a copy of King George's 1749 Articles*of* War, which was the Navy's rule book of crimes and punishments and was handed to him by Mr livery-coat Myers. Again he read out every word, which took some time. Then he gave us the speech we'd all been waiting for, which every Captain makes on taking command and whereby the crew learn what sort of man he is.

So off he went in a strangulated voice that was the best he could do with his mangled tongue. He gave all the fit and proper sentiments about England's glory, damning the French, and us as wooden walls, and shield of the nation. Every captain did that, the hands expected it and they nodded in approval. But then he came down to business.

'Now pay good heed, you men,' says he, 'In case you think I am soft, then learn that I am hard, damned hard, and mark you well that I have eyes every-where, and I shall by utmost diligence seek out the first lapse of discipline, and come down with exemplary force upon the guilty.'

That was it, and then he went below, leaving us to think over what he'd said, especially his last words. I supposed at first that he was attempting some feeble equivalent of my own practise in thrashing a ship's bully at first opportunity. But on reflection I didn't like the bit about 'eyes everywhere' and I saw the creepy crawlies smirk as Percy said it. So what with that, and my wondering what was bearing down upon me under Rowland's command. I didn't sleep much that night. So I got up in the dark and gave myself a little treat. I took Rowland's dagger in its fitted case, and heaved over the side. A brief pause, a small splash, and was gone for ever. It made me feel better, and I'm glad that I did it, but it didn't change much in the long run, and it certainly didn't change what Percy did next.

Chapter 6

'...*thus I have need of girls beyond the sophistication of any to be found in the provinces. They must be white swans, capable of acting out the part of virgins.*' (Translated from a letter of Tuesday 15th March 1796, from Madame Louise Shultz-Strauss, Maison Boules D'Or, Frangnal-sur-Longue, to Madame Henriette Le Clerk, 69 Rue Tire-Boudin, Paris.)

*

Colonel Claude Hector Bernard might be Inspector of Engineers to General Bonaparte, but he was also a man. He was a man with the needs of any other man, especially when that man was French. Thus even though Bernard had been happily married for over twenty years with three beloved children, he, being separated from them by duty and being in receipt of an enormous salary, was able to visit, each week, the luxurious Boules D'or, most exclusive maison close of the Loire valley.

The best time for Bernard, the time when duties allowed, was usually Tuesday morning, and on this present Tuesday morning he was relaxing naked in a huge, Lit-en-bateau bed, of golden yew-wood. He was draped in silk sheets, and reclined on silk pillows, with a little sunlight coming through venetian-shuttered windows into an opulently-furnished room that glittered in gilding and mirrors and ornaments. And best of all, Madame Louise herself lay in his arms, slowly tickling the hairs on his chest with the most delicious application of pointed fingernails. The sensation was so intoxicating that Bernard was dozing into sleep. He liked Madame Louise. She was voluptuous, smooth, unblemished and expert. She was a woman fitting his own age, because Bernard was too wise to think himself a boy any more, and the younger girls were beginning to seem...well...too young for a man of his dignity.

With effort, Bernard forced himself to think, and then to speak.

'Can you do it then?' he said, 'can you provide girls like that?' she laughed.

'You surely can't imagine that you are the first man to ask for that particular service?' he laughed, too.

'No, no, madame,' he said. 'I bow to your expertise. But how will you do it? Where will you get them?'

'First tell me about Bonaparte,' she said. 'You have actually met him, haven't you?'

'Yes,' he said, 'I've met him several times now,' Bernard shook his head. 'He's amazing. He has the gift to inspire. He makes you like him. Love him, even!'

'What's he like? Is he handsome?' she said. 'I've heard he's not specially tall.' Bernard had to think about that.

'I don't know,' he said. 'You don't notice. You just see the man,' Bernard thought deeper. 'He's quite small. But the energy of him. Mother of God! He never stops. I've seen him dictate letters on four different subjects, to four secretaries all at the same time. He goes from one to another, keeping each subject in mind, and the secretaries trying to keep up.'

'But is he handsome?'

'No,' said Bernard, and Madame smiled.

'And he's just married that second-hand tart, Josephine, that Barras dumped on him?' Madame sneered, 'Huh!' she said.

'Shhh!' said Bernard, suddenly nervous. Paul Francois the Vicomte de Barras was supremo of the Paris junta. He ruled like a tyrant. It was dangerous to say things like that, even in private. Bernard shrugged. No doubt that Bonaparte would deal with Barras soon enough, but it hadn't happened yet. Bernard changed the subject. 'How many of these girls can you get?'

'Tell me again what they're for. Why do you want them?'

'I've already told you.'

'Tell me again…or…,' she wriggled a hand down under the silk sheet, took hold of Bernard's most prized assets and squeezed, 'or I'll make you faithful to your wife forever!' There was a brief and hilarious struggle as Bernard threw her off and took possession of himself again. Both laughed. Then Madame filled two glasses from the bottle of excellent wine sat waiting on a bedside table. She handed one to Bernard.

'Seriously,' she said, 'tell me again in as much detail as you can. It will help me satisfy your needs.' He smiled at that.

'I think you've already done that for today.'

She bowed at the compliment.

'But tell me,' she said, 'Tell me the details.' Bernard nodded. He put his thoughts in order.

'I have a staff of Englishmen. Well, in fact Scotsmen.'

'Yes,' she said, 'But English or Scots, if they're working for France, they are traitors to their own people.' Bernard sighed. Madame was perceptive as ever.

'Yes, yes, yes,' he said, trying to brush away the ugly fact. 'But they're vital to France and that's all that matters.'

'Why?' she said, 'What are they doing for you in that Barracks?'

'I can't tell you,' she laughed and slid her hand down again, but he seized it. 'No,' he said, 'I really can't say.'

'So!' she said, and pouted. Bernard relented and went as far as he could.

'It's something clever,' he said. 'Something the English can do and we can't.'

'Go on …,'

'The fact is that we want them to make something, but we can't tell them exactly what it is for, because if we do tell them, then we will rub their English-Scottish noses right into the truth that they, really and truly, are betraying their own people.'

'So what have you told them? What do they think they are doing?'

'They are building some…things…,' he said.

'What things?'

'I can't tell you.'

'Oh, go on. You can tell me.' She put down her glass and came close and nibbled at his ear, and kissed his neck. Bernard shuddered with delight.

'Ohhhh,' he said and his eyes closed and he muttered softly, 'Steam things… to go on the road…,'

'Carriages?' she said. 'Carts? Waggons?' But Bernard remembered his duty. He opened his eyes.

'Things,' he said, 'things that we will use for something else.' She nodded. 'But the trouble is that these are very clever men, and they're talking among themselves and some of them don't entirely trust us, and are wondering what use we shall make of their…things.'

'And so?'

'So we must make sure that they are happy and content here in France. We're already providing them with the best accommodation and food they have ever known, in all their miserable English-Scottish lives, and good wine, and every help from England to get the tools they need for their work.' Madame was puzzled by that.

'Help from England?' she said, 'Tools? How can that be? We're at war with England.'

'Never mind,' he said. 'So they already have everything to make young men happy,' he smiled, 'except one thing.' She laughed aloud at that.

'Then bring them here!' she said. 'My girls will send them home dizzy and grinning,' she kissed him, 'Have you ever known me to fail?'

'Ah, but there's the problem,' he said, 'These are no ordinary men!'

'Oh, I see,' she said, 'Is that all? Well if it's boys they want, then that can be arranged easily enough. I know a house where...,' he interrupted.

'No, no, no. It's not like that.'

'Then what is it like?'

'They're strange men. Almost religious.'

'You mean protestants?'

'No, not that either. They're Freemasons,' she frowned.

'That's not religion,' she said, 'That's...,' she paused, 'Well it's...I'm not sure what it is.'

'Neither am I,' he said, 'But they have a lot of oaths and promises, these Freemasons, and they're true believers in the Revolution, and they don't get drunk, and they have their regular meetings which are all about noble values and a Supreme Being, and honest decency and the like.'

'And not going to the whorehouse?' she said.

'Yes. At least I think so, because none of them has even raised the matter. I think they're all ashamed to be the first one to mention it.'

'So what do they do for relief?' she asked, 'fiddle with themselves in quiet corners?'

'How should I know?' he said. 'But it's not good for a man to go without.'

'Indeed not!' said Madame, 'Or where should I be?' she smiled, 'So what's the answer?'

'The answer is something I said to a colleague in jest. The answer is that these youngsters - and they are quite young - must be made content, because if they're content they won't be asking difficult questions. So, Madame, I want you to provide me with some girls who can become pure fresh maidens again, and contrive to get these fastidious English-Scotsmen to fall in love. Then we can let nature take its course, because all the saints and angels will agree that there is no better way to bind them to France,' he grinned. 'We could even get Monsieur the Mayor to conduct marriages if that's what it takes,' she laughed, but he looked at her closely. 'So can you do it? Are there girls like that?' Madame considered this technical and professional question. She considered it very carefully. It was the numbers that might be a problem.

'Yes,' she said, finally, 'I think so. But you won't find them in the village market. It's going to cost a lot of money.' Bernard shrugged a French shrug, rich and deep in expression.

'Oh?' she said, 'Like that, is it?'

'Yes,' said Bernard, 'It's like that. Just get me the best.' Madame nodded.

'In that case I shall write to a friend in Paris. I shall write to her at once.'

'Good!' said Bernard, 'because our boys have to be happy,' he nodded, 'then we can use them against England.'

Chapter 7

It wasn't until a Friday – the twelfth of February – that *Serpant* upped anchor and set sail: not until then, despite every power that Rowland could apply and I suspect Black Dick too, because it's God that tells the wind when and where to blow and not the Royal Navy. In a way that was relief, because it gave plenty of time for packing *Serpant* with every last barrel of salt pork, powder, pickles, biscuit and rum and the rest, that the shore boats could bring out for us to cram aboard. That and the menagerie of livestock that any ship carried, on setting forth.

It's amazing what landmen don't know, so I won't be surprised if you are surprised to learn that as normal practise in those days – before freezing was discovered - the only way to keep meat fresh, as opposed to salted, was to take it aboard alive, in pens, coops and cages, stacked in every spare inch that could be found. Thus the maindeck of a man-o-war setting out on the King's duty, was a farmyard, with chickens clucking, sheep baa-ing, and pigs grunting. This meant feeding, watering, mucking out, and filth all over our clean white decks. But it gave us decent dinners, and some of the men made pets of the pigs and gave them names. Thus the lower deck had a prize porker by the secret name of Percy, which leaked out in the end, but our Captain didn't suspect anything, which shows you what a blockhead he really was.

A blockhead but a nasty one, as we found out the day before we sailed under his sealed orders.

Early in the forenoon watch, our final load of salt beef came aboard. I had the ship to rights by then, ably assisted by Mr O'Flaherty, a man I came to respect for his vast experience. He'd gone to sea as a common hand and worked his way upward. He was a devout Catholic who never touched a drop of drink except to toast the King's Health: a uniquely contrary mixture, for there's wonderfully few abstainers in Holy Catholic Ireland, and good luck to them say I. But I suppose the two matters were linked, because a Catholic couldn't be commissioned in those days, so O'Flaherty may have felt need to display loyalty even with no taste for drink.

That morning he and I were pacing the quarterdeck, leaving the work to Boatswain Douglas, and when the hands sent the last of the salt beef down below they deliberately left one cask on the deck by the mainmast, among the fowls and livestock there assembled. Then the hands got together behind the Boatswain, who came up to me and O'Flaherty, and saluted.

'Beggin' your pardon, Mr Fletcher,' says Douglas, 'but hands is mustered to Sing the Horse aboard. That's with your permission, sir?' That was new. I'd never heard that before. But O'Flaherty had, he saw me wondering and he helped out. That was his intention at least.

'Mr Fletcher, sir?' says he, and note the word 'sir' from a man over twice my age and ten times my experience. It made me uneasy at first, but a Lieutenant out-ranked a sailing master, and that was that.

'Mr O'Flaherty?' says I, and he nodded in reassurance

'Singing the Horse aboard ship?' says he, and smiled, 'Tradition of the Service, sir!' Coming from him, that was good enough for me.

'Then carry on Mr Boatswain,' says I.

'Aye-aye, Sir!' says he.

So the Boatswain's mates gave a long call on their pipes, and all hands gathered around the cask, grinning and taking off their hats. But then they adopted a pretend attitude of sorrow, with hunched shoulders and heavy sighs, and one man stepped forward: he was their Chanty Man, a title awarded by the lower deck to the one among them with the best voice and who led the singing when work was to be done. He was Jimmy Wilbur, a Yankee. It was common on those days to find Yankees on our ships and the men liked a Yankee for a chanty-man because a Yankee sings through the nose, which helps the voice to carry.

The ship's musicians were alongside Jimmy Wilbur, and they scraped and blew a melody, while he started clapping his hands and stamping one foot, in slow, deliberate time, and all hands followed him. Then, having got the time, Jimmy Wilbur began to sing. He sang to the old tune of Johnny Come Down to Hilo. He gave the first two lines, then they came in with the chorus, and so on. It would have been a heave-away song, had they been working, only they weren't working, but joking. It was a version of the ancient old tale that if you went past the Admiralty victualling yards where, supposedly, prime cattle were slaughtered for the Navy, then you heard nothing from inside the walls but dogs barking and horses neighing.

So these were the words they sang to the solitary cask:

Salt Horse, Salt Horse, we'd have you know,
That to the galley you must go.
Sing Johnny-o, Johnny-o, Johnny.
Poor old oss!
The cook without a sign of grief,
Will boil you down and call you beef,
Sing Johnny-o, Johnny-o, Johnny.
Poor oldoss!
And we poor sailors standing here,
Must eat you though you taste so queer.
Sing Johnny-o, Johnny-o, Johnny.
Poor old oss!

With that, all hands yelled out the words Salt Horse! Then they put on their hats, pulled shoulders back and walked off merry and grinning. It was only then that I noticed that O'Flaherty had taken off his hat, and was putting it back and laughing with the rest of them. So I smiled, too. But just then out of the corner of my eye, I saw someone scuttling down the after hatchway that led to the officer's cabins astern, and especially the Captain's cabin. It was Mr Myers, Poxy Percy's secretary. Down he went, and minutes later up he came again, following Percy himself, Lieutenant Chancellor, Dr Sir Richard, the two middies Copeland and Barclay, and Miss Maitland last of all. Percy was calm, almost smiling, and the two mids were mystified. But Myers, Sir Richard and Chancellor had all worked up the most powerful expressions of outrage.

Percy came straight up to me with his squadron astern of him. O'Flaherty and I saluted, and Percy returned the salute. But then he leaned forward at me as if addressing a child, and with that God-almighty superior look on his face, never raising his voice, and with Myers, Sir Richard and Chancellor right up behind him, yessing and gasping in support at every word he said.

'Fletcher! Fletcher!' says he, shaking his head sadly, 'and likewise, Mr O'Flaherty, of whom I would have thought better, given your many years of service,' he paused and shook his head, 'How could you, gentlemen ? How could you indeed?' he went on after this fashion without ever a hint of what had upset him, and all the while - scrawny streak of piss that he was – he had the gall to stand right up close, with that smile on his face, insulting me in front of the ship's people, and myself wondering if I could keep my hands off him. Finally it was O'Flaherty who asked the question because I was grinding my teeth too hard.

'Begging your pardon, Cap'n, sir,' says he, doffing his hat, 'But might we ask what's come adrift, sir? Or gone awry, at all?'

'You ask?' says Percy, as if in sorrow, 'when you and this officer,' he jabbed a finger at me, 'you two have stood by while the men contrive to insult myself, the Purser, the Admiralty, and all those set above them in law?'

'In what way, Cap'n, sir?' says O'Flaherty.

'In what way, you ask?' says Percy, 'Why, sir, in the way of the foremast hands insulting that which their betters have provided, at great cost to the public purse, for their benefit,' he turned to Myers who had a book open and his finger on a page. Myers stepped forward, bowed, and held the book. It was the Articles of War. Percy read aloud from it, 'Article nineteen,' says he, 'regarding mutinous assemblies or uttering seditious words,' he nodded and read on, 'if any person belonging to the fleet shall utter any words of sedition or mutiny,' Percy looked round to make sure we were all listening, then back to the book, 'if any person shall utter words of sedition or mutiny ... he shall suffer death!' He said it with a sad frown on his face, as if forced to do a cruel thing against his own, and merciful will.

This was met with utter silence on all sides. Only the gulls and the ship's creaking timbers were heard. The hands looked at one another in amazement, and this time even O'Flaherty had no words, so I spoke.

'What mutiny, Cap'n, sir?' says I, 'There's been no mutiny nor seditious words of any kind aboard this ship, as Heaven knows.'

'Aye!' said the hands.

'Loyal hearts and true, sir!' says the Boatswain.

'Oh?' says Percy, 'Then who was it that declared the salt beef to be salt horse? That is seditious mutiny and I am resolved to inflict full punishment upon the guilty.' If gaping jaws made sound, then the ship would have echoed with it. It took me seconds to react, so powerful was my incomprehension of what this preposterous nincompoop was saying. But O'Flaherty recovered first, and bless him for it because he was taking responsibility.

'But Cap'n,' says he, 'Tradition of the Service, sir. The hands was just Singing the Horse aboard. It's tradition. The hands always sing it when the last of the beef comes aboard,' Percy stared at O'Flaherty.

'Tradition, you say?'

'Aye-aye, Cap'n!' says O'Flaherty.

'Aye-aye, sir!' says the hands.

'Tradition, sir!' says the Boatswain.

Percy frowned. He turned on me.

'And do you know of this tradition, Mr Fletcher? Because I am sure that I have never heard of it.' That was a poser and no mistake, so I'd like to think that what I said next was out of respect for Mr O'Flaherty. But on top of that I still wanted to wring Percy's neck, and chose to defy him.

'Of course I know, sir! Everyone knows! It's tradition!'

'Aye!' says all the hands. Percy frowned a wounded frown.

'I'm not sure that I like your manner, Mr Fletcher,' says he. 'I think you'd best go below till you find better temper,' and after that things got worse by stages, with me answering back in a louder voice at every exchange, and Percy sticking hard to his threat to hang someone, never mind who, until even he finally lost his temper and screamed at me.

'Go below at once, you damned insolent puppy!'

Puppy? Puppy? God's blood and thunder, but the little prick-louse said that to me if you could only believe it. Me, that could lift up any man aboard and heave him over the side like a ship's biscuit! So...after that I can't remember what I said, though I do have a picture in my memory of Percy falling back, round-eyed, with his creepy crawlies sheltering behind him in fear as I raged and yelled, and the hands yelling loudly behind me. But thank God I never actually touched him. I kept my hands firm clasped behind me or I'd have throttled him, and been shot dead on the spot, because one of the creepy crawlies did his duty to Poxy Percy. That was Lieutenant bloody Chancellor of the Royal bloody Marines, who sent for his men at the double.

And so, and so, when I got some sense back, the ship was in two factions. Almost the entire crew was behind me and O'Flaherty, while Poxy Percy and his chums, plus the Purser and one or two others were backed up astern, facing me, but with Chancellor and a line of red marines between us, with muskets cocked and levelled at myself, and Chancellor with sword raised, waiting to give the signal to fire.

If you want to be pernickety, count Miss Maitland, Mr Midshipman Copeland and Mr Midshipman Barclay as a third faction, because they stood alone taking no part of the proceedings whatsoever, except that the two boys were knocking their knees in fright.

It was a very, very nasty moment indeed. One shot from the marines would have struck me dead, and dropped a spark into the powder barrel, because the good ship *Serpant* was as near to mutiny in that moment as any ship ever was. The men had taken hard against Poxy Percy, and here was Percy threatening death upon all hands and for nothing that they'd done wrong, and believe me my lovely lads, Jack Tar may have his faults but he likes justice aboard ship, and he turns very nasty when he don't get it.

Then Dr Sir Richard – a man I never liked – saved the day. He at least had the wit to realise the thing had gone too far. So he stepped forward into the grim silence and spoke.

'Now, Now, Lieutenant Chancellor,' says he, 'do tell your men to ground arms,' and he smarmed forward, patting Chancellor's arm, and smiling at the sergeant, and making little hand gestures at the red-coats, encouraging them to lower their muskets. 'We are all Englishmen here,' says he, 'And comrades in arms against the French. So lower your arms, my good fellows.' The men looked to their sergeant, the sergeant looked to Lieutenant Chancellor, the Lieutenant looked to Sir Richard – not to Poxy Percy mark you – and Sir Richard nodded.

'Stand at…ease!' says Chancellor, and there was a united sigh, as the muskets went back to half-cock, and the butts thumped on the deck. With that, hot passions were doused as Sir Richard took hold of Poxy Percy and whispered in his ear and led him below, while O'Flaherty did the same to me.

'Come away, Mr Fletcher,' says he, 'Let the pot go off the boil. I've seen the like before aboard ship. These things are best forgotten. Tomorrow will be different.' Meanwhile, Mr Douglas, the Boatswain, and his mates, chased the crew back to their duties such that all hands could likewise forget there'd just been a stand-up screaming argument between their Captain and First Lieutenant.

For some hours after that, there was an unholy truce aboard *Serpant*. There was still much to do before we could leave on the ebb tide next morning, and that was due just after dawn next day and the wind was fair. So there was plenty to do to keep the hands busy. But that was mainly the Boatswain's duty now, which he discharged well, giving the men no time for muttering and wondering. But I did have much time for muttering and wondering. For instance, had I committed mutiny? I tried to discuss it with O'Flaherty who was very polite, but clearly didn't want to talk: didn't or wouldn't.

As for Poxy Percy and his chums, I don't know what they were doing but eventually an emissary came forth from his camp, and the most unlikely emissary that could be imagined: it was Miss Maitland; in her redingote and fur hat.

It was dark when she came up the after hatchway, and she blinked and looked around before spotting me and O'Flaherty standing by light of the binnacle. She came straight up to me.

'Mr Fletcher,' says she, 'We must speak.'

'Ma'am!' says I and found myself giving a bow.

'Ma'am!' says O'Flaherty, doing the same, because that was Miss Maitland for you. Whatever her profession she behaved like a lady of quality and you couldn't help but respond. She was tall, too, which helped. Not as tall as me, but tall for a woman. She spoke again.

'I bring word from the Captain,' says she.

'Oh?' says I.

'Yes,' says she, as we stood together in a miserable cold night with miserable few stars. There were deep shadows everywhere, and the few men of the anchor watch were wrapped up in thick dark clothes looking on and hearing everything. So she wasted no time. She had the most compact manner of speech, and she looked at me with absolute confidence.

'No more of this,' she said. 'You and he have too much to lose, in the eyes of those who stand behind you.'

'You and he?' says I, 'You mean myself and Percival Clive?'

'Yes,' says she, 'Thus you have my promise that the matter is forgotten.' And that was it. She just stared at me like Queen Elizabeth giving Sir Walter Raleigh his marching orders. She was one hell of a little madam and no mistake. But O'Flaherty spoke up.

'No harm done, ma'am,' says he. 'Strong men have strong passions, but still can be shipmates.'

'Good,' says she. Then she nodded, and turned, and walked off and went below!

'Well I'm damned,' says I.

'No you ain't, Mr Fletcher, sir,' says O'Flaherty, 'All best forgotten, sir. I seen the like before, and we sails on the dawn tide, and no mistake.' Then he lowered his voice, 'I knows young Percy and I knows the lady,' says he, and he nodded. 'Trust me, Sir.' So I did, wondering profoundly what was going on. Who was this woman? How could she speak for Percival Clive? I didn't know. In any case we soon had far worse to worry about than a bit of shouting and temper, because once we did get to sea, the weather blew up and showed us something that few men had ever seen, and fewer still would believe you when you told them of it.

Chapter 8

(Letter dated Thursday 11th February, from Miss Sophia Maitland aboard HMS *Serpant,* at Spithead, to Mrs Amelia Maitland, 25 Blythe Crescent, off Blythe Square, Cadugann Road, West London.)

*

Dearest Mamma,

I have met Apollo and Hercules in one man. He is Mr Jacob Fletcher, the most magnificent male creature I ever saw. More of him later. Meanwhile the wretched Percival has all but provoked mutiny. He has done so within days of coming on to this ship. I therefore take comfort in my contract, as signed and sealed by you with P's father, Sir Reginald, the sugar millionaire. Likewise I renew my appreciation of the great sums involved. Be assured that the gold will continue to flow since I will continue in my duties.

Fortunately these duties remain light. P's demands are infrequent and he is easily persuaded into postures which cannot possibly lead to conception. I believe he actually prefers it and I am certain that he does not know the difference (once again I thank you for your advice in these matters, Mamma. Your years in our profession were not wasted!).

P's suite of followers presents more problems. Myers, Rogers and Chancellor would all advance upon me if they dared. But they are cowards except Chancellor who is vicious. He would beat a dog for the fun of it. The two midshipmen are children and of no account.

Meanwhile P knows that in me, his father has bought him the best. Thus P does not look beyond me and is thereby kept safe from entrapment of adventuresses. You may reassure his father in that respect, because I know that it worries him. In addition I have control over P quite sufficient to prevent him losing his fortune at cards, or over-indulgence in drink. Please reassure the father in that respect also. But as regards the utter incompetence of his son as a seafaring officer, the father cannot be reassured because his worst fears are made real every day. Consequently, if – as you report - his mother still believes P to be a gallant officer, then she is a bigger fool even than her son.

So to the mutiny. Today P took advantage of some peculiar tradition of the common crew,to pretend anger and accuse them of mutiny. It was all sham. His aim was to frighten them, then to demonstrate magnanimity. He wished to show himself as a hard disciplinarian. But Fletcher argued against this false accusation of mutiny, putting P in peril of genuine mutiny when P argued back against Fletcher.

This, because P did not know the strength of that which he was facing in the person of Fletcher, who is idolised by the crew. They would follow him down the cannon's mouth. They talk of him constantly: 'Mr Fletcher says this', 'Mr Fletcher says that'. He has their profound and total loyalty. Thus, when the quarrel began, the men instantly closed up in support of Fletcher. They cried defiance upon P with oaths and raised fists. They urged on Fletcher with such shouts as 'Jacky Flash!' and 'Give it him proper!' I saw this myself. It was remarkable. Where Fletcher leads, they follow.

Then Chancellor sent for his marines. They came in arms until Dr Rogers intervened, acting not out of courage –of which he has none -but out of fear for his own skin should violence erupt. He spoke, and persuaded the marines to lower their muskets. Not that this was any great triumph because the marines, like all the rest, admire Fletcher enormously. Thus I doubt they would have fired had Chancellor ordered them. But Fletcher, in his anger, did not see this and clearly believed himself threatened.

Later, when Dr Rogers took P downstairs to his cabin, I was able to speak to all of them. All, including P,were terrified of the anger they had aroused. They wanted peace at any cost. Only Chancellor demurred but the majority overturned him. All then accepted my suggestion that the matter should be forgotten on both sides. But none of them dared approach Fletcher excepting Chancellor whose temper could not be trusted. So I went myself and spoke to Fletcher who was pleased to agree. Thus we sail tomorrow as if nothing had happened. Men are such fools.

But Fletcher himself is a wonderful creature. He is huge and hand-some, dark and strong and has mysterious history. If I were free I would have such a man as him. But I am not. However, you and I Mamma are becoming very rich thanks to the contract. Thus I shall continue to fulfil it. Then once we are indeed rich, I shall indeed be free, and then who knows?

Your loving daughter, Sophia.

Post Scriptum. Do you recall Mr Rowland, the gentleman who recommended me to P's father as companion to the son? I encountered Rowland at the Portsmouth Hotel where P and I had rooms. He affected surprise but I suspect the meeting was contrived. He spoke of Mr Fletcher, whom I had not yet met. He advised me to take Fletcher's part if opportunity presented. He advised me to beware of treachery fromP. Quelle surprise? As if I needed warning!!? Rowland is old but most charming and has a powerful force of intellect. I wonder what lay behind his words?

With affection, S.

(Letter dated Thursday 11th February from Cuthbert Percival-Clive, Master and Commander aboard HMS *Serpant*, at Spithead, to Mrs Margaret Percival-Clive, Barrant Lodge Hall, Near Maidstone, in Kent.)

(NB that many spelling errors have been corrected, and that punctuation, capitals and paragraphs have been added, since the original has none.)

Mother,

I am beset with cruel, unjust, mutinous and disgraceful affronts and betrayed on every side by all those persons who a decent man might turn to for support. I therefore turn to you, my only friend in need and in adversity, begging that once again you would use your benign influence to persuade your brother, my uncle, Mr WilliamPitt, to use his high powers as Prime Minister, thus to smite down my enemies and lay them low.

Time is too short to tell all, for my ship sails tomorrow on the King's own orders. For now let it only be known that Mr Jacob Fletcher —once my companion and shipmate —is become a treacherous, mutinous, insolent dog not worthy of the rank he holds. I beg of you, therefore, mother, so to persuade Uncle Pitt, as to see Fletcher stripped of his rank and brought before Court Martial on a charge of foul and despicable mutiny.

Yours, in sure and certain anticipation of justice,

Your loving son,

Cuthbert.

Chapter 9

After the excitement of the previous day, our making sail and getting out of Spithead was unremarkable, since all parties really did behave as if nothing had happened. Thus, just before dawn when the tide was on the ebb, Percy and his chums came up on deck where I was waiting, O'Flaherty was waiting, the ships people were waiting, and even the hogs and chickens were nudging each other to see what might happen next.

So everyone saluted everyone else and never looked into one another's eyes. Then O'Flaherty and I stood back so Percy could take command, which he did, giving the order to up anchor and make sail. Then he gave the quartermasters their course to steer, because we were under sealed orders and only Percy knew where to head before he opened them. After that, he withdrew with his chums to the windward side of the quarterdeck, and left myself and the ship's people to do the rest.

I'll spare you the details of getting a ship under way. They were the commonplace of their time: hands to the capstan, anchors aweigh, massive cables coming aboard with mussel shells clinging. Gulls calling, fresh scent of the sea, salt spray on the wind, ship gathering way, decks heeling, sails filling: everything that poets dream of, and that bores the life out of me.

[Profoundly false. Fletcher adored the moment of setting sail. In later years his eyes would fill with tears as he described it. Even I was moved by his accounts of this moment, and ladies would fall into raptures. S.P.]

Then finally, some hours later, with the starboard watch on deck and the larbolins below: lines were coiled down, anchors secured, sails trimmed, and the good ship *Serpant* going steady on a stiff westerly. She was a fine ship and it was a joy to feel her rise to the swell without putting her bows into the ocean and throwing tons of icy water half way down the deck as some ships did. So the Brig Sloop *Serpant* was merry and bright, but the weather was not.

This was the deep of the winter, remember. It was early February and bitter cold, under a grey sky. The running ropes froze in the blocks, the sails were stiff as tin sheets, and the top-men – who went aloft with thick-mittened hands – couldn't expose their fingers long enough to do their duties properly, so the topsails weren't easily handled. Thus we had them close-reefed, O'Flaherty and I, and made do with a steady five knots of headway when she'd have doubled that and more, given the chance. So out we crept, with the Isle of Wight on the starboard beam, and a few sails on the grey-black seas around us, because even in winter, the almighty Royal Navy was about its business and we were far from the only ship at sea.

Orders from His Mightiness the Percy were to take *Serpant* out, then to cruise the coast of Hampshire and Dorset down towards Devon. So off we went, feeling cold and hard-done-by and never dreaming how sweet the weather was compared with what was to come. But first I had a little adventure. One that pleased me, though I freely admit it had to do with myself feeling somewhat cock of the walk, having faced down Poxy Percy and the marines.

Thus, coming up on deck after dinner I put my head over the companionway, just as Mr O'Flaherty – who had the watch – was yelling at the hands, because they too were feeling a little over-pleased with themselves. The rascals had taken to humming the tune Johnny *Come* Down *to* Hilo, in mockery, whenever any of Percy's chums were on deck. In this case it was Lieutenant Chancellor who received their music in company with Dr Sir Richard. The pair of them had gone up just ahead of me, and were standing by the mainmast. O'Flaherty didn't see me coming and he let fly.

'Avast that bloody noise there!' says he in a great bellow. The hands stopped at once, and put fingers to brow in salute, because they respected O'Flaherty for the man that he was: a salt-sea veteran bred up to command. But then little Lieutenant Chancellor stepped forward.

'Indeed!' says he, glaring at the hands, 'Just watch your mouths!' He was acting as if in support of O'Flaherty, but with his own nasty motives. He stamped around in his shiny boots with his chest puffed out and took a kick at one of the ship's boys. The nipper went over, with legs knocked from under, and Chancellor caught him another kick as he lay flat. Then Chancellor looked at Dr Sir Richard, and the pair of them grinned, especially Chancellor, as he seized the boy by one ear and hauled him to his feet.

'Owwww!' screamed the boy, 'Owww! Owww! Owww!' while O'Flaherty was wondering what to do, because his own status opposite a marine lieutenant was unclear. A sailing master was outranked by a sea service lieutenant, who was likewise senior to a marine lieutenant. But on most ships it wasn't rank, but social status that counted between master and marine lieutenant, and O'Flaherty had risen from the lower deck while Chancellor was a gentleman even if he didn't act like one.

Meanwhile, the ear-twisting went on too long, with torn flesh, a gaping wound, and a look on Chancellor's face that I didn't like, not one bit, because he was enjoying himself, having picked on someone smaller than his miserable self. Even the hands were frowning, and believe me they weren't gentle towards the ship's boys who usually got their orders with an oath and a clout. That's the way of the sea. But the ear-twisting went on too long, and I'd not forgotten who ordered men to point muskets at me, so I acted on impulse.

'Ah! Mr Chancellor!' says I in a big voice, and leapt up the companionway on to the deck, and everyone looked my way.

'Mr Fletcher!' says Chancellor, and the bugger knew he was doing wrong because he instantly let go of the boy's ear, and stepped aside as if the blood running down the child's chin was nothing to do with him. 'There you are, Mr Chancellor,' says I and put on my best smile.

'Ah, ah, Mr Fletcher,' says Chancellor, wondering what was coming – as well he might.

'Your advice, Mr Chancellor,' says I, 'I have a problem with the ship's pistols which I cannot solve by myself, and I would value the opinion of a soldier.' He blinked at that, sniffed a bit and pondered. Then he stood as upright as he could, and nodded.

'I will give whatever assistance is within my power,' says he.

'Splendid, sir!' says I, 'So perhaps you would follow me?' And he did.

There are few private places aboard a ship the size of a brig-sloop. The best I could find was the cable tier in the depths of the fore-hold. Even that wasn't entirely private as the ship's rats were somewhere underfoot, but mainly it was the stowage hole for the ship's huge anchor cables, cuddled up like mighty pythons and drying out over a grid that let water run into the bilges below. It was a dark, wet-smelling , low-roofed wooden cave, where the ship's motion always feels worse than it does on deck where you can see the horizon.

I'd picked up a lantern on the way, found a hook to hang it on for the light, and then I turned round on Chancellor who had the most woeful expression of doubt on his face. He clearly had little experience of ships, he'd followed me to this inexplicable place without question, and now I suppose he was wondering where the pistols were. He looked round, and his lips even started to frame a 'where?' or perhaps it was a 'what?' or a 'why?'

But never mind, because I took off the woollen muffler I was wearing, and shoved a fold of it into his mouth with my left hand, while my right hand pulled him up off his feet by the collar of his coat, got him fast against one of the oaken pillars that supported the deck-head, and swung my knee up into his galloping tackles, several times, and with great force. I was being careful, you see. The little sod deserved a chastisement but if I'd swung my fist I suspect I might have killed him, pitiful squirt that he was. But a swift knee up the privates takes a man's breath away but it don't ruin him. Anyway, it was the humiliation of it that counted.

'Uh!' says he, 'Uh! Uh! Uh!' one grunt every time the knee went home. He couldn't do better, not with his mouth full of wool. Then I dropped him and leaned over him where he lay, on the coils of a sixty-fathom hawser. Up came his own little knees, cringed together in agony, and the tears spurting from his eyes as they glistened in the yellow lamp-light, nasty little swine that he was.

'Listen to me,' says I, 'If you lay hands on anyone - man or boy - aboard of my ship again, then you won't only get another basting but I'll parade you round the deck stark naked, with your balls tarred black and a feather up your arse! Do you understand me?' He nearly nodded his head off and I never had a squeak of trouble out of him after that.

Then, later that day, after supper and well dark, Captain Percy finally opened his sealed orders, and was obliged to call a meeting of all his officers in the stern cabin. That was himself, myself, Mr O'Flaherty and Lieutenant Chancellor, who sat silent throughout, staring at the table top and nursing his aches. Those four, together with Dr Sir Roger, the two mids and Mr livery-coat Myers, who took notes, handed round the drinks and presumably cleared up afterwards. Since Percy had money, the stern cabin was now lavishly decorated and lit with dozens of candles hanging in patent shades that swung with the ship's motion and kept the candles from guttering. It was one of the best-lit cabins I was ever in. He had his own furniture, too, and paintings of his mother, his father, and their noble mansion bought with sugar money, somewhere in Kent.

He'd got back a bit of his self-confidence, and once the port had gone round enough times, he beckoned Myers to bring forward the now-opened orders and a map of the south west coast, so that he could explain what we were to do. Though there wasn't much to say, really.

'I am charged with intercepting and preventing the pernicious trade of

71

smuggling,' says he, 'a trade now working out of coves and secret harbours from Falmouth to Exmouth…,' and so on and so on. It was a very tasty posting for him; well away from French warships that might fight back, and exceedingly well placed to make prizes of smugglers with all the rich goods they carried. That's what you get when your father is a millionaire and your mother the Prime Minister's sister. Likewise it was very tasty for all aboard of us, because every man shared in the prize money. So we were all well pleased. We were indeed, and we grinned happily and laid hard into the port. In fact we as nearly had a convivial evening as could ever be, in Poxy Percy's company.

On the other hand, though perhaps it was the endless supply of port, but I felt as we sat together, that the sea was getting up and indeed it was. We had little sleep in our cots and hammocks that night, and I was on deck well before they sent for me in an evil black night. One of the middies was on watch: Mr Barkley, all wrapped up tight with a huge telescope under his arm and a keen expression on his face. He was happy. I could see it. He was actually happy to be on watch, in a real ship, on the real sea with the weather turning foul.

'Well, well,' thinks I, 'maybe there's a seaman inside of him.'

'Thank-you-mister-fletcher-sir,' says he, all in a gulp, 'because I'd have sent for you instantly, sir!'

'Quite so, Mr Barkley,' says I, 'You may consider yourself relieved, and I'd be much obliged if you would …,' I was about to tell him to summon Mr O'Flaherty, but I realised he was already standing beside me in the dark, having felt the ugly motion just as I had, and come up close behind me. The Boatswain had come up, too. I nodded. That was good. I spoke on, 'if you would summon the Captain, Mr Barkley.'

'Aye-aye, sir!' says the mid, and off he went at the double.

'All hands on deck, I think, Mr Fletcher?' says O'Flaherty, looking at the sky.

'Indeed, Mr O'Flaherty,' says I, and, 'All hands, Mr Boatswain!'

'Aye-aye, sir!'

Then there were boatswain's calls and heavy feet, and men turning out and the ship coming alive, and hands rushing to stations, just as the weather was rushing down upon us. Even Percival-Clive turned out and was as much use as a lead life-jacket, because in all reality I was in command of the ship from that moment, and he had the sense to keep out of my way.

But all of us, every one of the one hundred and twenty men and boys of *Serpant*'s crew, stood together on the deck or in the rigging, or ready manning the pumps as some were, and the carpenter and his men ready to sound the well, and the gunner's crew going from piece to piece to check the securing tackles, and even the loblolly boys – for the ship had no surgeon – ready with their knives and jollops in case any one got smashed or broken from what was so obviously coming.

Fortunately *Serpant* was snugged down for the night, like a lazy Indiaman, because we could barely work our canvas aloft, for the freezing cold. She spread just flying jib, and close-reefed topsails for comfortable steerage way, and was already braced up for a strong blow. But now I had the men rig hand-lines across the decks for us to cling to, and I doubled the gun tackles, sent down the upper yards, and struck everything but the fore topsail. It was hard work for all, even without cold fingers, and I doubt the hands would have done it without the practise they'd had while at anchor. Even so, they'd hardly finished before a great storm burst over us out of the black night.

'Here it comes,' says O'Flaherty, as dense clouds swirled around us and solid sheets of rain came down like waterfalls, and winds blew from all points with the ship, heaving and groaning and the rigging shrieking with each blast and blow of wind. It went on for hours, but *Serpant* rode it like a good 'un and the watches changed, and the men below got some rest, and the middies grinned and enjoyed themselves, bless their hearts. Then suddenly the clouds began to lighten. They moved at amazing speed, shifting off to the west like the drawing of a curtain on a stage, and the weather blew out in an instant, just like that, as the weather at sea does whenever it choses, and the storm went away, and the waves heaved rather than broke, and left us becalmed with a clear sky, moonlight and the brilliance of the planets and stars.

It was uneasy, uncanny, and after the fierce rain storm it caused a sensation of relief almost impossible to describe, and all the no-seamen came up on deck to see it: Miss Maitland – who nodded and smiled at me – and Mr Myers and Percy's servants. They all stood, pointing and gaping at the wonders above. You couldn't blame them. I've never seen such lights in the heavens. You felt you could reach up and take a star in your fist, or cut a slice off the moon with a carving knife. What wonders! It's why some men go to sea. But it couldn't last.

'Get those lubbers below, Mr Boatswain!' says I, pointing at Miss Maitland and the rest.

'Aye indeed,' says O'Flaherty, 'This ain't no honest calm. It's just telling us there's more to come.' And by George he was right, because I'd never seen anything like what happened next, and worse still, just when I was comforting myself that at least O'Flaherty would know what to do, he looked at me and shrugged as if helpless. 'God preserve us!' says he, 'All hands aboard of us,' and he crossed himself, as there came the most appalling rumbling noise, and the lookouts in the tops yelled in fear.

'Beware on deck!' they cried, 'Beware the wave!' But that's all I heard because soon, no human voice could carry over the roaring of the sea, and I looked up and saw the men in the foretop pointing in great sweeps from north to south, as if the whole ocean were rising against us. O'Flaherty shook at my arm and pointed, and I turned and saw the most appalling sight. The ocean had indeed risen against us: the whole ocean, because what was bearing down from the north east was one, single, colossal wave of enormous height, extending along the entire horizon. It came on faster than a galloping horse and I have never in all my days seen anything that struck such fear into me. Uttermost dread sank right down to the bottom of my soul. And it wasn't just me. There were men aboard who collapsed in fear, and some of them ran below. But not Mr Berkley, I would add. Not him, nor little Mr Copeland, the other mid. Maybe they were too young to understand. Maybe they were brave?

The monster came down on us like a mountain over a mouse, and I can't guess its height other than to state that it loomed high over the truck of our mainmast, which was over a hundred feet above the deck. The wave was smooth and shining and black and entirely un-broken at its crest. It was solid water, the wrath of the gods and the might of nature. It was like earthquakes and hurricanes which take hold of the works of man, and smash them to splinters and grind them to dust.

With no steerage way, it was only by luck that *Serpant* met the wave bow on. Had we been hit on the beam, we'd have gone over, rolled like a barrel, ripped out our masts, and most likely been broken apart and sunk. As it was, the ship went up, and up, and up, with all of us hanging on, until the deck was so steep that those astern, looked for'ard as if looking up the sides of a house, and I saw men lost and thrown overside, arms waving, legs kicking, mouths open, and all our livestock, in all our cages swept away, and the ship's boats amidships hanging in their lashings, and every gun in our battery fighting to break loose. Then the bows came down and the stern came up at shocking speed, and the ship groaned, and timbers cracked like gunshots as we reached the wave-peak, and saw the ocean below us as the gulls see it, with nothing on the face of the waters to match us for height. This held for an instant, then horrible, sickening, plunging nausea, as four hundred tons of ship dropped beneath our feet, down like a falling cannon ball, with lines parting, timbers sprung, and everything lost that hadn't already gone or wasn't nailed or battened down.

Down we slid to the level sea, and the ship wallowed and rolled, and the enormous monster that had lifted her up, went on its way, out into the deep of the ocean, and the roaring and weather went with it, leaving a clear sky with a promise of dawn. Who knows where the wave came from? Who knows where it went or what phenomenon of nature had caused it? But it was gone and we were left with nothing. No weather at all than a bit of rain, a bit of wind, some lightning in the sky following after the wave, and it was all over, unbelievably over, and the tempest gone and the seas empty.

So then, my jolly boys, we all of us looked around, to see who was still among us and who was not. And we looked at our ship to see if it was still there, which most of it was, and since I was in command – nobody including myself even thought of turning to Poxy Percy – I summoned the Boatswain, Carpenter, Gunner and Purser to find out what was left of us, and whether we had a ship fit to sail.

Which we did not. We were remarkably sound aloft: just the mizzen topmast carried away and some lines parted, but nothing the hands couldn't easily splice and mend. But she was opened up below.

'Leaking badly, Mr Fletcher, sir!' says the carpenter, as we gathered in our soaking clothing by the mainmast: a soused and dripping crew of the ship's technical experts, each come to report on his department. Poxy Percy was there somewhere I suppose, but who cared about him? 'Pumps going as hard as can be, sir,' says the Carpenter, 'and more men needed urgently.'

'Mr Boatswain,' says I, 'Send down as many hands as may be needed to man the pumps. At the double, now!'

'Aye-aye, sir!'

'Thank'ee, sir,' says the carpenter, 'It was the hogging, Mr Fletcher, d'you see? It was fierce bad when she was on the crest of the wave. I never knew a ship raised up in such a manner like that.' I nodded. Everyone nodded. Hogging was what happened when a ship was lifted up amidships leaving bow and stern to droop violently under their weight, pulling the ship's joints apart. We'd all heard the timbers crack when she was up high. 'I fear the ship ain't fit for service, sir,' says the carpenter. We might make port if the pumps keep ahead of the leaks, but she ain't fit for service.'

And that was that. Poxy Percy's wonderful, money-making commission was ended before it began. There was a groan from all hands, because it's not only pirates that relish the capturing of ships, but King's Navy seaman, too. That's the prize system for you, and you youngsters should note the legalized theft of it, which says that any ship captured by the Navy gets sold by Court of Admiralty, and the money shared out among those officers and tars that did the capturing. But we weren't going to have any of that aboard of poor *Serpant*, and I shook my head and wondered what might happen next. I especially wondered regarding myself. What about Rowland and his business in France? What about Percy's mummy and daddy, and all their influence? Was Percy really to be denied his tasty commission? I wondered and wondered.

Chapter 10

'It is with great satisfaction, my General, that I report the tremendous efforts that have driven the canal to completion.'
(Translated from a letter of Tuesday May 26th 1796, from General of Brigade Claude Bernard at Fragnal, to Generalissimo Napoleon Bonaparte, Headquarters of the Army of Italy.)

*

Bernard was awestruck at the extent and scope of the works, and he was cheerful because at last there was no rain, the sky was clear, and he rode a fine horse alongside the Commandant-General of Engineers and his staff of five officers to view what had been achieved in the name of France. Also, there was the pleasure of appearing in public in the uniform of his new rank - General of Brigade - as conferred upon him by the Paris Junta, at Bonaparte's insistence. Bernard had stood before the mirror in joyful delight when first he put on that uniform.

'And, so!' said the Commandant General, and wheeled his horse around, allowing Bernard to pass him. Bernard urged his horse forward, up on to a viewing platform built of neatly-squared timbers, neatly driven into a hillside, and fenced off for safety, with a neat, strong fence. Bernard puffed out his cheeks and dug in his heels. He wasn't an accomplished horseman, and his mount didn't like the booming timbers of the platform under its hoofs, not one little bit. So there were some whinnies and whimpers and stamping, but soon the seven horsemen were formed in a row, gazing out on one of the greatest military engineering projects in Europe.

Bernard stared. Along a vast, straight line the soil of northern France had been turned over, as if by the stroke of a colossal knife, run down a colossal ruler. Thousands of blue-clad military engineers had achieved this modern marvel, though of course they were all gone now. Gone to the Generalissimo's lightning war in Italy. Bernard looked up and down the long line. It was silent; it was peaceful, running as it did through the dense Forêt du Nord where hardly a soul lived. There was little to do now, other than clearing away rubbish, and that small task was left to a mere handful of peasants brought in for the purpose. But here Bernard corrected himself:

'Not peasants,' he thought, 'Citizens. Citizens of France,' He corrected himself because it was so dangerous to use the wrong words. And he wasn't even sure whether peasant was forbidden or permitted these days. Who could tell? For all he knew it was a compliment now! But you could never be too careful, and he knew that he was right to be careful because he saw the true belief shining in the eyes of the Commandant General. He was young. He was proud. He was inspired with the New Enlightenment. Holy Mary Mother of God! He was just like those English-Scottish freemasons back at the Barracks. But the child was speaking.

'Look, Citizen Inspector!' said the Commandant, 'All this great enterprise, for the common good!'

'Indeed!' said Bernard and he imagined the thump of shovels, the squeak of wheels, the pounding of mallets and the singing of the men as they'd worked for two years past on this vast canal, now running one hundred and sixty kilometres, from Frangnal de Picardy to the seaport of Lyommeville. It was indeed a vast enterprise. Something that only French engineering could achieve: so many heavy wagons to bring in food, drink, tents and bedding for the workforce; so many wagons to bring in the dressed stone for the canal banks, and the puddle-clay lining to make the canal waterproof. All this, together with the fodder for the draft animals themselves, and the Army doctors and field hospitals for the idiots who smashed one another's fingers with pickaxes, drove spades through their toes, or broke one another's noses in fights at night after too much wine. All this, overcome by French genius!

Bernard looked up and down the canal once more. He nodded. It was good. He even smiled at the young Commandant because the engineers were kindred to artillerymen like himself. They were technical men in blue, just like the artillery. The Engineers were builders and achievers, commanded by men of education. The French soldier fondly called them Les Génies, slang for engineers, but also recognition that they were like the genies of Arabia, when it came to taming of the wilderness with roads and bridges; or indeed canals. But sadly, the weather was all too good to be true, and the sky clouded as Bernard studied the works, and the first spatters of rain came down both on Engineer bicorn hat and Artillery bicorn hat.

'Bah!' said the young Commandant, and waved a hand at the sky. 'But if we are quick,' he said, 'I can show you our gate-works, before we go on to the Drawing Office.' Bernard nodded. The horses were turned and the seven riders came off the platform, down on to the military road, which was proof against any rain that ever fell. Thus they cantered steadily for a distance that Bernard judged to be about half a French League, because he didn't like the metres and kilometres of the New Order. He used them because he had to, but he didn't like them.

He cheered up when they reached an engineering camp where lock gates were being repaired. There were huge tents giving shelter, while saws were buzzing and red hot iron was clanging under hammers, and hearths were glowing and smoke rising, and busy work continuing. There were salutes, and men rushed forward to take the horses, and Bernard swung out of the saddle, and creaked and groaned on to his legs, with the young Commandant helping him, always talking, talking, talking.

'There's only one lock on this entire section,' he said, 'not like the locks outside Lyommeville. There's eleven of them down there!'

'Yes,' said Bernard, who knew exactly how many locks the canal had.

'Our's was one of the first locks installed,' said the Commandant, 'and some of one of the gates has rotted, so we're making a replacement.' He stepped forward and put a hand on the great timbers, and the workmen stood back respectfully. 'The way the locks work, Citzen Inspector, the way they work is like this: First you close the upper gates …,' Bernard stopped listening. He also knew exactly how a canal lock worked. He didn't need a lecture. But he took a good look at the near-completed gate. It was massive. It had to be. The canal was to be three of these new metres deep, and many more of them wide. Nothing less would serve the purpose. So the gates were massive, and strong and extremely expensive, and technically difficult to put in place. Bernard looked up at the tent canvas over the workshop. The rain was battering now, but it wasn't getting in. Good! The Commandant removed his hand, the carpenters, blacksmiths and hammer-men went back to work, and he continued his explanation.

'Citizen Commandant,' said Bernard, interrupting the flow, 'I've seen enough. Can we go into the Drawing Office? I need to speak to you in private.'

'Of course,' said the Commandant.

'Good,' said Bernard.

The Drawing Office was a brand-new wooden hut, built by Les Génies, who always did their utmost to produce the very best. It was big, dry, excellently waterproof and even had a vestibule with rows of hooks where sodden-wet cloaks and greatcoats could be hung to keep the damp outside.

Once inside, Bernard looked round at the desks, and cabinets and papers and drawing boards, and the big windows and the universal neatness and tidiness. This was the place where calculations were made, plans were drawn, and where the great canal had been brought into being. There was little to do now, and everyone here was standing to attention by their clerkish work. Bernard looked round. There was just the one big space, with no other doors than the one they'd come in by. Bernard glanced at the rain streaming down the windows. He certainly wasn't going out there again, to take the Commandant aside. So he checked one final time.

'Do you have an office, Citizen Commandant? Any quiet place?'

'No, Citizen Inspector,' Bernard shrugged. So be it. It was time to let these engineers know what they were building anyway. He judged that to be within the letter of his orders.

'The canal is a vital part of a project of utmost national importance,' said Bernard.

'Yes!' said the Commandant, and his men.

'As you know,' said Bernard, 'the canal was originally planned to link the city of Montfer with the coast,' all nodded, and Bernard continued, 'Montfer is famous for its coal mining and iron-working, and is connected by good roads to three of the greatest arsenals and storehouses in France.'

'And?' said the Commandant.

'And, citizens - thanks to your efforts, Montfer - and Fragnal, too - are now connected by your canal, and the road alongside it, to the seaport of Lyommeville.'

'Yes?' said Commandant and staff, and they thought hard because Lyommeville faced directly towards England across the narrowest part of La Manche: The Channel as England called it. Bernard nodded, he had them gripped in attention, now.

'The canal,' he said 'was planned for the general good of the Republic. But thanks to secret devices now being made at the Fragnal Barracks, a vastly greater opportunity has been perceived. It has been perceived and championed by Generalissimo Bonaparte himself!'

'Bonaparte,' said the lips of all the listeners, and Bernard reached the climax of his speech.

'So the new and enormous purpose of the canal is …,' But a door slammed open, causing all the glass windows to tremble, as a man dashed in. It was one of Colonel Sauvage's aides from Frangnal Barracks: a young ensign, fresh off the road, soaking wet, who hadn't even taken off his cloak. There was water running off it in streams on to the nice clean planking of the Drawing Office.

'My General!' he said to Bernard, and saluted.

'What is it?' said Bernard, much annoyed.

'It's trouble, my General,' said the ensign. 'It's the girls we got from Paris. Our English-Scottish have found out about them and there's trouble. Colonel Sauvage begs that you come back to Fragnal. He begs that you come at once.'

Chapter 11

We were lucky. *Serpant* held together despite uneasy winds that finally settled on a south easterly blow that tried hard to put us aground somewhere on the coast where Devon reaches down towards France. But on Saturday 17th April, we anchored safe and secure, among the lavish seafaring supplies of Plymouth: a fine thing indeed for a poor old ship, ruined below and having done her utmost best for her people. Though of course it was the ship's people that kept her afloat, with hideous labour turning the bars of our chain pump to heave the ocean out of her bilges. So I suppose that each gave best efforts to save the other.

When I say 'Plymouth' you youngsters should note that our anchorage was not Plymouth itself but miles away, in the Navy yard situated in the estuary of the river Tamar – the Hamoaze as it's known - on the east bank of the river. The yard was surrounded in its own thriving town, all devoted to the King's Navy. Everything there was straight lines and massive blocks of new masonry, with huge warehouses and magazines laid out like a fleet at anchor. Then there were dry docks, sheer hulks, mast ponds, spars, stores, cables, powder and guns in limitless profusion. All that and the shoals of skilled workers needed to re-fit a broken vessel, or build one from keel up. There was also a very great deal of naval shipping at anchor, mainly smaller ships: luggers, cutters and gunboats, but there were some frigates too, and a couple of old, worn-out ships of the line. There was much to see, and much to point out and admire.

Poxy Percy, of course, had to go ashore to make himself known to the Port Admiral, Lord Clyde-Jones, to seek further orders. But first Percy displayed the only piece of initiative I ever knew him capable of.

"Send the men to their dinners," says he to me, just before we piped the side for him to go down into a boat. He was all shiny and bright in his full dress, with his commission papers in a leather wallet and Dr Sir Rogers going with him to see he didn't wet himself when he sat on the pot. Then he gave a smile as if pleased with his own wit. "You may feed the pigs to the crew," says he, "including my own pig," and off he went.

All hands heard this, and it brought mixed feelings because there was only the one survivor of all the livestock we'd taken aboard, and that was Percy the pig: our Captain's own purchase, whom the men had adopted as a piece of the ship's luck. Percy was berthed in a solid pen on the lower deck, right for'ard by the hawse-holes: him and our other pigs. But Percy was alive, while the others had been smashed and mashed in the ship's motion. They were still edible, but they were very silent while Percy was grunting and snorting. But appetite conquered sentiment, because all hands were exhausted, we'd lost fifteen men overside, whose few possessions would be auctioned off among their mates, and fresh meat puts blood in a man's veins. So the ship's cook stepped forward with his knife, and poor Percy squealed and died and was butchered.

Meanwhile, the human Percy was away many hours, during which time various boats came alongside of us, the first bearing the tarts and traders that always flock down upon any ship new into harbour, especially a King's ship. Later, following Percy's damage report to the Admiral, a boat came out with dockyard shipwrights, to pronounce judgement on *Serpant*'s hull. These gentlemen I left to our carpenter and Mr O'Flaherty. But I stayed on deck when the first boats arrived, to watch over the hands - bless their innocent hearts - because if I'd not been there, who knows who might have taken the chance to desert? In those days, with crews largely made up of pressed men, desertion was second only to mutiny as the bogeyman that terrified Sea Service officers in the dead of the night.

But soon I got fed up with being the ship's jailor, and set little Mr Chancellor and his marines to the work. This I did mainly because I'd watched the men as they yelled and bargained with the boat people, and I could see that they weren't going to run. They bobbed and saluted to me and not a whiff of desertion was there about them. I suppose they were just happy to have survived the storm, and content to be aboard. But I'll never understand Jack Tar. He's a mystery to me and I can't explain him.

[The explanation is that Fletcher ran a happy ship, and his men never wanted to desert. But his affected prejudice against the Service prevented his ever understanding this; or so he maintained. S.P.]

Finally I record the only other thing of note that happened to me aboard the *Serpant*. As soon as Chancellor took over, I went below to wash myself. I'd not changed my linen in days and I was itching from the dried out salt on my skin from the seawater drenching. I wanted to be clean and put on something fresh, so I ordered a bucket of fresh water down to my cabin, and then, in the companionway coming out of Percy's stern cabin, I met Miss Maitland.

She looked at me. I looked at her. She was no more than six feet from me and there was nobody else about. So she gave me a look. Now, my jolly boys, there's many ways a woman looks at a man, and the looks are as meaningful as a hoist of flags. She looked at me, held the look just a second, then gave a tiny little smirk.

'You are in my way, Mr Fletcher,' says she, and raised her eyebrows.

'I suppose I am, Miss Maitland,' says I, 'Since there's only you and me here."

'Indeed, sir,' says she, 'But here is not a good place.'

'Are there better places?' says I.

'That, sir, depends entirely upon your own initiative,' says she, and she stepped forward, and the scent of her flowed over me as she brushed past, barely making contact, on her way up on deck.

'Huh,' says she, without looking back. Then she was gone. She'd never so much as noticed me before, but now, by George, she was signalling permission to lay alongside and it set the heart going and the thoughts racing. Skin and roast me, if it didn't.

Then things happened fast. Percy came back late that night, beaming and chattering out of his boat and on to the quarterdeck. He stared at me hard, as if in triumph, which puzzled me at the time, and Dr Sir Roger and all his chums and servants fell to fawning over him, and Miss Maitland was there too, and all hands came up to hear the news. So the whole crew of us was huddled in the dark, with the ship at anchor, and the night sky above, and the other ships in harbour sounding their bells as the watches changed. And then – in that moment – I had to agree that little swab seemed to have done well: him or his powerful relations.

"We are given a new ship!" cries Percy.

"Oh, sir! Oh sir!" cries all his chums.

"Well done," says Miss Maitland.

'Huzzah!' from all the hands.

'Huzzah!' from myself, would you believe.

'My commission is of such over-riding importance to the King …,'

'God save the King!' cries the Boatswain.

'God save the King!' cries the entire crew.

'We are to be given His Majesty's brig sloop *Lizard*,' says Percy, 'now lying at anchor nearby, with but three weeks left to come out of a complete re-fit, and then in need of a new company, which company is to be,' he drew himself up in vast self-admiration, 'myself!' says he, and swept a hand to indicate the hands, 'Myself and you, who are my loyal people.'

'Hmmm,' says the crew and they looked at me.

'So,' says Percy, 'You, my good crew, shall be taken off, and entered into the hulk Inquaestron for these three short weeks, until we are re-united aboard my new command. And then, we shall renew our persecution of smugglers, and traitors, and the King God-bless-him's enemies!' So he got a big cheer, and you can't blame the hands. I was pleased, too. But I was even more pleased with what Percy told us officers, down below in his cabin with the port flowing and the candles twinkling.

'We shall all be guests of his lordship: Admiral Clyde-Jones,' says Percy. 'The Admiral is a close colleague of my uncle, Mr Pitt, and it is Lord Clyde-Jones's wish that my officers shall be kept together, as the proven company of sea dogs that they are!'

'And as vindication of your own leadership, sir!' says Dr Sir Roger.

'Indeed, sir!' says Chancellor and Myers.

Prize crawlers the lot of them.

Next day, we were rowed ashore, and embarked aboard a set of vehicles from Clyde-Jones's own stables: a smart travelling-chaise for Percy and Miss Maitland, a barouche for Percy's chums, and a private version of a mail coach – a huge vehicle – that Clyde-Jones owned for swagger, since he fancied himself as a whip. This monster, driven to four horses, easily carried me, O'Flaherty, the two mids, and finally - turned out of the barouche and running up to us with his bags in his hand - we took up Mr Myers, too. He said he couldn't be got into the barouche. He said that although we all knew there was plenty of room but the Doctor and the Lieutenant were too finely bred to sit next to a servant.

It was a clear day and the five of us chose to ride outside: myself beside the driver, O'Flaherty and the mids on the seat just behind and a little higher, and Myers at the back behind the coach body, where he sat because we didn't like him and he knew it. So off we went, bags aboard, ourselves wrapped in our best winter gear, and looking down upon all those common creatures who walked or drove on the dusty road, with dogs yapping and chickens running clear of the hooves while we were on the hard cobbles of the town. So the iron tyres rumbled and the horses clip-clopped in the steady, mile-eating canter that a good driver gets out of his team.

It was exhilarating. We grinned and laughed at one another. We moved so fast and so high that it felt like flying, and the wind stung your ears and the tears streamed from your eyes with the cold and the dust, and the driver calling out to the horses.

'Goooo-on! Goooo-on!' says he, and a team of four stretched legs in front of us, and the long whip cracked in the air, and fields rolled past, and winter trees empty of leaves, and the dense, ancient hedges of old England, clipped and trimmed for centuries past until you could walk along the top of them and not even a bull could push through.

Then one of the middies - cheeky little devil - started humming Johnny *Come* Down *to* Hilo. I looked at him and he stopped. But then I laughed, and turned forward again and threw back my head and let fly to the same music:

'Oh I never seen the like since I been born,
Of big fat Molly with the sea-boots on!
Sing Johnny come down to Hilo, poor old man!

Everyone joined in with the chorus as I sang the old song, passed down aboard ship from ancient times, with verse after verse reporting fat Molly's adventures in ever-more bawdy detail.

[After dinner, in later years, Fletcher would subject the company to just such songs as this. His voice was deep and melodic but the words so improper that I was always mystified by the reaction of the ladies, who would fall into helpless laughter while blushing pink behind their fans. His appeal to the fair sex was profound, but totally beyond my understanding. S.P.]

I sang because I was happy, but also because I judged the song was something the mids should know for their education, to help them be the real seamen that they showed every promise of becoming. The coachman joined in too, and it was a happy time, especially when he handed round a bottle of brandy, kept hidden under his seat, and we all took a swig including the mids, which I insisted upon as being likewise good for them. Even O'Flaherty honoured the occasion with a tiny sip. But I didn't give any to Myers.

And so the seven miles soon passed, along a good turnpike, to Lord Clyde-Jones's ancestral home: Radbrough hall. This was a full and fair example of the mansions where the great nobility have their being. I'd been in some fine houses by then, in America as well as England, but never inside one of these giants, with wrought-iron gates painted black and gold, and a gatekeeper in his little house to let you in, and to bow and scrape at sight of his master's carriages. Then inside to a deer park and an avenue of elm trees, and finally the house itself. I'm told it was 'by *Robert* Adam *out* of Palladio' whatever that might mean, but it was a fine, white, smooth place, with a dome above, and pillars at the front, and broad steps and a battalion of servants, and a big, gravelled circle in front of the house where the carriages could come about in line astern, and drop anchor.

This we did and clambered out and down, and I shook the coachman's hand for the fine fellow that he was, and gave him a half crown, such that he saluted with his whip.

Then we were received with every honour by Lady Clyde Jones, a fine woman in her forties, and still worth while looking over. She was pleased to allow Poxy Percy to kiss her on both cheeks, and present his suite, who genuflected as only men can who are servile by nature and never miss a chance to prove it do.

"M'Lady!" says Dr Sir Roger, grovel, grovel, grovel.

'M'Lady!" says Lieutenant Chancellor, grovel, grovel, grovel. It fair turned my stomach.

'And Mr Fletcher, my First Lieutenant,' says Percy, and it was my turn to bow, and look her Ladyship in the eye. Perhaps I boast, perhaps my memory is flawed, but I think Lady Clyde Jones liked the look of me, and she presented her hand to be kissed. Then it was O'Flaherty, then the mids and finally Mr Myers, who wasn't received by her ladyship but by the butler, as was right and proper.

Inside we were all found rooms, mine with an actual bath laid out, with cans of hot water, and a wonderful view of the grounds, through enormous windows with thin glazing bars and panes three feet wide. Later there was dinner, in full dress, and superb cooking, and wine by the bucket. As to the wine, you must remember that this was King George's time when men didn't stint their appetites as they do today, and nobody thought the worse of a man who downed his second bottle.

[Or his third, in Fletcher's case. S.P.]

So I'm afraid the mids got drunk and fell asleep, and so did Poxy Percy once we'd withdrawn from the ladies and started into the brandy, while the Doctor and the Lieutenant were nodding and O'Flaherty looked tired too, though he'd taken no drink.

Then the ladies came in, and all stood, who were capable of such a feat at such a time.

'My dear gentlemen,' says Lady Clyde-Jones, 'I apologize yet again, that Admiral Clyde-Jones is unable, this night, to join us with so many and urgent duties bearing upon him in these dangerous times.' I heard the words, but I wasn't really listening. Instead I was paying close attention to the fact that she had entered arm-in-arm with Miss Maitland, who was at best a courtesan and at worst a common whore. Also I was looking at the pair of them, because you got a better look at the ladies when they were standing, than you did when they were sat at the dinner table.

I'm no expert on ladies' gowns, but as regards the manner of them you must forget all notions of our being at war with the French in that year of 1796. This because as far as ladies of fashion were concerned, we were not. Or even if we were, it didn't matter because the world's fashion – at least for the ladies – was set by Paris and nothing else counted. Thus they all looked at the fashion plates, smuggled in from France, and they all got their seamstresses and dress-makers to deliver up what they saw. Consequently here was a pair of England's finest beauties, both rich, both able to indulge whatever fashion they chose, and both having come out of dressing rooms full of servants ready to turn them out to best effect…and the effect was exclusively French! But by George, it was some effect. I shook the mids awake so they shouldn't miss the sight, thinking still of their education, d'you see?

Lady Clyde-Jones wore a shiny, brown-silk gown with a tight gold belt under her titties that shoved them up against a low neckline. The gown had tiny, tight sleeves down to just above her elbows, displaying naked arms. There was gold-thread embroidery at the hem of the skirts, and her hair was all in little curls, with a sweep of black feathers curling up above her head and dangling down to her shoulder. She might have been over forty, but she was fit to make the hackles rise on a stone statue.

Then there was Miss Maitland, who'd chosen skilful simplicity in a long, muslin gown – white with yellow flower patterns - with another low neck to show off her upper-works, and a long, yellow sash, belted tight in at the waist, and trailing five feet behind her as she walked. She, too, had a head-full of curling feathers, all mingled in with another sash, bound around her brow. And of course, she had the flower of youth on her side. Her skin was all creamy and smooth, and she smiled at us all, and we gaped.

We men just gaped, and later there was small talk, and laughter, and some remarkably well-informed questions from Lady Clyde-Jones about our perils at sea.

'A monster wave, you say, Mr Fletcher?' says she.

'Aye, M'Lady,' says I, very wary now because already at Plymouth yard men had smiled and sneered when we told the tale – as they still do now, all these years later.

'Did you see this wave, my dear Miss Maitland?' says she, seeking confirmation.

'No, My Lady,' says little madam, 'I was below decks. But I felt the ship rise.'

'Ah!' says Lady Clyde-Jones. But just when I was expecting the patronising smile, she nodded seriously.

'The sea has its mysteries, Mr Fletcher,' says she, 'And I believe that you are privileged to have seen one of the great ones.'

'Thank you, M'Lady,' says I.

There was more of that until it got quite dark, when Miss Maitland retired, the servants helped all those not quite capable, and I was left with her Ladyship for a most fascinating conversation. My Lady sent the servants away so there was just herself and myself in the enormous withdrawing room. It was a sight to see. It oozed in wealth, it was stuffed with furniture, laid with Indian carpets, lit with silver candelabra, and warmed by an enormous fireplace as elaborately wrought as the Parthenon of Athens. And then, to my great surprise, My Lady got up and joined me on the upholstered sofa where I was sat. Her gown rustled most wonderfully and a waft of perfume came with her as she settled beside me. She sat quite close and I even felt a bit of her warmth.

'Hallo?' thinks I, 'What's this?'

'A word, Mr Fletcher,' says she, looking me straight in the eye and putting a hand on my arm.

'My Lady?' says I, and thought deep thoughts. I thought them because she was over twice my age, but considering her big blue eyes, her luscious round arms, and the view down the neck of her gown, I wondered if it could be - could it really and truly be - that this noble and aristocratic lady was taking advantage of a husband away on the King's business and was about to have the britches off me? But no: damn, damn, damn. It wasn't that. She was far too serious.

'You are acquainted with Mr Rowland,' says she: a plain statement.

'Yes, M'Lady,' says I.

'So is Lord Clyde-Jones. He is closely acquainted with Mr Rowland and Mr Pitt.' I tried hard to follow. It was late. I'd taken a drop or two, and I couldn't see where this was leading. 'You must understand several things, Mr Fletcher,' says she, 'First that Cuthbert …,'

'Cuthbert?' says I.

'Cuthbert Percival-Clive.'

'Is that his name?'

'Yes. You must understand that Cuthbert is a nasty little toad.'

'I know that, M'Lady!'

'He is a nasty little toad who has been pouring spite into the ears of Lord

Clyde-Jones, accusing you, Mr Fletcher, of mutiny, and promising to denounce you to Mr Pitt.'

'How do you know that?' says I.

'A letter came from my husband in the hands of one of the coachman,' says she, 'Lord Clyde-Jones has thereby instructed me to warn you, and to promise that he will do all in his power to defend you.'

'Well thank you, M'Lady, but why?

'Because Mr Rowland is Mr Pitt's man, and so is my husband, and my husband – like other port admirals along the coast – is under orders to assist your commission by all possible means.'

'My commission?' says I.

'Well, not yours. It was intended for you, but politics prevented.'

'What politics?'

'Women's politics. Salon politics,' says she, 'Mr Pitt adores his sister. He can refuse her nothing, and she pesters him constantly to advance her Cuthbert in the Sea Service. Thus Cuthbert was given the command intended by Mr Rowland for you!'

'Me?' says I, 'Then just who the damned hell – I'm sorry M'Lady – just who is Mr Rowland? What is he?'

'Pitt's creature, but a creature of enormous influence. The plan to close down the west coast smugglers is his – Rowland's - idea, and his plan is to be given every assistance,' she frowned, 'How else can you imagine, that without notice, another ship was given you – or rather to Cuthbert – upon the instant of your arrival?'

'I see,' says I.

'So it is your duty, and Miss Maitland's, to ride over Cuthbert's failings and …,'

'Miss Maitland? What's it to do with her?'

'She was carefully chosen by Mr Rowland, to act as a brake upon Cuthbert's excesses – you do not know, Mr Fletcher, how nasty and depraved he was before her arrival.'

'She was chosen?' says I.

'Chosen, and employed at great cost,' she frowned again, 'Miss Maitland is not a person with whom I would choose to keep company,' she spread hands in reluctance, 'But these are strange times.'

And that was the extent of our conversation. I went to bed with much to think about, because politics is so mad a business. Here was Billy Pitt, the King's first minister, empowered to command fleets and armies, to levy taxes, pass laws and negotiate with Russia, Prussia and Spain. All that, yet he was subject to the will of his sister even if that meant putting a hopelessly wrong man into an important job. Don't ask me the sense of it. I just wondered if the French were as stupid as that? I certainly hoped so.

Just one final thought before I fell asleep. Obviously Rowland's plans were going forward after all. But why was it so important to close down the west coast smuggling trade? What did that have to do with Rowland's other plans? In fact that wasn't really my final thought, because I fell asleep sorrowing that I hadn't got my hands on Lady Clyde-Jones's nice round bum. Oh, the pity of it! Oh, the tender flesh that I would never squeeze! But never mind, my jolly boys, because an even better opportunity soon presented.

Chapter 12

'*Having seen the magnificent scale of the high pressure engines under construction I can assure you that the engines will serve your great purpose, provided only that the foreigners do not discover that purpose.*'
(Translated from a letter of Friday May 27th 1796, from General Bernard, at Frangnal-sur-Longue, to Generalissimo Napoleon Bonaparte, Headquarters of the Army of Italy.)

*

Bernard did his best to ignore the fierce quarrels going on around him. Instead, he stood in the Barracks yard and turned his eyes to the enormous atmospheric engine, now completed under a open-front timber shed that kept off the weather. At the very top an enormous beam rocked ponderously up and down, in near silence, driven by steam from the adjacent furnace-house with its smoke-billowing chimney. Gleaming-smooth drive rods transmitted the beam's motion down to gears, such that a giant iron wheel turned a drive-shaft, piercing the wall of the machine-shop, to power the devices within. The whole yard smelt of coal-smoke and steam and Bernard stood in amazement. He'd been away over a month to the canal works and other duties, and the progress made was awesome – which it should be, considering money and labour provided for these English Scotchmen.

The engine was wonderful to see. It was a close copy of a Boulton and Watt machine: the very latest English device, and now built here in France by McCloud and his Revolution true-believers. Bernard sighed. He dragged his eyes from the machine and switched from engineering reverence to melancholy gloom at the stupidities of mankind as expressed in the shouting and fighting all around him: shouting and fighting between those who should be close allies.

But Bernard was adept in more fields than engineering and had been chosen for his post by a man – Napoleon Bonaparte – gifted with genius for putting the right man to the right job. So Bernard's logical French mind gathered in the confusion and reduced it to order.

First, there were several companies of the 134th Regiment: shakos, greatcoats and muskets, who kept apart the various factions. These good soldiers stood fast and did not shout. Second, nearly half of McCloud's English Scotchmen were yelling at the other half across the hedge of the 134th's bayonets. Third, there was McCloud himself with one of his brothers, arguing loudly with Colonel Sauvage. Fourth, and loudest of all, and screeching over the deeper voices of the men, there was a good dozen of young women, all of them exceedingly pretty, in peasant blouses, embroidered aprons over blue skirts, and starched-linen caps hung with gold decorations. Bernard couldn't help but smile. They were too good to be true because they weren't true. They were dressed in some Parisian whorehouse -madame's idea of peasant costume and they looked like an opera chorus. They yelled, along with four of McCloud's English Scotchmen who stood in their front rank beside girls who clung most piteously to their men, weeping tears that only an old cynic like Bernard suspected of being false.

This opera chorus screamed at an off-shoot of McCloud's men: five of the oldest of them, who yelled across the divide of the 134th, stabbing fingers in a fury of outraged, righteous wrath. It was almost funny. Bernard couldn't understand a word the foreigners were yelling, but - by Father, Son and Holy Ghost - he understood what the girls were yelling, in their Parisian accents:

'Dirty buggers!'

'You shag on the quiet, though, don't you?'

'Can't you get it up, darling?'

'Ain't you got no dick?'

It had been like this ever since Bernard clattered on to the cobbles with his cavalry escort. He'd expected a briefing from Sauvage, but as word spread that he'd returned, the foreigners and the girls poured out from the buildings and everyone began shouting. At first they'd shouted at Bernard, but then they got down to the serious business of yelling at each other. They yelled at each other, and at a small band of French mechanics in leather aprons, that stood to one side, and yelled right back.

'So!' thought Bernard, 'Enough of this'. He beckoned the corporal holding his horse. The corporal came forward with the animal. Bernard pulled the carbine from the saddle holster. He cocked it and raised the muzzle.

Ka-Bang! Lock and charge fired. White smoke puffed. A ball went far away, and everyone fell silent and looked at Bernard.

'Colonel Sauvage, come here!' cried Bernard, 'Men of the 134th,' he pointed at the foreigners and the women, 'All these back into there,' he pointed at the Barracks block, 'Right now!'

'Yes, my General!' cried the corporals, sergeants and officers of the 134th.

'Get to it,' cried Bernard, 'Give 'em butt and boot if you must,'

'Yes, my General!'

There was a great outrage from the foreigners. They'd always been indulged before, but now there were kicks and blows. The girls screamed worse than the men, and fights broke out between some of the soldiers and those English-Scottish who thought they were protecting their women.

But McCloud shouted loudest of all. As he was pushed backwards into the big, grey building, he bellowed and roared and stretched an arm over the shoulders of the soldiers, and pointed at Sauvage and didn't stop until he was pushed inside and a door slammed on him.

'What was that about?' said Bernard, as Sauvage came up and saluted.

'Where shall I start?' said Sauvage.

'Is it that bad?'

'Yes!'

Bernard sighed. He looked round the silent courtyard – no, not entirely silent, because the yelling of the foreigners emerged muted through the thick walls. There was that, and the sound of horses' hoofs as Bernard's escort rode to the stables, and regular footfalls as most of the soldiers marched off to other duties. Also, Bernard noted that the Frenchmen in leather aprons, were walking towards the big steam engine as if to take charge of it. They saw Bernard's look and respectfully doffed hats.

'Who are they?' said Bernard, pointing.

'Some of our boys are learning the English tricks,' said Sauvage, 'Come inside, my General, and I'll show you.'

'Yes, but I want to know what's going on.'

'Of course, my General.'

So Bernard and Sauvage went into the machine shop, and Bernard gasped at the transformation since last he'd been there. The place was alive with wonder; a mere leather-aproned Frenchmen stood looking at Bernard, who stared fascinated at the big drive shaft from the engine outside, which rolled, steadily sending power by leather belts all up and down the long benches, to the finest array

94

of machine-tools in all of France. This was the English method whereby huge manufactories were driven by steam. It was the best of their mechanical genius and better, because something was taking shape under the lathes, hammers, and milling machines that not even England was making. But Sauvage was speaking, even if Bernard was not properly listening.

'They found out about the girls from Paris.'

'Oh?' said Bernard looking at the magical creation that was half-finished, half-made, and not yet brought together as a whole, but which was there in separate parts, all across the machine shop.

'At first it worked as we'd hoped,' said Sauvage, 'We told them the girls were cantinières like those in our army. You know, my General, the girls who run the canteens and provide the food?'

'Of course,' said Bernard, but most of his attention was now on the wheels. He looked at one of them. It must be one of the drive wheels. It was over three metres across, though of course the foreigners worked in English feet: say, twelve of their feet? It was machined from iron, and designed to be pushed by a piston and thereby turned.

'Well,' said Sauvage, 'Everything was fine, and the English-Scottish really liked the girls, and we let the girls run the canteen here, and all the English went there, and there was all manner of joking and laughing.'

'Yes,' said Bernard, looking now at the front wheels which, like the huge drive wheels, were not yet attached, and only one of them made up, as yet, and the other just a wooden pattern. The front wheels were a metre-and-a-half across, and designed to fit on to a swivelling axle. The wonderful thing was their lightness. These weren't heavy, lumbering wheels. They looked like the wheels of a racing carriage, yet made of iron.

'Then some of the English got hungry,' said Sauvage, ''cos they saw what our lads were doing.'

'What do you mean, what *our* lads *were* doing?' said Bernard, 'The girls were for the English!' Sauvage looked away. He shrugged.

'Didn't you tell our men that?'

'Yes. But well, you know,' said Sauvage, and shrugged again, 'some of the English decided they'd like a go. They wanted more from a woman than a laugh.'

'Wait, wait, wait,' said Bernard, 'these girls were supposed to be special. Supposed to act the part of village maidens.'

'Yes,' said Sauvage, 'they did at first. Then some of our lads tried their luck, and found out they weren't.'

'Yes, yes, yes,' said Bernard, and couldn't help walking across to the half-completed piston assembly. Sauvage smiled.

'So they had it away with the girls,' he said, 'The clever little foxes had some rooms in the back of the canteen: rooms fitted out with beds,' he shrugged, 'they are professionals, after all.'

'Hmm,' said Bernard, wondering what pressure the piston housing would withstand.

'Yes,' said Sauvage, 'and then there was some boasting, and some of the English had a go, and some of them really fell for the girls, and then McCloud found out – he's not touched any of the girls himself - and some of his men are like him, and they despise those who aren't.' Sauvage stopped. He saw that he'd lost Bernard's attention.

'Amazing!' said Bernard, marvelling at the neat complexity of the valves that let steam into the piston, and working out in his mind how all these components would be assembled into the complete carriage.

'My General?' said Sauvage.

'I'm sorry,' said Bernard, and turned to Sauvage,

'Then it all blew up,' said Sauvage, 'The English-Scottish fell to arguing among themselves, and with our lads, and McCloud guessed that the girls were tarts. And he came over all sanctimonious, and said I was a whoremonger, and all work stopped.' Bernard frowned in amazement.

'Do they really take it so seriously?' said Bernard, looking at Sauvage and forcing his attention away from the ironworks, 'Saints and angels,' he said, 'it's only natural. It's only what all men do. What are these English? Monks?'

'Yes!' said Sauvage, 'Well he is: McCloud. He's a fanatic. A real holy-Joe. He thinks the sun shines out of his arse and everyone else is a dirty fornicator.

'I know, I know,' said Bernard, because he did know. Why else had these foreigners betrayed their own people, except out of fanatical beliefs?' and he sighed as he saw the beautiful precision in everything these fanatics had made. It was artistry, not machinery.

'So,' said Sauvage, 'McCloud says there's no more work on anything, let alone the road engines, until this is settled, which is hardly surprising since half of his men hate the other half, and the other half hates them in return.' Bernard groaned. He shook his head at the madness of it. Europe was at war. Men were killing each other with cannon, muskets and bayonets. Bonaparte was planning to destroy the British nation. Meanwhile here came McCloud and his men, traitors to their own flesh and blood, yet detesting one another

96

because some of them had poked a tart and some had not! Bernard wondered if all the English were that stupid? He certainly hoped so.

Then logic got to work.

'What about them?' said Bernard, pointing to the leather-aproned Frenchmen standing by the work benches, 'You said some of our men are learning the English tricks, yes?'

'Yes,' said Sauvage.

'So can they take over if McCloud's men stop work? Can they put all this together?' Bernard looked at the mechanical parts laid out so neatly among the benches.

'No,' said Bernard, 'they know a bit, but not enough.'

'Why not?'

'It's harder than we thought. There's the language for one thing. None of our lads speaks English, and the English Scotchmen don't speak French.'

'But surely they can show our lads what to do?' Sauvage shook his head.

'Not now,' he said, 'They all hate one another, too.'

'What? Why in heaven's name?'

'It's the girls. Our lads don't like Englishmen going with French girls,' Sauvage spread hands helplessly, 'So there were fights. You know how it is. They're foreigners after all.'

'Holy Mary Mother of God!' said Bernard. But even in that moment his eyes were drawn magnetically to the boiler assembly with its glorious rows of copper tubes. He forced his mind back to logic. 'Sauvage?' he said.

'My General?'

'McCloud said: until this is settled, did he?'

'Yes, my General.'

'Then thanks be to God,' said Bernard. 'because I can work with that,' which indeed he could, even though most of his mind was calculating the size and scale of the engine lying here in its pieces. How big would it be? How tall? How fast would it run? What load would it draw? It was the little model made real. But then Bernard's picked on more of Sauvage's words.

'Road engines?' said Bernard, 'I assume that McCloud still talks of road engines, does he?'

'Yes, my General. We've been really, really careful not to mention anything else,' he pointed to the various mechanisms that had so captivated Bernard. 'Look what they've made. It's all for the road locomotive. They don't know what we really want the engines for.'

'Good!' said Bernard, 'Then let's leave things as they are for today. Let tempers cool down, and we'll talk to the immaculate Saint McCloud tomorrow, and let's see if we can satisfy the protestant bastard.'

'And now will you have dinner, my General?' said Sauvage, 'You must have been on the road for hours.'

'Yes,' said Bernard, 'Dinner!' and the two men walked off together, except that Bernard's mind was elsewhere, because Bernard was faced with a disaster entirely of his own making. It had been entirely his idea to bring the girls to Frangnal, and his idea had entirely failed. Thus Bonaparte would be incensed if he found out, and Bernard would be broken in rank, socially disgraced, and even at risk of his life. In such an extreme, some men would have collapsed into despair. But Bernard kept calm and made plans. He did so because he was an excellent officer, fiercely loyal to France. But before all else - as he trusted in God and hoped for resurrection - his engineering soul cried out to see McCloud's locomotive built and alive and breathing steam!

Chapter 13

When I say that I enjoyed my time at Radbrough hall, I make the greatest understatement of my career. But first I must explain the scope of my stay, because we were there nearly two months - myself and the others out of the old *Serpant* - since Admiral Lord Clyde-Jones's estimate of time to re-fit *Lizard*, over-ran by many weeks. Not that it was his fault. It was the lazy, idle swabs of dockyard people that you could get no work out of, and I'll give you one example.

We were constantly to and fro between the Navy Yard and Radbrough, kindly given use of his Lordship's travelling chaise, it being the fastest of his stable. By we, you will understand that I mean myself and Mr O'Flaherty as regards getting anything done, and Poxy Percy and his chums, for the chance to swan round the ship doing nothing, then quick ashore for the pleasures of Plymouth, leaving O'Flaherty and me to drive forward the work.

So, the first time we went aboard we were pleased to discover that *Lizard* was only two years old, a vessel of the same class as *Serpant*, and as exact a duplicate of her as could be made in those days of hand tools and rule of thumb. She was sound in the hull but had been months in repair after chasing a French privateer that had boldly come about and given a broadside that carried away enough sail aboard *Lizard* as to leave her wallowing. In this helpless state *Lizard* was pounded with long nines from outside the range of her carronades – the one flaw of carronades being short range. The result was dire: *Lizard* lost her captain, her master and half her crew killed or wounded, and would have had to strike, had not a British frigate hove in sight.

When O'Flaherty and I went aboard, the re-fit was complete as regards the shot-holes to her timbers, pumps and gear. Also, the re-rigging aloft should have taken only the few weeks the Admiral had guessed, except for the manner of idleness that we found aboard her as we came over the side. There was no Boatswain to salute us, since he and his mates had been killed in the action against the privateer. But the ship was full of men – landmen all - and was in chaos, with caulkers lazily hammering, idlers lazing in the rigging, and half those aboard cooking their dinners over charcoal braziers, with pint pots in their hands and the whole ship stinking of bacon and onions.

I was not pleased. Neither was O'Flaherty. So I drew breath and bellowed.

'Who's in charge?' says I, 'Step forward and step lively!' Nobody moved, except one of the bacon-fryers, who got up with a smirk, and all the rest looked up from what they were doing and stared insolent stares.

'I'm Harwich,' says the smiler, 'Mister Harwich,' but the smile went as I looked him in the eye.

'And what are you?' says I.

'Dockyard Foreman,' says he, 'And who are you?' I was about to put him right as regards respect for the Sea Service, when someone started sawing right next to me.

Buzz! Buzz! Buzz! The saw was a big one, and it made a lot of noise. I turned on the man holding it.

'Avast there!' says I and he stopped. He was a carpenter in waistcoat and britches and a folded paper hat to keep the sawdust out of his hair. He had a ship's spar mounted on trestles and was sawing off a two-foot length of it. He looked at me and blinked, all sheepish, and turned to Harwich for support. I didn't like the manner of him at all. 'What are you doing?' says I, and he said nothing, but licked his lips, and I noticed a collection of two-foot lengths of timber, fresh-sawn off a perfectly-good spar, and stacked by the trestles.

'Mr Fletcher,' says O'Flaherty, and politely took my arm. But I was annoyed.

'Come here, you lubber,' says I, as the carpenter tried to walk away, and I grabbed him by the collar. 'Mr Fletcher!' says O'Flaherty, more firmly.

'What are you doing with that spar?' says I, to the carpenter, 'You're ruining the bloody thing!' He tried to shake me off.

'Mr Harwich!' says he, all outraged, 'This matelot's took hold 'o me!'

'Matelot?' says I, 'I'm a King's officer, and you'll damn-well call me sir!'

'You let him be,' says Harwich, 'He ain't done nothing!'

'No he ain't neither!' says someone else.

'Leave him alone!' says another.

'Gerrof y'bleeder!' says the carpenter

'Mr Fletcher!' says O'Flaherty, 'Sir!' and he forcibly pushed between me and the carpenter. 'A word, Mr Fletcher,' says he, 'A private word.' I liked O'Flaherty so I nodded, let go of the carpenter, and walked over to the lee bulwark.

'Well?' says I. O'Flaherty looked round to make sure nobody else could hear.

'Listen to me,' says O'Flaherty, for once taking the tone of older man to younger. 'We can't touch these buggers. They ain't under the Articles of War, and if you lay hands on 'em, they just stop work and go ashore: all of 'em together. That's the way of it. That's how it's always been.' I frowned. This was news to me. But then I'd never had responsibility for a dockyard re-fit, had I?

'So what was he doing?' says I, and I looked at the carpenter with his sawn-up lengths of spar. O'Flaherty sighed.

'It's chips, Mr Fletcher,' says he.

'Chips?' says I.

'Perquisite of their trade,' says O'Flaherty. Any lengths under three feet, is regulated as chips, which they can take away and sell for firewood. That's dockyard law.'

'But he was sawing up a perfectly good spar,' says I.

'Mr Fletcher,' says he, 'every craft and trade in the dockyards has its own perquisites, and if spoiling timbers was the worst of 'em, I'd be a happy man.' I looked at the carpenter. He was grinning at me.

'And would he be a happy man if I kicked him round the deck?'

'No,' says O'Flaherty, 'It can't be done. It's been tried and it don't work.'

'Then what does work?' O'Flaherty drew me round, to turn our backs on the assembled audience so they couldn't even see our faces.

'Money, Mr Fletcher,' says he, whispering, 'Money works. You have to pay the bastards. So let's see what we've got between us, because if we left it to Captain Cuthbert, he'd pay too much, which is bad for the Service.'

'Ahhhhh!' says I, and the sun came out in his glory. Here was an opportunity to use the skills that I really value: the making of bargains, the getting of best value, the trading of one thing for another. That's what I was born for, not sailing the bloody ocean. So I cheered up wonderfully. 'Thank you, Mr O'Flaherty,' says I, 'I really am most deeply obliged.'

'Are you?' says he, amazed.

'Oh yes,' says I, 'And I do appreciate your most generous offer of monies, but you may leave the matter entirely in my hands.' I raised my hat to him, grand fellow that he was, and strolled across to the Dockyard Foreman. I was happy again, do you see? 'Mr Harwich,' says I with a smile, 'I do believe there has been a misunderstanding between us, but one which can be settled,' I paused, 'as a financial matter.'

'Ah!' says he, the greedy sod, catching my drift at once.

After that it was easy, and I do once more impress upon you youngsters to take note of your Uncle Jacob's experience. In this case the point is that there may be more than one way of getting what you want, and if a wiser man shows you the right way when you would have chosen a wrong way, then be sure to take his advice.

So Mr Harwich and I had the most congenial discussion - down in the stern cabin if you please - and I didn't squeeze him too hard: just enough to let him know I was his equal. And it didn't even take a lot of money, and in the end, Harwich sent for a bottle of rum – another perquisite of his trade I don't doubt – so we could drink on the deal out of tin mugs. You see, it isn't really the money that counts with the likes of Mr Harwich. What counts is that you give respect to him. You give him his due. You leave him satisfied that all's right in his dirty little world. As a man of business I disapprove of bribery, but sometimes it's the grease that eases the way, and with some people it's the only way.

And it worked, too. Later on, there were a couple more payings-out to other trades but from that day on, the re-fit on *Lizard* proceeded with the best goodwill that could be got out of an Admiralty dockyard in those days.

None of which explains why my time at Radbrough was quite so congenial. The reason for that was Miss Maitland, though I should first explain the way that life was lived in the great mansions in those days – and still is for that matter. We were handsomely entertained by Lord Clyde-Jones and his Lady: we were fed and watered and bedded down. There was breakfast, lunch, dinner and lesser meals during the day, with an enormous set of gardens to wander among, and golf, archery, croquet, and also the blasting of birds out of the sky with fowling pieces for those who fancied it, which I never did. All that plus billiards, cards and backgammon indoors when the weather was foul.

But the main entertainment was each other, and there was a great deal of very formal taking of turns about the garden with or without servants in tow, and the local gentry visiting. So, about a week after we'd arrived, I found I had a day spare, with nothing to do aboard *Lizard*, while Percy and his crawlers were off to Plymouth. Thus Lord Clyde-Jones, O'Flaherty and I made up a party with her Ladyship and some local ladies and gentlemen, together with Miss Maitland for a picnic dinner outside, in a choice spot with a fine view over the grounds. It was a grand day out, sitting on neat little collapsible stools, round a table set up by the servants, and we were well served, and all the little birds sang, and the sun beamed merrily.

The Admiral was with us on that occasion: a thoroughly decent cove in his seventies, and much older than his wife. He wore an old-fashioned full-bottom wig and had a stiff leg from a wound taken in the West Indies where he'd spent much of his service. He was another of Rowland's followers – if followers is what they were – and he treated me so generously as to have me tell the tale of the great wave, to entertain the visitors. So I did, and all the gents frowned in serious attention, and all the ladies oohed and ahhed.

'Were you not fearfully afraid?' says one of the ladies.

'Of course, ma'am,' says I, turning to O'Flaherty, 'Weren't we just, though?'

'Aye, sir,' says he, 'That we were, indeed!'

'I commend your honesty, gentlemen,' says Clyde-Jones, 'For only a fool would pretend immunity from fear, when the sea gets up.'

'Then could you give us further examples of your adventures, Mr Fletcher?' says another lady.

'Not in his Lordship's presence,' says I, looking to the Admiral. 'Not when his service is so much more distinguished than my own.' And yes indeed, that was myself crawling. But you have to say such things on such occasions. I was his guest and drinking his wine after all. But his Lordship smiled.

'Perhaps, Mr Fletcher,' says he, 'but some of your own service is quite singular, or so I believe.' I took that as a compliment and spoke on,

'There was the time,' says I, 'aboard the merchantman Bednal Green, when I was under fire for hours from a Yankee privateer.'

'Oh, do tell!' says all the ladies.

'Yes, Mr Fletcher,' says Clyde-Jones, with a grin, 'There is some,' he sought the right word, 'there is quite some discussion, in society, of your other, and submarine adventures in America,' and on the word submarine the ladies exchanged glances and stared at me with big eyes.

'Hallo,' thinks I, 'What's this? What discussion?' It was very strange.

[Note that Fletcher became notorious for his sinking, by submarine boat, of HMS *Calipheme* in Boston Harbour on October 4th 1794, as reported in earlier volumes of these memoirs. The occasion of the picnic party described here, may well be the first time Fletcher learned of his notoriety. S.P.]

But I thought it best to hold back on the subject of submarine navigation and told some other tales, and the matter passed. Then, when the meal was done and cleared away, Clyde-Jones, took us all on a tour of Radbrough's walled garden and his ice-well, and his orangery, which were all very splendid, and a corps of gardeners and boys standing by, touching their caps as we passed, and since each gentleman was supposed to lead one of the ladies, I somehow found myself with Miss Maitland on my arm. Later, we were some way behind the rest, leaving the two of us alone in the hot, bright, glass-house of the orangery. She was making polite conversation non-stop.

'What a fine construction,' says she, pointing to the high roof.

'How splendid to see full-grown orange trees.'

'Why do you suppose, Mr Fletcher, that the rear wall is painted white?'

'How tall do you think these trees might grow?'

Then quite suddenly she stopped, looked round, saw nobody but ourselves, and then stepped close, and looked me in the eye in a way that made my drum beat to quarters and ran out my lower deck battery. She came so close that I could feel the warmth of her and smell her perfume. What a moment!

'Cuthbert will stay in Plymouth tonight,' says she, 'He will drink himself senseless and not return until late tomorrow afternoon.'

By George and by Jove! And by whoever you please! I could hardly believe it. She'd barely looked at me most of the time; not a nod in my direction. But then I remembered aboard *Serpant* when she gave me the eye, and in any case I was young and full of fire, and by Heaven I wasn't going to waste time wondering.

'Well madame,' says I, 'Is this the better place you mentioned?' She laughed and looked round the glass house.

'No,' says she, 'but you will find my room – tonight - to be by the grand staircase, second on the right, past the Gainsborough portrait of Lord Clyde-Jones's father,' she leaned really close and brushed my chin with her lips, 'The one that shows the father with his sporting gun.'

'Sporting gun,' says I, and couldn't help but grab her, and lift her off her feet for a quick kiss. Quite long kiss actually, and her joining in. But that was all. Then I put her down and we tidied ourselves and smiled and moved on.

Well. How I contained myself over the next few hours I'll never know. I felt that God had stopped the movement of time. But in the end, the house all quiet and there was me, creeping out of my room, in nightshirt and dressing gown, and bare feet for silence, and making my way in the dark and my heart going like a hammer, and myself blessing the foresight that had set me finding out the way earlier on. Otherwise I'd have knocked Chinese pots off the side tables, Civil War breastplates off the wall, and in all probability gone arse-over-tit down the grand staircase and woken up the entire house. Even so, I stopped in fright several times at the creaks and groans that any house makes as it settles down for the night, and which sounded to me like gunshots.

But I found the door soon enough because, believe me my jolly boys, if you can find your longitude off Cape Finisterre in a gale - which I can - you can find a bedroom door in an English mansion at night.

Tap, tap, tap, on the door. A painful wait. Then click-rattle from the door handle and the door swung wide, and shut swift behind me, and there she was in the light of a single candle, utterly naked, utterly wonderful with hair brushed over her shoulders, and upright, arrogant, splendid and proud and snapping out her right hand, palm down. The gesture was magnificent. It commanded respect and I dropped on one knee, took the hand and kissed it. By God, it was exciting. I felt like Prince Charming having his way with Cinderella, 'cos I'd not planned to kneel. It was nothing of my making, it was the power of the woman, her skill and her magic. It was all so smooth and elegant, aside from some clumsiness on my part, as I stood up and heaved off my things and flung them aside, and swept her up, and felt the gorgeous, smooth warmth and carried her to the bed at the double, one-two, one-two, and look lively about it!

But now I'm going to surprise you. If you've read my memoirs you will know that Miss Maitland wasn't my first woman. There'd been many before, and would be many after. You will also know that I don't hold back in the details of these close engagements. But Miss Sophia Maitland was in a class of her own. She was an artist of her profession, and I'd never met the like before. She knew things and did things, that I didn't know could be done, and that I haven't got words to describe. I can only say that everything lasted longer, felt better, and reached its final conclusion like the French flagship L'Orient blowing up at the Nile when her magazine exploded.

Miss Maitland did all that, yet had the speech and manners of a lady, and you couldn't help but admire her for the woman she was. So later on we talked and I learned a bit about her, such as why she was in the company of such a nincompoop as Poxy Percy. I was surprised to hear that she was under an actual contract to be Percy's woman.

'His father pays,' says she, 'he pays excellently well, and the money goes to my mother who invests it with the bankers for our future.'

'What if Percy finds out about this?' says I, 'About us?' She laughed.

'I control him,' says she, 'If he came in now, I could later persuade him that he'd seen nothing.'

'Really?'

'Yes,' says she. 'He is a particularly stupid young man, and easily led.' So I wondered how she would lead him. Would she treat Percy to the exercises we'd just completed? But I had the sense not to ask. It was far better to be happy with her snuggled up and cosy, whatever she might do tomorrow. She was a most amazing woman. She even woke me up early next morning so I could be back in my own bed before anyone noticed.

That's how it went on over the next weeks, whenever Percy was away, and if I've referred to advancing the education of young middies in the Sea Service, then let me assure you that when I came away from Sophia Maitland's company, I was most wonderfully educated in the service of life, and in the tricks that men and women play to deepen their enjoyment of one another. For instance, throughout our exercises Sophia Maitland called me Mr Fletcher, never using my first name. In response I called her ma'am, and do you know it made everything all the more spicy for the naughtiness it conferred, by underlining that we were each supposedly committed to others and were plucking forbidden fruit. By Jove she was a clever 'un and no mistake. Though it all came to an end – or almost so - when we finally went aboard *Lizard*, and just before that I got a warning.

Just after lunch one afternoon, a man rode up the long gravelled drive, between the fine poplar trees that led to Radbrough Hall. I was sitting on the terrace with O'Flaherty with a pot of coffee and some sort of buns or other, and I saw the rider approach. He saw me, too, in my uniform, and raised his hat to me, then went on to the front door, where the butler received him and a servant led off his horse. Shortly after he came out with Lady Clyde-Cooper herself, with a sour look on her face and the butler astern of them. The three of them walked over to me and O'Flaherty. We stood and bowed to her ladyship.

'Mr Fletcher,' says she, 'Here is Mr Conway of the London, Bow Street Magistrate's Office. He is come on business that he may not divulge to myself,' she gave him a withering sneer. 'I therefore leave him in your company.' We all bowed again, and her ladyship came about, bore up under all plain sail, and swept off mightily displeased.

'Mr Fletcher?' says Conway, 'I spotted you at once, sir, but had to be sure.'

'Did you now?' says I and looked him over. He was a rough, tough man but well turned out, in a round hat with a curled brim, good riding clothes, a cravat round his neck, and tight pantaloons tucked into shiny top-boots.

'Are you a Bow Street Runner?' says I.

'A Principal Officer, sir,' says he, like a schoolmaster correcting bad grammar, because that was their proper name, although everyone called them Runners. 'This is for you, sir,' says he and took out a sealed letter from his coat pocket. 'I'm to say that it explains itself, Mr Fletcher, and all you need to know is within.' Then he touched his hat to me, and looked at the butler.

'If you'd follow me, Mr Conway?' said the butler, and off they went. I never saw Conway again. He'd done his job. He'd also put a considerable fright up myself, because what sort of letter was it that merited this sort of delivery? Then I saw the address. It said: Mr Jacob Fletcher, residing at Radbrough Hall, Near Plymouth in Devon. I recognised the handwriting at once, and I didn't like it.

Chapter 14

*'Even while suffering agonies of spirit in contemplation of my men fallen
victims to the sin of Lust, I myself fell victim to the sin of Pride at the sight of my
locomotive engine under steam.'*
(From a letter of Thursday June 23 1796 – sealed by never delivered -
from Donald James McCloud to his Father Mr Hamish McCloud, 15 Bream
Terrace, near Douglas Square, Edinburgh)

*

McCloud rejoiced. Considering all his other worries he tried to remain stoical,
but he couldn't help himself. So he rejoiced reluctantly. But standing beside
McCloud, Citizen General Bernard rejoiced and revelled and set no limits
upon the emotion.

'Open the regulator!' said McCloud, and the third man on the steel-grid
driving platform – the stoker whose job it was to feed the engine's furnace -
hauled on a lever and the whole great engine lurched forward, with McCloud
gripping the steering wheel, while Bernard cried out in joy.

'Voila!' he said, 'Elle marche!' and he threw his arms around McCloud's
neck and kissed the reluctant Scotsman on both cheeks, which normally would
have embarrassed McCloud most horribly. But now he was so happy that the
atrocious familiarity was not only tolerated, but almost welcomed, such that
McCloud delivered a miserly-rare smile.

But no such reserve held back the hundreds of men of the 134th Regiment,
lining the bright, white military road, under a bright, clear sky, nor even
McCloud's followers, now united into one team again, and cheering as
Locomotive Engine Number 1 rolled forward, for the very first time.

The engine was magnificent. It was thirty feet long and ten feet wide. It gleamed in shining metals and in disciplined lines of cunningly-driven rivet heads. It weighed two tons, the smoke-stack rose fifteen feet above the ground, the massive pistons hissed, the enormous drive wheels turned, and the long, barrel-shaped body was painted blue-white-red, in honour of the French Republic. The smoke-stack billowed white fumes. A great fly-wheel spun, smoke swirled, ash dropped from beneath the hot, shimmering furnace box, water dripped from the piston housings and above all, and before, all and to the eternal wonder of every man or woman who saw it that day … it ran! It ran with its tender behind it bearing coal and water.

'Alons enfants de la Patrieee-eh!' sang Bernard, and waved at the 134th's Regimental Band that marched behind the engine. They came on in excellent step, with mirror-polished brass instruments, drums beating, plumes waving, because this was a day of glory, a day never seen in the world before, and Bernard was determined to mark it in splendour. At Bernard's signal, the Drum Major raised his gilded mace and the band tremendously delivered La Marseillaise, and the men of the 134th roared out the words, and so did McCloud and his English-Scotsmen, good revolutionaries that they were, who'd long since learned the French anthem.

But Locomotive Engine Number 1 was built for speed. The band and its music was left behind in seconds, and soon the only men who kept up with the engine were those mounted on horses, first at the trot, then breaking into a steady canter, and the riders waving their hats and laughing and crying out in excitement. The locomotive shuddered and hissed, and ran faster and faster. The great drive wheels spun, smoke streamed from the stack, the stoker watched his fire, and shovelled and laughed and yelled and grinned, and the iron wheels crunched the road, and the shuddering grew and the speed became frightening. But still they sped on, leaving even the riders behind, and the Barracks lost, and gone, and far out of sight. The excitement was unbelievable. The engine sped on. The miles flashed past, and steadily, steadily, the machine went faster.

'Too fast!' said McCloud to the stoker. The engine was shaking badly and the steering wheel shuddered in his hands almost out of control. 'Slow her down!' he said, and the stoker eased back on the steam regulator, and the engine slowed. But Bernard was yelling in French into McCloud's face.

'Allons! *En* avant!' he cried. 'Pour*la* France! *Et* pour*toi, mon* Ecosais-Anglais!' But McCloud shook his head. Not a word did he understand, but it was obvious that Bernard wanted still more speed. Bernard was intoxicated. He was waving and pointing up the road and laughing and laughing.

'No, monsieur,' said McCloud. 'This is the first time under way. We may not take risks. We've done very well. Now we must turn back and examine everything.' Bernard understood. He laughed and patted McCloud on the back. At least there were no more kisses, and the engine slowed and slowed, and the horsemen caught up and clustered round them, pointing and chattering, and the horses rearing up at the hissing hot monster, the like of which they'd never seen before. But who could blame them? Who else had seen such a creation? Who else in all the world?

And then Bernard was almost overcome with fascination, and the horsemen too, gaped and stared as McCloud and the stoker performed the incredible feat of turning the engine in the road. They did this even though there was no room to turn in one sweep, and they did it only because McCloud's unrivalled genius had given the engine valves and levers to switch the motive power such that Locomotive Engine Number 1 could steam backwards as well as forwards! An unfathomable wonder!

The return to the Barracks was even more splendid than the setting out. McCloud, Bernard and the stoker, stood high over the road in the magnificent engine, the huge radius of the drive wheels on either side, the blue-white-red body before them and the dutiful tender behind. They were raised up and transfigured into heroes, as masters of this most miraculous construction of inanimate metals, which seemingly and magically was possessed of vigorous life. Thus the engine came home to cheers and flags and the band played every tune they knew in celebration of this enormous triumph for McCloud and his men.

McCloud waved to everyone as the engine came to a halt in the Barracks yard. He climbed down into a crowd of his own followers and French soldiers, with Colonel Sauvage – the one who spoke English - seizing his hand and shaking it fiercely.

'Wonderful! Magnificent!' said Sauvage, 'How did she run? How did the machinery perform?' But even before McCloud could reply, General Bernard was climbing down and embracing Sauvage and the two of them shouting at each other deliriously in delight. Meanwhile, McCloud's brothers pushed forward.

'Well done, Donald,' said one of them.

'Well done,' said the others. All were there. All shared in the moment. McCloud looked at them and looked at Sauvage and Bernard , laughing and embracing each other. He was grateful to the two Frenchmen. Especially so to Bernard, because Bernard - with Sauvage translating - was the one who'd argued and pleaded to make right what had gone wrong.

But then McCloud's mind darkened, recalling the disgraceful insult of Bernard's bringing prostitutes to Fragnal in the first place. McCloud looked at Bernard, and even with the locomotive proven and true beside him, even in that unsurpassable instant, McCloud's Calvinist, protestant, revolutionary-intellectual mind burned with resentment at what Bernard had done, and worse still the realisation that some of his men had welcomed the women. Some still did and could not be persuaded by any means to give them up. McCloud looked at his brother Jamie, now one of the worst offenders. But McCloud sighed, because Bernard had pleaded for the great cause of the French Enlightenment. Bernard had insisted that the building of the road engines was vital to the cause and must proceed at greater pace, which was excellent because the road engines were McCloud's dream, his purpose, and his own contribution to the cause. It was, after all, the very reason that he was here in France. Furthermore, Bernard had promised to send away the women, which was good, but then some of McCloud's own men had rebelled.

McCloud's chin sank to his breast in despair as he faced the ugly truth that it was not just 'some' of his men that had rebelled. It was more than half, and Jamie was one of them. They were defying McCloud by living in open and illicit liaison with French women. It was shameful – dreadfully shameful - but the wishes of so great a part of his men could neither be ignored nor suppressed. Thus a compromise had been agreed, sending some of the girls away and suffering some to remain.

McCloud looked back at the engine for comfort. He looked at it and was as nearly content in the matter as every he would be. There must now be the decent, engineering matter of examining the locomotive in detail, to check what might have worn, or come apart in this, its first use. McCloud would take the whole thing to pieces if necessary so that it might be improved, altered and perfected. McCloud managed a smile, because that safe and good path would surely lead to grace and contentment.

And so it did, until the evening.

McCloud had a suite of rooms on the first floor of the Barracks block. It had originally been intended for an officer: a major or a captain? McCloud didn't know, but it gave him room for his papers and for meetings with his men, who had their own and lesser accommodation along the same corridor, where they were close by for all eventualities. McCloud thought it a good arrangement, and he supposed that the French officer would have felt the same regarding his own men.

Now it was late, but still light, and McCloud was writing to his father in his living room, by a window that looked out over the Barracks yard. McCloud wrote to his father very often because he badly missed his father's advice. So he wrote to him, and constantly asked his opinion, though he never received a reply because his letters were never sent. Colonel Sauvage had explained the great need for secrecy and the impossibility of revealing McCloud's whereabouts, or what he was doing; not even to a father. But still McCloud wrote the letters, hoping that one day his father might read them, and because McCloud needed to express his dreams and fears, if only on a sheet of paper.

Thus, here in France, there was neither confidante nor comforter for McCloud, because – normally - his brothers and his men obeyed him with reverence, and there never had been any woman in his life. There was no wife, no sister, and his mother was long dead. There were only men, and McCloud was comfortable in the company of men. He greatly preferred the company of men to that of women, though of course there was no possibility whatsoever that any passions that lurked within him might follow paths other than those which the Lord God had ordained. Such a possibility was neither admitted, nor considered, nor even allowed to exist: not by a man who lived under such close, tight discipline as Donald McCloud.

Then someone knocked at the door and McCloud put down his pen.

'Come,' he said. The door opened, McCloud's brother Jamie was there, and with him was one of McCloud's followers, Anthony Dunblaine, a large and very handsome boy: quite young, and a fine craftsmen with a great eye for detail, but not gifted with great intelligence. McCloud liked him very much. Then he saw that Dunblaine had a French woman with him. She was almost hiding behind him, and clutching his hand. She was lovely of face, modestly dressed, and she constantly looked up to Dunblaine for reassurance.

'They've come for your blessing, Donald,' said Jamie McCloud, and Donald McCloud nodded.

'Leave them with me, Jamie,' he said, and Jamie went out.

'Come closer,' said McCloud.

'This is my Martine, sir,' said Dunblaine, and encouraged her to stand forward as if presenting her at court. He did so with pride, and with obvious fondness for the girl. McCloud thought that his movements were graceful, 'This is Martine Lejardin,' said Dunblaine, 'She don't speak no English, sir.' The girl curtseyed to McCloud and risked a smile, which instantly extinguished as McCloud frowned.

'Yes,' said McCloud, 'I know who she is. My brothers have explained your

111

relationship and your predicament,' he waved a hand as if to brush away a bad smell. 'So I must ask if you truly understand what you are doing? I also ask if this woman – being one of those brought here by General Bernard - is truly repentant?'

'Oh yes, sir,' said Dunblaine, 'Martine was sold as a child by her father, because they was starving and couldn't keep her, and so…, '

'I know,' said McCloud, 'I have heard the story. I wish only to be sure that she wishes to reform.' The girl frowned, and looked at Dunblaine, understanding nothing.

'*Quoi?*' she said, '*Qu'est que c'est que monsieur il a dit?*' Dunblaine explained. '*Monsieur McCloud, il a dit que …*'

'What?' said McCloud, 'Is that French? Are you speaking French?'

'Yes, sir,' said Dunblaine, 'She's been teaching me, sir. Me and Martine speak French every day now.'

'I see,' said McCloud, 'Then ask her if she repents of her past life.'

Dunblaine asked the question and Martine Lejardin responded with a torrent of French and a flood of tears that would have melted the heart of a statue hewn from ice.

'She says yes, sir,' said Dunblaine, when she was done.

'Indeed, she does,' said McCloud, 'And for your part, do you understand that if you wish to marry this woman, and live with her in France, you will have to become a catholic in full accordance with the laws of that most tyrannical faith?'

'Oh yes, sir,' said Dunblaine, and McCloud sighed from the depths of his Calvinistic soul.

'Then you may proceed,' he said, 'and on your own head be it, and for such as it may be worth: I grant you my blessing.' Dunblaine gave a huge, round smile, and turned and swept his lady off her feet so that her small shoes twinkled in the air. They looked so happy together that even Donald McCloud was moved. He was moved to polite conversation.

'So,' he said, once Dunblaine had put down the girl, 'Did you enjoy the demonstration this morning? Did you enjoy the sight of our engine under steam?'

'Oh yes, sir,' said Dunblaine, it was wonderful. Everyone thought so, but one thing puzzled me.'

'Pray tell,' said Dunblaine, giving a paternal smile. He was happy to explain any matters of engineering that might be troubling young Dunblaine. Dunblaine was so appealing, and engineering was safe and clean. It was entirely free from fleshly revulsions.

'It was the French gentlemen, sir,' said Dunblaine.

'Yes?' said McCloud.

'General Bernard and Colonel Sauvage.'

'Yes?' said McCloud.

'When the General got down from the engine, they was talking about it.'

"And?'

"Well. They was talking away to one another – in French of course – and I didn't follow all of it but here's what puzzled me, sir.'

'Go on,' said McCloud.

'Well they was ever so happy, but the General, he said, he said…,'

'Yes?'

'He said,' Dunblaine thought hard, to get the words right. 'He said…*it's a great pity* …quelle domage, *he said… it's a great pity we'll have to stop the English Scotsmen,*' Dunblaine smiled. 'That's what they call us, sir: English Scotsman. Isn't that funny?'

'Yes, yes, yes. Go on.'

'Well, sir, what he actually, said, sir, was: *we'll have to stop the English-Scotsmen building road engines, because now we've got to turn the engines to our real purpose.*' Dunblaine looked at McCloud in child-like innocence, 'What could they mean by that, sir?'

Chapter 15

The handwriting was Rowland's. I looked at the letter, then looked at O'Flaherty, and he read the expression on my face.

'Bad news, Mr Fletcher?' says he.

'Don't know,' says I.

'I'll excuse myself,' says he, 'and leave you to read it.' And he got up and wandered off. It was very polite of him and I was becoming very fond of him. He was a friend. So I opened the letter and read it. I've still got it, and this is what it said on a page spattered with ink from a pen that had scratched at high speed, and with heavy underlining for emphasis.

Fletcher,

In great haste, being drawn to other duties which prevent my coming to Plymouth. I send this news by trusted hand, when properly I should have given it you in person. You are to treat the contentof this note asabsolutely confidential & I cannot defend you if any of it should become public. Thus:-

You must take greater care oppositePercival Clive. Via his mother, he has almost convinced Pitt tha tyou made mutiny aboard Serpant, & my investigations confirm that you did indeed refuse a lawful command when he ordered you below & you disobeyed. I also learn of your assaultagainst LieutenantChancellor, giving Percival Clive still further complaint to use against you.

You must take no such risk again. I remain your ally, but there is a limit on my capacity to oppose Pitt's sister, since she is his elder & he grewup under her rule.

You must vigorously expedite Percival Clive's commission against the smugglers, since events across channel proceed faster than was anticipated, and threaten the existence of our nation by carrying steam machines into France to those English traitors of whom I have spoken.

You must act without further support from the Navy which believes that in time of war HM ships should engage the enemy, not chase smugglers, and I cannot yet reveal all that I know to convince the motherwise.

But I have contrived that other ships be given to your duties, which shall come under Percival Clive's command though you must take the lead. Use Miss Maitland as your route to Percival Clive. She is a clever woman & can be trusted. Rely upon her.

Know that the great length of coastline & the favour of the local population towards smugglers, means that none can be caught by random patrols. They can be caught only by following the advice of my agents as to the placing of your ships for precise interception. Percival Clive's orders require him frequently to communicate with the ports of Cawlo, Polcolm and Weyguard, from which my agents operate. You must ensure that he does this & takes heed of the information provided. I forbid absolutely that you should communicate with any local officials including the Customs and Excise men. Their loyalty cannot be relied upon, in the face of massive bribery.

Give your utmost.

R.

There was no such courtesy as 'Dear Fletcher' or 'sincerely yours' but that was Rowland. But cryptic as it was, the letter was so full of meat that it took a lot of digesting. It was only over some days that I calculated all the implications, which were that I was part of a plan - though by no means all of it - as conceived by Rowland, empowered by the Prime Minister and interfered with by his sister. Rowland was very obviously drawing secret information from informers everywhere: in France, along England's west coast, and even aboard *Serpant*, because someone must have told him of my part in the tale of the Salt Horse mutiny and my hammering of Chancellor's sweetbreads.

And now I was supposed to manoeuvre my ship's captain – the blockhead Poxy Percy - into chasing some very special smugglers, who may not themselves be traitors, but those Englishmen receiving them in France definitely were, yet Rowland would not tell this to the Admiralty, who therefore would not chase the smugglers, and meanwhile everyone else thought the smugglers were decent men who fetched brandy for the squire, lace for his wife, and God bless them every one! That normally was my own opinion, except that the steam-smugglers might lead, in some way that Rowland hadn't yet told me, to the destruction of England.

Faced with all this, my first conclusion was firm resolution that should I come safe out of the matter, I would never, never, ever again, be part of any such tangle of spies and dirty dealings. Fighting the French is only natural to an Englishmen, as is facing the perils of the sea. But espionage in all its forms is not natural except to such creatures as Frenchmen, and I despise it because you don't know who to trust and because – as I was to find out by personal experience – it might get you stood up against a wall and shot.

Then there was Rowland's surprising respect for Miss Maitland. I frowned at that, wondering if she'd treated him to the same exercises as myself? But no. He was too old. Or was he? Who knows?

So what was I to do? I pondered on all this and finally took comfort in Rowland's promise to get me out of the service. So in the end, since I could see no other way, I did as he wanted. And so, I believe his mighty influence worked on *Lizard* once she was fit for sea, even if it hadn't worked on the dockyard swabs. It worked through Admiral Lord Clyde-Jones who busied himself day and night, to get *Lizard* shipshape, provisioned, manned and armed. He did so officially, unofficially and every other way that got things done, because he was Rowland's man, though I never found out why, so don't ask me because I don't bloody know.

But there was still very much to be done by myself and O'Flaherty in getting *Lizard* to sea, and I wanted Percy completely out of the way, and took Rowland's advice, and spoke to Miss Maitland, who kept our Percy at Radbrough most splendidly, leaving me spending almost all my days and some nights aboard.

Thus we moved the ship's people aboard of her during the second week in June. The hands came happily from the old hulk they'd been inside, and there was some juggling among the standing officers, because in those days the Boatswain, Gunner and Carpenter – the big three of the warrant officers – belonged to a ship rather than the Service, and stayed with her for the ship's life unless they were promoted into a bigger ship.

With *Lizard*'s boatswain dead, our Mr Douglas and his mates were warranted aboard, but there was difficulty with *Lizard*'s Gunner and Carpenter because I preferred the men from *Serpant*. Also there was the luxury of choosing seamen from among the *Serpants* and those left of the *Lizards*. Finally I got the men I wanted, including even *Serpant*'s Purser, making best of a bad job.

You youngsters should understand that the Purser was a sort of shop-keeper aboard ship, providing food, drink, candles, clothes and other consumables to the men. He got his post by paying a huge deposit to the Victualing Office, and expected to make a profit on his sales. He was no sort of seaman, and ours was a mean little grub, adept at every twist and device to make private money. But I'd had the handling of him, and was used to checking his books once a month, which is pleasure to me because I do love a balance sheet, and because nobody who's ever tried once to get fraud past me, has ever tried to do so again. Oh no, indeed they haven't, my jolly boys. You just believe your uncle Jacob.

Finally we upped anchor on Tuesday June 14th, marking my entry into the Preventive Service as it was known in those days: a lesser and lower incarnation of His Majesty's sea forces, that was supposed to chase the smugglers, though the real Navy looked down on them in pity, while the good folk of old England drank a toast to the smugglers in French brandy. Despite this, *Lizard* went out of Plymouth with three ships in line astern of her, and Poxy Percy now rated Commodore – an inconceivable promotion which just shows what a domineering sister can screw out of her baby brother. None the less, those three ships were a sign of what Rowland could achieve against the inclinations of the Admiralty.

Two of our squadron were cutters: *Activity* and *Alderney*, each of ninety tons burthen, and not much more than big yachts. They were flush-decked, with a single mast stepped well for'ard, bearing mainsail and topsail with a spanker gaff and boom astern, and a spread of foresails to the jib. They were fast, handy, and excellent for any sort of coastal work. As few as twenty hands could man them, mostly needed to man the broadside of five, six-pounders, since the sails were so divided up into small individuals that a few men hauling on lines could achieve very much. Little beauties they were, and a fine sight to see when under way.

Our third companion was the lugger *Cornwallis* that had started life as the French Martinique until captured as a prize. I've never liked the look of luggers, and this one was no exception. A blunt, square, ugly bow with no curve to it, and a bowsprit sticking out flatly horizontal, and usually just two masts. But *Cornwallis* had three: fore, main and mizzen, with the mizzen stepped right at the stern with a huge boom jutting out behind the hull, and each mast bearing a pair of lug-sails, which are an ugly compromise between fore-and-aft and square rig. But having said that, I have to admit that this is a handy rig: ingenious and weatherly, giving similar driving power to that of a full square-rig, while taking far less manpower to manage. This makes a lugger well adapted for such duties as fishing, which are demanding of manpower while under way.

Cornwallis was bigger than the cutters, at 150 tons burthen, but less strong in the hull being clinker built for some mad fancy of her Froggy builders. You youngsters should note that a 'clinker built' hull is formed with long, flexible planks which overlap one another as in the longships of the Vikings: a flexible structure which eases as the sea heaves. The more usual hull is 'carvel built' in which stouter planks are fastened edge-to-edge giving a smooth hull of great strength.

A lugger was pure merchantman but often the type was taken into service for its virtues, and in this case, *Cornwallis* was armed with four nine-pounders and a row of swivels on her gunwhale. A useful ship, if bulldog-ugly and all the more so by comparison with the sweet little cutters.

All three, *Alacrity*, *Alderney* and *Cornwallis*, were based on Plymouth and had crews drawn from the west coast: Cornwall, Devon, Hampshire and Kent and their masters were Tarpaulins all three. They were wrinkled, old lieutenants risen up from the lower deck after years of service, and as innocent as babies where celestial navigation was concerned. They stood in awe of Mr O'Flaherty who, like them, had once served before the mast and yet had mastered quadrant, chronometer and spherical trigonometry.

I remember them coming aboard for the first time, which they did with *Serpant* and the squadron under easy sail, with St Austell off our starboard beam, and their boats bumping against our quarter. They were summoned aboard by Poxy Percy for dinner in the stern cabin, the first night at sea, according to tradition. So the Boatswain piped the side, the three old tars clambered over the rail, and O'Flaherty and I stood forward and doffed hats to greet them, Poxy Percy being too elevated in his own dignity to do so. O'Flaherty already knew them. He introduced them and I noted the way they bobbed and bowed at him, veteran old seaman that they were, in weather-stained uniform coats with the gold lace long since turned dark, and faces as brown as a mahogany sideboard. Their speech was the homely Devon burr so pleasing to the ear.

[As recounted in earlier volumes of his memoirs, Fletcher was born and raised in the Cornish town of Polmouth, but later developed the speech of a gentleman. S.P.]

'G'day to 'ee, Mizder Fletcher,' says the first of them.

'G'day, zurr,' says the next.

'G'day, zurr,' says the third, and 'Arrrr,' says all three together, in unison.

I'll spare you any further 'arrrs' and 'zurrs' since it's as tedious to write as it is to read. But that was the manner of their speech, and they were more at home on the lower deck than ever they were in the wardroom. They were all in their sixties, and quite open in their limitations as navigators; indeed, I believe they wanted it made clear at outset for fear of being given tasks beyond their skills.

'We b'aint like Mr O'Flaherty,' says one of them, to me. 'We be lead, log and latitude men.' What that meant, was that they disliked unfamiliar waters, preferring to find their way along coasts they already knew, by soundings, dead reckoning and the angle of the sun over the mainmast at noon: the primitive methods that seamen had used since ancient times.

'Aye,' says the other two, touching their hats to O'Flaherty, who laughed.

'Don't you take no heed o' that, at all!' says O'Flaherty to me, 'Why these men here, they know ever inch of shoreline from Portsmouth, to Land's End, and round into the Bristol Channel,' the three old tars grinned, 'See?' says O'Flatherty, 'They know that and every crafty cove where the smugglers come ashore.'

"Aye,' they said and would have blushed like maidens except that it couldn't show on their dark faces.

'Welcome aboard, gentlemen,' says I, and I'm right glad to have such men as yourself alongside of me.'

And so - later on - to dinner. We had to wait for that, which gave me time to tell the three men just what our duties were, and which was just as well, because Poxy Percy hardly mentioned that, preferring the drink and the food, and basking in Miss Maitland's radiance, and the dumbstruck awe of his guests, at sitting down in the presence of such a beauty.

The dinner itself was appalling: a Frenchified mangling of meat called a rag-oo.

[N.B. that in transcription I was obliged to render 'ragout' phonetically as 'rag-oo' since Fletcher violently rejected any usages of French spelling, and his attitude towards the French in general may be judged from the words immediately following. S.P.]

This was some vile sort of stew which – like every other meal Percy's cook delivered – most disgustingly had garlic in it: a vile herb which is contrariwise to all decencies of civilisation and against everything that distinguishes an Englishman from a Frenchman, a dog or a heathen.

After that, in the days that followed, I must say that I actually enjoyed myself. The weather was fine, Percy kept out of my way, and I had the running of the squadron, exercising them in signalling, manoeuvring, putting ashore landing parties on sandy beaches, coming to each other's aid in pretend emergencies, and even gunnery practise, to see who best could sink a floating barrel, as each ship bore past and gave its broadside. But mainly we just cruised up and down the coast, and occasionally north past Land's End, and I drew up a routine of visits to Cawlo, Polcolm and Weyguard to give Rowland's agents the chance to tell us where to find the smugglers.

This went on for a month, during which we had some fun swooping down on lone merchantmen, and firing a gun to stop them, so we could put men aboard to search for steam engines. The searching was mainly done by myself, face to face with the ship's master, and often over a glass of grog, on the assumption that any guilt or shiftiness might show in his face, because it just ain't possible to search a ship at sea, if you don't know where to look. Not with the cargo stowed one tier upon another down below, and a week's work needed in port to unload it. But no guilt did I see, nor engines did I find.

Likewise we spent much time, in the dead of the night, creeping into likely coves - the three old tars really did know where to look - where we hoped for lights on the headlands, and boats coming out with muffled oars to meet the smugglers hove too, for us to catch them. On these occasions all hands aboard of us were promised a flogging if any made noise to frighten the smugglers, but it was no use. After a week or two, I thought that maybe the Admiralty was right about not chasing smugglers, because I learned, as others had learned before me, that the main reason the smuggling trade flourished was that it was so damned hard to catch the smugglers, even if you tried.

So it was wasted time mainly, though we saw some sights such as a massive East India convoy outward bound, down-channel on the six-month's voyage to Bombay: dozens of enormous John Company ships, the biggest merchantmen in the world, with mighty spars and enormous masts, and a squadron of line-of-battle ships and frigates to keep off the French privateers, and a huge First-Rate with an Admiral aboard in command. What a picture that was to stir the heart of a man of business. What possibilities of trade! What wealth from the orient they'd bring back: spices, drugs, dyes, saltpetre and silk! All that and dusky maidens in sarees awaiting each jolly sailor. By Jove, but I wished I was aboard one of them, as they slid past, line after line, under vast and lofty canvas, and our little squadron having to back topsails and give honour to the great warships as they looked down their noses at us.

Then we carried on wasting our time until one of Rowland's men - the secret agent at Weyguard - put us in the right place at the right time, to find what we were looking for. We found that and much more, and not all of it was either good, or even safe, to find.

Chapter 16

(Letter dated Thursday June 30, from Mr Philip Charles Rowland, The Royal Charles Oak Hotel, Portsmouth, to Mr William Pitt, 10 Downing Street, London.)

Sir,

It is with the utmost respect for the many and heavy duties that fall upon you -as His Majesty's First Minister in time of war - that I trespass upon your time. None the less, I refer to that penetration of all arms, deep into France, which we have so long discussed, since I have now amassed definitive proof of the need for this expedition by which means —and by no other - we may extinguish the threat to our country, now under development atFragnal-sur-Longue.

I beg that you now devote all your powers and eloquence to driving forward this expedition since the latest information from my agents tells me that the enemy's plans are greatly further advanced, even than we had feared.

Viz:

1. A locomotive steam engine of miraculously cunning design and of full size has been built at Fragnal-sur-Longue and proven perfectin all its functions.

2. The canal is completed, to connect Fragnal-sur-Longue with the French sea-port and military establishments at Lyommevilleon the Channel coast.

3. Bonaparteorders that the manufactureof engines commence at other locations than Fragnal-sur-Longueto fulfil his plans.

4. General Bernard of the Fragnal Barracks, begs that more tools and model machines be brought from England to expedite the training of French mechanics in the manufacture ofengines at the newlocations.

In all this is revealed the one weakness of the enemy: namely that greater numbers of Frenchmen may not be trained up without items actually sent across to them from England itself in the hulls of smugglers. I am therefore redoubled in my efforts to prevent this trade, limited as I am with the ships available to me and I most urgently beg of you, sir, that you might influence their Lordships of the Admiralty into sending great numbers of His Majesty's ships into the Channel approaches, as only this will finally extinguish the activities of the smugglers.

Meanwhile some good news. I hope soon to direct my own squadron, according to information received, such that the most notorious of smugglers migh tbe detained. More of this soon, God willing.

Moving now beyond seafaring matters, I advise that the time is appropriate -nay urgent - to begin discussions with His Grace the Duke of York, Commander in Chief, to secure horse, foot and guns for the penetration into France, especially choosing our best engineers, and the intelligent, active men of our light infantry companies.

Finally and in closing, I most respectfully commend again to your attention that same Mr Jacob Fletcher whom we have much discussed, urging you once more to disregard accounts of his behaviour which I certainly know to be false. I recognise —as who could not? - the impeccable integrity of the person close to you who may especially be speaking ill of Fletcher, yet even integrity may honestly be mistaken, as indeed it is in this particular case.

I remain, sir, your servant in all these matters.

With respect and in hope,

P.C. Rowland.

Chapter 17

'No, sir!' says the leader of the three old tars. His name was Nathanial Benedict and he was the senior, having got his commission before the other two, who leaned back and nodded in total agreement.

'No,' says the second.

'No,' says the third.

We all peered down at the chart, held steady by glass weights on the great table of the stern cabin. Poxy Percy sniffed and looked first at Dr Sir Richard, who winced mincingly, and had the sense to keep out of the discussion, knowing damn-all of charts and navigation. But only when this prize booby failed, did Percy look to me and O'Flaherty. He looked like a high court judge forced to take evidence from the night-soil men.

'And what is your word in the matter, Mr Fletcher?' says Percy. He'd brought us all together to give us the shore news. We were hove-to in the Polcolm roads, wallowing heavily in a long swell, with the cutters and the lugger close beside. We'd come in for our regular appointment with whoever it was ashore – Percy wouldn't tell us who – that was feeding information from Mr Rowland. On earlier visits, a boat had come out from the Harbour Master, with ordinary letters and nothing important. But this time there was a special letter that left Percy hopping with excitement, and he summoned the captains of our squadron to repair on board of the flagship.

So there we were, sat round his table with the horizon rolling horribly through the wide-open stern windows, and the gulls calling and the waves lapping and Percy going slowly green, and Doctor Sir Richard too, which was pleasure to see. I nudged O'Flaherty when Percy wasn't looking and he grinned. O'Flaherty was immune to the sea sickness, and so was I – the only thing that's made life bearable all these years afloat – but I noticed that even one of the old tars was suffering, and there's the curse of seafaring for you, because the sea sickness affects even such splendid old veterans as him. At least it does when the motion changes, and especially hove-to, offshore.

'No!' says Percy, 'I will not have it,' he picked up the letter he'd had from ashore, taking care to fold it so none of us could see the signature, pompous little turd that he was. 'I have here the latitude and longitude of a headland,' says he, 'which lies off a cove from which a damned smuggler will set out, the day after next at dawn on the flood tide. Thus if we are waiting at dawn, we shall surely catch the rogue, and that's the first useful advice we've received this commission.'

'Might I ask the source of this advice, sir?' says I.

'A source ashore, Mr Fletcher,' says he, trying to display dignified authority. But his guts were now squirming and getting ready to spew, and it showed all over his pasty, wet face. 'A source,' says he, straining against the nausea, 'which - by the exchange of secret passwords - I know to be a true and honest source.' I could see he was telling the truth, and more than anything he just wanted to get himself on deck and lean over the side, for a good heave-ho and up comes breakfast.

I learned years later that it was the Harbour Master himself who was Rowland's agent, delivering accurate information except for the matter of shoreline geography. I turned to the tars, who were muttering to one another, and shaking their heads at the chart.

'Mr Benedict?' says I, 'What's wrong with this chart?'

'Nothing!' says Poxy Percy. 'The chart cannot be wrong. It is an Admiralty chart.'

'Mr Benedict?' says I.

'It be this here, Montmouth Point, Mr Fletcher,' says he 'which sticks out slantwise. The Chart ain't right, sir, 'cos Montmouth Point, her don't come like the chart say. Not her she don't, 'cos her goes t'other way.' And he ran a twisted old finger with a coal-black nail over the chart to show where it was wrong. 'If'n we lays off here,' says he, tapping the chart, 'Why! We won't see nothing when the bugger comes out. Where we ought-er lay off, be here off Barcolm Point: her with the gerty-great hill on her,' and he stabbed the spot with his finger.

'Aye,' says the other two tars and any fool could see that we should believe them. O'Flaherty was nodding furiously and so was I, though Percy was quite stupid enough to argue a paper chart against three men who'd sailed this coast all their lives. But the motion got to him first and he stood up quick, mumbled something nobody heard, and ran out. We heard his feet pattering up the companionway, then booming on the boards over our heads, and finally we heard his voice. We heard it clearly through the open windows.

'OOOOOOOOOO-RUGH!' says he, with great force and several times over, such that the good Doctor sweated furiously, went a hideous fish-belly white, and ran for the privacy of his cabin where he kept a chamber pot for days like this.

So we were spared further argument, and in the dark pre-dawn of Sunday July 3rd, our four ships were laid in wait off Barcolm Point somewhat to the south of Torquay. *Lizard* was in the centre of our line and Activity a cable's length off our starboard beam. *Alderney* was beyond her and *Cornwallis* to the larboard of us. The wind was northerly, which was good for a ship coming out to sea, and our ships had crept up in the dead of night, conned by Benedict aboard Activity with his vast local knowledge. All four ships were at general quarters, with guns run out, borders issued pistols and cutlass, and every man who had a glass was studying Barcolm Flood, the local name for the river mouth by the fishing village of Barcolm. We were there because that was where our informant had said a smuggler was loading a very special cargo that night: a cargo brought secretly down from the manufacturing North Country, for smuggling across the Channel into France.

Aboard *Lizard* we were in a thrill of excitement. There was dead silence other than the sounds of the sea, the creak of the ship, the wind in the rigging, and the two middies chattering which I had to stop with the threat of the Boatswain's cane, though you couldn't blame them. It was a wonderful moment, still dark, with our few sails black over head, the match-cords glowed in the gunners' linstocks in case flintlock triggers failed, and the ship's boys stood by to run cartridges up from the magazine. We were barely moving, with just enough canvas for steerage way, and the sun was getting ready to heave out of the ocean, far away to the East.

Slowly, slowly, the light came, and even Poxy Percy - standing with Miss Maitland and his familiars by the ship's wheel - had to admit the wisdom of going by Mr Benedict and not by the Admiralty chart because Barcolm Point with its gerty-great hill was to the east of us, and entirely shading us from the dawn light, which shone into Barcolm Flood, where numerous innocent fishing boats were anchored, and the dark little town sat behind them, and everything still and quiet, except for one neat, tight, splendid, middle-sized brig, remarkably heavily sparred for a merchantman, and obviously built for speed, now putting out to sea on the flood tide, with a great, bulging, spread of canvas aloft, and no lights burning.

'Make sail!' says I in a great shout.

'Yes!' says Poxy Percy, 'Make sail you fellows, and be smart about it!'

It was all prepared and rehearsed aboard each ship of our squadron. On sight of the smuggler – assuming that this was him - we would set all plain sail and converge on him, uncovering our own lights, and our drums beating a long roll. That and one more thing.

'Hip, hip, hip …,' says I.

'Huzzah!' says all hands in a great shout.

'Hip, hip, hip …,'

'Huzzah!'

'Hip, hip, hip …,'

'Huzzah!'

And the same aboard *Alacrity*, *Alderney* and *Cornwallis*: a trick I learned years ago on the slave coast, and which I commend strongly to you youngsters. Always go into action with a great noise and a big shout. It scares the shite out of your enemies, and puts heart in your own side.

On a north wind, we converged at a sharp angle to the brig. This, because he had the wind astern of him, while we had it on the beam. You must always remember the way things were before steam ships, so we couldn't run straight at the brig, and it was some while before we got close enough for a good shot in the dim light.

'Mr Gunner?' says I.

'Yes, yes!' says Poxy Percy, 'Mr Gunner!'

'Aye-aye, Mr Fletcher, sir!'

'A shot across his bows, if you please!'

'Yes, yes, across his bows!' says Poxy Percy, the useless dollop of dog dung.

Boom, says the foremost carronade, chop-splash, says the shot, hurling a hundred-foot column of white water into the air, before the brig's bow. But she never even slowed. She forged on at great speed, close enough now for us to see every detail of her, and the fine-lined craft that she was, and white faces looking at us from her rigging and her sides.

'Mr Gunner?' says I, and I don't know what Percy said because I was ignoring him by now, as was everyone else.

'Sir?' says the Gunner.

'One into the hull, if you please!'

'Aye, aye, sir!'

Boom! Crunch! But even that didn't stop him, and we gave him two more into the hull, until we got close enough for hailing. I got up in to the main shrouds and gave a good bellow.

'Heave to in the King's name! Back your topsail!'

'Aye-aye!' came back a voice from the brig, which was no more than a pistol shot from us, and she backed topsail and slowed. But she did it so fast and neat, and so expert in the manoeuvre, that the slower efforts of my own crew meant that we overshot. All four of us overshot, even the Devon-crewed cutters and lugger. Then, damn me for a bloody Frenchman, if the naughty rascal didn't come about so fast that she seemed to spin on her keel and her canvas thundered, as she backed and filled and hauled away splendidly, with every sail drawing hard, aiming to get between us and the shore and weather Barcolm point, and so out and away on to the empty ocean. By George it was some fine seamanship, and that wasn't the end of it.

The nearest to the brig, as she slid out of our grasp, was *Alacrity*. She was late to spot the brig change course, and was attempting now to come about to block his escape, which meant that she was caught bearing head-on to the brig, which was passing close by. In that condition none of her guns could bear, but every one of his could. Given that irresistible advantage, the brig couldn't restrain from proving that it was a wrong 'un, by giving a broadside into a King's ship.

And no King's ship could have done it better. I myself couldn't have done it better, and that's saying something. It was no ragged broadside discharged in haste. It wasn't actually a broadside at all. It was each individual gun - and I counted eight of them which was some battery for a supposed merchantman – it was every gun, fired in the time of its own captain, having taken careful aim. We heard the guns. We heard the ripping, tearing, splintering of shot running down the length of *Alacrity*, we heard the anvil clang of a gun struck and dismounted. It was dreadful to hear.

But meanwhile *Lizard* was coming about. No orders were needed. My men were not in the same class as those aboard that brig but they knew their duties, it was obvious what had to be done, and they were bursting for revenge. It was the same aboard *Alderney* and *Cornwallis*, and soon we were running past a helpless *Alacrity*. I was still up in the main shrouds as we went by, and I had a good view – which is to say a bad view – of the damage the brig had done to her. The brig had aimed low, into the hull, which is what you do when you want to kill men rather than disable a ship. To disable, you aim into the rigging hoping to knock away a spar or a mast, and bring down the sails. That's what you might expect a smuggler to do if he just wanted to get away. But not this particular smuggler. I looked down and saw the dead men, and the wounded men and the pieces of men on *Alacrity's* blood-stained deck. I was close enough even to recognise Mr Benedict though I'll give no description of the condition of him, which was not pretty, other than to say that he was well and truly dead. But there were plenty of men still alive, and waving to us, and she was safe afloat and sound aloft, so our clear duty was to chase the brig that had ruined her.

Which we did, and a long chase it was too, out into the Atlantic. It took us all day to catch that brig, and a cunning and slippery fellow he was and no mistake, displaying some of the finest seamanship I ever witnessed, and which can be told in words, but which – like the performance of an actor or a singer - must be seen and heard to appreciate, though here is what happened in plain language.

As we cleared the Channel, the wind backed steadily from north to north-easterly and steadied just a point short of outright easterly: a good, strong blow taking us far out into the Atlantic, and raising the waves till *Lizard, Alderney, Cornwallis* and the brig were plunging heavily. And now I must emphasise a truth not always appreciated by landmen, which is that each ship sails differently, under different sea conditions and depending on its own particular hull and rig – especially the rig – even leaving aside the skill of its crew. This means that a nimble, sharp-prowed little cutter, like *Alderney* would out-sail a brig under light winds and an easy sea. But when the wind gets up and the sea rises, then the cutter is disadvantaged as compared the greater sea-keeping qualities of the brig, which is more round in the bow and rises to the waves rather than piercing them. So if the cutter carries too much sail when the waves get up, then she'll drive her bows under, take the ocean aboard, and risk harming herself if she persists.

This is merely the simplest explanation of a very complex matter, but in principle, you youngsters should understand that this is the reason why *Alderney* had to shorten sail and fall astern of *Lizard* while the lugger *Cornwallis*, built for handiness and convenience and never for speed, had never had a hope of keeping up. So the brig raced ahead, *Lizard* strained every sail to follow, and the pair of us charged away from *Alderney* and *Cornwallis* and all sight of land went under the horizon behind us, and the chase went on for hours.

During all this time, of course Lizard's day ran its measured course, with the bell sounding and the watches changing. Not that anybody wanted to go below: not with such a sport in progress, and every hand who could, went aloft for a better view, except when I bellowed at them for spoiling the ship's trim. But there was no ill will amongst us, and nobody got my boot or even the Boatswain's: not with a chase in progress.

'Aye-Aye!' says the hands, doubling to obey and grins and smiles, except when I had to send them below at noon, watch by watch, for their dinners and grog, which normally they fell upon with delight. But this time they hung back to catch the last glimpse of the prize ahead. You couldn't blame them either, because any ship we took was indeed a prize, and that meant money in every man's pocket. Then just after six bells in the afternoon watch – say three p.m. shore time – there were growls of delight and cheers, and even the totally-useless-no-seaman Poxy Percy came up to me and clapped me on the back.

'Well done, Mr Fletcher,' says he. 'I've stood back and let you con the ship for your greater experience, but I see that you are doing well enough.' That's how the little bugger saved face, having been ignored by all hands since first we sighted the smuggler. Well, his toadies all smiled wisely, and Miss Maitland smirked as if in approval. But O'Flaherty winked his eye at me, and the Boatswain just laughed.

All this, because we were catching up with the brig. We definitely were. At first you had to judge it by measuring the height of the brig's masts with a quadrant. This you did by measuring the angle between the deck and the peak of the mainmast. The bigger the angle, the closer we got. Even the middies were making these measurements and squeaking to each other in excitement, and very good experience for them it was too, in the use of their instruments.

Soon you could tell just by looking, and the hands all cheered, and calculated the value of their prize money, and a merry ship's company we were too. But then the rascal proved even more clever, and an even finer seaman, than I'd thought.

Seeing that we were catching up, he hauled close on the wind – which means he turned so that instead of the wind blowing him from astern, he was as close to the oncoming wind as his rig would bear. Of course we had to do the same, but lost time in coming about as compared with him, and by that means he opened up the distance between us. But then, after running some while close hauled, we began to close the gap again. In response, the brig put up his helm, causing him to spin round again, so as to bring the wind astern of him, and he set every sail he could bear, and raced away before we could do the like. He did this again and again, running close hauled, and then running downwind, and switching from one to the other with marvellous skill.

It was a clever, yet dangerous way to avoid capture, because it depended entirely on his people being better exercised in his ship than mine were in ours. If it worked, he opened the gap each time he went about. But if he once missed stays, was taken aback, and left dead in the water, then we'd be on him with guns run out and matches burning. In the end he never failed but our lookouts got the better of him. I'm proud to say that they did so without any urging of mine, because they were seaman too, and of course they wanted their prize money. Thus they got better and better at spotting the brig's intentions as soon as his crew moved to their stations.

'Going about!' they cried, the very instant the brig's crew moved.

'Hands to the braces!' says I, because I too was now warned and had my people ready to follow the brig round.

A few more turns like that, and the brig gave up his cunning ploy because it wasn't working any more. Instead, and in desperation, he simply ran before the wind, heaving everything overside that would go, to lighten the ship and raise her in the water and gain some precious speed. First the guns went: sixteen of them with their carriages, then round-shot, powder, spars and anything else they could throw. The ship's pig would have gone too, if they'd had one which they didn't, and it damn well worked, as the gap between us opened up again, because in a straight sailing match the brig was now winning.

My men groaned, and bad farewell to the wonderful debauch that their prize money would buy in the tart-shops ashore. They groaned and sighed. But then, they cheered their hearts out as, in full view of all hands, the brig's foremast suddenly snapped forward in ruin, under the tremendous pressure of her sails, causing her stays and shrouds to part and all her beautiful spread of sail to blow out like washing on a line, and she staggered and slowed and rolled and lost way.

And so, my very jolly boys, His Majesty's Brig-Sloop *Lizard* 'came down like a wolf on the fold' to quote Lord Byron, who I met once and had to kick for ignoring the ladies and aiming his pretty smile too close at me. But even his curly-haired Lordship wasn't as devious as that smuggler once I got hold of him, because he was the most cunning sea-lawyer I ever met in all my life.

Chapter 18

'Facing total refusal by the English-Scottish to build further engines, I was compelled – against all previous inclination to divulge further details of our plans for these engines, in order to convince them that the Greater Cause was served.'

(Translated From a letter of Friday June 24 1796 from Citizen Inspector, General Claude Bernard, at the Frangnal-sur-Longue Barracks, to Citizen, General of Division Napoleon Bonaparte, Headquarters of the Army of Italy)

*

McCloud's room was packed. Most of his men were there, and those who couldn't get in were pressed forward in the corridor outside the open door. More than that - and beyond all understanding of Donald McCloud - some of his men had brought their women with them, and fiercely argued their right to be present.

'You can't refuse them, Donald,' said Jamie McCloud, who stood with his French girl jammed in the press beside him. 'You can't refuse them,' he repeated and this amazing statement brought a roar of approval from one side of the room - the side clutching girls in its arms - while howls of rage came from the other: the side that had elevated its chastity to religious fervour. Such was the ludicrous, laughable yet fearful chasm now dividing a once-united congregation. Donald McCloud turned for support to Colonel Sauvage, standing beside him, shoved as they were right up against the window in a room full of heaving bodies.

'Monsieur the Colonel,' said McCloud, 'You are a Frenchman, a servant of the new Enlightenment, and I call upon you to support me.'

'Quoi?' said General Bernard, on the other side of McCloud, not understanding a word. Sauvage shook his head. There was no time to explain. That would have to wait.

'Plus*tard, mon* General,' said Sauvage, 'Pas*de* temps.'

Sauvage looked at the mass of English-Scottish, nose-to-nose with himself, jostling and angry: angry more with each than either himself or General Bernard. Sauvage tried to think, tried to consider the mad, stupid, statement that Jamie McCloud had just made. He paused too long and Jamie McCloud shoved forward, yelling right into Sauvage's face.

'I say that the proclamation of the rights of mankind must clearly and logically include women as well as men, thus our women must stand with us, and debate with us, and vote with us!'

'Yes!' roared half the room.

'No!' roared the other.

'*Qu'est qu'il dit?*' insisted Bernard. This time Sauvage swiftly explained and the two Frenchman rolled eyes in disbelief that such metaphysical matters were consuming these English-Scottish. Didn't they consider practical reality? Didn't they wonder what they were doing in France? Did they even understand that England and France were at war? Then Sauvage and Bernard saw how the English-Scottish held on to their women – those who'd got them – and realised that it wasn't only politics working in the English-Scottish minds, but animal instinct. The fools were still in love with the girls and weren't going to be parted. That was it.

'Monsieur,' said Sauvage to Jamie McCloud, and did his best to smile and be calm, as he began a placatory speech, 'We have already agreed that all those women shall stay who have formed relationships with …' But he never finished.

'No!' cried Donald McCloud, 'No! No! We are not here to discuss the women …,'

A roar of anger from half the room drowned him out. The yelling was incoherent, deafening and in furious contradiction of McCloud, who was doubly horrified because he'd always been used to profound respect from these men: respect to his every utterance. For a moment he was stunned. But he came back.

'No! No! No!' he repeated, 'What is at issue here,' he said, glaring at Sauvage and then at Bernard, 'What is at issue is the treacherous plan – in the face of all that we have understood and agreed – to transmute our road engines into some other purpose, as yet undeclared.'

That brought silence. The yelling stopped. The division of the room disappeared.

'Yes,' said a dozen voices, and everyone looked at Sauvage and Bernard, and then closely at Bernard, because Sauvage instantly turned to his superior for guidance.

'*Qu'est que c'est?*' said Bernard, though he'd already guessed. Sauvage explained and Bernard started to speak but was interrupted.

'Be warned,' said McCloud, 'Be warned that if we are prevented from building our road engines, then the whole purpose of our work here is laid low, and neither I nor any of my men will lay hand on tools again,' he looked at his men and raised his voice in a final flourish. 'We are here in reverence of the Enlightenment,' he cried, 'and in no other cause.'

'Yes!' roared the entire room. McCloud had sounded a true note. The matter of the women was set aside.

*

Sauvage and Bernard spoke rapidly to each other in French.

'What in God's name are they talking about?' said Bernard.

'They've found out we're going to use their engines for something else,' said Sauvage.

'I know that.'

'And they're saying that if they can't make road engines they won't work at all.'

'Saint and angels! And why not?'

'Who cares? They just won't!' said Sauvage, then tried to explain, 'It's the God-damned Enlightenment,' he said, 'all that shit and corruption from the revolution. They actually believe it. They're mad. We've always known they're mad.' Bernard groaned.

'I know,' he said. 'Holy Mary Mother of God, it was so much easier in the King's time. We were loyal to him and to France and that was enough,' Sauvage agreed. He agreed from the bottom of his heart. Meanwhile Bernard looked at the English-Scottish, hoping that some understanding of them might be granted him. 'Can they really be so crap-head stupid as to stop work if they can't make road engines?' he said. 'What do they care what engines they make?' But Bernard knew that they did care, and that he, Bernard, had deceived the English-Scottish. He'd told them one thing while planning another, and now he was caught out in a lie. But Bernard was loyal to France under whatever rule.

'So!' he said, 'this is what we tell them. What you tell them, Sauvage.'

Sauvage listened, nodded, and switched to English.

*

'Gentlemen!' he cried, 'My friends! We all serve the same great cause and your magnificent engines will serve that cause. You have my word and my promise

133

on that.' Sauvage looked particularly to Donald McCloud. He looked most seriously at Donald McCloud, and Bernard did the same. The two men did their best to appear honest and sincere. The noise in the room faded. Everyone looked at McCloud for judgement. For the moment McCloud's men gave him again the respect they'd given him in the past.

'Will you explain yourself, Colonel Sauvage?' said Donald McCloud. 'If we may not make road engines, how can we serve the cause?' Everyone looked at Sauvage. Sauvage looked at Bernard who nodded, understanding men's faces if not their words. Sauvage spoke.

'The movement of goods and vital supplies within France, which was the destined purpose of the road engines, is now better done by canal transport, because of the great programme of canal building now under way. Thus the engines that you make will best serve the great cause of the Enlightenment, if they are used to drive not road locomotives, but boats.'

Sauvage paused to see the effect of his words, which were very largely true. The engines were indeed going into boats, but the boats were destined for waters far greater than canals, and that greater truth must be kept as far away as possible from the English-Scottish.

Chapter 19

I said that the smuggler was he, but to my uttermost amazement he wasn't he, because he was she. The smuggler brig's name, carved and gold-leafed at the stern, was *Molly Monckton* and the person in command was a woman in man's clothes - master mariner's long coat plus cocked hat and sea-boots – who stepped up right in my face and defied me.

'First of all, mister,' says she, I'll have you know that I out-sailed you fair and square, and you'd never have caught me at all, but for the cowardly shot you put into my foremast as I made sail out of Barcolm!'

'What?' says I, stopped dead by the cheek of the woman.

'Aye!' says she, 'such that the mast finally failed, and even such as yourself could finally crawl up alongside in your own lubber's time.'

'Aye!' says all her crew.

'What?' says I again.

'So just what d'you think you're doing?' says she, 'Speak up now, For I'm Captain Sally Combes, of Falmouth in Devon, out-bound on lawful business.'

'Aye!' says her crew, and for an instant I stood gaping as she acted the injured party and damned me for a villain. But then I answered back.

'None of that!' says I, 'I called on you to heave-to, in the king's name, and you refused and then fired on the British flag like a bloody pirate.'

'Pirate?' says she, 'And how was I to know in the dark that you weren't a pirate yourself or a French privateer? Anyone can call out in the King's name. And as to firing, you fired first. That's how you wounded my mast!'

'Aye!' says her crew, nudging one another and grinning, while she stamped her foot, and folded her arms across her chest, and stared me out, because by George she was one hell of a woman. But here I must avoid giving false impression. I don't want you youngsters imagining Cap'n Sal as some kind of fantasy pirate queen: a saucy minx with tight britches, boots and a riding crop, swaggering across the pantomime stage, slapping her thigh and declaring:

'Where is that naughty boy, Jack?'

Oh no, my jolly boys - tasty as the image is - because that wasn't Sally Combes, not when you got to know her. In the first place she was a fine seaman, and I insist that the word applies to a woman because she truly had out-manoeuvred my squadron, trained her crew better than mine, and ruined *Alacrity* with a single broadside. But neither was she one of those odd-little, wizened females of my young day that cherished the sea life, and got themselves aboard ship by pretending to be men. Every seaman came across one of these in his time, and since they worked hard at being shipmates they were usually accepted as such, and it was only when someone new came aboard and pointed them out, that we got reminded that they weren't really men.

Sally Combes wasn't either of those, because she was something unique. She was a womanly woman, with tits and hips to prove it, and quite young. She was about five foot six, with a blond, Baltic look: high cheekbones, slanting eyes, and a strong jaw. Nor was she one of those females that don't like men, because she did, but in that she was doomed by the unfairness that falls upon a strong and dominant woman, since there's nothing about being strong and dominant that makes a woman attractive to men. Some men are instantly frightened off – not that I ever was – but some are, and even if they're not, then no man ever fancies a women, deep down in his loins, because she's a fine organiser, gets things done, and makes folk jump. Indeed they don't because men look for other things in a woman because that's the nature of men.

On the other hand, this undoubtedly explains how Sally Combes kept discipline over two hundred prime seamen in the full vigour of their youth, including a gang of six of the finest toughs I ever met afloat, who stood firmly around their Captain, as the elite of the ship's company. They were bruisers every one, that stared at me with fixed hatred, led by a man even bigger than myself. He was like father Neptune, with big fists and a full beard: black and streaked with grey around the mouth.

Which left myself with a boarding party of a mere dozen behind me, and *Molly Monckton* hove to, rolling on the big Atlantic sea, with her foremast half gone and her rigging ruined, and her decks packed with Captain Sal's men, pressing ever closer and getting more insolent with every word she spoke.

'I'll have the law on you mister,' says she.

"Ayyyye!' they roared.

'I'll make you pay!'

'Ayyyye!'

'We'll start with the cost of a new foremast!'

'AYYYYYYE!'

With that the rascals were fingering their knives and slipping the belaying pins out of the rails. One word from her and they'd have been all over us, and she knew it too, because she looked round and winked at her people, and they roared and stepped forward, and she turned and sneered at me.

'So what'll you do now, mister?' says she.

'Make ready, lads!' says I, in a great shout.

'Clack-clack-clack!' says two dozen of pistol locks behind me, as my men drew, cocked and levelled, such that Captain Sal's people, blinked and stood still. If we'd not had the only firearms aboard ship, then I don't doubt that I'd have been slit, gutted and dumped in the ocean: me and all my boarding party. But I take credit for certain precautions in that respect.

*

When *Lizard* first came alongside *Molly Monckton* and hove to, we wallowed up and down of one another, rising and falling such that first we looked down on their deck and then they looked down on ours, and the masts waved circles in the sky as we rolled. It gave both sides an extremely good view of the other at less than twenty yards range, and our crew were overjoyed with the neat, smart beauty of the brig, and what a fine prize she was to put money in all our pockets. So all the *Lizards* peered at the brig and laughed at her scowling crew and her empty gun-ports, while *Molly Monckton's* people looked at our main battery, run out and ready to deliver 32pound shot at spitting distance and mash them all to splinters, while all parties on both sides knew that the brig was entirely ours to play with, and to do with as we pleased. And yet I was careful.

For one thing, there was a very large crew aboard of her - far bigger than *Lizard's* - and we'd had plenty of opportunity to judge their quality. They were prime seamen every one, and they stood fast and glowered at us and stewed in their anger.

'An excellent body of men, Mr Fletcher,' says Poxy Percy, who'd looked them over and drawn all the wrong conclusions. 'What a pity they cannot be brought into the King's Service, don't you think?'

'Indeed, sir,' says Dr Sir Roger.

'You are right as ever,' says Mr Myers, neither of whose opinions was worth a pint of piss.

'If you please, Captain?' says I, worried that Percy might do something stupid, and I raised my voice before he did. 'You there, aboard the brig?' says I, good and loud, 'Do you hear me?'

'Aye-aye,' says a voice.

'Then heave your small arms over the side. I'll see a cutlass and a pair of pistols go over, for every man of you, or I'll open fire!'

'Fletcher!' says Poxy Percy, 'Do you really judge that necessary? It would be a tragedy to ruin her.' Miserable little swine. We'd have to go aboard her sooner or later, and put our men's lives at risk, outnumbered as they'd be, and Percy was thinking only of the prize money, of which he – as captain – would have the greatest share. I managed not to sneer, because I knew I had to be careful with him. I'd been warned by Lady Clyde Cooper and Rowland both, hadn't I?

'If you please, Captain,' says I, and pointed at the brig's crew, 'These are the men that fired into *Alacrity* and killed Captain Benedict.'

'Ah,' says Percy, and bit his lip and stood back. He stood back and let me take responsibility. So much the better, because there was no movement aboard the brig. None at all. I frowned.

'Small arms over the side!' I cried, 'Do it now!' But they didn't. As when we'd first caught her, they didn't give up at first warning. Thus some of them huddled together on the quarterdeck and spoke to one another but nobody moved. 'Right,' says I, 'Mr Gunner, put a shot over her decks. Fire on the upward roll. Just to warn the buggers and make 'em show respect.'

'Aye-aye, sir.

And so he did. The detonation must have been appalling aboard the brig. Guns are hideously loud even behind or to the side, while being in front, blasts the eardrums and singes with powder grains. But that was merciful compared with sending a shot into her. So when the smoke cleared, all hands aboard her were clutching their ears, but all of them were alive.

'Small arms over the side!' I yelled, 'Or I fire for effect.' That did it. There was a bustle of movement, and men were pulling pistols from their belts and throwing them over the rail, and cutlasses too. I turned to Poxy Percy. 'Permission to go aboard her, Captain?'

'Oh, yes,' says he, 'go indeed,' and he stood back and gave his best superior smile, 'It will be a test of your initiative, Mr Fletcher,' and he pointed at the brig, 'You may go aboard to take her surrender, but be aware that you shall be in my eye the whole time.' All his creepy crawlies murmured their approval and they nodded as if listening to the wisdom of Nelson. 'So get about your business, Mr Fletcher,' says Percy, 'and be prompt about it.'

'Aye-aye, sir,' says I. What else could I say? But I saw Mr O'Flaherty trying not to laugh at Percy, and that made me feel better. So we swung out a boat, and I called for boarders, and had a quiet word with our Gunner before I went over the side. He didn't like what I said, but he nodded, and later he had a word with our people.

*

So: it finally came down to Captain Sally's people working up their anger to charge into our pistols because we could never kill all of them, and those at the back would leap over those that fell. But I had one final trick to play. I turned away from Sally Combes and her six bruisers, and called out to *Lizard* close alongside.

'Mr Gunner?' says I.

'Aye-aye!' says our gunner.

'What are my orders, Mr Gunner?'

'In case of treachery aboard the brig,' says he, 'I shall giver her as many broadsides as may be needed to sink her!'

'And will your men deliver?' says I.

"AYE-AYE!' says *Lizard's* lower deck in a great shout.

And that was the end of it. Captain Sally looked at me and nodded. She'd got the point. She spoke to Black-Beard and he went among the crew and spoke to them, and all was as peaceful as ever it can be when a large crew of strong men, is forced by foul circumstances to haul down their flag: which is to say that *Molly Monckton* was still highly dangerous.

Meanwhile, Sally Combes looked at me and spoke with something approaching civility.

'So who are you?' says she.

'Lieutenant Fletcher of his Majesty's Ship *Lizard*,' says I, 'Here to search for contraband.' She frowned and her next words were a surprise.

'Fletcher?' says she, 'Jacob Fletcher?'

'Yes,' says I, wondering what this meant, and she nodded.

'Then we'd best go below, Mr Jacob Fletcher,' says she, 'So you can see the ship's papers.'

[As mentioned earlier, Fletcher, had by this time acquired a reputation both afloat and ashore, the extent of which he seems not to have realised. S.P.]

So that's what we did, once I'd had our boat go back and forth a few times to put more armed men aboard the brig in case of naughtiness. Down in the stern cabin, everything was all neat, tight and scrubbed, like everything else aboard *Molly Monckton*, and Captain Sally observed the usual traditions, sending her steward for a bottle and some glasses, so we could talk properly. She sat in one chair, with Black-Beard in another beside her. He'd come below with us, and was behaving himself for the moment. He gazed at Captain Sally with fathomless respect, keeping quiet and nodding fiercely at everything she said, but taking no part in the business himself. It was like seeing a gorilla on a lead. Mind you, he furrowed his brow at me, and the two of us eyed one another up, as men do on first meeting, and I felt more than I've ever done in all my career that I'd have to put a fist in his face sooner or later, and the sooner done the better. The only problem was that for the first time in my life, I had some hesitation. He had the most enormous hands: far bigger than mine, and was at least as heavily muscled as me. So I truly did wonder if I could do the work, when it came to it. And that was new to your Uncle Jacob, my jolly boys, so think on it, and think hard.

'This is Mr Longridge,' my First Mate, says she, introducing the gorilla. I nodded, with them on one side of her cabin table and me on the other, while the ship rolled deeply and the bottle slid to and fro with the motion and had to be caught by one or another of us – which a sailor does without even knowing - and so we went on.

'Your health, Mr Fletcher!' says she.

'Your health Ma'am,' says I, but she frowned.

'Captain!' says she.

'Captain,' says I, and so begun a most remarkable conversation.

'You're Fletcher that sank the *Calipheme* in Boston Harbour,' says she, and Longridge nodded.

'How the damned hell d'you know that?' says I.

'From the size of you, and from seaman's gossip.'

'Well Captain,' says I, 'Who I might be, ain't hardly the matter in hand, because what I want to know is: what have you got under hatches, and which I must examine in the king's name?' She nodded at that, cool as you please, and took another sip, and looked me straight in the eye.

'I'm carrying a cargo of iron ware,' says she, 'and very special it is too, being worked up into clever machines intended to make other machines, and make them to a very great exactness.' There she paused and gave a little smile as you might in chess when you make a clever move. 'I'm carrying that, and half a dozen of other devices, which are something even more remarkable, because they are the miniature imitations of actual, road-running engines, driven by steam for the purpose of drawing carriages behind them, without ever the need of horses.' She smiled again and had the cheek to raise her glass at me. 'So there you are, Mr Fletcher, and a very good health to you,' says she.

Well: in that moment I thought Christmas and my birthday were both come on the same day, and I must have sat up in my chair with triumph all over my face. But then I thought a bit and looked at her calm expression, and I wasn't so sure.

'And where might you be carrying this cargo?' says I.

'To America,' says she, 'To Messrs Carter, Cooper and Brown of Long Island, who are in trade as machinists to the Governor of the State of New York,' and Longridge laughed, a deep rumbling in the belly, like a prize porker digesting.

'What?' says I, 'Don't you try to fox me, for I know you're a damned smuggler carrying goods to the French, and that's the truth, ma'am.'

'Captain,' says she, correcting me again.

'Bladderwash,' says I, 'Where's your papers? Your bills of lading? Commission from your owners...,' She raised a hand.

'And where's my contract from Carter, Cooper and Brown?' says she, 'And Where's my Banker's receipt of monies paid in advance?' she pointed at one of the cupboards, carpentered into the bulkheads all round, 'You will find all that in there, Mr Fletcher,' says she, 'All that and more, all shipshape and Bristol fashion, set out in black and white,' and she wasn't done. Not by a long way, 'So you'll find, Mr Jacob Fletcher, that everything's in order, and that my ship is legally bound on a legal cruise, and,' she smiled and filled our glasses again before she continued, ' and, you'll find that my lawyers in London will fall upon you like the tigers of Bengal, and will tear you to shreds in demanding utmost reparation for the damage done to my ship. So! I'll see you in court, Mr Fletcher,' says she, 'and I'll see you ruined.'

Chapter 19

'The betrayal is final and absolute. The French lies are revealed and yet even my own brother refuses to recognise them but now works in an evil cause which turns our engines to the devil's own purpose and that devil is Bonaparte.'
(From a letter of Friday July 15 1796 – sealed by never delivered - from Donald James McCloud to his Father Mr Hamish McCloud, 15 Bream Terrace, near Douglas Square, Edinburgh.)

*

Donald McCloud screamed at his brother Jamie, and the younger brother fell back, shocked and shaken, while all their compatriots looked on in horror. The sun shone bright and light into the great workshop at the Fragnal Barracks, and the little birds sang in the dawn of a lovely day. But to those inside everything felt like miserable rain in the deep of winter.

'Traitor!' said Donald McCloud in a voice twisted in anger, 'Judas! Our Daddy will disown you! You'll never go home! I curse you to die an outcast in a foreign land!' Jamie McCloud blinked and blinked. He was a big man, like his elder brother. Both were used to hard work, and hard muscles. Both had a temper. Now Donald's was up, and Jamie's was brewing, just as everyone's tempers had been brewing ever since yesterday, when Colonel Sauvage announced that they were to make engines for steam boats. Everyone had argued the meaning of that all night, and now they must come to a decision.

'Donald,' said Jamie McCloud, mastering anger and attempting reason, 'What difference if we make road-engines or water-engines? It's all part of the cause.'

'You, child!' cried Donald McCloud, 'You infant! You stupid, idiot, moron. Can't you see you're being led by the nose?' he stabbed a finger at Colonel Sauvage and General Bernard, stood with a large body of soldiers behind them,

'They've deceived us. They knew we came to make road engines for the great Enlightenment, but they have some other scheme entirely. What will they do with water-engines? Do you know? Do you think they've told us everything? Can you ever trust them?' Jamie McCloud blinked and stumbled over his words.

'I...I...,' he said, 'That is ...,'

'Ah!' cried Donald McCloud and jabbed a finger hard into Jamie's chest. 'There, sir!' said Donald. 'Caught out, sir. Caught out in your own lies.'

'I'm no liar,' said Jamie, and struck Donald's hand away, but he looked away from his brother's eyes.

'Ah! Ah! Ah!' cried Donald, 'So that's the way of it, sir. I see it in you. You damned bloody liar, I see that you have reasons of your own!' and Donald went white in the face, and Jamie went white in the face, and they stared with wild eyes. 'Traitor!' said Donald, and stabbed a finger at Jamie again.

The second jabbing finger broke the thin wall of reason that had been holding the brothers apart, and they leapt on one another in the ferocious combat of big men gone mad in anger. They tumbled and fell and rolled and kicked and punched, and throttled and fought. They fought without art or skill, but with total and hysterical aggression. They would have done each other real harm, but for the 134th Regiment, whose soldiers - at Bernard's command - put down their muskets and rushed forward, and hauled the two English-Scottish apart, and very effectively kept any other of the English-Scottish from joining in with the fight, which some of them would otherwise have done.

Eventually the struggling ended, and left the workshop full of panting, gasping men, with opposing factions held apart yet again by the disciplined French such that Sauvage and Bernard despaired. Bernard spoke rapidly in French to Sauvage, who nodded and stood forward.

'Enough of this,' he cried, 'I'll have no more of this fighting,' he pointed to one side of the big workshop, 'It comes to this: every man of you who still wishes to build engines, must stand over there.' Nobody moved at first, and Sauvage almost lost his own temper. 'Over there, now this instant!' he said, 'because all the rest of you will be placed in confinement.'

There was a long silence, then Jamie McCloud spoke.

'I'm for building the engines,' he said, and shook off the French soldiers holding him, and they looked at Bernard, who nodded, and they let McCloud go, and Jamie walked to the side of the room.

'Traitor!' cried Donald McCloud, and there was another lively bout of struggling, and yelling, and Bernard shouting orders in French, before just fourteen of the McCloud followers stood with Jamie, and the rest were dragged off with Donald.

Eventually there was silence and Sauvage and Bernard looked around the Fragnal workshop, because it, at least, was ready, even if the English-Scottish were not. Hand tools and materials were ready in profusion, the great stationary engine outside was under steam, and the engine's drive-shaft turned silent and smooth, where it pierced the wall and came inside to drive the belts that would run all the machine tools now ready and waiting. The machine shop was something entirely new to France: something assembled to the best Soho-Manufactory standards.

But the only men who could really operate these technical wonders, were the mad English-Scottish, and just fourteen of them, and their new leader Jamie McCloud stood with his chin on his breast in despair.

Sauvage saw that and – nudged by Bernard – he stepped forward, placing an arm around Jamie McCloud's shoulders. Sauvage was a clever man with intuitive understanding of human nature. Thus he knew instantly what was gnawing at Jamie McCloud's soul, because Sauvage and Bernard had calculated exactly what to say, to keep McCloud happy and working.

'My dear McCloud,' said Sauvage, in the kindest and most understanding voice, 'I understand your distress. But this is what happens when a great, and new idea takes hold of men. There are always some who cannot see the way: the new way. There are some who will be left behind. So we must pity them, but not be miss-led by them. We must ourselves remain true to the Great Cause…,'

Bernard stood back and watched as Sauvage droned on:*etcetera, etcetera, etcetera* and blah, blah, blah.' Bernard didn't understand the words, but he saw the expression on Jamie McCloud's face – he saw the nods and finally the smile - and he concluded that McCloud was believing the rubbish that Sauvage was offering. After all, McCloud was a fanatic, was he not? Bernard shrugged. Who cared, just so long as the work went forward?

Finally Sauvage finished his prepared speech and stood back, and offered his hand like an Englishman. Bernard nodded slightly as McCloud instantly took the hand and shook it, and something like a cheer came from the English-Scottish standing with him. Then there was much more talking in English, and then all the foreigners were standing round a table, and McCloud was pulling out a long, rolled-up, sheet of paper, the size of a large map. Busy hands flattened the paper on the table and everyone – including Bernard – pressed forward for a good look.

'Ah,' thought Bernard as he looked at the beautifully-drawn diagram. It showed a boat, a large boat, as seen from bow, stern, each side and above. The boat contained a steam engine and a most fascinating and complex structure stood out from the stern of the vessel. Bernard wondered what that structure might be.

He wondered but Jamie McCloud revelled and gloried in it, because although Jamie McCloud did indeed respect the French Enlightenment, there were other passions within him. Jamie had seen Anthony Dunblaine marry Martine Lejardin in the local church, and Jamie was living with his own French girl and learning French. Thus his loyalties to family, and even to country, were shifting. So, while Jamie had despaired when his Elder brother disowned him, and while Sauvage had helped Jamie overcome that despair, in fact Sauvage had merely given the final shove to send Jamie where he already wanted to go, because more important than any of these personal emotions – and most simple of all - Jamie McCloud was an engineer and he wanted to drive a boat by steam.

As far as he was concerned, the road engine had run and was done, and that was Donald's triumph. So he, Jamie, now wanted to drive a boat by steam. He would annihilate the primordial dependence of the mariner upon wind, tide, and current. He would save lives, abolish shipwreck, and increase the trade of all the world to the universal benefit of mankind. He was intoxicated, fascinated and enthralled with the idea and especially by his own, inventive proposal to drive the boat not by oars or paddles, but by something vastly better.

Chapter 21

I got myself out of Captain Sally's cabin at the double. Everything she said rang false as a cracked pot, but she'd said it with such confidence that just possibly, just maybe, there might be appearances in court for all hands. In fact, even then I thought that unlikely, but if matters did come to law then far better Poxy Percy should stand in the dock, rather than young Jacob Fletcher just newly promoted. Percy was the officer in command, after all.

I took Captain Sally with me of course, who first insisted in gathering up her ship's papers and stuffed them in an oilskin bag, and I took Mr Blackbeard Longridge, too. I certainly wasn't leaving those two out of my sight, and I made them go first because I wanted Blackbeard where I could see him: a wise precaution because he did indeed try to get behind me as we went through the cabin door. So I gave him a hefty push to send him first, and he turned and snarled at me, and the pair of us levelled eyes, measuring each other up as men do before they smash one another. I held back only for fear of a Court Martial, with myself arraigned by Poxy Percy who might consider the battering of prisoners to be as wicked as the grinding of Lieutenant Chancellor's balls. At least I hoped it was only fear of Court Martial that held me back, because Longridge laughed.

'Not got the bottom for it, sonny?' says he, ''Cos I've eaten things like you and chewed on the gristle.' In reply I stuck a sixteen-bore pistol in his belly.

'Get up on deck!' says I. But he just sneered and so did Captain Sally.

'Got suddenly brave, have you sonny?' says he, 'With a barking iron in your fist?'

'Leave him alone, Mr Longridge,' says she, 'He's too small for you.'

'Aye-aye, Cap'n,' says he, and gave another leer and went out.

It made my hands shake, which was something new, and I didn't know whether it was the closeness to pistoling Longridge in cold blood, or was I actually frightened of the bugger? I even wondered if I should have pulled the trigger when I had the chance, because while Poxy Percy was resolved to see me hanged if I used my fists again, he might have accepted a pistol shot as just retribution against a violent smuggler, which is bizarre but probably true. I didn't know what to think: I was confused and I was troubled, and all this was swirling in my head because I'd finally met a man as big and fierce as myself. Finally I stuck the pistol in my belt, shook my head, and followed Captain Sally and Longridge up on deck.

There was much to do, with boats passing to and fro, since the Service has its ways in dealing with well-manned prizes, and even Poxy Percy knew the drill: which is to say Poxy Percy as advised by Mr O'Flaherty. So *Molly Monckton's* crew were sent below, with our marines at the hatchways ready to shoot any who tried to come on deck. Meanwhile Captain Sally and her officers were made prisoners and taken across to *Lizard*: that's herself, Longridge and his five bruisers, together with their carpenter and gunner. In return, as many of our hands as could be spared came aboard *Molly Monckton* well-armed, to help keep her people under hatches, and to work her back to Plymouth, which was the nearest Naval Dockyard. In addition *Lizard* kept close company, ready to dismast *Molly Monckton* with chain shot if need be.

That's the way to do it, my jolly boys, and it works, except that it left *Lizard* under-manned, which seemed acceptable at first, but turned out bad in the end.

Meanwhile the sea got up, and the wind turned foul for a run back to England, and it took us five days to cover the distance we'd flown in swift hours during the chase. Also, with the heavy seas and the failing light, all boat work had to cease and I was unable to go back aboard *Lizard*. I was left in *Molly Monckton* along with Mr O'Flaherty to whom Poxy Percy had given command of our prize: a calculated insult twice over to myself incidentally, because such a privilege should have gone to me as First Lieutenant, while a ship's sailing master supposedly never left her, being responsible for all matters of navigation aboard of her. But marooned I was, and stayed marooned for two days because that night, even with lights showing, we damn near lost *Lizard* and found her only as a dot on the horizon when the sun came up, and would never have caught her at all if she hadn't been looking out for us in return.

We went on like that over the next two days of bad weather, sighting more and more other vessels on the way since we were in well-travelled sea lanes, and even – by the most fortunate chance – encountering the lugger *Cornwallis* left behind and still patiently looking for us, and which took station astern of us, with much waving and cheering on all sides. We never met *Alacrity*, but the sea is mighty and ships are small and that's all there is to it. She came home to harbour eventually but I never saw her again.

Eventually, on July 6th the seas eased, our little squadron hove to, and *Lizard* hoisted out a boat to take me aboard. It was a relief since I'd had no clutter of my own for days, was unshaven, unkempt and as glad to be home as any sailor is when he comes back aboard. But as the tars heaved the boat dripping out of the water I found Mr Douglas, our boatswain, with the two mids, Copeland and Barclay, waiting by the main chains as I came over the rail.

I raised my hat to salute Poxy Percy at the binnacle, and Mr Douglas sidled up and muttered out of the side of his mouth, while the two mids nodded furiously in support. I frowned at that, but I said nothing because I could see the hands looking fixedly at me, from their duties. They stood among the two rows of guns, and the lines and gear and rigging, and all the complexity that is a ship of war at sea. They stood and they stopped what they were doing and looked at me as if expecting something.

'Watch your back, Mr Fletcher,' says Douglas, 'Things is gone bad. Bad and mad, sir.'

'Bad and mad, sir,' says Copeland, muttering like Douglas.

'Yes, sir,' says Barclay.

Well that was a facer and no mistake. But there was worse. I was astonished to see Blackbeard Longridge and his mates, actually on deck and among *Lizard*'s people, acting as if they were part of the crew. And having spotting him, I noticed that all hands were constantly looking from him to me and back again, and whispering to one another. Longridge laughed at this and took a step forward and caught my eye, and slowly raised a finger to his brow in salute. But the salute was so slow and the look on his face so offensive, that the salute was both insult and challenge. My temper boiled and he nearly got it right then and there. But Douglas stopped me.

'Back your topsail, beggin' your pardon, sir,' says he, 'Things is changed sir,' and he nodded at Poxy Percy. I followed his gaze and I saw something I'd missed the first time. Percy had his little circus around him: Dr Sir Richard, Mr Myers, Lieutenant Chancellor – who'd not gone aboard *Molly Monckton* with his men - plus servants and Miss Maitland as ever. Chancellor was a midget, but Sir Richard, Myers and Miss Maitland were tall, and someone stood out from behind them: Captain Sally Coombes herself, who instantly tipped her hat and smiled at me in the greatest self-satisfaction that could be imagined.

'What's this?' says I to Douglas and the mids. 'Why isn't she in irons? Her

148

and the rest of them?' But Percy himself was advancing towards me, and he explained everything, in his own stupid way.

'Mr Fletcher,' says he, 'I rejoice that you found courage at last, to risk the crossing.' He looked over his shoulder, and his minions smiled in adoration.

'Oh, sir!' said their faces, 'Such wit!' Percy laughed in reflection, then turned to me and shook his head and put on his infuriating expression of more-in-sorrow-than-in-anger. 'Fletcher, Fletcher,' says he, 'I fear you are gone wrong again,' he pointed to Captain Sally, 'Captain Coombes has explained everything. She has documentation clearly establishing her legal right to carry machinery to the Americas.' He turned and beckoned Dr Sir Richard, Myers and Chancellor. 'To me, gentlemen,' says he, and they trotted forward like the good little boys that they were. 'Bear me out, gentlemen,' says he, 'Hasn't Captain Coombes proved her right to go about her honest business?'

'Oh yes, indeed sir,' says Chancellor, the stupidest of the three.

'It appears so, sir,' says Myers, more carefully.

'Hmmmm,' says Dr Sir Richard.

On impulse I looked beyond them to Miss Maitland, who slightly shook her head, while Captain Sally saw the gesture and laughed. It was a lot to comprehend and I couldn't follow it all, so I fixed on the part concerning me.

'You said I was wrong, sir?' says I. 'In what way was that, sir?'

'Why, Mr Fletcher,' says he, as if instructing the simple-minded, 'By firing into an innocent British merchantman, even though I warned you not to.'

'Indeed, sir!' says Sir Richard, Chancellor and Myers, now united in voice.

'But we knew that ship was a smuggler,' says I, 'You yourself, Captain, acted on orders brought out from Polcolm.' Percy raised a hand, and briefly closed eyes in exasperation.

'I acted on orders now proven false,' says he. 'I acted properly in challenging the brig *Molly Monckton* and in pursuing her.' He looked at me with his nasty-little, twisted face and frowned, 'In all this I am free of blame,' says he, 'but it was you Mr Fletcher that caused shot to be fired into Captain Coombes' ship, and you who will face any consequences,' then he sniffed, frowned, and stood back and looked at the dishevelled state of me. 'Meanwhile, Mr Fletcher, you have not the appearance of a gentleman. You will go below and not come on deck again until you are properly cleaned and dressed.'

And it got worse. Percy constantly repeated his concocted, truth-twisting tale, to get him out of legal blame – which clearly he feared as a real threat. The only trouble was, that I had indeed given the order to fire, and done it over his head, and in the meanwhile a more immediate threat bore down in the person of Blackbeard Longridge

The two mids explained a lot more to me that day, during the first dog watch, when the sea was calm and *Lizard* under easy sail, with *Molly Monckton* astern of us, and *Cornwallis* astern of her. They picked a moment when Percy and his minions were below, and nobody was about.

'It's Mr Percival Clive, sir,' says Copeland, 'He's taken to Captain Coombes real strong, sir.'

'What?' says I, 'Her? Compared with Miss Maitland?'

'No, sir,' says Copeland, 'Not like that, sir.'

'Then what?'

'He believes it, sir,' says Barclay, 'All of it, sir. About carrying machines to America.'

'Oh, that,' says I.

'Yes, sir,' says Copeland, 'And he wants Mr Longridge and his mates for his boat's crew.'

'WHAT?' says I, 'His boat's crew? That parcel of bloody pirates?'

'Yes, sir!' says Barclay. 'They've all declared for the Sea Service, sir. They say they want to better themselves and become King's men.'

'God spare us,' says I, 'And does Poxy Percy actually believe that?' Which incidentally really was mutiny on my part, in calling our captain by such a name before the ship's people. But the mids just grinned.

'He does, sir,' says Copeland, and frowned. 'And then there's Mr Longridge, sir, he's been going about saying that you don't dare face him, sir,' The two lads looked at me with big eyes, and I was amazed to see that the little tinkers actually regarded me as a hero. I wasn't just amazed but astounded: me that would turn bloody cartwheels to get out of the Service if only I could.

'Not that we believe him, sir,' says Copeland.

'Not us, sir,' says Barclay, and paused, 'But the hands are all wondering, sir. And they're laying wagers as to who shall win, when the moment comes.'

Which it nearly did several times that first day back aboard, whenever I passed Longridge, who repeated the insolent salute, and looked round to make sure that all hands had seen the gesture, and all hands duly took note. He did that, and then stood aside to let me pass but managed to stand close so that I brushed by him and even smelt him. I remember the sweat and stink of him even now.

I learned even more that evening when Percy gave a dinner in his cabin, inviting everyone of importance but myself. Even Lieutenant Porthgain, commander of *Cornwallis*, was summoned, and Captain Sally Coombes, too.

At least Longridge didn't sit down to dine. Percy's in-bred snobbery saw to that. But when the dinner was still under way, with the usual songs and cheering round the table and many bottles emptied, I was up on deck idling for a while with no duties, and suddenly found Miss Maitland beside me. It was dark, the ship was heeling to a favourable wind at last, and the hands had little to do. Mr Midshipman Barclay, officer of the watch, raised a hand in salute to the lady, then he and everyone else acted as if she weren't there. It was better that way with a creature not even supposed to be aboard ship.

'Come with me,' says she.

'What? Now?' says I, mistaking her purpose, for there'd been nothing between us since we came aboard. How could there be?

'Just come with me,' says she, 'Is there any private place aboard this ship?' So it was the cable tier again, though this time for quite another purpose. We couldn't help but be noticed as we made our way there, though the Lizards just gave salute, glanced at Miss Maitland and assumed Mr Fletcher was a lucky bastard. We didn't meet any of Captain Sally's men though, and I was grateful for that.

Once we were alone with the great, coiled ropes, she produced the oilskin bag that Sally Coombes had brought with her out of *Mary Monckton*.

'I took this from Percy's cabin,' says she, 'That damn woman's a liar but he's believed it all, and now he'll be drinking himself unconscious as ever he does when I'm not there to stop him.'

'Why aren't you there?' says I.

'I have the headache,' says she, 'Can't you see?' I smiled, 'Here,' says she, 'take it. We mustn't stay long.' So I took the bag, went close to a lantern, and pulled out the contents. It was everything Captain Sally had said: bills of lading, letters from Carter, Cooper and Brown of Long Island, permits and bills of every kind. 'I thought you should see all this,' says she.

'Thank you, ma'am,' says I and took a good look. I looked at every sheet and held them up to the light. It was all very nice, and very proper, and very neat… and all entirely fake. But here I take no stance as a cunning detective agent. It's just that I am a man of business, with a deep love of the paperwork that goes with business. Remember that I served my time as a counting house apprentice in Polmouth, and I'd run my own businesses in London and in Jamaica since then. So I'd grown used to the manner of business correspondence, and the craft of record keeping. Most folk – now as then – seeing only the brute size of me, would never dream of the inky clerk that lives within my soul. But he's in there, my jolly boys, just you believe your Uncle Jacob.

[For once Fletcher is profoundly truthful. He had the most investigative eye for detail in written records such that every accountant that acted for him, stood in fear of Fletcher's judgement of their reports. S.P.]

'It's deceit, ma'am,' says I, 'It's all made up and invented, and I truly doubt that any such enterprise exists as Carter, Cooper and Brown of Long Island.

'Oh?' says she, 'How can you know that?'

'Look,' says I, holding up some sheets to the light, 'It's all in the same hand.' She frowned.

'Are not some in different handwriting?'

'That's not what I mean,' says I, 'Look at the style of the writing: the hand. It's common for a business to have its own hand: its particular way of forming the letters. See how every letter d has a curl at the top, not a slope? It's all like that. Every single document is written in the same hand, though someone has made the attempt to disguise his writing, within that hand.'

'I'm not sure what you mean,' says she.

'Never mind,' says I, 'Trust me.' She nodded, and I carried on. 'And look at the paper: it all has the same watermark.' I held some more sheets to the lantern to show her.

'Oh, yes,' says she.

'You see?' says I, 'There should be several kinds and quality of paper, bought by all these supposed clerks, from their local stationers,' she nodded, 'Look,' says I, 'Even this pretend-American document has the same watermark, and that just can't be right.'

'Ah!' says she, much impressed.

'Someone has cut the sheets to different sizes,' says I, 'to make them seem different, but it's all the same paper!' I looked at her lovely face shining with admiration for my cleverness, and by George it's a shame we weren't somewhere more congenial than the cable tier.

'Mr Fletcher,' says she and moved closer.

'Yes?' says I.

'Do you realise what this means?'

'It means that Captain Sally is a smuggler.'

'Yes, but more than that.'

'What then?'

'Well,' says she, 'If you can see at a glance that these papers are false,' I nodded, 'If you can see, then so would lawyers in a courtroom.' I nodded again. 'Which means,' says she, 'That these papers aren't meant for a courtroom. They're just a first line of defence to bamboozle those who don't know documents. It worked with Percy because he's an idiot, and it would work with those old sea captains aboard *Cornwallis*, *Alacrity* and *Alderney*. From what I've seen of them, I doubt they can read and write properly, let alone judge watermarks or the preferred hand of a counting house, and I'd guess they are typical of the sort of officer that might catch a smuggler if ever one were to be caught.'

'Yes,' says I, thinking of poor old Benedict, the log, lead and latitude man, 'you're right.'

'So that means,' says she, 'That the real defence of smugglers, when they get caught, is not these papers but something else: either bribery and corruption ashore, or something worse afloat.'

'Meaning?' says I, though I'd already guessed it from the swagger of Longridge and his men.

'Meaning,' says she, 'that the papers serve merely to distract the Revenue men ...,'

'Or the navy!' says I.

'Causing them to release the smugglers, or to be unready with their arms ...,'

'While the smugglers pick up their own ...,'

'And settle the matter by violence,' says she.

And that was Miss Sophia Maitland for you. Mr clever-cunning Rowland had told me she was intelligent and that I should rely on her, and he was damn well right and I damn well did. But first I had to face Mr Blackbeard Longridge, because he came looking for me.

Chapter 22

(Letter dated Thursday July 7th, from Mr William Pitt, 10 Downing Street, London, to Mr Philip Charles Rowland for whom no address was given.)

My Dear Rowland,

The game's afoot! The documents and testimonies placed into my hand by yourself have proved eminently eloquent, such that doubts within my cabinet are overcome, the malicious machinations of the Whig opposition are supressed, and the entire cooperation of their Lordships of the Admiralty and His Grace the Duke of York are now both of them assured.

Even now chosen men of the 27th Light Dragoons, together with the light companies of our guards and other regiments are ordered to Portsmouth in company with those musterings of the Royal Engineers which you named as our best choice, while Col. Maitland's Troop of Horse Artillery is to follow. Simultaneously Their Lordships have provided a strong squadron of frigates and transports for the venture itself, and are in process of rehearsing off Dungeness, a landing on the French coast.

When the time is close, a powerful and further squadron, including escorting frigates, will command the local waters off the landing site in France, so as entirely to obviate any possibility of the Naval Forces of our enemy, from interfering.

In all this, my dear Rowland, I place my trust in yourself and conjure of you in the words of our enemy Bonaparte: that you should be lucky! Be lucky, my friend, because if you should fall, then the Kingdom may fall and even if it does not, then you and I certainly shall, following the extremity of persuasion upon which we have extended ourselves, thereby becoming prey to our political opponents, should this bold enterprise fail.

In that, and for the further summoning of good luck, it is my strongest personal wish that you should yourself embark with the landing force, and take personal command of those special matters concerning treason (seebelow) which you have identified. A written commission, signed for Their Lordships and for the Duke of York, follows this letter and grants you the authority to take command at your discretion.

And now I kill two birds with one stone. Thus I respect your advocacy in behalf of Lieutenant Jacob Fletcher and stress the vital importance of keeping locomotive engines out of the hands of the French. You therefore have my assurance that Fletcher shall be promoted high and swift, thereby encouraging him to remain in the King's Service.

Finally, having given you the authority to do so (see above) I leave to your judgement the manner of restraining permanently those British subjects in France who are delivering up steam engines to our enemies. I charge you to prevent their despicable treason, while trusting that you will behave throughout as a Christian, English gentleman should.

None the less, note that all such actions are entirely your responsibility and that of Fletcher.

Yours sincerely,
W. Pitt.

Chapter 23

Fast as I could, I got Miss Maitland back to the cabin that Poxy Percy had given her for decency's sake, to pretend she wasn't nightly tucked up with him, even though all hands knew that she was. The noisy dinner was still going on nearby, as I put her into the little thin-walled cabin.

'Take care,' says she, in the dim light, and actually put her arms around my neck and kissed me. It was extraordinarily pleasant because she did it because she liked me. She never smiled, though. That was her, I suppose.

I went straight back up on deck, which was a mistake because I should have gone to my own cabin for my pistols and sword, but I wanted to warn the mids and Boatswain Douglas, and I nearly reached the ship's wheel, aft of the mainmast before anyone stopped me. *Lizard* was bounding along, the stern lights of *Molly Monckton* were ahead of us, and a night sky above with the moon behind clouds and few stars. The ship was dark, but alive with motion, lines taught, sails drawing, bow plunging and a fine spray coming aboard. My eyes were just getting used to the dark, and the few figures on deck were shadows, as were the tight-lashed guns, hatchways, capstan and all the other impedimenta that would trip a landman helpless.

'Mr Fletcher, sir?' says a voice, and a huge shadow lumbered forward. It was Longridge. I heard him and smelt him. He always stank of sweat. 'A word, Mr Fletcher, sir,' says he, 'Very hot and important, like. Cap'n Sal's orders, Mr Fletcher, sir.' And a dark hand went up to a dark brow. That was odd. He was polite. He was saluting properly.

'What's this?' says I, 'Explain yourself.'

'Not here, sir,' says Longridge, 'Not where the common hands might hear,' and a dark arm pointed towards the taffrail at the stern. I looked around, saw Mr Copeland and Mr Barclay by the binnacle, with the quartermasters at the wheel, and Boatswain Douglas with them, all of whom saluted, and everything seemed proper and comforting. So I shrugged.

'Lead the way,' says I, still wary but wondering what Captain Sally might have to say. Also, and I freely admit it, I was demonstrating to myself that I had no fear of Longridge, and was not afraid of being in his close company: a stupid vanity which I cannot too strongly recommend you youngsters against, because if you fancy yourself to be in danger then you probably are. So off he went to the very stern of the bounding vessel, braced on the deck as only seamen can, and the figures at the binnacle hardly seen and the two of us as nearly alone as two men can be aboard of a vessel the size of *Lizard*.

Then he turned to face me, and the moon popped out and shone on his face: all big and fat and bearded, and the two of us eyed one another up just one more time, and my heart hammered and thundered till my head shook.

'So what do you want, mister?' says I.

'Cap'n Sal's orders,' says he, "Cos you've got to be the first,' and out came a pistol, clutched in his fat, hairy hand. A total surprise. I was fairly taken aback. I was cursing myself for being unarmed. But the big fat hand was shaking! His eyes were blinking fast. He was fumbling to cock the lock with his left hand, which was hard since his hands were enormous, and the pistol a small one, and all this seen by me in seconds.

'So,' says I, 'Who's the rollicking boy now, hiding behind a pistol?'

'Sod you!' says he and stretched out his arm with the pistol ready to fire.

'So now it's you that hasn't got the bottom for it,' says I, 'I thought you chewed on the gristle of men like me?'

'Sod you!' says he, and the arm with the pistol wavered and shook, and damn the perversity of the human mind, because in that moment I was actually disappointed. Here was myself having had the horrors of Blackbeard Longridge since ever I'd first seen him, and wondering if I'd finally met a better man than me, and searching myself for fright like a beggar after a lost sixpence. All that and now - I read it in his eyes - he was more afraid of me than I was of him! He'd kept it well hid, but when it came to the moment, he was afraid ... or was he? Was I reading too much? My own heart was bounding so perhaps his was too, and shaking his hand? I didn't know and my words came out without thinking.

'What's the matter Longridge,' says I, 'Can't you do it man-to-man?' and I beckoned him forward, 'Come and try it, you swab, and see what you get.'

'Orders is to kill you,' says he, 'Cap'n Sal's orders.'

'Bollocks,' says I, 'You're afraid. You're a coward!' and I took up a pugilist's stance, right forward, close to him, stood sideways on with fists raised and legs

157

braced.. He saw that and he wavered, because perhaps he wasn't so frightened after all and he did want to fight. So he lowered the pistol. 'Come on then,' says I, 'If you've the heart for it,' and he frowned and fought a battle inside of himself. There was a man's pride within him that wanted to smash me with his fists alone. But he was under Captain Sally's orders and on top of that, he was wondering if he could actually do the job with fists alone.

At first pride won, and down went the arm with the pistol. Then up it came again as fear and duty won. Then down, then up, then down, such that I never learned which parts of Longridge would have won the argument, because he dithered too long and instinct took hold of me, and the next time the pistol went down … I hit him with every atom of weight in my body. My fist landed square on his left, lower jaw, and with the blow coming too fast for him to prepare, his head went back and the snap of his neck shuddered all the way up my arm to the very shoulder. Then over he went, flat on the deck, and lay there with arms spread out and mouth wide open.

I stood and looked down at him. He didn't move: not a twitch nor a shudder, and huge emotions surged in my head. First came the deep and primeval satisfaction of besting the swine. Got you, you bastard! How d'you like that? And I danced on the balls of my feet in a pleasure as physical as that of having a beautiful women. But then came awful doubt, because Poxy Percy, the perverse and useless creature that he was, and backed by political power, would see me hung at the yard-arm for this. I knew it, I knew it, I knew it. He hated me and there'd be no justice and I'd be hanged.

Perhaps I was wrong? Perhaps my thoughts were clouded? But in that moment, that's what I believed. So I fell to my knees and put my ear to Longridge's face in the hope that he wasn't quite dead. I listened hard. He wasn't breathing. He was warm and stinking but he was dead. I looked around. It was dark and the ship was working noisily. Perhaps nobody had seen, or heard?

Instinct drove me again. I hauled Longridge to the lee side – that's the bottom of the down-sloped side to you landmen – and tried to heave him out through a carronade port. But a dead body is a devilish awkward thing to move, especially one so big as Longridge's. So I made the near-impossible effort to lift him up, and heave him over the rail, just aft of the hammock nettings. But that didn't work, either. He was too heavy, even for me. Then others were at my side, come from nowhere in the dark.

'At my command!' Says Mr O'Flaherty, 'One, two, three: heave.'

'Aye-aye!' says Mr Douglas.

'One, two, three: heave!' says O'Flaherty, and with three of us working like jolly tars together, then over the side went Longridge and the pistol fast in his fat fingers, and a bloody damned accursed good riddance to him, too.

'Back to your stations, lads,' says O'Flaherty.

'Aye-aye!' says Douglas. So we stood by the wheel, and the two mids gaping awestruck at me, and the quartermasters too, and even Mr Douglas. Then O'Flaherty spoke.

'Nobody saw nothing,' says he. 'D'you hear that, all of yous?'

'Aye-aye!' says the mids, the quartermasters and all hands in earshot.

'Mr Fletcher,' says O'Flaherty, 'I have to go back to the Captain's table,' he looked at the younger mid. 'Mr Barclay, here, ran down like a good lad and summoned me when you went off with Longridge. He told the Cap'n there was a blow coming on …'

'Which there was, sir!' says Barclay and everyone laughed, though it was a false laugh releasing wild emotions.

'No!' says O'Flaherty, 'This ain't funny. Nobody saw nothing and nobody says nothing. Remember that before all else, and may sweet Jesus save the bugger that blabs!'

'Aye-aye!' says all hands. Then O'Flaherty looked at me. He nodded quietly.

'You did right, lad,' says he, 'and we're all shipmates together here, and will stand by you come what may.'

'Aye-aye!' says all hands, and it was wonderful to see the way that everyone took my part, and heart-warming, too. But there was a hot and feverish mood on the lot of us because I'd just left a man dead. It left me thick headed. Had I just committed murder? Had I justifiably overcome mutiny? Had I even mistaken what Longridge said? Had he actually meant to kill me, or was he just trying to frighten me? It all sounds strange now, to tell of such doubts, but imagine how you might feel, my jolly boys, if you'd just killed a man with a single punch and felt the limp warmth of him as you threw him into the sea, and this aboard one of King George's ships, under King George's law, and answerable to Lord Howe who didn't like Jacob Fletcher at all.

So I didn't summon all hands and arrest Captain Sally and her people because I was confused, and worried that Poxy Percy and his minions would damn anything I attempted, and call me a liar, and order the crew to disobey my orders, and probably put me in irons rather than the smugglers. Who knows? Later the dinner ended, O'Flaherty and Porthgain were rowed back to their commands, and eventually I went down to my cabin and fell asleep in my hammock just before I fell over with tiredness.

159

But I was turned out at two bells of the morning watch, just after dawn, when all hands were summoned on deck and the brig-sloop *Lizard* turned itself inside out searching for Longridge, and Captain Sally gave me such glances as told me that she knew exactly where he'd gone. But *Lizard's* people delivered their best act of diligent searching, and Poxy Percy consoled Captain Sally when no Mr Longridge was to be found aboard ship, and even hailing *Cornwallis* and *Alderney* had failed to discover him, in the unlikely event that he'd taken it into his head to swim across to one of them in the night.

'He was a most splendid man, ma'am,' says Percy to Captain Sally, 'and a grave loss to the service, for I'd intended he should be the coxwain of my own barge.' And so she nodded and so they chatted like the good friends they'd now become, and Dr Sir Richard and Lieutenant Chancellor, and Mr Myers joining in.

'He must have been lost overside,' said Sir Richard, 'for such things happen at sea.'

'Indeed,' says Myers.

'Quite,' says Chancellor.

Blockheads the lot of them. How did they know what happens at sea? They were just land lubbers following Percy's lead. They were treating Captain Sally as if she were the parson's wife who'd lost a beloved child. But Sophia Maitland stood off to one side, looked at me and raised eyebrows in disgust.

Later at noon observation, I was instructing the mids in using their quadrants - or trying to with my mind elsewhere - and Captain Sally came to find me. I left the mids and she and I spoke by the foremast, with the deck-watch looking on and fair winds blowing *Lizard* home, and England only just under the horizon.

'Mr Fletcher,' says she.

'I'm him,' says I, because I wasn't going to call her ma'am or Captain.

'So!' says she, and blew away any doubts regarding my actions last night. 'I sent him to kill you, and you killed him,' She tipped her hat. 'You're some bonny lad, Mr Fletcher, and your mother'd be proud if you had one.' As she spoke I couldn't help looking at Poxy Percy. 'Don't worry,' says she, 'he knows nothing. Your men kept quiet but one of mine told me.' She touched her hat again, in salute. 'Looks you struck fear in Longridge,' says she, 'I wanted no noise, and he said he'd do it unarmed. But it seems he weren't sure,' she shook her head, 'I didn't know about the pistol.'

'What do you want?' says I, 'Come to the point.'

'The point is, Mr Fletcher of Polmouth in Cornwall, who once was apprenticed in a counting house…,'

160

'Yes, yes, yes,' says I, becoming impatient.

'You want to be out of the Service, don't you?' I frowned.

'How would you know that?'

'You talk too much,' says she, 'and people listen.' I said nothing. 'So,' says she, 'I've an offer for you.' Again, I said nothing. 'Don't you want to know what it is?' I shrugged. 'Ah!' says she, 'How'd you like to come away from this ship, free of the Navy, with a pile of gold, and all the world open in front of you? 'Cos I ain't bound for America this voyage, but I might be the next, and I'd be pleased to take you.'

'What gold?' says I, wondering at my own motives.

'A-hah!' says she, 'You don't think, do you Mr Fletcher, that I embark upon such ventures as I do, except for rich payment?' she looked at me closely, 'In fact, Mr Fletcher, being the man you are: why! There might be a future for you in my very trade, which I really do assure you is most highly profitable.'

'And would you do all this, for me, out of kindness?' says I.

'No, Mr Fletcher,' says she, 'I'd do it for the price of your looking the other way when I leave this ship, or better still of coming with me!' and she leaned close and lowered her voice. 'I've heard a lot about you, and I like what I've heard. Look how you dismissed my papers as false, which they were. And I've seen your seamanship and you've proved you can fight. But more than that I value your abilities as a man of business.' She stood back. 'Come and see me when you've thought it over, Mr Fletcher, but don't leave it too long.'

[Note this proof of Fletcher's growing notoriety, since Captain Sally Combes could not have possibly have learned of his proficiency in business during her brief time with him aboard ship, but only from earlier gossip around his reputation. S.P.]

Well, my jolly boys, all my life folk have praised me as a seaman, a gunner and a demon in a fight, none of which makes my heart sing. But here was Cap'n Sal wanting me for the very thing I was born for. She admired me as a man of business, and was pointing the way to America, which of all lands beside England I most greatly love, and the thought filled up my mind with wonder. It filled it so much that I did the very thing she'd warned me against. I left it too late. I did my duties aboard ship that day, in half a mind or less, because most of my mind was already in Boston, or New York.

And so to the consequences.

Of all *Lizard's* people, there were only thirty hands aboard: nine seaman of the larboard watch, ten of the starboard watch, and the rest idlers: followers of the various trades that had no deck duties: carpenters, sailmakers and the like. With *Molly Moncton* being so full of men, we'd sent most of our people aboard of her to make sure the smugglers didn't find ways to get up on deck and take back the ship in the night. So we'd sent them and all the marines too who, of course, were the only men in the ship armed with firelocks all the time.

That left Captain Sally with seven men: all now on the ship's books, with three supposedly serving in the starboard watch, and four among the larboard, and her own good time to plan what she did next, and nobody to interfere, and myself most guilty of all because I'd been warned something was coming and did nothing about it.

So, eight bells sounded the turn of the first watch, which is midnight shore time. The larboard watch were in their hammocks as were the idlers, and the starboard watch on deck: just ten loyal men awake and alert. I was likewise in my hammock, and was roughly woken by little Mr Chancellor, who was holding a lantern, clad only in a shirt. Cabins are tiny on brig-sloop. Mine was just seven feet long by four wide. I rolled out half asleep, hauled on boots and coat by instinct, with yelling and commotion all round, and Mr midshipman Barclay's voice crying out, and still more yelling, then someone hit me on the head fit to crack my skull and I stumbled and fell. I was down for a while. I don't know how long. Then I got up and reached for the sword hanging on my cabin wall.

'Avast!' says a voice, 'Belay that or you're dead!' The light was bad, there were Chancellor's big round eyes, and behind him one of Captain Sally's men, with a belaying pin and a large knife, and another man behind with a pair of pistols. I was dazed and staggering and a voice was bellowing at me.

'Get on, you fucking bastard! Go where you're fucking bid!' and there was more yelling from up on deck, and Mr Barclay's voice again, then one big voice and then quiet.

'Oh God, oh God, oh God!' says Chancellor, clutching at me. 'The Captain is took and we're all done for.'

'Shut fucking up!' says the man with the pistols. 'Get on, the pair of you! First the little bugger then you, Mr fucking Fletcher, and I'm right astern of you to blow your fucking liver through your fucking backbone, if you won't fucking go!' and with prodding and threatening, and Chancellor gibbering in front of me, I was forced into the stern cabin and there was Captain Sally, with a bright forest of candles burning, and everyone else trussed up nice and tight. I noticed Sophia Maitland first, tied hard into a chair, with ropes cutting into her skin. That looked ugly, but I thought how much worse it could have been for a woman in the hands of pirates, or outlaws or whatever these men were, and at least she'd been spared that. In my innocence, that's what I thought.

Dr Sir Richard, Mr Myers, and of course Poxy Percy himself were tied into chairs just the same, and not only tied but gagged as well to keep them silent. They were all sat at table, as if for dinner, with Captain Sally at the head of the table, and they stared and stared and stared: eyes turning from me to Captain Sally and back again.

'Fletcher,' says she, 'Come in, sit down, and make no noise or you're dead.' I hesitated, and got another such clout round the head, that I thought I'd been shot.

'Sit fucking down, you fucking sod!' says someone, and limited as he was in vocabulary, he was very persuasive. So I sat down.

'Here's his box of pops,' says one of the men behind me, and put my shiny new case of pistols on the table in front of Captain Sally, who opened it with delight, and loaded swift and neat while talking to me all the time.

'Your arms locker was empty,' says she, 'all gone away to *Molly Monckton*. But gentlemen has their own barkers, unlike the common hands,' She glanced at Percy, Dr Sir Richard, and Myers, 'So we took their 'uns when we nabbed 'em, and your bold marine lieutenant's too,' she grinned, 'All done nice and quiet with them full of wine, and then we came for yourself. We got your midshipmen too, and their nice pistols courtesy of their Mammas and pappas.' She smiled, 'they woke up and fought back,' says she, 'bright little sparks the pair of 'em, and a credit to the service. But it's all neat and tidy, up on deck now and no shooting to bother the squadron.' She finished her loading and pointed my pistols at me. 'We had to stick some of your crew, in the doing of it, but you'll never miss them, not nohow.'

She stared hard at me and rocked back in her chair.

'So here's the way of it, Mr Fletcher. We'll soon be in sight of England, when you will signal those vessels in company that we've a leak below, as must be pumped out while we heaves to, and takes the way off her, and themselves to go ahead, and us to follow. And then you'll sail where I tell you, Mr Fletcher, to a nice quiet cove where you'll lower a boat for me and my men. And then ourselves and yourselves shall go our different ways and no harm come to any one of us. D'you hear me, now? For that's what you must do.'

I blinked. My head was still aching from the battering it had taken.

'And what if I won't?' says I, and she just laughed. She nodded at one of her men: the one with the knife.

'If you won't, Mr Fletcher,' says she, 'Then there's going to be blood all over this table as we start cutting throats,' she looked at Sophia Maitland, 'starting with her, 'cos she's neither use nor ornament to me, but I hear that she is to you.'

Well, my jolly boys, she'd have got what she wanted with that alone, but Captain Sally, wasn't yet done. She leered at me in a way that wasn't nice to see. 'Of course, Mr Fletcher, you might think my lads wouldn't kill a woman, what with them being jolly tars and her so fine a lady,' she cocked her head on one side. 'And so Mr Fletcher, we'll put away the knife for the moment,' she looked up and her man instantly shoved the knife back in its sheath. 'There,' says Captain Sally, 'Now ain't that nice?' She paused, and I knew that worse was to come, 'But if you don't behave yourself, Mr Fletcher, then I'll let my lads take Miss Maitland into your captain's sleeping cabin where there's a cosy bed, and they can have her any way they chose, in any order they chose, and that's all seven of them. So how d'you like that, Mr Jacob Fletcher of Polmouth in Cornwall, who I made a good offer to, which you refused?'

Chapter 24

'Treason is a mighty evil.'
(From a letter of Wednesday 27th July 1796 – sealed by never delivered -
from Donald James McCloud to his Father Mr Hamish McCloud, 15 Bream
Terrace, near Douglas Square, Edinburgh.)

*

Donald McCloud was divided within his own mind: divided and worse because
so many ideals were in conflict. The Enlightenment said one thing, while celi-
bate puritanism said another, and the engineer within in him fought against
the patriot. He looked to his brother Jamie, he looked to Colonel Sauvage, he
looked round the Fragnal workshop at the fourteen leather-aproned craftsmen
who'd once been his followers but had taken Jamie's side. Perhaps most of all he
looked at the leather-aproned Frenchman, standing among and beside Jamie's
people, and indistinguishable from them, such that a newcomer, entering the
workshop - with its steadily-turning power shafts and drive belts - would never
know who was a Frenchman and who was not.

'Look, Donald,' said Jamie McCloud, 'Look at what we've achieved. But now
we need your help.' The McCloud brothers stared at one another in silence. Each
was on the limit of his tolerance and patience, because the quarrel between them
was not forgotten but merely set aside. Thus each was now on his best behaviour, with fierce emotions held back behind polite faces. So Donald McCloud
turned and looked at what his younger brother had achieved, and the engineer
within him was impressed because on the bench in front of him was a device
of such novelty that there was nothing like it in the whole of Europe. It rested
on steel supports, and was connected to a canvas drive-belt such that one push
of a lever would set it in motion. It was a steel shaft ten feet long, at the end of

165

which was something that looked like a bronze daisy flower two feet in diameter, with just four petals, and the petals smoothly twisted.

'It's a water-screw, isn't it?' said Donald McCloud.

'Yes!' said Jamie.

'Yes!' said everyone else, or 'Oui!' according to inclination, because everyone was speaking some French these days.

'Of course this isn't new,' said Donald McCloud.

'Oh no,' said Jamie McCloud, 'There were others ahead of us.'

'Bushnell, for one,' said Donald.

'Who?' said Sauvage, 'Who is Bushnell?'

'He's...,' said Donald McCloud.

'He's...' said Jamie McCloud simultaneously.

'After you,' said Jamie.

'Thank you,' said Donald. Sauvage was delighted to see the brothers treating each other with such respect, and there was a united gasp of relief from the onlookers because Jamie and Donald McCloud were charismatic idols to this intense community. But what nobody saw - because it was hidden deep - was that the behaviour of the brothers towards each other, was the behaviour of a man who steps barefoot over a venomous reptile: ever wary of harm, and in hatred of the creature that may bite him.

'David Bushnell is an American engineer,' said Donald, 'who devised a submarine boat to attack the British fleet in New York harbour, during the recent American Revolution.'

'Ah!' said Sauvage, 'I remember. The event was much discussed at the time. Didn't Bushell attempted to place an explosive charge under milord Howe's flagship?'

'He did,' said Donald McCloud. 'The attempt failed but the craft worked well enough.' He turned to the bronze daisy, 'Bushnell's craft was driven by a device like this: a water screw.'

'But his was driven by hand,' said Jamie McCloud, 'It was driven by one man turning a handle, whereas we shall apply the power of steam!'

Now, Sauvage held his breath as Donald and Jamie McCloud looked at one another. Sauvage was profoundly weary of the work needed to keep the English-Scottish working, and ten-times-over weary of the work of keeping the McCloud brothers sweet. It was Sauvage who had interceded, and persuaded Donald McCloud's of the humanitarian mission to save the lives of mariners and to increase the trade of the world by steam navigation. The ideas were all Jamie McCloud's but Donald would not listen to Jamie, and only reluctantly

166

to Sauvage. Fortunately, Donald McCloud was nodding, and Sauvage truly believed that he had healed the division between the brothers.

'Yes,' said Donald McCloud, 'We shall improve upon Bushnell.' He turned to the assembled mechanics. 'We shall do this together,' he said, and there were smiles from those who understood him. But soon the Frenchmen smiled when their English-Scottish colleagues explained in French. Meanwhile, Donald nodded to Jamie, who threw a lever to engage a drive belt, and the water screw began to turn - smooth, quiet and perfect - in its bearings. 'We shall utilise the water-screw because it is more efficient than the paddle wheels or oars that others have employed,' said Donald McCloud, 'Others like the Marquis de Souffroy,' he nodded to Sauvage, who bowed at this courtesy to French inventiveness.

'Yes,' said Jamie McCloud,' looking at the turning screw, 'but we must first find the best design. This one is just a guess.' He looked at his brother, 'And we need you for that, Donald.' The elder McCloud nodded.

'So,' said Donald McCloud, looking to Sauvage, 'I believe that the plan is, Colonel, that we shall equip boats with steam engines, here at Fragnal,' Sauvage nodded, 'and that those boats shall pass, under steam, down a great canal to the seaport of Lyommeville, where they will be tested for ocean navigation?'

'Indeed!' said Sauvage, hoping that the McCloud would not guess what France intended to do with the steamboats, because it certainly wasn't to save the lives of mariners and increase the trade of the world. But Donald McCloud nodded again.

'Therefore,' said Donald McCloud, 'I will design a test jig so that different shapes of water-screw may be compared for efficiency. We'll do that with small models, then build full-sized when we have the best design.'

'Bless you, Donald,' said Jamie McCloud and stretched out his hand to his brother.

'Bless you, Jamie,' said Donald McCloud, taking the hand, and there was applause from the onlookers: applause and cheers, and in that little moment, and for that little moment, there briefly existed the possibility that Donald and Jamie might be united again: united in the fascination of delivering a shining new creation - an engineering creation - into being upon the face of the Earth.

But sadly and unfortunately, there was something other than applause from the audience. There was lively discussion too, because the Frenchmen – who spoke no English – wanted to know what Donald McCloud had said. So the English-Scottish, who were gathering fluency in French, explained and smiled. They even waved their hands like Frenchmen, all the better to express themselves. After all, they were used to speaking French to their wives.

Donald McCloud saw this and at first he smiled.
But then he saw how very French his compatriots had become.
And the engine of his strange mind slipped a gear.
And a truly appalling understanding fell upon him.

Chapter 25

They kept me in the stern cabin, they locked Sophia Maitland in Percy's sleeping cabin, and he and his chums were put in irons down in the hold. Then, at first light, Captain Sally sent me up on deck with a warning.

'I'll be at your side,' says she, 'and a man ready to shoot your captain and his mates, and another outside missie Maitland's door, to get aboard of her if I says so. D'you hear me?'

'Yes,' says I.

'And the word's spread among your men for their good behaviour, too.' So up we went to a fair, fresh wind and all hands on deck, the two mids both heavily bandaged, and everyone saluting me with dread on their faces. But some of our people weren't there.

'Where's the Boatswain?' says I.

'He's below, Mr Fletcher,' says Barclay. 'They stabbed him, sir. Him and three others. He's dreadful bad sir,' he stared at me. 'The bastards killed three of our men, sir,' says he.

'I shouldn't worry, my lovely lads,' says Captain Sally to the mids. 'You've both been wounded in the King's service. So I shouldn't wonder if they don't make admirals of the pair of you.' She laughed and turned to me, 'Make your signals, mister,' says she. So I did. What else could I do? I gave the order, and up went our signal flags ordering *Cornwallis*, *Alderney* and *Molly Monckton*. In curt Navy code they read the equivalent of:

'Proceed urgently to Plymouth while Flagship under repair.'

All three vessels hoisted the acknowledge, but Mr O'Flaherty in command of *Molly Monckton* backed his canvas, to come alongside in hailing distance, and the two vessels heaved up and down, a biscuit's toss from each other, and *Lizard's* people lining Molly *Monckton's* rail, with cutlass and pistols, and ourselves aboard *Lizard* unarmed and not daring to raise a hand for fear of what might happen to those of us took hostage.

'Ahoy, Mr Fletcher,' says O'Flaherty, 'Can I be of assistance, sir?' Captain Sally was beside me. 'Is there trouble in the ship, sir?' says O'Flaherty, seeing the bandages on Barclay and Copeland, 'Shall I send men aboard?' Captain Sally eased close. She smiled and lifted her hat to O'Flaherty, and whispered to me.

'Watch your mouth, or missie might be spared a galloping and get sliced after all.'

'All's well, Mr O'Flaherty,' says I, stretching my brains to find words to warn O'Flaherty. But I failed. 'There's a leak below,' says I, 'for which we must take the way off her, to give the pumps their chance. Then we'll make all good and follow you to Plymouth.'

'Shall I not send men aboard to help man the pumps?' says O'Flaherty.

'Careful now,' says Captain Sally.

'Not needed, Mr O'Flaherty,' says I.

'Tell him to proceed as ordered,' says Captain Sally, 'Tell him!'

'Proceed to Plymouth as ordered, Mr O'Flaherty.'

'Aye-aye, sir!' And soon he was under way and gone.

'Well done, Mr Fletcher,' says Captain Sally.

'I've got to go to Mr Douglas,' says I, 'the Boatswain.'

'Oh him,' says she, and shrugged. 'He's all done for, but talk to him if you must,' she stared at me with nasty emphasis. 'But tread careful, mister, or I'll kill one of the prisoners just for the fun of it.' So I went below, down on the berthing deck. It was empty of men, but Boatswain Douglas was in his hammock with one of the hands in attendance: Jacky Gearing, our loblolly boy – that's a surgeon's mate to you landmen – who'd done his best for poor Douglas, laid out with the stubble sprouting on his chin. There were the three of us, and one of Captain Sally's men with pistols, keeping guard.

'Mr Fletcher,' says Douglas's lips, with hardly a sound. But then he winked at me and nodded his head at Gearing, who winked in return, and spoke to the guard.

'Oi!' says Gearing, 'Matey? I've got to go for a piss.'

'You ain't going nowhere without me,' says the other.

'Then come along,' says Gearing. The guard nodded.

'Don't you do nothing,' says he, to me and Douglas, 'Neither of you,' and off they went and Douglas beckoned me close.

'I'm all right, Mr Fletcher sir,' says he. 'The sods aimed at my kidney but missed. So I bled a bit, but it ain't mortal 'cos Jacky says so, and he knows.'

'Glad to hear it, Mr Boatswain,' says I, thinking that Jacky Gearing was good for slopping out and stitching up, but his judgement on survival after stabbing was another matter. 'Happy to have you back among us,' says I though he was deadly pale and he'd obviously bled a lot more than a bit.

'Sir!' says he, 'I knows where there's some firelocks.'

'What?' says I.

'Down on the orlop, where the Master at Arms has his tools and gear. There's pieces down there under repair, and powder and ball besides.'

'Are they fit for service?' says I.

'No, sir,' says he, 'but they could be fixed.'

'Good,' says I, 'then I'll get down there.'

'No good, sir,' says he, 'them buggers won't let nobody go anywhere alone, and not everyone can do the fixing.' He clutched at me with a feeble hand. 'But I can do it, sir. You let it be known on deck that I'm done for, and I'll do the rest.' I looked at the state of him and thought I'd be telling no lies to say he was near death.

'Good man,' says I. 'Well done, Mr Boatswain.'

Poor Douglas indeed, but now I knew where arms were to be had if only I could get at them, and hope is a bright candle on a dark night. And there was more, because all my worries over Poxy Percy's vengeance were gone, because there was no doubt now that Captain Sally and her men were villains, and that I was in the right. But more important than all the rest put together, a great light shone, and I saw my own stupidity in believing that something I had accepted as a tremendous threat…was no threat at all!

So now it was a matter of waiting for the right moment, which nearly came that very day at noon observation, when I took my sight beside the two mids. And here I point out to you youngsters that navigation must proceed despite all else, because the unrelenting violence of the sea remains forever your worst enemy. Thus we were not in sight of land, and must fix our position, come what may.

Captain Sally was keeping close company with me as ever, and took note of what I was doing.

'I hear you're a longitude man, Mr Fletcher,' says she.

'Yes, ma'am,' says I, now entirely happy to address her. 'I can make landfall within five miles of my destination.' That was some exaggeration, but well justified.

[Perhaps no exaggeration. Fletcher was a superb navigator finding longitude by chronometer as well as by the older method of Lunar observation, even performing the calculations in his head. In this he was indeed a prodigy. S.P.]

171

'Hmm,' says she, and I realised that she was another one who preferred familiar seas, and the crude old practise of running down the latitude. So her promise to take me to America was puff and wind. Or was it? Perhaps she'd do it, with me as navigator? Her next words confirmed that. 'Are you entirely sure, you're on the right course, Mr Fletcher?' says she, 'and in the right service?'

'Are you offering your service, ma'am?' says I, and shook my head. 'What about *Molly Monckton*'s crew that's to be hanged as pirates? They were in your service, and who'd choose to be in a service like that?'

She just laughed.

'What?' says she, 'And them prime seamen and the Navy gasping for 'em? No, mister! They'll say they was forced into it, and they're loyal hearts and true just wanting to serve King George. And the Navy'll take 'em 'cos it needs 'em.' I nodded because it was true. So I took a step in her direction.

'See here, ma'am,' says I, 'if you just bring Miss Maitland up here on deck, and give me back my pistols, then I do believe that we can talk.' And by George she nearly did, because I meant what I said and she knew it. So she thought and blinked and chewed her lip. It could have been a turning point in my life. But finally she smiled and shook her head.

'No, Mr Fletcher,' says she, 'because then I'd be in your power, and I like it the other way around.' So that was one path blocked, but others still open, though Captain Sally was very careful. She even did as I'd done, in making us throw all conceivable weapons over the side: knives, hatchets, boarding pikes, and even the spare belaying pins. Despite this, my moment finally came, at night, off Shaker's Point in Cornwall. Captain Sally might be ignorant of longitude, but like the three old tars commanding *Alacrity*, *Alderney* and *Cornwallis* she was masterful skilled in the south west coast, having been bred up to it.

So she got what she wanted: safe passage to a quiet cove of her choice, with a good beach for boats, in the moonlight. *Lizard* was hove to, with a triple block on the mainstay and all hands hauling out our cutter from its berth amidships. Captain Sally was with me and the mids at the ship's wheel, and her men were placed as follows: one outside Sophia Maitland's cabin, two watching over the men hauling out the boat, one as personal bodyguard to herself and one at my elbow where he'd been these past days watching over me except for his calls of nature. But worst of all, the remaining two, on Captain Sally's orders, had brought up the prisoners from the hold, with hands tied behind them, and Mr Myers and Dr Richard unable to stand for the harsh treatment they'd suffered, but laid on the deck like rolls of carpet.

Captain Sally had presented them to us earlier, when they were brought up staggering and stumbling.

'Here they are, then,' says she, and twisted Percy's nose and he made no sound. She turned to us *Lizards*. 'He don't say much no more, don't this one,' and she twisted his nose again, very hard.

'Ah!' said Percy.

'He talked a lot a first,' says Captain Sally, 'so we slapped him round the head till he shut up. Ain't that right, lads?'

'Aye-aye, ma'am,' says they.

'The rest of them took note and kept mum,' says she, and looked at Dr Richard and Lieutenant Chancellor who cringed in fright.

'Knives, lads!' says Captain Sally, and her two men got behind Percy and Chancellor, and put blades to their necks. 'So,' says Captain Sally, 'The rules is that all hands behaves themselves and launches a boat, and I goes down into it, and my lads too, and all the prisoners, including missie below, and then off we pops, and nobody follows, and nobody gets cut,' she looked at Percy. 'Not him nor nobody else, d'you hear? And we let them go all nice and safe once we're ashore.' She smiled and bowed. 'You have my solemn word on that!' It was all very simple. Either we did as she bid or two men got murdered before our eyes. As for her promise: that wasn't worth a rat's turd, but who were we to argue? She had all the advantages. But I'd had a word with the loyal hands when my guard was performing his motions, because there were still some weapons that Captain Sally had forgotten, and more important I'd come to an understanding within myself.

Meanwhile, *Lizard's* men seemed to be having trouble with swaying out the cutter. The boat wasn't rising as it should. It seemed to be stuck half way up.

'Mr Barclay! Mr Copeland!' says I, 'take command! Get that boat moving!'

'Aye!' says Captain Sally, impatient to be away. So the mids ran off and everyone watched as they, too, yelled at the men to heave harder.

'Heave away…together!' cries Barclay, which word was the signal I'd given the men, and so the triple block whirred, and the lines rumbled as the hauling team let go the line, and the boat came down with an almighty crash that drew all eyes. At once I darted past the man guarding me, who wasn't expecting it, and I was down the companionway towards the cabins. The swab guarding Sophia Maitland saw me and tried to shoot me, but failed, and I battered him senseless in seconds. Then I was kicking in the door to the sleeping cabin which was flimsy and went in a trice. So there was Sophia Maitland, all terrified in the dark.

'Here!' says I, taking one of the fallen man's pistols, which instantly told me why I'd not been shot. It was a fine London piece with safety bolts against accidental firing, which common pistols don't have, and the guard hadn't known about! So I slid the bolt and shoved it into Sophia's hands. 'Shoot any who's one of them,' says I, and grabbed the second pistol, and ran up on deck to a great commotion, with the mids acting their part among the loyal hands, urging them to haul, and everyone yelling, which had drowned out the noise below. But one swab saw me and pulled a pistol, but I fired first and he got an ounce ball through his bowels and over he went.

'Monkey tails!' says I in a great shout. 'Give it to 'em lads!' and all hands cheered and ran to the carronade carriages, and pulled out some ironware that Captain Sally had forgotten. Thus carronades are trained side-to-side by inch-thick iron bars over three feet long. In action they fit a socket at the back of the carriage, but otherwise they are slung on hooks beneath, and drawn out and swung hard, they crack skulls like nuts.

So there was a fierce fight on *Lizard*'s main deck. Whatever orders they'd had, the men with knives abandoned their prisoners and drew pistols, as did Captain Sally's bodyguard and the men guarding the hauling team: that's five men with a brace each and cutlasses, too. But there were twenty-five loyal hands, plus myself and the midshipmen, even if there were only sixteen monkey-tails to go round.

I took up the pistol of the man I'd shot, and someone screamed and ran at me and I fired and missed but the muzzle flash dazzled him and he couldn't see, and I couldn't get the second pistol from the man I'd shot, all wriggling and groaning. But Mr Midshipman Barclay swung two-handed and brained my attacker with a monkey tail, while pistols were banging all round, and I got the cutlass out of the wriggler's belt.

Then it was hand-to-hand, and men going over on either side, and our unarmed lads taking weapons from the dead, and I had a terrific swing at Captain Sally herself, but I stumbled over a body and she blocked it with her own cutlass and ran off. I got up and pitched into the fight, finding one swine backed against the rail trying to hurl empty pistols, and I split him from brow to chin, and my cutlass stuck as he went over. It jerked from my hand and I picked up a monkey tail someone had dropped and looked for someone to kill, and found it was all over, apart from some of *Lizard*'s men, in their anger, still beating the brains out of enemies already flat on their backs, such that none of Captain Sally's men survived, not even the one I'd left below because all seven were entirely mashed by the *Lizards*. But three of our lads were groaning on the deck and another four made no sound at all, being dead. One of these, I record in deepest sorrow, was Mr Copeland, the younger of the two mids, shot through the middle of his shirt, and laid as if asleep with not another mark upon him.

There was powder smoke everywhere, I was heaving with effort and dripping with sweat, and in that mood that follows a fight, when you can't believe you are alive, and knowing that the wrong ones were killed – like Mr Copeland. Men moved like the living dead, and it was time for me to take command and put the ship to rights.

But a lone pistol fired. A bright, sharp, crack and flash in the night.

'All of you listen here,' says a voice. Captain Sally's voice. We all looked and there she was, cuddled up against Poxy Percy, stood with a knife under his chin and the other hostages crawling away.

'This business ain't done!' says she. 'Do as you're bid or I'll slice bacon off this one here, until nothing's left,' and she jabbed the knife-point into Percy's cheek and twisted till he screamed. So all hands looked to me. They were exhausted. They'd have rallied if the French were coming over the side, but this was different. So I dropped the monkey tail and stepped forward. I was twenty feet from her, but she screamed aloud.

'Not another step!' says she and put the edge to Percy's throat.

'Fletcher,' says he, 'help me.' It was pitiful.

'What do you want?' says I to her, with *Lizard* wallowing in the night, and dead and dying men all round us.

'Get that boat in the water,' says she, 'and me aboard with Percival Clive, and two men to man the oars.'

'And what if I say no?' says I.

'Then I cut this bloody lubber from ear to ear!'

Well, my jolly boys. That's when the light shone over me again, only stronger, because I knew now that the threat that had ruled me these last days past had never been fear for Poxy Percy's miserable life; no indeed and not a bit of it! I could have roused the hands to fight any time I chose and they'd have followed me. But I couldn't do that because the real threat had always been to Sophia Maitland. That's why I'd gone for the man outside her cabin before anything else. Then once she was safe, Percy could take his chances; him and the rest, and especially Lieutenant Chancellor. So I looked at Captain Sally and shouted aloud.

'Cut and you're damned!' says I.

[Here we are at the root of Fletcher's notoriety. Ever afterwards he claimed to have spoken the above words in a tone of stern warning, to prevent murder.

But witnesses among *Lizard*'s crew maintained that what he really said was, 'Cut and be damned,' in contempt of Percival Clive's life, actively inciting the woman Combes to kill him. S.P.]

'I'll count to three!' says she, and she clutched Percy close. 'One!' says she.

'Sir,' says Mr Barclay, 'what are we to do?'

'Stand fast!' says I.

'Two!' says Captain Sally.

'Wait!' says Barclay. 'Don't!'

'Three...,'

'Bang!' a gun flashed and fired in the dark, from forward of the mainmast, and Percy twitched as a ball struck. Captain Sally let him fall, and she stood and turned and looked, as we all did, to see who'd fired. But a deeper gunshot boomed and Sally Coombes fell across Chancellor and Dr Richards, who moaned and cried, bound as they were. Just forward of the mainmast, Mr Douglas the Boatswain was pulling himself into sight, hanging on to the mast, with a smoking blunderbuss dangling in one hand and a musket on the deck beside him. The men cheered and ran to him. But I wanted sight of Captain Sally, and there was plenty to see: plenty of blood and plenty of holes in her, from a multiple discharge of pistol balls. You can get up to a dozen of those down the muzzle of a 4-bore blunderbuss, and she'd taken the lot. So she shivered and shuddered and glared at me in hatred. She tried to speak, with lips all twisted in anger and probably wanting to curse me. Then her eyes went dull, and she died and said nothing. But Percy was slumped beside her, likewise breathing his last, and he did manage some words.

'This is all your fault, Fletcher,' says he. Then his mind wandered, and he smiled and shared a confidence as if with a friend. 'I am to rise high in the Service. Very high.' Then he closed his eyes and sighed as if finished, but blinked and rallied. 'Mother says so,' he added, with infinite assurance, and then he was gone. So I went to Boatswain Douglas, held up by his mates.

'Mr Fletcher, sir!' says he, 'I crawled down day by day, to fix the firelocks, and kept it secret.'

'Well done, Mr Douglas,' says I.

'I fixed 'em and charged 'em, and when I heard the shooting, I got 'em and came up astern of the buggers, through the fore-hatch.'

'Well done, Douglas.'

'I got that bloody cow, didn't I, sir?'

'You did indeed!'

'But I didn't hit Mr Percival Clive by mistake. Did I, sir?'

'No, Mr Douglas,' says I, 'she had another pistol and shot him.'

'Oh?' says a few voices.

'That's what happened,' says I, 'and that's how it shall appear in the ship's books.'

'Aye-aye, sir!' says all hands.

Which ended my adventures in the Preventive Service and pitched me into something even worse.

Chapter 26

*'Having this day inspected the staircase of canal locks I can promise you, my
General, that the first steamboat will be brought down for a sea trial before the
end of August.'*
(Translated from a letter of Saturday July 30th 1796, from Citizen
Inspector, General Bernard, at Lyommeville, to Generalissimo Napoleon
Bonaparte, Headquarters of the Army of Italy.)

*

Bernard rode with the elite of Lyommeville: the Commander of the garrison
with his aides, together with the Port Admiral with his aides, the Colonel-
General of Artillery with his aides, and three captains of warships anchored in
the harbour, all these, and greatest of all: Citizen Plombier, the mayor! Himself
above all others, with his acolytes and councillors in train. A troop of dragoons
rode behind and ahead, for protection in these dangerous times, but the senior
man was Plombier, who reeked of politics. He spoke of the Paris Junta members
by name, as if they were his intimate friends, and nobody dared interrupt
him. He was a fat, red-faced man, marked by the small pox, but magnificently
dressed in fine clothes draped with a tricolour sash, and a hat with blue-white-
red ostrich plumes.

'We stop here!' cried Plombier, to the dragoon trumpeter that rode behind
him – Bernard noting the fact that the trumpeter rode behind this civilian
and not the Captain of the escort. The trumpeter raised his instrument with
a flourish and blew a call that brought the whole company to a standstill; the
horses tossing their heads, and snorting and stamping, in a settling of dust and
a jingling of harness.

'Citizen General!' said Plombier, 'Everything may be seen from here.' Bernard marked Plombier's accent and speech: they were the authentic tones of Versailles. Obviously Plombier – if that was his real name - was another one who'd started life as a nobleman, and greased his way up in the new world. He was just like Citizen Barras, head of the Paris Junta who was now so proletarian but had once been Monsieur le Vicomte de Barras.

'Citizen Mayor!' said Bernard, and rode forward. Plombier had chosen a good viewing site, half way up the steep hill on which the ancient fortress town of Saint Germaine was built. It was the smaller, older half of the combined town of Lyommeville, which looked across the gulf of the river Lyommes to Abbeyvaux: the larger and newer half. Bernard looked all around. The weather was fine and the view magnificent at this elevation. The air was marvellously fresh and clean, and scented with the sea. Bernard could see to the very horizon in bright, sharp clarity, and gulls called and wheeled, and the land stretched green, above and below Lyommville, in a north-south line facing La Manche, while vast, yellow flats of beaches extended on either side of the deep-water channel leading out from the harbour. The day was beautiful, tingling and invigorating.

'Citizen Inspector,' said Plombier, 'I draw your attention to the ancient walls of Saint Germaine: fortified with twelve bastions once named - by religious superstition - for the Christian apostles. But now they are gloriously renamed as months of the Revolutionary calendar.' Plombier drew breath, and pointed out the bastions one by one: 'Vendémiaire…Brumaire…Frimaire!' he cried, reciting the new, pagan month-names, as his acolytes cheered and waved their hats.

Bernard tried to ignore them. He looked up at the ancient, medieval walls and especially at the tower that rose from within them. That was the spire of the Cathedral of Our Lady of the Ocean, once a beloved centre of pilgrimage and miraculous healing. Bernard sighed, because the Revolution had forbidden the practise of religion, and turned the cathedral into a military arsenal. Fortunately Plombier was coming to the end of the list, which he marked with an upsurge of passion.

'Messidor…Thermidor…Fructidor!' he cried, and Bernard joined in with the cheering because it was wise to do, since Plombier was studying faces to see who was full of Revolutionary fire and who was not. Bernard followed his gaze and was pleased to see that some of the soldiers were unsmiling in their cheers, while the Port Admiral simply looked away. He was an old man – perhaps a survival of King Louis' navy – who remembered the days when honest men did not have to believe that shit was gold.

Plombier frowned at the Admiral, but then replaced his feathered hat and

179

continued his exposition. 'Look down, Citizen General,' he said, 'and take note of the new and excellent port, so recently built.' Bernard duly took note. How could he not? He was looking fifty metres straight down upon the fresh stoneware of an excellently extended harbour, fit to accommodate ships of the line, and not just the fishing fleet now present: those small craft plus a frigate and two sloops. The harbour was a glittering disc of water enclosed by Saint Germaine to the north and Abbeyvaux to the south. Bernard nodded in approval and unconsciously looked towards the junction of the two half-towns.

'Ah!' said Plombier, 'I see how anxious you are, Citizen, to view the magnificent locks of our new canal. How keen you are! How full of enlightenment!' Plombier laughed at his own words as if to mock them. But it was a false laugh because he looked round again, searching for dissidence. The old admiral actually sneered this time, which pleased Bernard greatly. But Bernard stood up in the stirrups for a better look because there was a great sight to be seen. It was the ocean terminus of the Montfer – Lyommeville canal.

The harbour was about a hundred metres wide at its entrance, swelling to nearly six hundred metres within the harbour walls, before narrowing to the mouth of the River Lyomme. The harbour was ancient, though recently extended. But to one side of the Lyomme river mouth, there was something entirely new: a vast staircase in gleaming water, built because inland of Lyommeville, the ground sloped upward to a range of hills so great that their local name was Massif du Nord, and the staircase was the eleven locks that would lift boats over one hundred metres to the level of the inland canal.

This complex construction was necessary because even though Lyommeville was entirely enclosed by the Massif, no other seaport suited Bonaparte's plan. But fortunately, once raised up, the canal waters could run through land that was level almost all the way to Montfer, needing just one more lock in one hundred and fifty kilometres. Bernard thought deeper, because the innate French genius for organisation was only half of the magic which had built this wonder of the modern world. The other half was Bonaparte himself: whose will had poured fathomless expense, and the toil of a hundred thousand men, into completing these works, which would become a cannon aimed at the most deadly enemy of France. All that was needed now was to load the cannon by bringing steamboats down the canal.

Bernard nodded with justified patriotism. No other people in the world could have delivered this masterwork of mechanism. It was an heroic achievement placed right on the sea shore facing England, which fact was a mighty strength.

Chapter 27

"The French are calling it an heroic achievement,' says Rowland, 'But it has a mighty weakness.' He turned to a big map pinned to a board on an artist's easel. The map, tinted in watercolours, showed the French coast around the port of Lyommeville. 'See here,' says he, tapping the map with a cane. Rowland was stood in front of us, with a whole series of maps and plans set up on artists' easels, and two very senior officers seated beside him, to give authority to his discourse. Also, there was a large trunk that I thought I recognised, on the floor beside him. 'The weakness is,' and he smiled at his audience, 'that they've built this great lift of eleven locks… right on the sea shore facing England!'

'Ahhhhh!' said the generals, and admirals, the captains and colonels, the commanders and majors, and myself at the back as the lowest form of life present. We were in the Riding School of Ramilles Barracks, Portsmouth, a vast, high space where equitation was taught in bad weather. It was guarded outside with fixed bayonets, and one small end of it was occupied by a cluster of navy blue, army red, and a sprinkling of Orders of the Bath.

Under Rowland's orders, I was fresh off a post-chaise from Plymouth, where Mr O'Flaherty in *Molly Monckton*, was already anchored beside *Alderney* and *Cornwallis* when I brought *Lizard* in. Our dead were all buried at sea, except Poxy Percy who our loblolly boy gutted, and pickled in a brandy barrel for his family to bury him ashore, as was common practise in those days, and the same was done to Nelson after Trafalgar.

Now in the Riding School, everybody grinned at one another, and drummed the table with their fists, because we were seated behind rows of tables - strictly according to rank - and each one of us with a packet of papers in front of us as personal versions of the plans on Rowland's easels, and provided by his detailed efficiency. So we drummed the table, because the mood among us was that of a wolf pack finding the farmer's lambs unguarded.

'So,' says Rowland, 'Would you be so kind, my lords?' he turned politely to the two senior officers: Field Marshal Lord Cutler-Sheif and Admiral Lord Oliver, and the mighty men nodded. Rowland continued, 'Would you be so kind, my Lords and gentlemen, to turn to document number three, of those set before you?' Heads bowed, papers rustled, and we all took out number three. Like the rest it was a printed sheet, a diagram with codes, words and instructions, and all neatly tinted like the big map on the easel. No expense had been spared.

'Document three,' says Rowland, 'gives a detailed plan of the lift of locks that the French have built, to connect the sea with the canal – now completed – from Montfer, to Fragnal, and to Lyommeville.' Rowland had a real gleam in his eyes. He was a happy man if ever such as him was ever truly happy. 'So, yes indeed, My Lords and gentlemen, this lift of eleven locks is an heroic concept, but the French, or rather Bonaparte whose plan this is, has made a mistake of colossal proportions and one entirely new to the art of warfare.' More table drumming followed, and some hurrahs. It really was like raw meat to wolves, because apart from myself, everyone else in that room was a lifetime dedicated officer, and totally bred up to fighting the French.

Field Marshal Cutler-Sheif smiled and raised his hand. Silence followed.

'My Lord,' he nodded to Admiral Oliver, 'and gentlemen, I rejoice to see such spirit among you, and I will therefore ask Mr Rowland, to continue his address, by revealing to you that which previously has been the deepest of secrets.' Profound silence fell, such that we could hear from outside, the crunch of boots and the bawling of a sergeant-major as some company or other was drilled.

'Leff-right-leff! Leff-right-leff! Pick your effin feet up you effin barstids!' The Field Marshal smiled at that, and continued.

'I will ask Mr Rowland,' says he, 'now to reveal the purpose for which the French have built these, ' he paused, 'these heroic works.' Everyone laughed. 'Mr Rowland!' says he, 'please continue.'

'My Lord!' says Rowland, turning to the audience, 'And now gentlemen, I do not refer you to any papers, because what I have to say is not to be written down.' We all shifted in our seats, and gave Rowland utmost attention, because it was like a piece of theatre. Indeed it was a piece of theatre. It was a huge drama because something enormous was about to be spoken. In fact, I'm surprised that Rowland hadn't got a band to give a drum roll, and a clash of cymbals before he spoke. 'The purpose of the Montfer-Lyommeville canal,' says he, 'is to enable boats to pass from Fragnal, where they are being made, down to the harbour of Lyommeville. The boats are of a most special and new kind, being propelled not by oars nor sails, but by steam engines.' This caused a growling from the Sea-Service officers.

'Steam engines?' says someone, as if sniffing a bad egg.

'Can't work!' says another.

'Been tried and failed!' says another.

'Gentlemen!' says Lord Cutler-Sheif, 'Pay close attention to Mr Rowland, who has my complete confidence and that of the Admiralty, the Horseguards and the Prime Minister.' The growling stopped. Rowland continued.

'Thank you, my Lord,' says he, and turned back to the audience, 'Bonaparte's plan is to assemble a considerable fleet of sea-going steam boats, in the harbour of Lyommeville.' The growling rose again.

'Gentlemen!' says Cutler-Sheif, 'be silent and pay heed!'

'Once a sufficient fleet has been assembled,' says Rowland, 'the French will fill the harbours of Boulogne, Calais and other ports, with barges equipped to carry men, horses and guns. Then the steamboats will pass up and down the coast, and choosing a day without wind when our Navy cannot sail, they will tow the barges across the sea to England, with an invasion force embarked of such size as to be irresistible. They will defeat, conquer and take…our country, our people, and our King.'

Only the first half of that sentence was truly audible. The outrage was too great. There wasn't growling but roaring and both Lord Oliver and Lord Cutler-Sheif had to get up and shout for silence because - and you youngsters take note - things under King George weren't the same as they are now. Nobody held back his feelings. You loved your friends and damned your enemies. You drank deep and lived full, and while every man was entitled to his opinion, every other man was entitled to knock him down for it. So there was uproar in that room that you wouldn't believe today, and men shouted in Rowland's face.

'Steam don't work and can't work!' cries a Post Captain.

'We'll beat the Frogs come what may!' says a Guards officer, and there was more.

'Nothing can get past the Navy!'

'There's never a flat calm in the Channel!'

'God save the King!'

'God bless England!'

But their two Lordships got silence in the end, and everyone sat down, red and puffing and muttering to one another.

'Mr Rowland?' says Cutler-Sheif, 'Give 'em some proof. Show 'em your machine.'

'Yes My Lord,' says Rowland, and looked straight at me over the heads of the rest. 'Mr Fletcher?' says he, 'Will you step forward?' So I did, and joined him at the front, with everyone staring at me. 'My Lords, gentlemen,' says Rowland, 'May I introduce Captain Fletcher of His Majesty's brig-sloop *Lizard*, who is fresh landed at Plymouth, having just intercepted the most dangerous smuggler in England, capturing a shipload of machinery illicitly bound for France, and who - with his own hand - despatched three of the smuggler's villainous crew.'

'Oh?' says the audience, and I bowed thinking it the proper thing to do.

'Fletcher,' says Rowland, 'shall we get this beast under steam, as we did before?' he pointed to the trunk, which was indeed the same as he'd brought aboard *Neptune* when I was examined for Lieutenant. 'Over there, if you please,' says Rowland, and pointed just behind where everyone was sat, where there was an area neatly planked over. It was Rowland's efficiency again. We had to be in a large enclosed space for this secret demonstration. But the riding school had a sandy floor that wouldn't suit a locomotive steam engine. 'My Lords? Gentlemen?' says Rowland, 'If you would follow me?' So they all got up and gathered round the planking, and one of the engineer majors had the decency to help me with the trunk which was too heavy even for me to drag over sand. But we got it onto the planks and I thanked him.

'If you'd be so kind, Captain Fletcher,' says Rowland. And so I gave them the same show as I'd given aboard *Neptune* and the model engine spoke a truth greater than words: one that couldn't be countered neither by prejudice nor argument. I was quicker this time in getting it under way, even though I was close pressed by men marvelling at the beauty of the thing, and its arcane technical construction.

'It's like a chronometer!' says a Sea-Service officer.

'Or a cylinder-boring engine,' says the helpful engineer.

'Marvellous!' says another.

They shook their heads in delight when the little wonder ran round with its tender and carriage in tow, and seeing the actuality of the machine, and the smoothness of its operation and - I emphasise this last as being no small matter – the very beauty of the thing, with its steel and brass and bronze, and all its twinkling, whizzing mechanism. Then, seeing all that, the doubt and scepticism was drained out of the audience.

Finally, when we ran out of the small store of charcoal that was left in the trunk, I stopped the engine, loosed off the steam with a great hiss, and stood beside Rowland.

'My Lords! Gentlemen!' says he, 'You have seen the model?'

'Yes!' says they.

'And does it convince you of the power of steam?'

'Yes,' they said, though with slightly less conviction.

'Then now believe me,' says Rowland, 'that British traitors at Fragnal have built a full-sized version of this engine, which runs and functions perfectly, and they are now working to equip boats with steam engines working exactly as the engine you see here,' he pointed at the model, 'with the advantage that a boat has far more space for machinery than a road engine, and needs no wheels and is therefore much easier to build.' The audience fell silent. Most nodded.

'Mr Rowland?' says one of them, 'I have a question.'

'Ask, sir!'

'How can you tell us what happens in France? How can you know the plans for the locks at Lyommeville, or the building of road engines at Fragnal?'

Lord Cutler-Sheif answered first.

'Gentlemen, I must first remind you that Mr Rowland has the full confidence of the Prime Minister and Government. Is that understood?'

'Yes,' says everyone.

'Then I can assure you that Mr Rowland has sources,' says Cutler-Sheif, 'and agents - in France and elsewhere - upon whose reports we may rely.'

'Hmmmm,' says everyone. They didn't like that. Not sources not agents, nor spies of any kind. That wasn't British, my jolly boys, it wasn't the way these blue-clad, scarlet-clad men went about their work. That's what they supposed, at least. Rowland saw that and threw them something else.

'In addition, ' says he, 'the lift of eleven locks has been observed by our ships, off Lyommeville,' he smiled, 'and I think we may trust in the Navy and its telescopes.'

'Ah!' says all the Sea-Service officers. That was much better.

'And so, Mr Rowland,' says Cutler-Sheif, 'what are we to do with this lift of eleven locks.'

'My Lord,' says Rowland, 'we shall land in force at Lyommeville – which landing the Navy has been practising these several months past.'

'Ahhhhh!' said the Sea-Officers, so that's why they'd been putting boats ashore at Sheerness, trying hard not to drown the redcoats and horses embarked aboard of them.

'We shall land in force,' says Rowland, 'taking advantage of the catastrophic error that Bonaparte has made, in concentrating in one small place - and that place next to the sea which Britannia rules - a military work of such importance as to constitute a thing new to warfare: a target that a relatively small force may destroy at enormous loss and cost to the French. So gentlemen,' says he, 'we shall land at Lyommeville, capture the town before the French can respond, and blow up the staircase of eleven locks, before re-embarking and returning in triumph to England!'

That brought a great cheer, and much more talking followed, with the handing out of responsibilities, and the planning of times and dates and ships, and careful study of tides and currents. It was all very thorough, and not just Rowland thorough, but Navy thorough. The army may have been a load of numbskulls, whose officers bought their commissions with money, but the Navy – or most of it anyway- had officers that knew no other way than the right way, thus demonstrating the eternal superiority of the Sea Service over the Land Service.

[Prejudice. Pure prejudice. S.P.]

The meeting went on all day, with a stop for lunch, and then more work, and myself getting steadily more puzzled as to why I was there at all, since no task was allotted to me, nor did it seem that I was entered into any ship, or had any place in the expedition. But late in the afternoon, Admiral Lord Oliver was on his feet, pointing Rowland's cane at a plan of one of the squadrons that would form the expedition. Oliver had a rasping, mumbling voice - odd among seamen who usually bellow – because an old wound to his throat had spoiled his speech so you had to pay close attention to hear him.

'Here,' says his Lordship, 'is the Red squadron under *Pondorous*, of ninety guns, in company with the frigates *Domentira* and *Apollo* to ward off interference from the French navy.' This brought a laugh of contempt from the Sea-Service officers, who regarded the entire Channel up to the beaches of France as a British lake. Oliver smiled indulgently and continued. 'These ships shall protect the bomb-ketches *Fuego*, *Saltpetre* and *Brimstone*, each mounting a pair of thirteen-inch mortars, which will bombard the batteries of Boulogne.' Oliver moved to the next easel. 'The Blue squadron is exactly similar: *Cartagena* of ninety guns, *Kent* and *Suffolk*, frigates, and the bombs *Eruptor*, *Vulcan* and *Thor*,' he turned to the audience, 'which squadron will entertain and divert the batteries of Calais.'

He moved to another and quite different plan: a map showing bold red lines connecting the Channel ports of France, and running inland.

'See here,' says he, 'This represents the French semaphore telegraph lines, whereby a signal may pass a hundred miles within minutes, and even to Paris itself. We shall use this ingenuity against itself, since it will transmit the news of our bombardments, causing the French to look in the wrong places!' Everyone laughed, and Oliver moved to his final plan, again representing ships. 'And finally, the White Squadron,' says he, 'which shall embark our expeditionary force: the light companies of the three Guards regiments, plus those of the 11th, 23rd, 49th and 50th foot, together with Brady's troop of the 27th light dragoons, a troop of horse artillery, and detachments of the Royal Engineers.'

'Ahhhh!' said the audience in delight.

'The White squadron, in overall command of the expedition, shall be led by the seventy-four gun *Proctalymion*, a prize taken from the Dutch and of shallow draft fit for inshore work. She shall be in company the frigates *Thranite*, *Thalamite*, *Zygite*, each of thirty-eight guns, and *Euphonides* of forty. These ships of the White Squadron shall embark the troops, horses and guns, and shall be commanded by…,'

But this was too much for the enthusiasm of the officers in blue. These last frigates were the talk of the service. The thirty-eights were superior to even the latest French equivalents, while *Euphonides* was a magnificent heavy frigate, one of the finest ships in the fleet, and the dream of any seaman to command. She was too fast for any ship that could beat her, and too powerful for any ship she chose to catch. There was a great gossiping as these ships and their captains were named, and I wasn't paying attention to Lord Oliver's mumbling because the helpful artillery major was sat beside me, who didn't know what all the fuss was about, and I was explaining. I did notice some of the Sea-Service officers looking my way, and frowning, but nothing more.

Much later there was a great dinner in the officers' mess. I'm told it was an elaborate occasion with silver, crystal, a dozen courses and gallons of wine. But I didn't attend because Rowland advanced upon me, as the Riding School meeting finally ended, and seized my arm.

'Wait a bit,' says he, as everyone else went out, talking non-stop, and marines came in at the double, and cleared away all the plans and easels, and the trunk with the model engine.

'Back tomorrow, Mr Rowland, sir?' says their sergeant, saluting smartly.

'Back tomorrow,' says Rowland, 'with the second batch of plans and papers.'

'They'll be there, sir!' says the sergeant. 'As per your orders, sir!'

'Good,' says Rowland, and, 'Come on, Captain Fletcher.'

'Captain?' says I, but he just grinned. He had a closed carriage outside to take us to The Royal Charles Oak Hotel, finest in Plymouth. It was only a ten minute journey but the conversation, in the swaying, clip-clopping vehicle was most profoundly interesting.

'You called me captain,' says I. 'You did it before.'

'That's right, captain,' says he. 'You've been promoted.' By Jove, but I've never met a man that could throw me sideways as he did. I looked at him in silence as the carriage passed through the evening traffic, and a dark, lamp-lit Portsmouth slid past.

'Aren't you going to say, Oh?' says he.

'Not this time,' says I. 'How can I be a captain? The next step for me – even if I get it - is to commander.'

'Really?' says he, 'Didn't Lord Uxbridge's son go from midshipman to captain in four months? And wasn't Lord Rodney's son made commander, then captain, on *the* same*day* in October 1780?'

[Note that these are true examples of grossly accelerated promotion in the Georgian Navy. S.P.]

'Yes,' says I, 'But they had powerful men behind them.'

'So do you,' says he, 'You have the Prime Minister.'

'Oh,' says I, and he rocked back in his seat and laughed.

'But I thought he was against me,' says I.

'Not any more. You don't know how important was the cargo in *Molly Monckton*! So I hope you'll like your new command?'

'What command?'

'*Euphonides*. You're posted captain into *Euphonides*.'

'Oh,' says I, and he laughed and laughed and laughed.

'And you're wealthy,' says he, when he'd done laughing, 'I am informed that *Molly Monckton* had such a cargo as we're still trying to calculate the value of, having never seen the like before. There were four model steam engines, each worth their weight in diamonds, plus a hold full of machine tools, and ingots of bronze, copper and tin, plus the considerable value of the ship herself, and you're senior surviving officer, so will get a huge share of the prize money.' He looked at me, 'Won't you say Oh?'

'What about Percival Clive?' says I, 'Doesn't any go to him? I mean his family?'

'That's for the lawyers to decide, but there'll be plenty for you...Captain Fletcher.'

I sighed. I didn't want the money; not earned this way. It took away the joy a man gets from making it by himself. Worse still it was obviously Rowland who'd spoken to the Prime Minster and got me hoist up the ladder and given *Euphonides*, and Rowland wouldn't give anything for nothing.

'So what do you want in return?' says I. He ignored the question.

'By the way,' says he, 'Miss Maitland thinks well of you.'

'How do you know that?'

'She reports to me. By special courier.'

'Does she though.'

'Yes. She is grateful that you were her champion.' I smiled because I knew that already. She'd shown her gratitude several times on the brief voyage from Shaker's Point to Plymouth.

'What will happen to her?' says I.

'She will please herself,' says he. 'Her contract provides a generous lump sum in the event of his death in the King's Service.' Then the carriage stopped. 'Ah' says he, 'Here we are.'

We were outside a smart new building built of Portland Stone, with a pair of marble columns capped with a gilded pediment, framing the steps leading up to the entrance. Wigged and liveried servants stood smartly forward to let down the steps of the carriage, and grovel us through a pair of huge, glossy doors into a bright-lit opulently furnished interior. One of the servants seized the luggage I'd brought with me, and we went inside. A senior servant in gentleman's evening clothes emerged from behind a counter, and bowed low.

'Mr Rowland,' says he, 'good evening, sir.'

'Good evening to you,' says Rowland, 'my companion's luggage should be taken up at once.'

'Of course, Mr Rowland.'

'And we'll have dinner as soon as you please.'

'Of course, Mr Rowland.' Rowland turned to me.

'Up to our rooms, perform ablutions, and down for dinner in ten minutes,' says he.

'What do you want, Rowland?' says I, this time seizing his arm and drawing him away from the servants. 'Tell me what you want.'

'You,' says he, 'because the destruction of the canal locks is only half the solution; perhaps less than half because the French can always re-build them. We have much to talk about this evening, but I'll begin by telling you that while the army and the engineers are busy blowing up locks, you and I,' he paused. 'Did I tell you that I'm coming with you aboard *Euphonides?*'

'No!' says I, because of course he hadn't.

'No?' says he, in return, 'Well, never doubt that I'm coming, because you and I - with a chosen band - are going all the way inland to Fragnal, which journey is made easy by the fine military road alongside the canal. So we'll be in and out like tailor's needle!' He paused, 'once at Fragnal, we shall have a final reasoning with the traitors who are making steam engines for their country's enemies, and that's what I want you for; you and your special talents.'

Chapter 28

'I cannot be more precise, as high matters of secrecy are involved, but the man I seek must be capable of examining steam machinery and identifying any superiority that it may have, over devices made in England.'
(From a letter of 16th July 1796, from Mr Philip Charles Rowland, The Royal Charles Oak Hotel, Portsmouth, to Mr James Watt, The Soho Foundry, Near Smethwick, in Staffordshire.)

*

'Kershaw,' said James Watt, 'I cannot tell you where you will go, because I do not know myself.'

'Yes Mr Watt,' said Ronald Kershaw, a highly-skilled toolmaker just out of his apprentice time. He was nineteen years old; slim, small, dark and active, with the look of a Celtic Welshman about him, even though he was Staffordshire born and bred. He was also much addicted to the sport of beagling, at which he excelled for his stamina in following the hounds on foot.

'Nor can I tell you how long you will be away,' said James Watt, 'nor even what perils you might face.' Kershaw grinned. He leaped gates, he ran for miles, and more than that he was famous among his friends for fighting for shillings against the boxing-booth men at the county fair.

And now he stood before Mr Watt, in the sanctum sanctorum of the Soho Foundry: Mr Watt's own private office, deep within the counting house, on the first floor of Block One, with a marvellous view of the entire works from its large and expensive windows. Mr Watt was enthroned behind a huge desk, with clerks in lesser chairs on either side, guarding neat stacks of documents, from which they passed examples to Mr Watt, at his command, while a third, and most senior man, stood behind Mr Watt and whispered into his ear, while looking at Kershaw the whole while.

'Yes, yes,' said Watt to the senior clerk, then 'Kershaw?' he said.

'Yes, Mr Watt?'

'Do your parents approve of this matter?' The three clerks gasped. Kershaw frowned, and the senior clerk hissed words into Watt's ear.

'Ah!' said Watt, 'My dear Kershaw, I do so much apologise. For the moment I had forgotten. How inexcusably rude of me! Your late father was a most respected and decent man.'

'That's alright, Mr Watt,' said Kershaw, and he meant it. Because it wasn't Mr Watt's fault. His Pa and his brother Peter had both been killed when the McCloud brothers - those revolutionary bastards and traitors to England, God damn them - had burned down the West Block. They shot Peter dead, and Pa was burned so bad you didn't know him, and it took him a week to die. Kershaw hated the McClouds with a deep hatred. But it wasn't Mr Watt's fault. Not at all. He was a good man.

'Your mother, then?' said Watt, hurrying on, 'What does she think?'

'Well, Mr Watt,' said Kershaw 'You say my wages will be paid, in double, to my Ma and my sisters for as long as I'm gone?' Watt and his clerks nodded.

'Yes,' they all said.

'And it's a year's pay in golden guineas when I get back?'

'Yes,' they all said.

'Then my ma and my sisters will be happy and so will I.'

'Indeed you will!' said Watt and smiled. He looked to one of the clerks, 'the list of requirements, if you please?'

'Yes, Mr Watt,' and a paper was passed to Watt which he gave to Kershaw.

'You will need these clothes and other items for your travels.'

'Yes, Mr Watt.'

'Everything will be provided for you at no cost to yourself.'

'Yes, Mr Watt.'

'Then give me your hand, Kershaw, and I give you my blessing.' Kershaw and Watt shook hands, one of the clerks showed Kershaw out, and a few minutes later Watt stood looking through one of the windows as Kershaw walked across the flagged courtyard, merry as could be, and all but jumping for joy. Watt smiled.

'Mr Watt, sir?' said the senior clerk.

'Yes?' said Watt.

'Are we entirely correct in our choice?'

'Oh yes,' said Watt.

'But the young man has certain defects of character.'

'I know,' said Watt, and the senior clerk persisted.

'He has great alterations of mood and behaviour,' he said, 'and would have been dismissed for fighting, except that we indulged him for his father's sake.'

'Yes,' said Watt, 'but also because he is a remarkably gifted draftsman.'

'Yes, sir,' said the clerk, 'But he is also a prize-fighter.'

Watt said nothing and the senior clerk hesitated, because he did not wish to cast darkness upon a young man whose family had already suffered badly. But truth is truth and the clerk finally spoke.

'Mr Watt,' he said, 'Sir, I would fail in my duty if I did not draw your attention to the fact that Ronald Kershaw may change in an instant from respectful deference, to violent temper, which he cannot control.'

'I know, I know,' said Watt, who was becoming impatient.

'He acts as if more than one spirit resides within him, and in the fury of his anger he did real harm to one of the boxing booth-men at the fair.'

'That is the risk these men take. They are shaven-headed savages.'

'His brother Peter was the same. It was he that struck the first blow against Donald McCloud's men. He killed one of them with a blow from an iron spanner, and…,'

'Enough!' said Watt, 'Give me that letter from Rowland!' The letter was put into his hand and Watt ran a finger over the writing. 'Listen!' he said, 'these are Rowland's words: the man you chose must be fit to keep up with a light infantry march,bear loads over rough ground, and not mind sleeping out of doors.' Watt looked at his clerks. 'Every other man we considered was too old or otherwise unfit, and Kershaw is highly intelligent and a constant user of our lending library, who seeks to better himself in every way: mathematical and philosophical as well as practical. He has furthermore generated improvements of mechanism which we have patented to the betterment of our business. He is an ideal choice, and there's an end of it. Do you agree?'

'Yes, sir,' said the clerks, seeing how firmly Mr Watt's mind was fixed.

But they did not agree. They knew Ronald Kershaw.

Chapter 29

I went aboard *Euphonides* on July 26th, which was a Tuesday. Mr O'Flaherty and Mr Midshipman Barclay were with me and I was glad of the company because I was nervous. I was painful, serious, dreadful nervous such that my past worries over Blackbeard Longridge were nothing by comparison. And the reason for that, my jolly boys, is that it's one thing to be given command of the finest ship in the Royal Navy, but quite another to go into that ship and expect all hands to respect you or even accept you. Not when you're replacing a captain who they'd loved so much that if even the next captain had been the baby Jesus, they'd have hated him by comparison.

So there came us three *Lizards*, with all our goods and luggage, being rowed out into Portsmouth harbour in an immaculate-smart cutter, pulled by an immaculate-smart boat's crew with an immaculate-smart lieutenant in command: a boat out of *Euphonides* bringing myself - her new commander - aboard. Clank-clank went the oars, heave-ho went the tars, moving in a rhythm as perfect as a steam engine's pistons. The gulls called from above, and even the English ocean was blue for once. It was like the Mediterranean. It was like a holiday, and yet my guts were in spasm.

Then the anchored *Euphonides* was bearing straight ahead, and by God and all his little angels but she was lovely. She stood out from every ship of the host of warships anchored in their measured lines. This was especially so because *Euphonides* was anchored alongside of the lumpish, round-stern, old seventy-four *Proctalymion*, that had once been the Dutch *Jan Tromp*, and which would command the White Squadron for the coming expedition. The other White Squadron companions, the frigates: *Thranite*, *Thalamite*, and *Zygite*, were close by, and were excellent ships in their own right. All four, and *Euphonides* herself were fresh from weeks of exercises off Sheerness, in constant practise of landing troops, horses and guns.

But neither the White Squadron nor any other ships in harbour looked so fine as *Euphonides*. She was first of a brand new class. From bow to stern she was as long as a line-of-battle ship, and nearly two thirds the tonnage, with lofty masts, a huge bowsprit and – for a frigate – a truly massive battery of forty, twenty-four pounder long guns plus twenty, thirty-two pounder carronades. Even the two chase guns mounted under the bowsprit were eighteen-pounders, as compared with the nines or twelves of ordinary ships. And she was fast. By George, she was fast. She was famous for having once heaved the log in a strong blow and found she was going fifteen knots, which was lightning speed before the clippers and steamers came along, and no other ship in the Fleet could match her.

Her full crew was up to four hundred and fifty men and boys, including fifty Marines, and five Sea Service lieutenants, plus a Marine lieutenant, a dozen midshipmen, two master's mates and every other seagoing trade from butcher, to barber and the boy that fed Jimbo, the ship's cat, which animal was celebrated for the number of rats he killed and mangled and always left under his favourite gun for the hands to clear up.

I could go on. I could say that her guns had tangent sights for better aiming and that her drinking water was stored not in casks but the latest iron tanks from Maudsley's Ironworks. I could say she set skysails over t'gallants. I could say all that and more, but that doesn't explain why this ship was lovely and others are not. It's exactly the same with a lovely woman. You can't put into words what it is that makes her lovely. You have to see her, and so it was with *Euphonides*. With ships as with women, I've been in love quite a few times, and this was one of them.

The trouble was that *Euphonides* was also famous for the captain who'd gone before me: Sir Edward Perrenporth, one of the great, buccaneering captains of British history, who'd captured enough prizes to make an armada, and made himself and his officers rich, and given all hands a fat share in the loot. Old Sir Edward had gone to sea when George The First was a lad, and served ever since, and had for years manoeuvred mightily not to be promoted admiral, but to stay a frigate captain. Thus he claimed to be sixty but was over eighty, and when he really did get too old to carry on, his four grandsons – renowned Sea Service officers, every one - came aboard under Admiralty orders to drag him out of the ship for his own good, at which the entire crew wept oceans of tears and were so helpless with grief that the ship could have been bested in battle by a boat-load of Quakers armed with Bibles.

Such was the man I was replacing.

Such was the love of his crew.

So just think on that, my jolly boys.

It froze the cockles of my heart to wonder how ever should I compete with Sir Edward, or have authority over the ship's officers, who would all have more service time than me, and were the elite of the Service. So I looked at the lieutenant in command of the boat, who instantly raised his hand to his hat in salute, though without the least warmth in his eyes.

'Never mind,' says O'Flaherty, sitting beside me on the thwart. I looked at him and he smiled and patted my knee like an old uncle. 'You'll do it, my lad,' says he. 'You've faced worse than this, and come out right.' He'd guessed my thoughts. They were written on my face. 'And we've got plenty of friends aboard,' says he, 'the which will count, because they'll put the word round the lower deck.'

That helped, because we did indeed have friends aboard. Even *Euphonides* was short of men in wartime, and I'd seized on the privilege of a newly-promoted captain to bring men out of my old command and into the new. That's why Mr O'Flaherty and little Barclay were with me, though in O'Flaherty's case there was a genuine vacancy to fill, since Sir Edward's sailing master had been a lifetime shipmate, as old as himself, *and* had gone ashore with him. But in addition, two dozen prime seamen out of *Lizard* were already transferred into *Euphonides* to make up her full complement, and they, at least might, think well of Captain Fletcher.

Captain Fletcher? Could that be true? The words were strange. What had I become? I feared that I was in too deep and might never get out.

But then we were alongside *Euphonides's* quarter where a neat and immaculate set of stairs had been rigged with neat and immaculate white handrails, and up I went in my full dress, first out of the boat because that's Service tradition: the senior man goes last into a boat and first out of her. My heart was thumping hard, and I was over the bulwark to another neat set of steps so I didn't have to clamber down, and there they all were, hundreds and hundreds of them, lined up in silence, and the smartest crew that ever set sail, and everyone in his finest, and the marines presenting arms, and the Boatswain and his mates piping the salute, and my hat off to salute the quarterdeck, and every other hat in the ship off to salute me, and every part of the ship gleaming and shining and neat and whitened and polished and scrubbed and buffed, and even the cat Jimbo, lined up with the rest, on a lead held by a ship's boy and the cat with a little blue jacket and a little tarred hat secured on his head by a line.

I gaped. I must admit it. I gaped at the smartness. I thought I'd always run a smart ship. But not like this. Then O'Flaherty and the rest were out of the boat and behind me, and the ship's First Lieutenant - always known as Number One - nodded towards the ship's band of music, which was a substantial gang of twenty men with dazzling brass and gleaming wood and four marine drummer-boys mustered among them. The bandmaster waved a baton, and they started with *God Save Great George Our King*! They gave it with gusto and volume and all hands joined in with a will. It was my first introduction to this ship's customs and practise, of which it seemed that a strong one was music. So I sang along with all the rest.

Then once we'd sung all three verses there was silence, as Number One - whose name was Pyne and who was old enough to be my father - stepped back, enabling me to complete the ceremony of taking command.

O'Flaherty handed me the paper he had ready. It was my commission. I took it and looked at it, and then looked up at the hundreds of faces. Then I looked down again, and a great fear settled upon me, and all the world shrank into the writing on the paper, because although I'd known fear before – as every seaman has – this was a new kind of fear. It was fear that I wasn't good enough, because I'd never been in full command of a ship with commissioned officers. I'd been in command of *Serpant* and of *Lizard*, and other ships. But there'd always been lesser men beneath me, either swabs like Poxy Percy, or lower deck hands who knew less than me of seamanship, navigation and gunnery. Even O'Flaherty was a foremast hand made good who instinctively deferred to my commission. So I looked at the paper with its fine words, inscribed with a flourish by some clerk in a bold round hand.

I've still got it, and this is what it said in its antique and traditional style:

*By the Commissioners for executing the Office of the Lord High
Admiral of Great Britain and Ireland etc. and of all His Majesty's
Plantations, etc.*

   *To Captain Jacob Fletcher hereby appointed in command of His
Majesty's Ship the Euphonides*

   *By Virtue of the Power and Authority to us given, We do hereby
constitute and appoint you Captain of Euphonides willing and
requiring you forthwith to go on board and take upon you the
Command of the ship, strictly Charging and Commanding all the
Officers and Company belonging to the said ship, to behave themselves*

jointly and severally in their respective Employments with all the Respect
and Obedience unto you their said Captain …

I stopped there, with my attention fixed on the last words: the words whereby Their Lordships of the Admiralty compelled all hands aboard *Euphonides* to kiss my arse every day of the week and twice on Sundays. The words could not be more precise. They could not be challenged. But hadn't Poxy Percy read out the same words aboard both *Serpant* and *Lizard*? And hadn't he been treated with contempt ever after? So was that going to happen to me, Jacob Fletcher, who'd sunk a British ship with an undersea mine? Jacky Flash who wasn't a proper sea officer at all, because he didn't want to be one?

I looked at the faces again. Now they were blinking and wondering. Some were shuffling their feet, and the hands were glancing at one another sidelong. So were the officers. The moment stretched. It lasted forever. Then O'Flaherty nudged my arm.

'Sir,' says he, 'Read it.' I said nothing. I did nothing. I was frozen. 'Sir!' says O'Flaherty, 'Read it!' I still did nothing. I couldn't move. Then O'Flaherty came really close. 'Jacob,' says he, very slowly and deliberately in his soft Irish voice, 'Read…the fockin…paper.'

God bless O'Flaherty. I read the paper. I read it loudly and to the end, and that stirred memories. I might not have been a real sea officer, but I'd served under some who were, and I remembered the captain of the first ship I was ever in: Captain Bollington of the frigate *Phiandra*. I remembered him and took him as my model. So when I'd done bellowing out the words of my commission, I handed the paper back to O'Flaherty, clasped my hands behind my back, and took a step forward and glared at them all. It was an act, a complete act, and my legs were shaking, but that soon stopped as even I came to believe in the act.

'Now pay heed!' says I, in a huge voice, 'For I am Fletcher, and it is my heart's desire to smash, wreck, sink, burn or destroy everything French that goes upon the face of the waters!' That was a good start and there were nods of agreement on all sides, because – as I've said elsewhere - that's what every captain said in those days, and the men expected it. But then I was blessed with inspiration. 'So you and I shall do this together,' says I, 'We shall do it for King George and for England, but most of all we shall do it for Captain Sir Edward Perrenporth,' they all jerked up straight at the name, 'so here's three cheers for Sir Edward: Hip hip hip..,'

'Huzzah!'

'Hip hip hip…,

'Huzzah!'

'Hip hip hip…,'

'Huzzah!'

Best thing I ever did aboard that ship, believe me, because if I'd not mentioned Sir Edward, he'd have hung over me like an undead spirit. But calling for cheers in his name released the men's emotion and opened their minds to fresh thoughts. So I damned the French a bit more, blathered on about homeland and duty and saving the women from rape, and then concluded as Bollington had done aboard *Phiandra* years ago, because I do exhort you youngsters that if you can't think of a good idea of your own, then copy somebody else's!

'So,' says I, 'all hands below to put on sea-going rig, then stand to quarters, and we'll see how fast this ship can clear and run out!' That was enough. They were a smart company. No questions were asked, no more orders were needed. Officers and men doubled to the order, and were back in minutes in working clothes, and Number One with a big gold watch in his hand. The ship was ready, all hands were ready. Number One saluted me.

'Permission to clear and run out, Sir?'

'Clear and run out!' says I.

So they did. They did and I was enormously relieved. They were good. They were very good. No commands were needed, every man did his duty and got in the way of no other man. They heaved with a will and all together, and the guns rumbled out, and all the ritual was served, of casting off securing tackles, fitting flintlocks to the guns, sanding the decks for firm footing, marines at the hatchways to stop unauthorized persons going below: all that and the rest. It was all done quick and neat. They were a fine team and yet they weren't perfect. They weren't magic. They weren't like the gun-crews of Bollington's *Phiandra*. But Bollington was mad for his guns, and even paid for powder and shot out of his own purse, for practice firing. So I was delighted to see that there was, after all, something I could teach these men, because I'd seen better than their gun drill, and I could show them how to improve.

When they were done they stood by the guns looking my way, and Number One came forward, touched his hat in salute and showed me his watch: a fine stopwatch by Hargreaves of Liverpool.

'One minute and thirty-five seconds, Sir,' says he. I nodded. Because it was a good time, even allowing for the fact that it was done in harbour, when the guns could not be loaded or fired.

'We'll have it faster next time, Mr Pyne,' says I, 'With live firing so soon as we're at sea, and I'll want three broadsides in five minutes.'

'Aye-aye, Sir!' says he, and I could see he didn't like it, but he'd just have to get used to it because - come the day when the enemy was bearing down with drums rolling and guns run out - you could never clear for action fast enough, and Mr Number One Pyne knew that in his heart, whatever his face said.

After that there was an astonishing number of people to meet, and things to see, some of them familiar, some new, some even bizarre: at least to me. Thus I had no less than four servants to look after me and my quarters: all lower deck seamen told off to this duty. I also had a personal cook, separate from the ship's cook. To my surprise, this man, whose name was Pringle, was first on the list that Number One presented me of persons needing my attention.

'It is the matter of the dinner, Captain,' says Pringle, in the large and immaculate stern cabin, where I sat behind a table to receive those brought in by Number One's minions. Pyne stood by me throughout, with a pen-pusher sat at my side taking notes. This was the Ship's Chaplain the Reverend Mr Goodsby, who also acted as Captain's secretary. With him was some sort of secretary's mate to keep his papers, while one of my servants constantly came in and out with refreshments.

'Dinner?' says I, to Pringle.

'Dinner, Sir,' says Pringle, bowing respectfully. He had the look of a successful tradesman. Good clothes and not a sign upon him that he did any of the menial work himself.

'Dinner, Sir,' says Number One, and the Reverend Goodsby, both nodding firmly.

'Oh yes,' says I, recalling that as captain my first duty would be to entertain my officers to dinner, something I'd never had to do before. 'Deal with it!' says I, to Pringle. 'Draw up a menu, show it to me, then buy whatever you need ashore. But show me all the receipts.'

'Receipts?' says Pringle, the word sprung out of him by surprise, and I felt the same word coming from the Reverend too, which reaction told me that Old Sir Edward had never checked his bills. But Pringle recovered fast.

'Of course, Captain!' says he and bowed again, and went out. After him, Pyne fetched in the most amazing number of people to show their faces: the lieutenants, the mids, the masters mates, the Surgeon, the Purser, the Boatswain, the Gunner, the Carpenter and others. Later, when this first wave of introductions was finished, and after coffee and rout cakes were served, Pyne excused himself, doing it in a most peculiar way. He looked to the Reverend Goodsby with an inquiring look on his face, and Goodsby nodded, and Pyne nodded back, then spoke as if he'd just been given orders: orders from the ship's chaplain to the First Lieutenant!

'Ship's business calls, Sir,' says he, to me, 'So if I might leave you in Mr Goodsby's hands?'

'Carry on, Number One,' says I, and out he went with the Secretary's Mate in tow, astern of him.

'Hallo,' thinks I, 'What's this? There's some private business afoot here,' and I wondered what it might be. So I looked closely at Rev. Gent., in his black clothes and clerical band and old-fashioned powdered wig, which all proclaimed what a virtuous man he was, even as he proceeded to run through some accounts which were very far from virtuous.

Well, my jolly boys, there've been occasions in these memoirs when I've taken the back off the clock of Old England and revealed the works within, just to show you how they used to grind. So stand easy and pay close attention, because here comes another such revelation. But first I must refer you to the works of Captain Frederick Marryat the novelist. He was a friend of that pompous windbag Charles Dickens whose characters had fatuous names like Dr Dickywinkle and Miss Pratt. But Marryat – who'd served at sea – had proper characters who were brave and skilful Navy heroes. There are other authors too, with brave and skilful Navy heroes. But these fictional officers differ utterly from the real ones – including even Nelson himself – who were indeed brave and skilful, but were also busy making money by corrupt and devious means, and I'm not just talking about prize money: because yes indeed, that's no more than legalised piracy, but at least it's out in the open.

Contrariwise, there was a dark current of money that flowed beneath the surface of the Georgian Navy and though I'd always known it, I'd never dreamed the extent to which a big ship like *Euphonides* was a commercial enterprise with the captain taking most of the profits. All this was revealed as Goodsby went through the books and I suddenly realised why the Navy's officers tolerated the dockyard hands sawing good spars into useless chips. It was because they understood and sympathised with such practises, being profiteering sinners themselves.

'Freight money, Sir,' says Goodsby, with a deferential smile, passing me a document. 'We have a standing arrangement with Messers Cooper, Slim and Goldbeater, bankers of Lindemann Street,' he smirked. 'We get one percent.' Now what that meant was that should these bankers wish to send gold coin overseas – say to Lisbon – and should our ship be ordered to Lisbon, then we would carry the treasure safe in our hold, and the captain would get one percent of it. A nice practical arrangement whereby the treasure was protected by the ship's guns, in order that gold might flow and trade prosper. The only problem was that no warship should have been carrying any cargo at all at the captain's profit … because that was illegal!

'Likewise we have similar arrangements,' says Goodsby, 'with The Honourable East India Company, and other institutions.' His neat, clean finger pointed to a list and I goggled at the sums of money involved. He turned to other papers. 'Here are your Servants Allowances, Captain.' says Goodsby. 'The rating of the ship allows you ten servants,' he waved a smooth hand, 'but of course you need only four, and the salaries of the remainder, go to you.' He moved on, 'Then, there are the so-called Widows' Men, Sir, of which the rating of the ship allows twenty,' he smiled, 'who do not exist but are on the books that their pay might be used to the betterment and health of the crew. Your share is twenty percent.' And there was more. There was much more. But then there were expenses.

'The band of musicians is in your service not the king's, Sir,' says Goodsby, 'and these are their salaries, to be paid by yourself, together with costumes and instruments and repair of same. Though they are of course, fed and bedded at the Ship's expense.'

'Are they now?' says I because that was plain fraud. But Goodsby continued without the least hesitation.

'Mr Pringle, your cook, is likewise in your service.'

'Is he?' says I, 'We'll see what sort of a dinner he delivers tonight.'

'Quite so, Sir,' says Goodsby, and then he looked nervous, 'Ahem,' says he, 'meanwhile, Sir, since Captain Sir Edward has removed his wine, his larder, his table wear, and cutlery, I have taken the liberty to replace them…ah…in your name…ah … at these…ah…costs,' he faltered at the expression on my face, but I looked at his figures and nodded. In fact he was efficient and honest - at least with me. He had to be, because his employment depended on me. His rating as Chaplain came from the Admiralty, but his tasty job as secretary was in my service. He saved up his own costs and salary till last, and they weren't small.

So there it was. My official salary and prize money plus Rowland's Spanish dollars, had already made me wealthy. If I then added the peculations and embezzlements Goodsby had laid before me, then I was seriously wealthy even allowing for the costs of himself and my cook and musicians. So I was – in effect - a man of business again, which thought considerably pleased me.

'Well enough, Mr Goodsby,' says I, when he'd done, 'but I'll see all your accounts and everyone else's aboard this ship.'

'Of course, Sir,' says he, hardly believing me. 'But there are many such accounts. Dozens, Sir. There are so many trades and professions aboard.'

'I know that,' says I, 'So you just give me a list of them, and I'll pick one every so often, just to keep the others warned.' I did too, as long as I was in that ship, and you youngsters should do the same, because if a man is spending someone else's money and nobody checks his books, then he falls prey to wicked temptation: and we wouldn't want that, now, would we?

So I was happy for the moment, but then Pyne came back and took me on a tour of the ship, where a very considerable surprise was waiting for me.

Chapter 30

*'I report with infinite satisfaction, that the seemingly endless period of dispu-
tation is ended among the English-Scottish engineers, who are not only united in
purpose, but becoming more visibly French every day.'*
(Translated from a letter of Thursday July 28th 1796, from Citizen
General Claude Bernard, at the Frangnal-sur-Longue Barracks, to Citizen
General of Division Napoleon Bonaparte, Headquarters of the Army of Italy.)

*

'We've found him, my General.' The young ensign of the 134th was very young indeed; too young even to grow a moustache. A sergeant and corporal stood behind him, and a few men of the regiment's light company. The rest were out in the woods.

'Go on, my boy,' said Bernard, 'tell me the rest.' Jamie McCloud and Colonel Sauvage stood with Bernard in the Barracks courtyard. The workshop was silent, the engineers – French and English-Scottish – stood clustered at the door. Even the men manning the big steam engine were looking away from their monster and towards the ensign.

'He's in the trees, my General. He must have gone out by himself during the night.'

'And?' said Bernard, 'tell me, boy. It's all right. You can tell me.' The ensign blinked and paused. He fumbled for words.

'He's…ah…he's dead, my General. He's hanged himself.' There was a groan from all present.

'Oh!' said Jamie McCloud. Just that single, expressionless sound. But Sauvage and Bernard crossed themselves and Bernard put a kindly arm across McCloud's shoulders. It was what they'd all feared. Donald McCloud had left a note on his desk. It was scrawled in the nervous writing of a disturbed man. All it said was:

I am a traitor. I am guilty beyond redemption and go to my punishment.
Pray for my soul if you will.
Donald McCloud

So everyone had been searching for Donald McCloud since breakfast when he didn't appear as usual. The engineers had searched the buildings, and the light company of the 134th searched the woods around them. So now McCloud was found, and now he was dead. But Bernard, ever practical, asked a practical question.

'Are you sure he's dead? Did you cut him down at once? Did you feel for a heartbeat?' The ensign nodded.

'He was cold, my General. He'd been out all night. His clothes were soaked with dew. His face was grey,' the boy thought carefully. 'He had a chair with him, my General. A chair and a rope. And he must have stood on the chair, and reached up to tie the rope to a branch, and then tied the rope round his neck and jumped off the chair,' he paused before giving the final detail. 'His tongue was sticking out, my General. Like this,' and he mimed the distortion of features. The onlookers sighed. 'And we did cut him down, my General, and he was dead. Really dead.'

'So where is he now?' said Bernard. 'Did you just leave him on the ground?' The ensign mumbled something that nobody heard. 'Bah!' said Bernard, 'Go and fetch him! Bring him back. Do it properly and with respect. He must have a decent burial,' he turned to Jamie McCloud with great sympathy. 'I regret that you must organise this, Monsieur McCloud. 'It's not something we can do for you…I mean for him.' Jamie McCloud frowned, uncomprehending.

Bernard led him aside and spoke softly to avoid broadcasting a shameful thing because – in the sorrow of the moment – Bernard had abandoned the political correctness of La Revolution, and reverted to the honest Catholic faith of his upbringing.

'Monsieur l'Abbè at the church can't bury your brother,' whispered Bernard. 'He can't do it because a suicide is damned by Holy Mother Church,' Bernard crossed himself again. 'A suicide, can't be laid in consecrated ground or receive holy rites.' His eyebrows rose hopefully as he looked at McCloud, 'but perhaps your religion is different?'

'Yes,' said Jamie McCloud, and stood up straight. 'We'll bury him. We'll bury him and all these troubles with him.' Bernard was surprised, almost shocked. Here was a man whose brother had just hanged himself, yet there were no tears in his eyes. Bernard stared at Jamie McCloud. The man wasn't actually smiling: not quite. But by Saint Denis and Saint Joan, he surely wasn't broken with grief! McCloud seemed relieved, satisfied, content even. Bernard drew back the arm that he still had around McCloud's shoulders.

*

Much later, Bernard and Sauvage had dinner and a bottle of wine. They discussed the day.

'So they're all back at work,' said Sauvage.

'Just as if nothing had happened,' said Bernard, and Sauvage shook his head. 'What do you make of them?'

'Pah!' said Bernard, 'I gave up wondering, long ago.'

'Me too. I'm fed up with them and their quarrels. I'm sick of them.'

'Who can understand the bastards?'

'Who cares? Who wants to understand them?'

'Not me. It's not worth the effort.'

'At least the one who hanged himself understood that they're a bunch of traitors!'

'Shhh!' said Bernard, 'What if the rest think the same?'

'Not them!' said Sauvage, 'And I can prove it to you.'

'How?'

'Easy! Haven't you noticed that I don't have to speak English to them any more.'

'Oh yes. They're all speaking French.' Sauvage nodded and raised a glass.

'So I salute you, my General.'

'Why?'

'Because your plan worked after all.'

'You mean the girls?'

'I mean the girls,' Sauvage grinned, 'Did you know some of them are pregnant?'

'Are they?'

'Oh yes,' said Sauvage, 'And I can promise you that whether or not these little shits of English-Scotsmen, understand it and know it, they've become French English-Scotsmen with French wives and French children on the way, and they're busy fitting a steam engine into a barge, and sticking a water screw up the barge's beam ends, ready for Bonaparte's plan of England.'

'Have another glass, mon ami,' said Bernard, reaching for the bottle. 'I shall write to the Generalissimo this very night to give him the good news.'

Chapter 31

When I'd done talking to the Reverend Goodsby, Pyne took me on a tour of the lower deck to see the men's living quarters where we found that the hands had made certain preparations, egged on by the two dozen who'd followed me out of *Lizard*.

The rascals were grinning and eager, but raised fingers to brow in respectful salute, and everything was neat and tight, with the mess tables rigged and each mess's pots and pans on display, shiny polished. Everything was proper except that just forward of the mainmast, they'd cleared a space, and rigged it with ropes. It was a boxer's ring, and the biggest man on the lower deck was standing in it, stripped off to the waist with fists raised. His name was Ned Pugin, known to his mates as Pug. As Pyne and I saw this there was a cheer, led by the old *Lizards*. God knows what Pyne thought, and even I was surprised. But then the *Lizards* started yelling.

'That's Pug! He's the ship's bully!'

'Baste him Mr Fletcher!'

'Give it the bugger!' But others yelled differently.

'Go on, Pug!'

'Pug's the boy!' and there came the deep, slow chanting of hundreds of voices:

'Who's, the boy that knocks 'em down? Our Puggy!

Who's the boy that breaks the bones? Our Puggy!

Who's the boy that wins the crown? Our Puggy!'

In reply to this, the two dozen *Lizards* did their best with a united barking of:

'Jacky Flash! Jacky Flash! Jacky Flash!'

I looked at Pyne, who frowned monstrously. But the younger lieutenants had appeared behind him, and the masters mates and others, and they were all for it. It was sport, d'you see? All the world likes sport, and bets their fortunes on it, especially young officers, such that the only thing that exceeds sport in all-consuming fascination, is getting their leg over a tart. And as for the lower deck, all hands were uproarious and the *Lizards* were urging me on, and it was obvious that what I'd thought of as a private tradition, had become something public. The noise was tremendous, and every eye was on me.

'Well,' I thought, 'Why not?' and a truly colossal cheer went up as I gave my hat to Pyne, and started to unbutton my coat.

Pug was ready and waiting and he did his best because the *Lizards* – bless their hearts – had told him that's what I'd expect. So he fought hard, but he was a useful seaman for any task involving bullish strength and rank stupidity, so I'm pleased to say that afterwards, once they'd picked him up off the deck and emptied a bucket of water over him, he was back to his duties within days, with no more than bruises and a closed eye, and even that opened up soon enough. As for me I had to retire to my cabin to wash off the sweat, and Pyne - who was embarrassed by the matter - didn't mention it afterwards, acting as if it had never happened. Since he didn't mention it, nobody else did, because the First Lieutenant is a great man aboard ship and sets the tone that others follow. So he swiftly led me on to still more ship's business, like meeting the Master at Arms and other warrant officers, and nobody even thought about Ned Pugin, nursing his bruises, and with vinegar and brown paper slapped on his eye. Mind you, I ordered double grog for him and his messmates, just to show there were no hard feelings and to speed his recovery.

Later we had a lavish dinner in the dining cabin, though you landmen should note that the meal was properly named supper, not dinner, and was served at the turn of the afternoon watch: say 4 pm shore time, when the hands were fed and got the day's second ration of grog.

Fortunately Pringle the cook proved he was a good 'un, and had the sense to try nothing foolish with the cost. The mood round the table in the big dining cabin was polite, but not warm, though I think the officers, led by Number One, were genuinely surprised that I had the manners and speech of a gentleman, because they were expecting someone like the highwayman Macheath from *TheBeggar's Opera* – a swaggering rogue with pistols in his belt and his feet on the table. Also I was pleased to find that not all the lieutenants were older than me. Two of the five certainly looked quite young, and only Pyne was grey and wrinkled. O'Flaherty was there too, with the rest of the ship's gentlemen, which made a large gathering, and once the port had gone round a few times, there were some red faces and some whispering.

I'd taken a drop myself by then and was feeling comfortable because now

I was actually in the ship, things weren't as bad as I'd feared. It was like swimming in cold water after dithering on the bank. So I smiled to myself at the whispering, because as with the memory of Sir Edward, there was a ghost here to be exorcised. So I banged on the table for attention, and everyone blinked and looked my way. It was time for the Loyal Toast anyway.

'Gentlemen!' says I, 'The King!'

'The King, God bless him!' says everyone, and raised glasses.

'And the sport of kings,' says I, and paused before delivering the clincher. 'Which for me…is fisticuffs!'

O'Flaherty lead the laughter. He laughed and all the rest did too, even Mr Number One Pyne, and thereby was my battering of Pug formally acknowledged by this proud company, and was recognised as Captain Fletcher's novel behaviour which duly replaced the accustomed usages of Captain Sir Edward. So now I was part of the ship's history, and while that ship never loved anyone quite like old Sir Edward, at least it was giving me my chance.

So far so good, but there was still one more test before I could be accepted into command, and that test was music, because the tradition aboard *Euphonides* was that – weather and enemy permitting – the ship had an hour of music after supper. This meant that officers and all hands turned out on the main deck, and the band played, and all those who could sing would do so, and by George they were good. I doubt that many professional artistes could have matched them for the songs they sang and the music they played, which was mostly popular airs from the Drury Lane theatre, because when seamen set out to entertain it isn't chanties that they sing, because those are work songs. No, my jolly boys, what Jack Tar wants for entertainment, is ballads and sentimental love songs: that or something patriotic, though aboard *Euphonides* the band was perfectly capable of delivering works by Mozart and Handel.

That afternoon, anchored in Spithead, with fine warm weather and a sunny evening the ship could really excel with its music, and all other ships within hearing, lined their rails and filled their rigging with men to listen in. So I stood with my officers around me, and joined in as need be, and quite a few of the officers stood forward to sing, the last of which was Pyne who had a decent tenor voice and gave *Heart of Oak* to great applause. When Pyne was finished, he turned to me and bowed, and all hands paid close attention.

'Captain,' he said, 'the ship would be honoured to hear you, if you would so graciously condescend as to give us an air?' He was full of applause from his own song, and he still didn't entirely like me, so while he was as respectful and subordinate as could be, I felt that this was his last chance, subtle and covert as it might be, to put Jacky Flash in his place as a lesser man than Captain Sir Edward, who among his other talents had been a fine singer. So I looked round. Hundreds of faces: blue uniforms and scarlet, bandsmen, seamen, boys, and Jimbo the cat. I thought the mood was fair. I'd won over the lower deck by beating Pug, so they were on my side.

'I'll sing happily and with a will, Mr Pyne,' says I, and turned to the bandmaster.

'D'you know *Spanish Ladies?*' says I.

'Aye-aye, Sir,' says the bandmaster, 'And if you would begin, captain, we will match your key and follow.' That was a poser. I'd have to start cold, with no music behind me. Ah well. Ah well. It was better than facing a French broadside. So I lifted up my voice and sang.

What followed was one of the happiest moments, not just of my Service career but of my entire life. It was the closest I ever came to abandoning my desire to give up the sea. It was idyllic. The evening was fine, the ship was lovely, the hands in their hundreds were entranced in the music and they gave the chorus with true voices. Even the men aboard other ships joined in since the song is a superbly fine one much beloved of seamen, because it tells of the sorrows of parting, which are as much part of the sea life as the ocean itself.

I make no boast of my performance, because having a strong deep voice is not something achieved by virtuous effort, but is merely the gift of fate. So I did my best, and supported by the musicians and all hands aboard, the music was wonderful: it was slow, deep and melodious. I hear it in my dreams still now, and those dreams are precious sweet to me, and very dear indeed:

'Farewell and adieu to you fair Spanish ladies.
Farewell and adieu to you ladies of Spain.
For we're under orders to sail to old England,
And we may ne'er see you fair ladies again.'

So that was my entry into the good ship *Euphonides* and I had nearly twenty four hours as the man in sole command until next day, just after noon observation, when a boat came out bearing Mr Philip Charles Rowland, and his luggage and gear, and a bright, grinning, merry young fellow called Kershaw, who was as fit as a poacher's whippet and who, later on, raced the middies up the rigging to the peak of the mainmast. He looked a promising lad, who might well have the makings of a seaman. At least, that was my first impression.

Rowland being Rowland, he had to have best accommodation, which meant my day-cabin, usually reserved as the office for the Captain's business. But there

209

was no arguing with the inevitable, not once we'd had a private meeting in that cabin, and he'd shown me the authority in which he'd come aboard. He was looking his age, and had climbed aboard only with effort. He was fighting for breath and rubbing his left arm. But he ignored over these infirmities of the body and vanquished them with strength of will.

'You will take note of these,' says he, 'Copies of which are in the hands of the Admirals in command of the three squadrons comprising the fleet for the Enterprise of Lyommeville, and likewise in the hands of the senior Land Service officers.'

'Is that what we're to call this business?' says I, 'Enterprise of Lyommeville?'

'Yes,' says he, 'Now take a look at these papers.' So I did, and most extraordinary they were, too: signed and sealed for the Admiralty and the Horseguards, giving Rowland the right to take precedence over all other officers at his discretion. And just to be sure, each document was counter-signed by no less than the Prime Minister himself.

'What's this?' says I, 'Are you to be admiral and general combined?'

'Not at all,' says he, 'I shall leave these technical matters to those better qualified than myself,' he smiled, 'Including you, Captain Fletcher, who'll have no interference from me as regards navigation and command of this ship.'

'Very decent of you,' says I, and he laughed.

'But there may be a need for my authority to be unchallenged, when it comes to the main purpose of this expedition.'

'Hmm,' says I, thinking of what was be done with traitors.

'Indeed,' says he.

So who is this lad Kershaw?' says I.

'He is our expert on steam machines,' says Rowland, 'provided at my request by Mr Watt's Soho Manufactory.'

'What for?' says I.

'So that he might examine any machines made traitorously at the Fragnal Barracks, to seek for any superiority over the equivalents made in England, in order that we might thereby improve our English machines.' Rowland smiled and looked round the cabin with its lavish fittings, because Old Sir Edward might have taken his dining tackles but he'd left all his furniture and ornaments out of love for the ship.

'How do you find your new command, Captain Fletcher?' says Rowland.

'Where's Fragnal Barracks?' says I, with deep suspicion, and Rowland laughed.

'It's where we're going, you and I,' says he, 'And young Mr Kershaw, too.'

And so we did, but not for well over a month while there was the most exasperating business of bringing aboard the landing force for the expedition. First, all five ships: *Proctalymion*, *Thranite*, *Thalamite*, *Zygite* and *Euphonides* suffered butchery at the hands of their carpenters and the dockyard hands, in fitting them out below decks to accommodate a vast load of soldiers, horses and a battery of six-pounder field guns. This load was spread between the five of us, with each ship embarking a share of each branch of arms, in case any ship were lost or strayed, which meant horse-stalls on all our lower decks, and some of our own guns sent ashore to make room, and messes and hammock-space provided for the troops. Worse still was all the damnably complicated business of entering touchy young army officers into a ship's hierarchy, such that Land Service lieutenants should understand that they were outranked by Sea Service lieutenants, which some of the army were too weak-minded to comprehend. Equally abrasive was the fact that there wasn't enough wardroom space for everyone aboard that had a commission, thus some of the redcoat officers must mess elsewhere, accompanied by some of the ship's officers to show goodwill but - fearful horror - perhaps within actual sight of the lower deck hands shoveling down their vittles.

We likewise had to be careful how the lower deck behaved itself, when a rival service come aboard. So, in *Euphonides*, I threatened dire punishment for any man who took such liberties with the soldiers as telling them that the ship's bog houses were to be found up in the maintop.

Then the boats came out in swarms from the shore, with red-coat troops on the thwarts, muskets grounded between their knees, muzzles up, and the horses kicking and screaming as they were swayed aboard in slings, and the field guns easy and neat by comparison, because they made no complaint, and were tiny compared with naval guns. They came up and aboard like feathers, to the sound of boatswain's pipes, and pitying grins on the faces of the men hauling on lines.

'Call that a gun?' says a hand, 'I've one in me britches what's bigger than that!'

But the job was done, and well done, because the Navy had been doing it for hundreds of years and the Navy's tradition knew the way, right down to the heave-ho buckets prominently secured throughout the ships, for the convenience of all the poor, sea-sick landmen and which provided innocent amusement for the ship's people, later on, as the green-faced soldiers lined up for their go and the tars offered helpful encouragement:

'Is that your dinner that's just come up, mate? You don't want to waste it, so if you pick it out of the bucket while it's still warm…you could eat it again.'

None the less, it was a grand sight as the Expedition of Lyommeville finally upped anchor and got underway, on the ebb tied of the morning of Monday September 5th. We went out in our three squadrons with *Euphonides* in line astern of the flagship *Proctalymion* under command of Admiral of the White Lord Oliver, and our comrades *Thranite*, *Thalamite* and *Zygite*, astern of us. The Red Squadron and Blue Squadron followed, under their flagships *Cartagena* and *Pondodrous*.

Our mission was supposed to be profoundly secret, but the redcoats all cheered and waved, the anchored ships manned their yards and cheered, and there was a great flotilla of small boats, with ladies and gentlemen aboard to see the fleet go out: the rich and the poor, the high and the low, and – without my orders I would add – aboard *Euphonides*, our band of musicians mustered on a deck, already heaving with red coats, and the bandmaster saluted and looked to me. All my officers were grinning. Even Pyne was grinning, and the army officers were beaming.

'Go to it, bandmaster!' says I, and they gave it their mightiest: *Rule Britannia*, *Britons Strike Home*, *The British Grenadiers* – this one very popular with the redcoats - and every lively tune from *The Lincolnshire Poacher* the, to *Sweet Lass of Richmond Hill*. As I keep telling you youngsters, this was the Georgian world, not your middle-class world of today, and we followed our hearts and our feelings in those days.

So we went out in splendor, and the wind was as kind as it knew how, which means only moderately malignant, with weak and variable winds, so we got ourselves up Channel and off Lyommeville, after a tedious slow passage, by Wednesday September 7th, where doubtless the Frogs ashore must have seen us with their telescopes. But they were used to the Royal Navy parading offshore, where their own navy was too feeble to stop us. So they doubtless puffed out their cheeks and shrugged and told one another that Monsieur Le Rosbif was up to something, but who knew what?

Well they found out in the dawn of Thursday September 8th. They found out in very deed.

Chapter 32

*'The steam barge is a working reality. It is far more powerful than expected
and we estimate that it could tow a fully rigged ship.'*
(Translated from a letter of Thursday August 23rd 1796, from Citizen
General Claude Bernard, at the Frangnal-sur-Longue Barracks, to Citizen
General of Division Napoleon Bonaparte, Headquarters of the Army of Italy.)

*

This time there were no cheers. The technical problems of adapting a high pressure engine to marine propulsion had been greater than expected. The barge had
sunk three times now, and been hoisted out with capstans, hawsers, and heavy
lifting frames, by the men of the 134th Regiment. Three times it had sunk, and
been lifted out, and repaired and improved and re-floated.

'It's the sealing of the screw shaft,' said Jamie McCloud, to General Bernard,
brought here by the good news, along with Colonel Sauvage and a cavalry
escort. 'It has to pass out through the stern, and be able to rotate smoothly, yet
the bearing must keep out the water. And we had to adapt the piston drive,
to pass at right angles so as to turn the screw shaft, and do all that within the
space available.' He glanced at the barge. 'This is all new, my General. We're
learning by our mistakes, learning as we go.'

Bernard nodded, no longer even noticing that McCloud was giving this
explanation in effortless French.

'But the job is done,' said Bernard. 'You have made it work, haven't you?
That's what I was told.' Sauvage and the cavalrymen looked on expectantly.

'Oh yes,' said McCloud, 'And it's under steam, ready to show you what it
can do.' Bernard smiled. He sniffed the now-familiar scent: steam, coal, smoke
and oil. He looked at the barge. It was big and broad, nearly filling the wide

canal that ran from here at Fragnal de Picardy, all the way to Lyommeville and La Manche.

The barge reminded Bernard of a Noah's Ark, but with the deck house partly open, to let out a big funnel and some of the fierce heat from the machine within. The barge crew – all French – stood in oil-stained, coal-streaked overalls, bare-chested and sweating on a summer's day with a live furnace making even more heat. Some were wiping their hands on scraps of rag. Bernard smiled. They were always doing that, these steam engineers: always wiping their hands. Meanwhile the steam engineers looked back at Bernard. He thought they seemed confidant, though not cheerful. There had been too many false starts, and last time the barge sank, it drowned a poor devil who caught his foot in the engine compartment, and didn't get out fast enough, which probably wouldn't have happened on a normal canal because it was too shallow. But this canal was nearly twice the depth of a normal canal. It had to be, because the steam barges had to have proper keels, not flat bottoms like canal boats: not if they were to work on the open sea.

Bernard shook his head at the thought of the drowned man, horribly gripped by scalding iron and brass as the water rushed in and filled his lungs. Then he noticed something new.

'What's that?' said he, 'Have you given it a name?'

'Her,' said McCloud, 'She, my General,' and at last the English-Scottish and the barge-crew smiled. Bernard read out the name at the stern in gold lettering on a neat white plank.

'*Michelle Justine*,' he said, and turned to McCloud, 'Would that be Michelle Justine McCloud? Madame McCloud?'

'Yes, my General. Michelle Justine is my wife,' said McCloud.

'So,' said Bernard, 'Let's see what Madame Michelle can do,' and he looked to the stern of the steam barge, where a line of normal canal boats was waiting, all grimy and dark, and their draft horses standing by idle, with lads patting their heads in reassurance that today they would not need to haul any loads. That's what these boys had been told, but they didn't really believe it.

Aboard the barges, each crew gazed in superstitious ignorance at the steam barge, wondering why they'd been brought here, in this outlandish, unheard-of concentration of so many barges all together, and taken away from their normal occupations. But Bernard knew why they were here. He knew that it was the will of Bonaparte that they should be here, and that no expense was too much to bring them here, each one laden with some thirty tons of stone ballast, to give something for the steam barge to strain against, and to show what sort of a load it could pull.

'Make fast the tow line,' cried Jamie McCloud to the steam barge crew.

'Yes, Monsieur the Chief!' said the crew.

'We'll start with just one barge, and work up from that.'

'Yes, Chief!'

'Take it slow and steady as the load comes on, then give full power.'

'Yes Chief!'

The steam barge drew just one so easily that McCloud brought up another and another until the steam barge was hauling a load of five, starting them from full stop, and moving down the canal at a speed too fast for a man to keep up while walking, and the steam barge easily capable of pulling even greater loads. By then, there was some cheering, and some utter, dumbfounded amazement on all sides.

Bernard spoke quietly to Sauvage.

'That's a hundred and fifty tons,' he said.

'Yes,' said Sauvage, and a thousand troops with all their campaign gear weigh under eighty tons.'

'I know,' said Bernard, 'So just one of those,' he looked at the steam barge, 'could pull a string of invasion barges, with thousands of men.'

'We won't even need very many of them,' said Sauvage, 'A dozen? Twenty? Fifty?'

'Maybe more on the open sea,' said Bernard, 'It won't be so smooth as this canal.'

'Yes, but it can be done. We really could do it. Wait for a day with no wind, when the English navy can't sail, and it could be done We could tow an invasion force across La Manche and conquer England!'

Chapter 33

The slow passage from Portsmouth to Lyommeville, at least gave Admiral Lord Oliver the chance to bring his commanders aboard the flagship for final discussions of our plan of attack. *Proctalmiyon*, being Dutch built and shallow draft was a heavy roller, and the day was warm so it was far from a comfortable meeting when so many officers of the two services got crammed into the flagship's stern cabin, and large, coloured diagrams were laid out before us, like those used at our first meeting in the riding school at Portsmouth.

Rowland was there, too. He sat behind the big table with Oliver and the other two flag officers, plus a General of Brigade, and some colonels. He was accepted as an equal by Oliver and the rest, just as he'd been when first I met him at my examination for lieutenant, which seemed so long ago.

'Now, gentlemen,' says Oliver,' coming to the important business, 'Lyommeville is protected by guns in the twelve bastions of the fortress of St Germaine.' He pointed a crooked old finger, at a big map on the table, and we all strained to make sense of his crooked old voice. 'So it's ruin to any ship that sails straight into the harbour.'

The sea officers nodded wisely. Wooden warships didn't like forts, because forts were almost immune to shot while ships were not. Also, forts didn't pitch and roll so their fire was accurate, and forts were usually high above the sea, giving their guns greater range. So if dire need compelled a ship to fight a fort, then the best the ship could do was hope the smoke of her guns would hide her, and that a few lucky shots would enter the fort's embrasures to hit the guns behind. But that was Tom-fool dreamery, and it was an accepted fact that five heavy guns in a fort would defeat the hundred guns of a first rate line-of-battle ship.

'But, see here,' says Oliver, and we all leaned forward, including those at the back who hadn't a chance of seeing what was on the table, 'the sweep of the batteries is limited by this headland, to the south of the Lyommville, and beyond the headland there are open beaches upon which we shall make our landing, out of reach and sight of the enemy's guns.' Everyone nodded. 'It will mean a march of three miles for our landing party,' says he, 'from the landing site…here,' he stabbed at the map, 'to come round the headland and into the town…here.' he stabbed again. 'The march to be undertaken at night, such that our force – which in daylight would be in plain sight of the batteries once round the headland – will not be seen and shall capture the town at a stroke!' There was a growl of enthusiasm, and the military men all smiled. Meanwhile, Oliver continued. 'I now invite Mr Rowland to confide details of how the fortress may be entered and taken, to prevent it's being able – thereafter – to interfere in any way with our plans.'

'Thank you, my Lord,' says Rowland, 'and with your permission, I will address myself especially to the Royal Engineers among us.' All the engineers sat up straight. 'I know that you engineering gentlemen have prepared charges for the destruction of the canal locks, and also for fortress gates.'

'We have indeed, Sir,' says the senior engineer, 'as previously agreed.'

'Quite so,' says Rowland, 'and if you would now consult the diagrams concerned,' there was a rustle of paper as the engineer officers flattened papers on their knees. 'The fort has twelve bastions,' says Rowland.

'Hmm,' from the engineers.

'Counting from east to west: bastions number three, five and eight, have gates approached by draw-bridges, across a dry earth moat.'

'Hmm.'

'You must ignore bastions three and eight!' says Rowland, with strict emphasis. 'These have strong, new-built gates, with a second set, equally strong, behind them. Also, the space between the gates is roofed over and provided with murder holes in the ceiling – ancient works but still deadly – enabling the garrison to drop grenades among our men if they are delayed there.'

'Hmm.'

'But Monsieur the enemy has been lazy with regard to bastion five,' says Rowland

'Ahhh!'

'The outer gate of bastion five is old and rotten, and can easily be blown in by a demolition charge, while the inner gates are gone completely, enabling our light companies to effect swift entry, to overwhelm the garrison – which is not large – and spike the guns.'

'Huzza!'

'Mr Rowland?' says the senior engineer.

'Sir?' says Rowland.

'What about the draw-bridge? Does not bastion five have a draw-bridge?' Rowland smiled.

'It does, Sir, but the lifting mechanism is rusted and jammed such that it cannot be raised.'

'Ahhh!' says everyone. But the senior engineer wasn't done.

'I have two further questions, Mr Rowland.'

'Ask, Sir!'

'First: why is the enemy so ill-prepared, with his jammed mechanisms and rotted gates? And second: how have you, Mr Rowland, come by so detailed an account of these matters?' That brought considerable muttering and nodding of heads.

'As regards the enemy being ill-prepared,' says Rowland, 'the French are ill-prepared because they do not even dream of a landing by our forces. And that is obvious because if they feared an attack on their priceless and wonderful canal locks, they'd place an army of ten thousand in Lyommeville, to make an attack impossible. As it is, the total French garrison of Lyommeville is less than two hundred men.'

'Ahhh!' says everyone.

'But how do you know all this?' says the senior engineer. Rowland looked at Lord Oliver and said nothing. Oliver sniffed as if at some odd smell, and looked at the admirals and army officers beside him. They reacted much the same, mostly frowning as they did so.

'Huh!' says Oliver, and turned back to the rest of us. 'Gentlemen,' says he, 'I must remind you that Mr Rowland has the confidence of the highest in England. I must also remind you that we may not enquire as to his sources.'

'But, my Lord,' says the engineer officer, 'I ask because I must send men, at night and in the dark, with explosive charges in hand for the demolition of the enemy's gates, and with two hundred men of the Guards, close behind, ready to advance at the double...,'

'Enough, Sir!' cried Olivier, as best he could with his feeble voice.

'Enough!' says the admirals and the Brigadier.

'...advance at the double through the smoke of our explosion,' says the engineer, 'such that any failure or betrayal, would place us under the enemy's guns and a devastating blast of cannister shot!' This brought on another very loud, and very Georgian, argument, with pointing and shouting and sweating – it being sickening hot in the great cabin. But Oliver had his way in the end, and Rowland kept mum. You could see that nobody liked Rowland, especially among the soldiers. I didn't like him either, and for the same reason which was the fact that my life - like theirs - would depend on the accuracy of the information Rowland had swept in from his network of spies, paid informers, and two-faced royalist Frogs who couldn't make up their minds which side to be on.

In the end, we all had to take Rowland on trust, and Oliver served up a very poor dinner for the most senior of us, and hardly anyone ate it because of the ship's sickly motion. Then it was back to our various ships, and by George was I glad to stand on a deck that didn't roll the milk out of tea. After that, in all the ships of the White Squadron, there was much to do and much to worry about, and it was pure relief when we put the soldiers ashore that night, because never had I been so awestruck at what the Navy could do when it set its mind to it, and I stress that none of this tremendous task was of my doing, since it'd been planned and tested off Sheerness for weeks before I came aboard.

So: first imagine yourself in a ship on a moonless night, hove to and with topsails backed. The ship heaves and breathes. She rises and falls. She creaks and groans. The sea splashes and patters against the hull. The decks are full of all the usual gear, so arcane and obscure to landmen: guns, capstans, binnacles, pin rails and hatch coamings. As you look up, you can just see the yards and rigging, black against the stars and sky. Now the matelots go smartly about their duties slipping through ranks of poor bloody infantry burdened with all their impedimenta: knapsacks, canteens, cartridge pouches, bayonets and Brown Bess muskets on slings. And then there's horses – anxious and afraid – being comforted by their riders – and field guns and carriages, and hand-carts for the engineers to carry their explosives, and redcoat officers with plumed hats, swords, and glittering epaulettes. There is, altogether, such a jam of men and gear that no landman could believe that any job of work whatsoever, could be done.

But up goes a boat, hoist by the seamen! Up it goes and out and over the side, and the boat's crew scrambling easy and barefoot, down by the main chains and into the boat, and oars tossed and all made ready. Then the soldiers in their hobnailed boots and heavy kit, are going nervously down into the boat, by scrambling netting, and their sergeants cussing and blinding to keep them going. But the cussing is soft and low because every soul aboard – including even Jimbo the cat – has been threatened with flogging if they make any noise.

'Give way!' says the coxwain. Oars dip, and the first boat is gone on a black sea and a velvet night, and on the instant the next boat is ready. This time it's a nag that goes over the side in a sling, cinched and buckled into its saddle and gear, and its rider begging the tars to be gentle. Then more horses, and that boat gone as well. Then it's a six-pounder gun with shot, cartridges, rammers, sponges, buckets and tools.

And all this repeated on five ships: *Proctalymion, Thranite, Thalamite, Zygite,* and *Euphonides* until an entire flotilla of longboats, launches and cutters is pulling for the shore in the darkness, visible only by the white foam of the oar-strokes and bow waves, and the starlight reflecting off the wet oar shafts.

On the beach it was the army's turn to show what they could do, and even I will admit that they did it well. I know because I was there to see boats grinding into the sand, seamen leaping forward to haul them safe out of the waves, soldiers lumbering out, splashing knee-deep through the water with muskets held muzzle-down to keep the flintlocks dry. Every man moved to a purpose, with no confusion nor milling about, because an advance guard had gone ashore first: picked men who took up their positions with white flags and lanterns, and the flags numbered to show the different units where to form up, which they did, and with credit, and in profound silence.

But the thing to remember before all else, my jolly boys, is that the Navy put ashore over a thousand men, two hundred and fifty horses and five six-pounder field guns complete with caissons, limbers and carriages, plus the engineers' hand carts, and did all this off a hostile shore, in the dead of night...without losing a single man or so much as a fingernail broken! And yet folk still ask how it was the Navy always beat the Frogs and every other nation who dared oppose us. How did we do it indeed? We did it because that's what the Navy did!

So there we were, formed up on the beach, with the Sea Service saluting the Land Service before stepping back into its boats, and pulling for the squadron, and there was myself standing among the redcoat clump of officers who were now in full command, because I'd bad farewell to Pyne and the rest on *Euphonides's* quarterdeck, just fifteen minutes earlier, noting the extreme anxiety on Pyne's face as I shook his hand.

'Do take care, Captain,' says he, which did not at all mean that he worried about me personally, but that he worried about the traditions of the Service, which insisted that no captain ever went ashore at such times. Rather he should send one of his officers instead, because the Captain's duty was to his ship before all else. But I shook Pyne's hand, at which the other lieutenants came forward wanting to do the same. I must admit I was a little touched, and even more so when the Boatswain came forward.

'Beggin' your pardon, Cap'n Sir,' says he, saluting, 'but on behalf o' the hands,

Sir, they want you to know that we'd give three cheers, right full and hearty, and we'd pipe the side as you go, only we're ordered silent.'

'Aye!' says a deep murmuring from the shadows.

Now, on the beach, the officer commanding the raid was speaking. He was Brigadier General Sir David Lavery, a baronet whose family owned much of Berkshire. His regimental commissions had all been obtained by purchase, but he was a good soldier who knew his work.

'Gentlemen,' says he, 'you will now by set your watches to…,' he held his own watch to a lantern, '…ten minutes past the hour of one, ante-meridian, of this Thursday 8th of September.' There was a stirring and fumbling with watches. 'And now,' says Sir David, 'to your duties! But remember that the Navy will stand offshore, waiting to embark us aboard their ships, until noon on Monday September 12th. Remember that! Noon of September 12th, because we must assume that by then, the French will have discovered us and sent powerful land forces against us.' The plumed hats nodded. 'Mr Rowland?' says Sir David, 'It is particularly for you and your Flying Column that we shall hold the beach. Our destruction of the canal locks cannot take more than a day, but we are aware of …,' he sought the right word, '… the importance of your work,' says he, with a strong hint of disapproval. 'The importance of your work, which will take some days.'

'I am obliged, Sir,' says Rowland

'Quite,' says Sir David, 'But know that once the canal locks are destroyed, the Navy will take off all forces except the light company of the Coldstream Guards, and a battery of six pounder guns, which will secure the beach within entrenchments, awaiting your return until …,'

'Noon on Tuesday, September 12th,' says Rowland.

'Quite,' says Sir David. 'Meanwhile your flying column, Mr Rowland, shall follow close behind our foot, into the town, and you may proceed about your responsibilities, as soon at the way through the town is secured.'

'Again, I am obliged, Sir,' says Rowland. 'Then have I your permission to mount up and stand ready?'

'You have, Mr Rowland!' Sir David peered among the officers around him, 'Captain Brady?' says he, 'are you there?'

'Here, Sir!' says an officer in a fur-crested Tarleton helmet. He was in command of a troop of the 27th Light Dragoons. Captain Vasily Brady his name was, because his daddy, Sir Edwin Brady, was an English diplomat, but his mother was Russian. She was a great beauty and a Countess; a lady I got to know most exceedingly well in later years, though of course I didn't know her then. Young Vasily looked just like her, and was very handsome in a pretty-face sort of way. He was a man I didn't quite admire. He was certainly brave, and certainly a competent officer – at least when he had a good sergeant major to provide the depth of technical knowledge that he lacked. But he was too much the sauntering, theatrical cavalryman, dressed up exquisite to please the ladies, and he was religious too – which I am not – brought up in his mother's Russian Church. He even kept a saint's fingertip in a locket round his neck, that the countess said he must wear for the good of his soul.

So this was the gallant creature that stood forward at Sir David's command, and Sir David eyed him over, perhaps thinking the same as me.

'Get your men mounted, and consider yourself under the orders of Mr Rowland,' says Sir David.

'Yes, Sir!' says Vasily, saluting.

Then there was a lot of bustling about, with me and Kershaw following Rowland, to where the horses were held: you could smell them before you saw them as you fumbled forward through the dark ranks of men. A dark-shadowed dragoon trooper led us to them.

'This'n's your'n, Mr Rowland, Sir,' says he, 'and this'n's your'n, Cap'n Fletcher, and this'n's for Mr Kershaw.'

It was all very efficient because I later found that my horse's saddle bags had my own travel things packed, and my Nock pistols were in the saddle holsters. So I was very well armed since there was a carbine too, in a scabbard by my right knee, and I was wearing my Tatham sword. Better still, being inside the blue cloth of the King's uniform, I was safe from any charge of espionage. But Kershaw was in civilian dress like Rowland, which I shrugged off as being his trouble, not mine, because I wasn't too sure of Kershaw by then. Payne had berthed him among the mids for want of where else to put him, and he'd blacked a few eyes in fights; common enough when young gentlemen sort out whose arm cracks the walnuts, and some of the mids were bigger than him. But ship's gossip was that he'd caused the fights and was far too cocksure for a landman who wasn't even on the ship's books.

And so, with much reluctance, I clambered aboard a horse, which isn't and never will be my choice of transport, since the beast often desires to set his own course which seldom agrees with mine, and he's displeased with me in the first place since I'm such a load to carry. Worse still, I never have mastered the art of rising *to* the trot – if that's what they call it – and as for jumping, I'd rather

222

jump from the main truck in winter. The plain fact is that I don't like horses and they don't like me, and these days my preferred means of land travel is a Pullman's railway dining car with female company on either side of me and a decent dinner in front of me.

But that particular choice wasn't available on that particular night of September 8th 1796. Not on an open beach in Revolutionary France, and neither was there any choice of avoiding what happened when finally we did come alongside of the traitors of the Fragnal Barracks.

Chapter 34

'Pay no attention to her mad delusions! They are entirely harmless, entirely fictitious, and cannot have caused her to take any actions that would be harmful to France.'

(Translated from an undated letter believed to have been written by Colonel Antoine Sauvage, and sent to Dr Raoul Charles of the Hôpital des Invalides de Frangnal-en-bas, though the letter is signed only by 'A' and addressed only to 'R' without any other detail.)

*

General Bernard looked at the woman stood bolt upright and shouting, between two men of the 134th, in his office. He wished she would stop shouting, because his head ached.

The women was over seventy, but plump and very pretty, with a smooth face and big eyes. She was immaculately dressed in female military uniform: white apron and blue skirt under an army coat with the same insignia as those of the 134th Regiment, but all tailored and neat and fitting, and the red feather in her hat was bright and bold.

She was Madelaine la Cantinière: Old Madelaine, Mamma Madelaine, the regimental sutler who'd served drinks and dinners in the army canteens since time began – or so it seemed – because a Cantinière was no mere camp follower but a full and proper part of the army. She was respected as such, dressed as such and – in the Case of Mamma Madelaine – loved as such. She'd been known to generations of soldiers, who'd come to her with their troubles and tears, and she'd listened and smiled, and sometimes done very much more, and they'd always gone away happy because she was a woman who appealed to men.

Bernard thought deeper. Madelaine had been in the army since the dark ages; the ages before the Light of the Revolution shone down upon men: the supposed dark ages and the supposed Light of the Revolution. That bright and shining light that justified a thousand strokes of the guillotine each day, if that's what it took to sustain the light.

Bernard looked round the room. Mamma Madelaine was still shouting treason for all to hear, even though everyone tried to look away and not hear. There was a captain, a lieutenant, a sergeant and two soldiers, not to mention Colonel Sauvage and the two clerks who always worked in Bernard's office: them and everyone outside the office who could hear what Mamma Martine was saying, and every single one of these profoundly embarrassed men was looking to Bernard, for some way out of this.

'Holy Mother of God,' he said in despair. He looked at the captain, who was so young, because they were all so young these days. 'Are you sure?' said Bernard.

'Yes, my General,' said the captain. 'We searched her quarters and found a forbidden altar – a religious altar – and some prints of the man Louis Bourbon …who …who was…,' the captain hesitated.

'Go on!' said Bernard, 'Say it! The King!' The Captain's eyes gaped at these poisonously dangerous words.

'Yes, my General,' he said, 'The king. Him and his wife, the queen.'

'Saints and angels!' said Bernard, 'Get on with it! What else?'

'A letter, my General. I have it here.' The captain stepped past Mamma Madelaine and her two guards, and put the letter on Bernard's desk. Bernard and Sauvage looked at it. They read it in silence. Mamma Madelaine might have been mad, but the letter was written in a bold, clear hand, giving precise details of work on the steam barge, and of the numbers of men, women, engineers and soldiers present at the Fragnal Barracks.

The Captain waited politely until Bernard and Sauvage finished reading and looked up at him again. 'It's proof, my General,' he said. 'It's proof that she's a spy.'

'Not a spy!' said Madelaine, 'A patriot!' and she wriggled free of the young soldiers who hadn't the heart to grip her arms too hard. She pushed forward and spouted words into Bernard's face, along with a waft of perfume and fine soap: the familiar scent of Mamma Madelaine. 'God save the King!' she cried, 'God save and keep the King. I served him once, I serve him now, and I will never, ever change! I don't care if you cut off my head and put it on a stick, because my King's allies will soon be here to avenge me, and you'll all be very sorry!'

She ranted on. There was more. There was very much more. There was not the slightest doubt that Madelaine La Cantinière was a royalist counter-revolutionary of the very worst kind: the kind that kept secret and worked against The Enlightenment.

'Oh God, save us all!' said Bernard, 'Shut up, woman. Shut up and let me think.'

'Why?' she yelled. 'You've found me out and I'm going to die, so I don't have to be quiet any more! And I don't care because God will roast you all in Hell, and I will go to heaven with my King!'

'Oh, take her away,' said Bernard to the captain, 'Find her a clean cell in the defaulter's block and lock her in,' he waved a hand. 'Make sure she's got food and drink and whatever else she needs. See that you make her comfortable.'

'Of course, my General!' said the young captain. 'Of course we'll make her comfortable,' and his men scowled at the very suggestion that they'd do anything else! Thus Mamma Martine was dragged out with much more yelling and screaming from her, and pleading from the soldiers that she might come quietly, as Bernard turned on the two clerks.

'And you can get out as well,' he said, 'and close that damned door behind you!' he looked at Sauvage, 'Holy Mary!' he said, 'there's a bottle of cognac in the cupboard over there,' he pointed. 'For God's sake get it out and a couple of glasses!'

Bernard and Sauvage sat quietly down with the cognac. The life of the Barracks went past the windows and the sounds of men and beasts came faintly inside. Neither man said anything for a while. Then Bernard spoke.

'D'you think there's any real harm in her?' he said.

'No!' said Sauvage.

'What about this chain of letters she talks about?'

'Fantasy,' said Sauvage, 'Can't be real. D'you really think that she can pass a letter to one man, who passes it to another and another, and it ends up with the smugglers and gets to England?'

'It's fantasy,' said Bernard, 'And even if her letters did get to England, who'd believe them? Who'd take any notice?' Sauvage nodded.

'Are we to suppose.' said Bernard, 'that there is some master spy who reads what she says, and then reports to their head of government? What's his name? What do they call him in England?'

'Pitt, their Prime Minister.'

'Anyway,' said Bernard, 'What if the English really did know all about our steam boats here at Fragnal, what could they do about it? We're deep inside France. We're a hundred kilometres from the coast. What will the Rosbifs do?' he grinned, 'send their navy up the canal?' Sauvage smiled.

226

'The idea's mad,' he said, 'and she's mad, or she'd never have boasted about what she was doing and got found out.'

'Yes,' said Bernard, 'she's mad,' he reached for the bottle. 'Another?' he said. But Sauvage was staring into the misty distance. Then he thumped the table, and turned to Bernard.

'I know what we can do,' he said. 'I've got an old friend from the days when we were boys in our village. We used to hunt rabbits and make camp in the woods. His name is Charles Raoul. He's Doctor Raoul now, and he has a hospital that takes in mad people. It's his life's work,' Sauvage gave a little shrug, 'and he's even a bit mad himself! But he's a good man,' Sauvage lowered his voice, 'he's a good catholic. He's a true Christian.' He nodded, then spoke normally. 'He doesn't put the loonies in chains or beat them. He's kind, and if I asked him, I think he'd take Mamma Martine, and then we wouldn't have to report her, because if we did…,'

'It'd be the guillotine!' said Bernard.

'And we don't want that!'

'So we'll tell the men she's mad and they'll believe it.'

'Because nobody wants Mamma Martine under the guillotine!'

'So will you write to your friend the Doctor?'

'Straight away,' said Sauvage.

'Then the job's done!' said Bernard. He poured two more large measures, and shook his head, 'Poor old soul. How could a woman like that send letters to England?'

'How indeed?' said Sauvage.

'Pah!' said Bernard.

227

Chapter 35

Half an hour after Sir David's words on the beach, Rowland and I were aboard of our horses in station behind Captain Vasily Brady and his officers, with Kershaw astern of us, and the dark, French night glowing in flashes of musketry up ahead. The firing echoed all around us, and a great confusion of cries and shouting arose as the French realised that they were under attack.

'Boooom!' went a heavy explosion.

'Ah!' says Rowland, 'I hope that was the gates of bastion number five.' He looked at me, and I think he smiled, though it was too dark to tell. We were well around the headland that hid the beaches from the French guns, and all of us were staring at the twin towns of Abbeyvaux and St Germaine ahead, that together made up Lyommeville. It was all black, black, apart from the musket flashes. It was black, but with twinklings of light appearing, because the towns that had been sleeping were now woken up. Apart from that you could see stars, the gleam of the river Lyomme, the gleam of the sea, and earlier we'd seen and heard the crunch-crunch-crunch of light infantry going past us at the double: hundreds and hundreds of them, with the officers clutching their sword-scabbards as they ran, and the sergeants chanting:

'Lef' *right* lef'! Lef' *right* lef'!'

It was desperate thrilling stuff to see those elite men go forward, with the engineers ahead of them, hauling their hand-carts laden with powder charges, and now there were British cheers coming out of the dark, and an intensified crackle of musketry in the night, and an alarm bell ringing somewhere, and then French yelling, and it all seemed confusion and lurid powder flashes in the narrow streets of these ancient towns, and lanterns and shadows and women crying, and children too. We could see nothing clearly and had no idea what was going on, and could only hope that the soldiers did know. Then there were more heavy explosions and the ground trembled and the echoes leapt, and there was even more cheering, and if that weren't enough, out from the sea to the north and south, came further detonations: this time not rumbling demolition charges but the flat, reverberating thud of naval gunfire.

'Ah!' says I, because that was familiar sound, 'that'll be our bomb ketches commencing fire on Calais and Boulogne,' which indeed it was, because long seconds after – as the thirteen-inch projectiles arched high up and plunged down on their mile-long flight with fuses burning – long seconds after, there came the entirely-different sound of the shells bursting.

'Aren't they a bit early?' says Rowland.

'No,' says I, looking to the first, pink light in the sky. 'Orders were to open fire at dawn, and our ships certainly wouldn't fire until then.'

'Why not?' says he.

'Well,' says I, 'the shore is to the east, and our gunners would want the dawn light behind the target, so they can see it against the glow. Otherwise they'd be firing into the dark and wasting shot.'

'Thank you, Captain Fletcher,' says Rowland. 'I defer to your greater knowledge of these maritime affairs.' He really was a most sarcastic sod. I'd liked him once, but not now. 'In whatsoever case,' says he, 'let's hope their fire deceives the French such that they do not notice our actions here.' Fortunately, his wish was granted. It was granted because our plan worked beautifully, with the steady fire of the Red and Blue squadrons keeping the enemy's mind well away from the White Squadron. By later accounts, once the sun was fully up, the ingenious French telegraph system was alive with messages to Paris: messages which entirely concerned Calais and Boulogne, and not one word about Lyommeville. But nothing is perfect in this wicked world, and we were delayed until late in the morning by the only stumble in the whole affair.

This was stubborn resistance by the few French troops in Lyommeville, or rather in the newer, lower town of Abbeyvaux where the blighters got themselves behind the thick walls of the one really old, really strong building in the town. In ages past, it had been a place of refuge complete with loopholes for musketry and battlements on top, but was now conscripted into service as the Town Hall, which the Frogs most strangely call the Mary.

[The word is of course la Mairie, but nothing could persuade Fletcher to set down French in any other way than the dismissively phonetic. All corrective advice was met with intemperate abuse. S.P.]

The new town was laid out in typical Frog fashion, in a boring and supposedly logical grid pattern with the Mary in the centre commanding a view up all the main avenues. So the Frogs could now direct musketry from safe inside, at anything attempting to pass, which they did with energy once there was daylight. So there they sat until our horse artillery brought up four pieces, and blew in the Mary's doors, and plastered the loopholes and battlements with canister so that eventually the tricolour came down and the white flag went up. But they didn't give up until every man of the little garrison was killed or wounded, which took a whole morning's fire from the six-pounders. In the end, our gunners were so impressed that they offered the Frogs the Honours of War, meaning that they could march out with colours flying, but none of them could get up on his feet to march, being wounded, which I suppose is to their credit, even if they were Frenchmen.

Finally though, our Flying Column was given leave to pass, clip-clopping through the lower town, with the iron tyres of our guns and carriages, rumbling on the stone sets, then up the sloping road that led to the inland canal. The town was full of people, mainly clumped in families, with the men scowling and the women clutching their children and most of them waving their fists and cursing us. But we got a fine big cheer from the redcoats now occupying the twelve bastions of the old castle, and we were thankful to see them there, because as we looked up at the ancient grey walls we realised how totally vulnerable we would have been to the guns now looking down on us, with spiked touch-holes and totally silent.

So up we went, a troop of dragoons clattering and jingling and two six-pounder guns, each with six horses and associated gear. It was a fine force for a quick dash in and out of the enemy's territory, and there were about one hundred and fifty of us all told. Our troop of the 27th Light Dragoons was as follows: one captain – Vasily – two lieutenants, one cornet, one sergeant-major, one farrier, four sergeants, four corporals, one trumpeter and eight-five men. The gunners and their gear made up the rest: together with carters, in light wagons bearing special food for the horses: oats or some other grain I suppose, not that I bothered to look.

But I did have a very good look at Lyommeville and the astonishing works the French had built with their great staircase of eleven locks that could lift boats up and down the three hundred feet, between the waters of the harbour and the inland canal. I had a good look, and we all did, because the road that wound uphill beside the locks gave the most wonderful view. It really did look like a flight of enormous, shining steps marked out at each end by massive lock gates, and jutting, oak beams to lever the gates open and shut. It was all bright and clear in the September light, and as we climbed the hillside, all of us looking down on the busy ants that were our engineers, planting the first of their charges: those that that would blow out the lowermost pair of gates.

Down there, all was shouting and protesting from a crowd of French civilians and some officials – Frenchmen – in dark uniform waving their arms, and our troops shoving everyone back with musket butts. Then one of our men was stripped off to his drawers and plunging into the lowermost lock.

'See that?' says I. 'What's that fellow doing?'

'He's placing the first charge, Captain Fletcher,' says Rowland.

'Is he now?' says I.

'Yes,' says Rowland. 'The matter has been explained to me, and it seems that the best and most destructive plan, is to place the charge hard up against the closed lock gates, on the inside – that is the high-water side and actually under water if possible, which means enclosing the charge in a waterproof cask, with some means of fixation – perhaps spikes – to be driven into the gates by a man who is himself more under water than swimming upon it.'

'I see,' says I, thinking of certain past adventures, and Rowland laughed.

'I should've thought you'd have understood these matters, Captain Fletcher,' says he, 'as the submarine navigator who sank a British ship in Boston harbour last year?' I said nothing. 'And wasn't that done with gunpowder?' I still said nothing. It's all in my earlier memoirs if you youngsters want to read it, but in that moment I wanted the matter forgotten. Then he changed the subject anyway. 'Ah!' says he, 'And now the fellow is climbing out by rope ladder, and they are igniting the fuse.'

Which indeed they were, with our redcoats shoving everyone back double quick, to even more yelling and arm waving from the French, and all along the hillside our mounted column slowing, because all hands wanted to see the fireworks, and it was some show when it came. First the dazzling flash and the bulging, fat cloud of white smoke. Then seconds after – for us on the hillside – the huge roar of a ninety-pound powder cask exploding. It couldn't have been less, and by George it was some wallop of a bang. Tons of water heaved into the air together with tumbling shards of gate, and much of the stonework that had been the canal banks. Down by the harbour, men who'd fancied themselves safely clear were thrown over, shoved flat by the blast, while stones, earth, spray and splinters were coming down on all sides, and I'll tell you what a force was let loose, because bits and pieces pattered down on the road around our horses, even though we were hundreds of yards away from the lock gates, and at least a hundred and fifty feet above it.

Then, when the smoke cleared, there was ruin and desolation where the beautiful lock-gates had been. Our engineers hadn't just blown up the gates and let loose the waters; they'd gouged a massive, jagged crater where the gates had been, and comprehensively smashed the canal banks, because that was their entire purpose. There was no point to our expedition if we did some piddling little damage the Frogs could repair in five minutes. Thus comprehensive destruction made good sense. But I took no pleasure in watching the proceedings because it was dismal to see such noble engineering reduced to wreckage. It was horribly like the moment when a ship goes down: a tragic and appalling sight which no seaman ever wants to see, not even if it's the enemy's ship.

So I was not in merry mood when our column got itself up into the high land above the town, and set off inland down the fine military road that the Frogs had built beside their fine canal. As for the engineers in Lyommeville, they got on with their works, and every so often – I'd guess it was about once or twice an hour – the thunder of their explosions came to us ever more faintly with us getting further away, as they worked their way up the staircase, blowing out another and another gate. But we saw none of that. We saw only the blue skies and the green fields and the little birds and bees of rural France, which was like England and yet not like England. The hedges and trees were different. Don't ask how because I'm not a farmer. They were just different.

And so to the march inland, because march is what the Army calls an advance even by mounted men, and in the unlikely event that there is any further need for me to warn you youngsters off a career in the Army, then pay attention now because an advance by cavalry isn't what it's supposed to be. I would ask you first to consider that wonderful piece of music called *The Light Cavalry Overture* which captures the entire spirit of what a cavalry advance should be. It goes:

Diddy-dum,*diddy-dum!*
Diddy-dum, diddy-dum!
Diddy-dum, diddy diddly-ah dah!

It rouses you out of your chair, and makes you grin, and it is precisely the sort of music that I like and it's by some German called Soup.

[In fact, Herr Franz von Suppe who is Austrian. S.P.]

So there you have it. The spirit of that music says that a cavalry advance should go forward at a rollicking canter, with wind in the hair, plumes tossing, swift speed and devil take the hindmost. But does it? Does it bloody damned hell! What a fraud. What a disappointment. They don't even ride all of the time but stop every fifteen minutes, for all hands to get off and walk to spare the horses, and then get back on again fifteen minutes later. And then everyone stops entirely for ten minutes out of every hour for the beasts to rest. And then the horses have got to have hours out of the day to forage and eat bloody grass, or get stuffed with oats from nose bags. And then they've got to be watered, and you mustn't let them gorge themselves. And then the Farrier has to examine them all for saddle sores. A man on his own two feet could go faster. Look at that Greek that ran from Marathon to Athens. He covered twenty six miles in no time at all.

Mind you, all that care and attention for the horses is what was supposed to happen, and I learned it because this time it wasn't actually done. I learned the art and mystery of cavalry movements from a discussion held during the first of our ten minute, hourly stops. Rowland beckoned me to join him, with Vasily Brady and his officers by the roadside, while the men were looking to the mounts, and generally chatting and gazing at the Froggy countryside. We officers stood in a little circle and discussed something that I didn't like, despite my views on riding horses.

'Captain Brady,' says Rowland, 'We have sixty miles to cover to reach our destination and sixty miles to get back to the beaches.' Everyone nodded. 'So,' says Rowland, 'Will you explain how these distances can be covered and our mission accomplished, all within three days?' Brady smiled. Rowland smiled. Then Rowland winked at me and I could see that Brady had been got at. Rowland had got at him.

'Certainly, Mr Rowland,' says Vasily, and gave a graceful little bow to his officers. 'We shall proceed at utmost pace, without regard to previous precedent, and will aim to reach our destination by midnight tonight.' That brought on a frantic, anguished discussion when all the details came out of how a troop ought to advance so that its mounts were fit for action at the end of the march, and everyone spoke at once, and the men standing by their horses, all turned to see and to listen, and didn't like one word of what they heard.

'Can't be done, Sir!' says one officer.

'We'll rub sores into the horses backs!' says another.

'Half of 'em will fall lame!'

'They're still weak from the sea-crossing!'

Brady nodded, smiled, and raised his hand. The rest fell silent.

'Gentlemen,' says he, 'There will be no cavalry action when we reach Fragnal. We shall dismount and fight on foot.'

233

'Oh?' says everyone.

'How do we know the enemy has no cavalry?' says one voice, and everyone nodded.

'Mr Rowland assures me,' says Brady, 'that the enemy's total strength is less than sixty men, all infantry, with no cavalry or guns.' Another argument followed, but Rowland and Brady remained calm, though I'm sure I wasn't the only one who wondered how Rowland could be so sure. Did he have some spy at Fragnal writing letters to him? Knowing him, he probably did. Then he caught my eye.

'And what do you think, Captain Fletcher,' says he, in pure devilment probably, because I knew nothing of cavalry and horses.

'What about Dick Turpin the highwayman?' says I, for want of anything else, 'Didn't he ride his mare Black Bess from London to York? Wasn't that two hundred miles in one day? And we've only got to cover sixty to get to Fragnal.'

'Dick Turpin?' says a voice, 'that's just a tale.'

'And the horse would've been ruined at the end of it,' says another. But such is the perversity of human nature, that my nonsensical mention of a folk-tale actually silenced the opposition to Brady's proposal. Perhaps it was sport again? Perhaps these young officers felt challenged to beat Dick Turpin's record? On the other hand Brady took me seriously and gave a serious – and very cruel – reply.

'You are all correct, gentlemen' says he. 'To advance at such a rate will ruin some or all of our mounts. But what is that compared with the security of England? So we shall march on, at whatever cost to the horses, and I am assured,' he turned to Rowland, who nodded vigorously, 'I am assured that new mounts will be provided on our return to England. Fine Irish hunters, gentlemen, think on that!' They did think on that, but Brady wasn't done. 'Mr Rowland,' says Brady, 'I believe you have more to say?'

'I have, Captain Brady,' says Rowland, 'Gentlemen,' says he, 'We shall pass through some of the least populated areas in France,' everyone nodded, 'but should we encounter any French presence, whether civilian or military, then I will explain us with documents prepared in advance, stating that we are Dutch troops with French officers, in the service of the French Republic.'

'Won't they spot us as English?' says I. Rowland smiled.

'Not at all,' says he. 'Could you, Captain Fletcher, tell French from English cavalry uniform, let alone Dutch?' I thought about that and frowned.

'No,' says I, because all cavalry uniforms were gaudy and bright, and they very much copied one another. Thus all nations had so-called Polish lancers with square-top caps, just as they had so-called Hungarian Hussars with fur-trimmed jackets, and they all had dragoons, and I certainly couldn't tell an English one from a French one. So if I couldn't, I suppose some rural Frog couldn't, either. What a clever bastard was Rowland and no mistake.

'Captain Brady?' says he.

'Sir?'

'Do any of your officers speak French?' Brady laughed.

'Of course!' says he, and off he went in Froggy goobledegook, and Rowland gabbled right back, and they both laughed and shook hands. God knows what they said to each other, but it was French all right because Vasily Brady had been born in Russia and lived there till he was thirteen, with his father on diplomatic service. Since all educated Russians spoke French, little Vasily had grown up speaking French, English and Russian in that order. As for Rowland, of course he damn-well spoke the enemy's damned language, because it was just the sort of damned, cunning trick to be expected from him.

Bloody foreign languages! I see no use in them. Why can't everyone speak the King's English like sensible men? Look at the Americans: fully equal to ourselves as the two greatest nations God made, and the Americans speak English. So if we can do it, why can't all the lesser people? Damn them all, say I! Damn all foreigners! Rule Britannia and God bless America!

[I stress with insistent emphasis, that the foregoing paragraph is a mere edited summary of a ferocious and prolonged ranting by Fletcher, which was heard by every servant in the house, and even those in the gardens and stables. Only his exhaustion at the end of it, allowed me to escape the unspeakable task of setting down a full transcription. S.P.]

Eventually, off we trotted after our ten minute rest and it was hard pounding from then on, and steaming, sweating horses and men bleary-eyed in the saddle and my arse pounded so that all I cared about was any chance to get off, not that there was much chance of that as we steadily inflicted cruel harm on our horses in England's name to cover sixty miles at cruel speed.

And then it got even nastier.

Chapter 36

'*It is with utmost pride and honour that I report to you - my General, my Chief, my Caesar Augustus - that our first, fully working ,fully tested steam boat, is proceeding down the canal to Lyommeville.*'
(Translated from a letter of September 9th 1796 from General Claud Bernard, at the Fragnal Barracks, to Generalissimo Napoleon Bonaparte, Headquarters of the Army of Italy.)

On the neat stone quayside beside the Fragnal end of the canal, the regimental band of the 134th played every patriotic and cheerful tune in their repertoire. The few dozen men of the regiment who were present, all cheered and waved shakos on musket muzzles, while the wives of the Scottish-French waved handkerchiefs and shamelessly blew kisses that everyone pardoned in the happiness of the occasion, since the previous profession of these girls was almost entirely forgotten.

General Bernard stood with Colonel Sauvage, and the regiment's officers, and the leaders of the Fragnal engineers: principally Jamie McCloud and the newly-promoted Frenchman Oliver Fournier, the first of the purely French trainees to be raised to supervisory rank as a qualified steam engineer. Fournier's rank represented an achievement and an emphasis of the progress made at Fragnal in training of the French staff, though these days, Frenchman and Scottish-Frenchman mixed indistinguishably in speech, bearing and loyalties.

Bernard and the rest stood on a wooden stage, put up for the occasion draped in blue-white-red, right next to the canal, and with a gangplank neatly furnished with white rope handrails, giving easy access to the bright-painted steamboat, which now displayed so many tricolour flags that the hull could hardly be seen. But who cared about that? Who cared when steam was up, easy smoke rose from the funnel, and heat shimmered from the deck house?

Bernard gave a speech that everyone cheered, then Sauvage passed Bernard a cap of Liberty emblazoned with a blue-white-red rosette. Bernard raised it high.

'Monsieur Alasdair McCloud!' he cried, 'With this, I proclaim you as Captain Commander of the Republican Steam Launch *Michelle Justine*!' Everyone cheered. Next, Sauvage passed Bernard a document rolled up and bound with blue-white-red ribbon. Bernard gave the document to Alasdair McCloud, third oldest of the McCloud brothers, and one of the most fluent and eloquent French speakers among all of the Scottish-French. 'Here are your orders, monsieur,' cried Bernard, 'your orders to take the launch to Lyommeville and place it under the command of the Admiral of the port!' Alasdair McCloud took the document, and emotion swamped him for the moment.

He thought of his tragic eldest brother. He hoped that Donald would have been proud of all that had been achieved, in conceiving and building their wonderful steam boat. He looked to Jamie McCloud – now head of the Fragnal Engineers – who was proud beyond doubt. He looked to his two other brothers and to all the good comrades and friends of this magical, wonderful place, where Scots, Englishmen and Frenchmen were united…and French women, too! Jamie's wife Michelle Justine, was now visibly pregnant and blooming, and Alasdair's own wife thought that she, too, was expecting. Alasdair looked at his wife, standing with the women. She waved and Alasdair waved back with the scroll and its ribbons. Then he stood straight, and turned to General Bernard and lifted up his voice.

'You do me great honour, my General!' said Alasdair McCloud, 'And it will be honour to do my duty to the Republic, the Enlightenment …,' he paused, and thinking of his newly-conceived child and his beloved wife, he added, '…and to France!' Bernard stepped forward and embraced Alasdair McCloud, kissing him on both cheeks. Then he stood back, still clasping McCloud's shoulders with outstretched arms.

'I see that you are a Frenchman now, monsieur!' he said.

'I am a citizen!' said McCloud, with pride, 'a citizen of the Enlightenment!'

'Citizen?' thought Bernard, 'Enlightenment?' and even in that joyful moment, a large splinter ran under the fingernail of his contentment. 'God save us,' he thought, 'God save us from these intellectuals, and republicans. And is it really worthwhile to deal with these Scottish-English traitors, just to get the steam boats a bit quicker, when some decent Frenchman would build them in due time? Men like the Marquis de Jouffroy who invented the damned things in the first place?' But Bernard shrugged, and then nodded to Sauvage, and Sauvage nodded to the band, and the band gave La Marseillaise, and the music at least was splendid, though it was the fourth or fifth time it had been played that morning. But who knew? Nobody was counting.

Soon after, the steam launch *Michelle Justine* was out of sight of those left behind. She made steady progress at a speed of about four knots. She was manned by a Commander, two engine men, a stoker and a boy. She had coal aboard for one hundred kilometres of steaming. She was twenty metres long, five metres wide, with a deep keel and up-rising bow for ocean-going work. She was no mere flat-boat fit only for canals. At full steam she was expected to make eight knots at sea, and was proven capable of towing fully laden ships. Her machinery was efficient and reliable and she was fit for purpose and ready to do her duty.

Chapter 37

So we didn't canter with the wind in our hair, but the *Flying Column* did move at reasonable speed, and by late on that Thursday we managed to get about half way down the canal – some thirty miles – before the real action started. But the ride was eventful in several other ways. Thus Rowland spent a long time riding alongside Vasily Brady, and the two were soon chatting like old pals, and paying the most amazing close attention to each other's words, while Mr Ronald Kershaw the steam expert from the Soho works, was brought to my close attention. He was brought to my very discreet attention by Sergeant Major Gerald of the 27th who came up to me during one of the few breaks in the march, when most people were gulping drink and the horses stood trembling and sweating.

'Cap'n Fletcher?' says the sergeant major, 'Might I have a word, Sir?' He was a real old veteran. Grey hair, scarred cheeks, immaculate turnout, and chin shaved shiny by years of razor-work. He looked like a good man. I'd have employed him in any business under my command.

'Certainly, Sergeant Major,' says I.

'Might we talk private, Captain?' says Gerald. I looked round. There was nobody close: Rowland was talking to Vasily Brady again, and the troopers were all busy with their horses.

'Why not talk here, Sergeant Major?' says I, 'There's nobody listening.'

'No, Sir, but might I ask you to follow me, Sir? It's for the best, Sir.'

'Lead on, Sergeant Major,' says I, because I was intrigued.

The land around the canal had been cleared by the Froggy engineers for about fifty yards on either side of the canal in most places, but we were now by a hill with a stand of trees on it, and these were quite close to the stonework of the canal banks. Sergeant Major Gerald led me to just inside the trees where there was a sergeant and three men, and there was Mr Kershaw as well, sat on the ground with carbines pointed at him. He looked up as I approached, and stood and would have spoken, but I saw that another of the troopers – one who did not hold a carbine – was out of his jacket and helmet and had blood round his mouth. Also, Kershaw had the gall to leer at him so I guessed what had gone on.

'You!' says I to Kershaw, 'Not a word! Put a hitch on your jawing tackle!' I turned to Sergeant Major Gerald, 'This gentleman answers to me,' says I, pointing to Kershaw, 'He answers to me, and nothing like this will happen again. Not ever. Not on my watch!' the Sergeant Major nodded.

'Likewise for him,' says he, looking at the trooper with the bloodied mouth. 'It's a thousand lashes for them as fights each other when we're in the face of the enemy.'

The trooper shook with fear.

'It was him, Sar'nt major,' says he, pointing at Kershaw. 'It was him started it.'

'Shut your trap!' says Gerald. 'It's a thousand lashes,' He turned and looked at me, 'A thousand lashes,' he paused, 'if Mr Brady finds out…,' I saw his drift at once and nodded.

'You did right in coming to me, Sergeant Major,' says I, 'I'm sure that you and I can manage this affair.'

'Quite so, Sir,' says he, 'But with the utmost respect for your rank, Sir, and for the Sea Service,' he saluted me again, 'I would most humbly beg to point out that this here gentleman,' he put the most wonderful sneer into the word as he looked at Kershaw, 'has been chancing for a fight with my men, ever since we came aboard your ship, Sir, and I do most respectfully advise you, Sir, that I think him responsible for this one.' He was obviously speaking the truth and I thought actions more eloquent than words. So I walked over to Kershaw and gave him a clap round the ear that knocked him flat. Then I hauled him up by the scruff of his neck and held him with his nose next to mine. He was stunned by the blow and didn't quite know whether it was Monday or Friday. So I shook him a bit and spoke.

'Is that you making apology, Mr Kershaw?' says I, "cos I can't properly hear you.'

'Yeah,' says he.

'Say sorry to the Sergeant Major,' says I. 'Say it properly!' and I shook him a bit more.

'Sorry,' says he.

'Ah, Sergeant Major,' says I, 'that's Mr Kershaw apologising to you. Did you hear?'

'I did, Sir,' says the Sergeant Major. I turned back to Kershaw.

'And is that you now apologising to the trooper you hit?' He'd learned the rules by now, clever little chap that he was, and spoke up nice and clear.

'Sorry,' says he.

'And we don't want this poor trooper flogged, do we now, Mr Kershaw? So was it you that started the fight?'

'Yes,' says he.

'Yes, Sir!' says I.

'Yes, Sir,' says he.

'And have you ever actually seen a flogging, Mr Kershaw?'

'No, Sir,' says he.

'Then don't make me show you one.' I let him think about that for a bit, while Sergeant Major Gerald nodded in profound approval.

'Spoken like a gentleman,' says he, 'I do declare.' I shook Kershaw a bit more and finally let him drop. He went down gasping and heaving and rubbing at his neck, and gazing up at me with the oddest expression on his face. But Sergeant Major Gerald was delighted.

'Thank you, Sir,' says he, 'else otherwise I'd have had to punish a man that wasn't at fault. So if you're happy, Sir, then I'm happy, and perhaps we may declare the matter is closed?'

'Entirely closed, Sergeant Major,' says I, and took out a gold piece from my purse. 'And would you kindly accept this on behalf of your men, Sergeant Major? As a sign of the goodwill of the Sea Service?'

'Gor' bless you, Cap'n Fletcher, Sir!' says he and whisked away the coin on the instant.

That was all there was to it and I dragged Kershaw off, back to our horses, without another word. But here's the strange thing: After that, we were off again and riding hard, and I couldn't keep Kershaw away from me. I'd seen hero worship before from youngsters like little Mr Barclay and poor young Copeland, and now it was shining out of Kershaw. Very odd. Very odd indeed that you should shake a man like a rat, and he thinks the better of you. Perhaps it was his love of fighting, and of seeing all his ideals incarnated in myself? I don't know. I leave such speculation to philosophers. But that was Kershaw and the odder thing still, was that his conversation was interesting. He lived and breathed for steam engines, field sport and boxing, and he spoke of these things with great knowledge.

He did grovel a bit, but he was amusing and impertinent all at the same time, not being properly in the King's Service and under discipline, and he had a great talent for cheeky vulgarity, so after a while I just let him talk. There was nothing else to do and it kept me from concentrating on the pain being directed up my beam ends by a leather saddle.

'When you hit that Pug, Captain Fletcher,' says he, 'why, the hairs of his dick dropped out and his bollocks begged for mercy!' And on the fitting of pistons into steam cylinders: 'They has to be slick as a tart's tongue and tight as a virgin's arse.'

The words are coarse, but he had a way of saying them that amused rather than affronted. I thought he would have made a famous clown on the London stage, and was deceived into thinking well of him, as a naughty chappie with a bit of a temper but not much worse. He was a very fine steam engineer after all, and discoursed on such abstruse matters as the mechanical equivalent of heat. 'Count Rumford!' says he, 'Do you know, Captain, that during the boring-out of cannon barrels in Prussia, he found by actual measurement...,'

I never did learn who Count Rumford was, or what he might have measured, because just at that moment, about six hours into our journey, men started shouting that the water level in the canal was going down. Rowland fell back to ride beside me, and Kershaw touched his hat and got out of the way. It quite galled me to see that, because while Kershaw regarded me as a hero, he was respectful of Rowland in a way that he wasn't to anyone else including me. But I suppose Rowland truly was one of the ruling class: bred up to look down on lesser folk, and them to look up at him.

'Captain Fletcher!' says Rowland, pointing to the canal, 'Do you see that?' and of course I did because we were all staring. 'That means they've blown the last lock gate,' says Rowland, 'and the water must be leaping out like a waterfall, all over Lyommeville,' he raised his voice into a shout, 'and that, in turn, means that the main task of this enterprise has been achieved!' The company raised a cheer in response. But it was a quiet cheer because we were all nearly as tired as the horses.

Then events moved faster. We'd already met a few French people as we moved along the canal road, but they'd been simple rustics who didn't know what our uniforms meant, and Rowland didn't even bother to speak to them. He just raised his hat to the women, or let Vasily Brady give them his smile and make them blush, when he said bong-jewer madame.

But then up came a man in uniform, on a good horse going at a good trot. He came towards us, from inland, heading towards Lyommeville. Vasily Brody signalled for the column to halt, and he and Rowland advanced to meet the man, who was highly agitated and yelled at them in French, while pointing to the canal, which was now almost drained of water. He stopped, Vasily and Rowland stopped, and there was a conversation that nobody else understood, what with it being in French. Then the Frenchman started shouting, and Rowland produced a paper from his saddle bag and thrust it at the Frenchman, who looked at it, and then he stared hard at our column, and pointed at Vasily's Helmet, and tried to draw a sword. So Rowland dropped the paper, pulled a pistol from his saddle holster, and shot the Frenchman.

The pistol barked, the Frenchman twitched at the impact of the ball, toppled off his horse, and fell to the ground, with the horses prancing all round him, in fright at the shot and the smoke. There was a united gasp from the column. Even I was shocked. I'd seen death before, and so had the men around me, but we'd suddenly gone from a peaceful ride in the country to shooting men dead, and all without any declaration of war. I couldn't help but ride forward to see what had happened. The Frenchman, in some sort of dark blue uniform, was quite dead, with Rowland out of the saddle and searching him.

'Fate!' says Vasily Brady, nodding at the dead Frenchman, 'His time was come, that's all,' He smiled, and the blood of his Russian Countess mother spoke up: the mother that owned serfs. 'Don't worry, Captain Fletcher,' says Vasily, 'He wasn't a real officer – only a peasant in uniform.'

'So why did you shoot him?' says I to Rowland, who ignored me and completed his search of the Frenchman's pockets and pouches.

'He recognised us as English,' said Vasily, 'Or at least not French or Dutch.'

'But you said that couldn't happen,' says I to Rowland.

'Well it has,' says he, standing up, 'But never fear, because although this gentleman was an outstanding connoisseur of uniforms, he was no more than a lock-keeper riding to find out why the canal waters are gone.'

'But you shot him,' says I.

'Would you have preferred that I let him kill me?'

'What were you talking about? You were talking for some while.'

'Yes,' says Rowland, 'we were, and very interesting it was too,' he looked down at the Lock-Keeper. 'He was full of news, was this man,' Rowland pointed along the canal. There's a steam-boat down there, Captain Fletcher.'

'What?' says I.

'A steam-boat. An actual working steam-boat, all decked out in French flags and on its way to the sea at Lyommeville,' he spread hands expressively. 'They've done it, gentlemen! The French have done it. They have a working, sea-going, steam-boat.'

'What?' says I.

'You're repeating yourself again, Captain Fletcher. I do wish you would desist.'

'Well what's it doing?' says I, 'this steam-boat'.

'It's stuck,' says Rowland, 'There's one final lock on the canal up there,' he pointed, 'and there's water on the inland side of it and the steam-boat is stuck there, unable to proceed.'

'Good God almighty!' says I, 'then hadn't we better get to it?'

'We had indeed,' said Rowland, and so we did. We pressed on at even greater speed, and I rode right up in front with Vasily and Rowland, and Kershaw right behind me, and the whole column behind us, and the bouncing gun carriages and the fodder wagons astern. It was exciting. It really was, and I don't know which of myself and Kershaw was the more fascinated with anticipation in waiting for our first sight of the steamer.

And then there it was! Up ahead on the ruler-straight line of the canal, there was the last pair of lock gates, holding back the last of the water, while on our side the canal was down to a thin layer of mud, weed, and a few flapping fish on the waterproof lining. By George but that steamer was a sight to see, as I gazed between my horse's ears and the wind whistled round my hat, and my poor damned bum got a heavier basting, and all the thrilling noise of a cavalry charge was all around us, because by then we were damn near galloping. Then there were a few forlorn figures looking at us by the steam-boat and the lock gates, and the neat little keeper's house, with two women, one young, one old, standing at the door. And above all and before else there was the steamboat, with a few men around and in it, and it was a lot bigger than I'd expected and had a fine, rising bow, and a deck house, and no masts, sails or oars, because it was a steamer. There was a big funnel rising overall, and steam and smoke rising up, and that scent of steam that first I'd smelt when Rowland and I got the model road engine under way. It was the scent that always ever since, has stirred that part of me that would have been a steam engineer, and not a seaman or a man of commerce, had things been different and opportunity presented.

Then we were alongside and dismounting, and Vasily and his officers were shouting, and the troopers spreading out to secure and protect, and a third of them out of the saddles with carbines, while another third, spread around us still mounted, and another third held the horses of those with carbines. It was all very smart. But I barely noticed. I was getting aboard the steam boat and gaping and gazing and goggling. I just about heard Rowland chattering away in French, to the two women, both of whom threw their apron over their faces and fell into tears. The lock keeper's family I suppose.

Then some fellow was speaking to me in French. He was a tall man in his twenties, with a French liberty cap on his head, decorated with red, white and blue rosette. He was half looking at me, and half at Rowland, and had obviously heard whatever Rowland had said to the women. Now he was questioning me, and in bloody French, too! I was about to put him right, when Kershaw got in first.

'Here!' says he, actually pushing past me to face the man with the rosette. 'You're one of them bastard McClouds! You are, aren't you, 'cos I've bloody met you before!'

'Huh?' says the rosette man, and switched to English as neat and smooth as you please, though with a Scottish accent. 'Aye,' says he, 'I am Alasdair McCloud.'

'You fucking bastard!' screams Kershaw, 'You're one of them that shot our Peter and burned our Pa! You're one of them treacherous fucking McClouds!' and I'll not record the rest of what he said because it was such filth as would shock a sailor. As for the rosette man, he flinched, as anyone would, but you could see in his face that the words struck home. He was blinking and guilty because whatever it was that Kershaw was screaming about, then it looked as if Mr Rosette – McCloud – had really done it. I saw it. Kershaw saw it. And Kershaw went mad.

He frothed at the mouth, he growled like an animal, his limbs shook, his face went white, and then he went for McCloud with total, animal ferocity: not just punching and kicking, but spitting and biting and beating his brow into McCloud's face. Down they went on to the neat-clean, fresh-new planks of the steam-boat's deck, snapping the little poles that rose up everywhere with French flags, and they rolled and fought, and tumbled into the gaping, amazed troopers and the others on board who I took to be the steamer's crew.

I say that they fought, but it wasn't a fight. It was Kershaw trying to rend, tear and rip McCloud into shreds, with McCloud – by far the bigger man – reduced to a feeble defence that could never have saved him. By God, but I'd got Kershaw wrong. In later years I was advised by scholars that the man was what the Vikings called a Berserk: normal most of the time, but out of his mind with violence when something triggers him. So he'd have killed McCloud for sure if I hadn't stopped him.

But I did. I stopped him. I stopped him because I am a very big man and I am enormously strong. I say that not as a boast but as fact. It's like the colour of my hair or the shape of my nose. It's born into me. So I threw off my hat and coat and got down and got hold of Kershaw, and hauled him off McCloud by brute strength. And then the little swine turned on me. He was so deranged that he turned his full force on myself, just as he had on McCloud, because the devil was in and the sense was out, and he was utterly gone and was fighting mad. I'd have smashed him a blow with my fist if I could have risked letting go of him. But I couldn't. The only way I could keep myself safe, was to clutch him to my breast and hold him there, while he struggled and howled and kicked and bit. I held him like that until he exhausted himself, and damn near exhausted me, too. Again, I do not boast when I state that there are not many men who could have done what I did, and when finally he relaxed: all spent, delirious and moaning, I don't know which of the two of us was sweating more, because it was coming off us in a united stream, and forming a pool on the deck.

So I dropped him and stood back and saw that there was an entire ring of men around, all staring, and there was I with my shirt in rags, my britches torn half off, and my arms and shoulders livid with the marks where I'd been bitten. And there was McCloud, Mr Alasdair McCloud, plainly and obviously guilty over whatever it was that he'd done in the past, and now sat looking up at me, crawled away from the fight with his back to the boat's deck house, and blinking and wondering whether we were enemies or friends. He was in a worse state than me, and bleeding from the wounds Kershaw had inflicted with his bare hands, boots and teeth.

It was an ugly moment, and I looked for the comfort of an ally: not Rowland, not Vasily. I wanted the someone I liked.

'Sergeant Major Gerald?' says I, looking for him. He was there, standing on the path by the canal, with his men.

'Sir?' says he.

'Sergeant Major,' says I, 'D'you think you could find me some clean water and a towel, and some clothes that'll fit me?'

'Yes, Sir!' says he, 'Right away, Sir.' I pointed at McCloud.

'And would you guard this man so that I can have a word with him?'

'Yes, Sir,' says Gerald, but Rowland took over with the effortless authority that he wielded without even trying.

'You can leave Mr McCloud to me, Captain Fletcher,' he said, and smiled, and helped McCloud to his feet. McCloud blinked and looked at Roland with extreme nervousness.

'Are you Mr Alasdair McCloud?' says Rowland, 'younger brother of Mr Donald McCloud, late of the Soho Iron Works?'

'Yes,' says McCloud.

'Ah!' says Rowland, friendly as can be.

'Then you are one of the very men I have come here to see.' McCloud said nothing. Rowland turned to me. 'Leave this to me, Captain Fletcher,' says he, 'You just go and put yourself to rights.' He smiled again in the most reassuring manner and put a friendly hand on my arm, and thus I was deceived. So I went off with Sergeant Major Gerald, who most efficiently got me the necessaries to clean and dress myself, which I did – for decency – with the men and horses between me and the two women. But before I was done, there came the sound of a gun-shot…crack!

I half guessed what it was, and damned myself for an idiot and ran shirt-less, in bare feet and britches, and found men looking towards the side of the lock-keeper's house that was out of sight of the troop. I ran round, and there were Rowland and Vasily Brody, in the long shadows of the evening, standing over the body of Alasdair McCloud. He was face down with arms spread out. He'd been shot in the back of the head, and Rowland held a pistol, with the powder smoke swirling around him.

Chapter 38

I urge you to send a troupe of horse to re-inforce my small detachment.'
(Translated from a military despatch of September 9th 1796 from
General Claud Bernard, at the Fragnal Barracks, to The Office Commanding
the People's Republican Garrison of Montfer.)

*

It was late afternoon, but the Fragnal Barracks heaved with the action of desperate men trying to turn it into a fort. The buildings were already strong: the main block and its walled courtyard were like a castle keep and ring-wall. But now, soldiers were standing ready to reinforce the gates with heavy timbers, once the women were brought in from the little village of wooden houses, outside the Barracks, where they lived with their Scottish-French husbands. The women chattered and laughed and made eyes at the soldiers, because they didn't understand the danger. They didn't even believe it. But their husbands did, and they hustled their women forward, and into the protection of the thick-walled Barracks building. Then the gates slammed, the bar went down, and the engineers moved in with augers and bolts and hammers and set to work.

Sauvage and Bernard stood in the centre of these works, in the evening light, as other men with crowbars tried to knock loopholes into the walls, which was exceedingly heavy work, given the thickness of the stones and mortar, while Bernard faced the four men who'd volunteered to stay outside as pickets to give warning of the enemy's approach.

'My brave boys,' he said, with real emotion, and kissed each man on both cheeks. 'My General!' they said, and out they went and the gates were closed behind them. Then Barnard saw the futility of trying to pierce the heavy walls for loopholes.

'No! No! No!' said Bernard, 'Stop that! We've got plenty of timber, so build a framework against the wall, and a firing step so we can shoot over the top.' The sergeants saluted, the men dropped the crowbars. 'But leave some big beams for the gates,' said Bernard. 'They're too thin. They were never intended to stand siege. Damn, damn, damn,' he said, 'We've got so few men! We're less than eighty even if you include the Scottish, and all we've got is muskets.'

'But we can't be sure they're coming,' said Sauvage, who wasn't convinced.

'Sauvage,' said Bernard, 'The water's drained out of the canal all the way from the half-way lock to the coast.' Bernard turned to a thin, gangling lad stood politely holding his hat, and with nothing to do in all this activity. 'That's right, boy, isn't it?'

'Yes, my General,' said the boy. 'The water level started to go down this afternoon, and Papa rode to the coast to see what was happening, and sent me here to tell you, because it must be something serious, because the upper gates at Lyommeville are double-gates: one set behind the other, and both sets double strength, and they can't just fail all by themselves. Not both sets.'

'See?' said Bernard, 'And what did Mamma Madelaine say? She said … *my King's allies will soon be hereto avenge me*…that's what she said, and we all thought she was mad. Well what if we were mad and she was right? What if they are coming? The damned English and their damned navy, that goes everywhere and does everything? If they put men ashore at Lyommeville, they could blow up the lock gates and then use our own damned road to come straight here to us!'

'My General!' said an officer, pushing forward and saluting. 'I need your permission.'

'What for, damn you?' said Bernard.

'I want to use the English-Scottish. We need more men.'

'Get on with it, damn you, I've already told you to do that!'

'Yes, my General,' the officer hesitated, 'but I want to issue them with muskets in case it comes to fighting. It could make a difference,' Bernard sighed.

'Do they know what's going on?' he said. 'Do they understand?'

'Yes, my General, and they've got more reason to fight than anyone. Their people will see them as traitors, and they know it.' Bernard sighed. He sighed because he felt sick. This wasn't the way wars were fought under King Louis. In those days a French officer didn't give muskets to English traitors to use against decent English soldiers. But that was then, and this was now, and now was the time of the God-damned Enlightenment.

'Go ahead,' said Bernard, finally, 'a musket for every one of them.' Then he took Sauvage by the arm, beckoned to a couple of ensigns who were standing by as runners, and led them all into the his office. There, candles were already burning and maps laid out on a table, but the two clerks were gone. They were getting their clean, white hands dirty, out with the working parties.

'Look,' said Bernard, pointing a map of the Fragnal region. 'We're here, right?'

'Yes, my General,' said the rest.

'And here's our little quay on the canal.'

'Yes, my General.'

'The branch road runs from our quay to us here, just two kilometres, while the main road and the canal goes straight on to the main terminus at Montfer, which is another fifty kilometres, and the nearest reinforcements are at the Montfer Barracks, and we've sent a galloper to beg their assistance.'

'Yes, my General.'

'But that's half a day's ride even in daylight, and it's late now, and our man will soon be riding in the dark, provided he doesn't fall off and provided his horse doesn't go lame! And then, even if they send help at once which they might not, that's another half a day so we can't expect any help until this time tomorrow, and they might not even take us seriously and they might delay, so we don't know when they'll come, if they come...' And then Bernard stopped sharp as he remembered something important. 'Holy Mother of God!' he said, and ran out of the office and into the Barracks yard, with its giant steam engine, and its machine shop with belt-powered precision tools, and all the other advanced and precious equipment that made this place such a tempting and wonderful target for the enemy to take, capture and destroy. 'Stop! Stop!' he cried, 'Leave the gates! I want them open again!'

The men who were labouring to seal the gates, stopped work. They looked at their General, then they looked at one another and they wondered what was going on. 'Open the gates, just once more!' cried Bernard, 'There's something more to do!'

Chapter 39

'He tried to escape,' says Rowland looking down at the dead man. 'I gave warning but he persisted,' He turned to Vasily Brady, 'Isn't that so, Captain Brady?'

'Oh yes,' says Vasily, 'he tried to run,' and he smiled.

'You bastard,' says I to Rowland, 'You murdered that man!'

'Not at all, ' says Rowland, 'I gave fair warning, then prevented the escape of a creature – who would undoubtedly have been condemned for treason if ever he were brought back to England, and which is precisely the reason he tried to run.' He gave a small gesture with his hands, as if to say 'what else could I do' and then calm as you please, he gripped his walking stick between his knees, produced a cartridge and proceeded to prime and load his pistol, before sticking it back into his belt.

Then others came and joined us: Sergeant Major Gerald, the lieutenants and other officers, and a few of the troopers, all staring at the corpse. I was full of anger, but there was little I could do, and every chance of making a fool of myself, with accusations I couldn't prove. So I said nothing, and Rowland took over again.

'Captain Brady, Captain Fletcher, gentlemen,' says he, 'this man,' he looked down at McCloud, 'was shot while trying to escape,' he looked round, 'Sergeant Major?' says he.

'Sir!' says Gerald.

'Find some spades and get him buried.'

'Yes, Sir!'

'Good,' said Rowland, and so confident and assured was his manner, that not another word was ever said about McCloud by anyone. 'But first,' says Rowland, 'You will find Mr Kershaw, rouse him, put pencils and sketch-book into his hands, and tell him to record whatever is of interest in that steam-barge. Tell Mr Kershaw to make his drawings steadily and with care, because he has plenty of time. We shall camp here, and not resume our march until tomorrow.'

251

'But, Sir?' says Vasily, 'Should we not press on at our best speed? I thought that was our plan, even if it means a night march?'

'It was, Captain Brady,' says Rowland, 'But the steam boat's presence here, is an unexpected and tremendous bonus. It is the very essence of the French plans against England. It is the prototype of the boats that they would use to tow their invasion fleet to England, and since we cannot take it home with us, it is vital that Mr Kershaw has adequate time to record its complexities in full.' Everyone nodded at that. It made sense. 'Also,' says Rowland, 'it would be best to avoid a night march if we may, and to take advantage of resting our men and horses. Thus we shall move off tomorrow in daylight, and shall camp again tomorrow night, to rest our men further before attacking Fragnal at dawn. The men will fight all the better for that.' Everyone nodded again, except me.

'What about getting back to the beach at Lyommeville before the Navy leaves?' says I. 'Today's Thursday the eighth, if we march tomorrow and attack on the tenth, then even if we're ready to march that afternoon, that's less than two days before the navy abandons the beach. If we've fought a battle on the tenth, will we be in a fit state to get back there in time?'

'Hmmmm,' says everyone.

'Thank you for that maritime perspective, Captain Fletcher,' says he, with just enough sauce in his voice to make these army officers smile at the Sea Service, 'But needs must when the Devil drives, and we shall just have to do our best before the Navy abandons us.' Again they all smiled. 'Now, gentlemen,' says Rowland, 'Will the officers step aside with me, so that I can impart my latest information. Quick as you please, now gentlemen! And troopers go to your duties.'

Note the manner of him: the confidence in ordering men about. The Duke of bloody Wellington couldn't have done it better, even though Rowland had never actually been in any kind of military service, as far as I know. So we stood round him as he gave his little lecture. 'The man Alasdair McCloud,' says he, 'Was one of the brothers who led an attack on the Soho works in September last year. All these men are fanatical republicans, who subsequently took their steam expertise here to France. It was during the attack on the Soho Works that Mr Kershaw's father and brother were killed.'

'Ahhh,' says everyone.

'Yes,' says Rowland, 'Hence Mr Kershaw's anger, since he was present at this attack and recognised Alasdair McCloud.'

'Ahhh,'

'But before his attempted escape, Mr McCloud confirmed that there are seventeen others like himself – all traitors to England – working at the Fragnal Barracks, now converted into a steam manufactory, and which is defended by a total of only eighty men. We may therefore be confident of our ability to capture and take Fragnal.'

Everyone grinned, the talk turned to practicalities of making camp, and when it was done I got myself properly dressed, and being fascinated by steam, I went on board the boat, and down into the engine room to see the machinery. But Kershaw was there, at his drawings, and a great embarrassment followed.

'Oh Mr Fletcher, Mr Fletcher, Mr Fletcher!' says he, and dropped his pencil and papers and lunged at me, and fell to his knees and threw his arms around my waist, and buried his face into the region of my fruit and nuts, which action was decidedly unwelcome. 'Oh, Sir! Oh Sir! Oh Sir!' says he, and he sobbed and snivelled and wept and the snot and tears soaked into my britches, and I shoved him off.

'Be done with it, man,' says I, 'Stand up and give an account of yourself.'

'Oh, Sir,' says he, wringing his hands, 'It's the fury that comes over me. I can't help it, Sir. So can you find it in your heart to forgive me?' There was much more like that, which I do not bother to set down.

'All right,' says I finally, 'I forgive you, you bloody nasty little bugger. But Christ help you if ever you try that again!' I said it to shut him up, but he accepted these fine words as absolution, and poured out his thanks until I threatened to kick his arse if he didn't stop. He really was an odd little swab because you never knew what he was going to do next, and I almost preferred him as a berserk. But then he picked up his pencil and book, and he made the most wonderful engineering drawings. He worked with great speed, recording whatever it was that was novel, and his drawings were so good, and looked so real, that you'd think you could pick them off the page and handle them. Mind you, it spoilt my innocent desire to have a look at the machinery and puzzle out its workings. I didn't feel comfortable doing that with Kershaw half glancing at me all the time. So I left, and coming off the boat, I met Rowland,

'Feeling better, Fletcher?' says Rowland, as if I were a maiden aunt who'd tried to fart and fainted.

'Huh!' says I. He just laughed, looked around to see nobody was listening, and spoke quietly.

'Let it lie, Fletcher,' says he. 'The record will show that Alasdair McCloud was shot while trying to escape. That's a manly death and better than being hanged at Newgate and anatomised by the surgeons.' He was a clever bastard was Rowland, and a fierce man to oppose, even when – as now – he was gasping for breath and wincing at the pain in his arm. What's more, there was some truth in what he said and I couldn't deny it. 'And why do you think I brought you here?' says he, 'Or have you decided – despite all your love of trade – to stay aboard your nice new ship, so you don't need my help to get free of the Admiralty?' He said that and more, and he was devilish persuasive. He shut me up and made me think, which indeed I did.

Meanwhile we camped the night, and were up on the morrow, when Rowland ordered that Kershaw's vastly important sketches be sent back to our forces at Lyommeville, at once, and in two lots carried by two riders who rode an hour apart, so one might escape if the other were captured. I had to admit that he was thorough. Then off we went at a more steady pace then yesterday's, though still it was more than the horses liked and some of them were falling out every hour our so, with pistol shots to despatch those most grievously ruined, and others left with feed bags in the hope of retrieving them during the retreat. Also, one of the six pounder carriage-wheels was shattered, as a horse fell, and the gun went into a ditch. So that gun and all it's gear had to be left behind, which at least freed six horses, not that they were in much better state than the trooper's mounts.

We camped the next night too, just short of Fragnal, and were up before dawn with a breakfast of biscuit and butter, dried meat and a tot of rum. We camped by the canal, but rode a mile or so in the dark down a branch road, then we dismounted, and tethered the horses, except those drawing our remaining six-pounder. It was just about possible to pick out the dark bulk of the Fragnal Barracks buildings against the night sky, some hundreds of yards off.

Rowland had left it to Vasily Brady and Sergeant Major Gerald to plan the attack, and he was right to have done so. Vasily and his officer already had a map of the Barracks building and walls, provided by Rowland from whatever spies he used. So the 27th came with its plans prepared, and we all took off out hats and wrapped white cloths round our heads, so we shouldn't split one another by mistake in the dark. Then the troopers drew carbines, fixed bayo-nets and primed and loaded, and I checked my pistols and felt the edge of my sword. Then I followed Vasily, Rowland, and Sergeant Major Gerald, to lead the attack with the gun coming just behind us, as quiet as such a vehicle can be. God knows how Rowland kept up, with his stick and his infirmities, but he did. Force of will again, I suppose.

The men followed the gun, just over one hundred and fifty strong, marching by sections behind their lieutenants and sergeants, and we got quite close before we were challenged. Someone yelled out in French from the dark, because they'd had the sense to put out sentries to keep watch. Rowland shouted back in French, all easy and merry to deceive the sentry, and we went forward with him. We were just on the threshold of dawn, there was enough light to see the French soldier come out from behind a tree, with his shako and Charleville musket. Then Rowland was laughing as if at some joke, and the Frenchman was lowering his musket, when one of the artillery horses whinneyed and pranced and all its gear jingled. The Frenchman frowned, gabbled at Rowland, and Rowland replied. But it was no good and up came the musket again.

Bang! The musket flashed, but Rowland had got close and slashed with his stick, and knocked down the barrel so the ball dug itself harmless into the ground. Then Vasily and I were on the Frenchman with our swords, and finished him in an instant.

After that it was all too fast for proper words to convey. Vasily yelled at the gunners, the team galloped forward, dragging the bouncing gun behind, and in the growing light I witnessed the stirring sight of a horse artillery piece wheeling into action: the six horses charging round in a half-circle to bring the gun to bear on its target. Then the gunners were leaping down from horses and limbers, to free the gun and train it on the gates of the Fragnal Barracks. But the enemy was warned now, and bugles sounded from inside the walls and a drum rolled, as two of the artillerymen ran forward with a prepared charge to blow in the gates, as our first and best means of doing so.

But a thick volley of musketry came from the walls around the gate, and our two men fell, and there was a brief pause, then a huge flash and roar as the charge – with fuse already burning – lit the world in fierce light, but all wasted and clear of the gate. So it was heavy work for the six pounder, sending shot smashing into the timbers to do the job the charge had failed to do.

After four or five rounds of solid ball, the gates seemed knocked into splinters, and the gunners switched to canister to clear the defenders from the wall tops over the gate, and Vasily gave a cheer and led from the front, and I went with him followed by men with axes and mallets to knock a way through the ruins of the gate. And that was the really nasty part. The gate had been strengthened within, and the round shot hadn't done a full job, and there was a need for smashing and hacking, while the defenders tried to shoot out through the ruined timbers and I emptied both my pistols, and men were beside me firing carbines back at the French.

Finally, Vasily was yelling to everyone to get out of the way as the gunners brought the six pounder to within a dozen yards of the gates, and gave two more rounds of canister that finally blew a clear, practical hole, big enough for men to pass. The muzzle-blast alone would have done it at such a range, and it certainly blew away all the defenders, while we attackers were all deafened, but Vasily was first man through the hole, with me right behind him.

*

'D'you think they'll ever come?' said Sauvage.

'Who?' said Bernard, 'the English or our reinforcements from Montfer?'

'Either of them,' said Sauvage, and smiled. He still wasn't sure that Bernard was right, and was putting too much trust in the ramblings of a mad woman. But then he frowned. He was believing his own lies! Mamma Madelaine wasn't mad. He'd just said that she was, for her own good. He was about to mention that to Bernard, standing next to him on the firing platform behind the walls, when they heard the challenge. So did the twenty infantrymen alongside them, with muskets levelled over the wall.

'Who goes there?' cried the sentry, invisible in the dark.

'A poor old soul with a broken wagon!' said a voice in excellent French, laughing as he spoke. 'We're going to need some help, Citizen, because there's a woman in the cart who's ready to give birth, so can you please help us?'

'What?' said the sentry. 'What wagon? Where?'

'Horse shit!' said Bernard to Sauvage. 'Nobody comes here at this time of...,'

Bang! A musket flashed and roared, and there was fighting and commotion outside the walls.

'Alarm! Alarm!' cried Bernard, and the bugles and drums sounded the General Alert to bring the off-duty watch to their duties. Down there!' yelled Bernard. 'Fire!' Twenty muskets roared, two men fell outside the gates, then there was huge explosion, everyone was blinded and deafened, and then an artillery piece was thundering away at the gates.

There was great confusion. Bernard did his best. Sauvage did his best. The men of the 134th did their best, but they were outnumbered to begin with, and the field gun performed deadly work for the English. More than half the men on the firing platform were blown into ragged meat by canister shot, and many more were killed as they tried to defend the gate. Finally, when the English came storming through the wrecked woodwork, the main fight for the Barracks took place in the cobbled yard, as an ugly melee of butt, bayonet and sword, once the firearms had been discharged without hope of reloading in a struggle.

Bernard's men fought hard, but less than forty brave Frenchmen were left standing, and could not prevail over three times their number of Englishmen, and soon, in the dawn light, Bernard and Sauvage, both dripping blood from wounds, were backed up against the Barracks block wall, with dead and wounded comrades all around them, and a ring of sharp bayonets in front of them. For a while there was silence as all these exhausted, shaking men – English and French equally – panted and gasped for breath, with their hearts still thumping from hideous combat.

Then an English officer stepped forward with an enormous man beside him, a man in a blue uniform and white cloth bound round his head like all the rest. The officer bowed elegantly and spoke in fluent French.

'Messieurs,' he said, 'I am Captain Vasily Brady of the 27th Light Dragoons. I ask who is in command here?' Bernard stepped forward and returned the bow.

'Monsieur the Captain, I am General of Brigade Claude Bernard, and I have the honour to be in command.'

'Monsieur the General,' said Brady, 'I call upon you to surrender, to save needless bloodshed. You have already done all that brave men can do.' Bernard groaned because never in all his service had he been obliged to surrender. But there was a duty yet to perform. He stood straight, gripped his sword and spoke with a firm voice.

'Monsieur the Captain, there are women behind us in the Barracks, and I cannot strike my colours without your solemn word as a soldier that they will be respected. Without that, my men and I will fight and die where we stand!'

'I give you my word,' said the English Captain, 'as an officer in the service of my King.'

'And do you give your word as a Christian?' said Bernard, who had to be sure.

'I give my word as a Christian,' said Brady, and crossed himself in the manner of the Russian Orthodox Church, touching brow and breast with the thumb and two fingers that symbolise the Holy Trinity. Bernard was surprised at this oddity in an Englishman, but at least the man wasn't a protestant. Meanwhile Bernard's men were all looking at him. They were all listening. His decision was life or death for them, but he was a good officer, they were loyal, and none of them flinched. Every man on either side waited until finally General Bernard sheathed his blade, unhooked the scabbard from its baldric and offered his sword, hilt-first, to Captain Brady.

*

The fight in the courtyard was like a boarding action at sea: dense, fierce and short. I laid on with my excellent sword, and if I've not told you youngsters before how to do it, then listen now, because the way of a sword fight is to swing left and right as hard as you can, bellowing madly as you do, and taking the attack right into the enemy's face, and never even attempting any fancywork fencing because that'll get you killed. So that's what I did, and a few Frenchmen got the sharp end of it, and then it was all over, and the Frogs – those left alive of them – were up against a wall, and Vasily Brady was speaking French to the French commander whose name was Bernard: Bernarrrr as the Frogs say it.

I couldn't understand what they said, but it was slow, and formal, and surprisingly stirring of the emotions. Then Vasily made some sort of religious gesture, which seemed to impress Bernard, and the French laid down their arms, and we all sighed in relief. But after that if we'd thought that the fight was hard work, what followed was worse.

Tired as we were, we had to lock up the French soldiers with men to guard them, and we had to find the seventeen English traitors among them, which wasn't hard because the blighters stood out in their civilian clothes, but with military cross-belts for cartridge pouches and bayonets. We caught some of them trying to get rid of these, but it was too late for that. In fact there were just twelve of them, the rest being dead and – according to Rowland – thereby saved from an English hanging. But these twelve had to be guarded, and kept separate from the Frenchmen. Then we had to find the women, who were indeed present, inside the big Barracks, and we all knew they'd been found when they started screaming and screeching, at which moment, Vasily Brady had to find reliable men to guard them, under pain of hanging should anyone lay hands on them.

To his credit, Vasily – and his officers, too – did a fine job of separating these various groups, though finding places to put them was done with much smashing of doors to gain entry, and boots running up and down the corridors of the big Barracks, which rose up on three floors and took plenty of searching to make sure there were no hidden threats. It was done rough and noisy, because it had to be done fast.

And of course we had to deal with the wounded. There was no surgeon among us, but the 27th's Farrier could dig out shot, sew up wounds, and clap on dressings. So he was put in charge, and found a large dormitory where the seriously wounded – over thirty of them – could be laid in the comfort of actual beds. He and his mates put the French and English side-by-side, because it did no harm and made less work. Though any of the Frogs who could walk once the Farrier was done with them, got roused out and put in with their fit and active comrades.

I have to record the sad fact that Sergeant Major Gerald was one of those worst wounded, and died a few hours after the battle in the courtyard. As I've said before, it's common among fighting men to say that the wrong ones get killed in action, but in his case it was as true as it was for little Mr Midshipman Copeland. Gerald was a good man, and others worse than him survived. At least the Farrier made him comfortable for his last moments.

I had nothing to do with any of this, because that was the army's work, and I could spend time captivated by the machinery in that Barracks yard. To begin with there was the most enormous steam-powered beam engine: the manufactory kind that in England would power a whole mill. It was hot and alive, with coals in the furnace and steam in the boiler, and it was rigged so as to turn a shaft that ran in through a wall, to give power by canvas belts to the most wonderful, magical machine shop of lathes, milling machines and precision calibrating gear that ever I saw in my life. It was the very ultimate in mechanical-technical invention, and it was beautiful, too. It was just like seeing *Euphonides* for the first time. When I first got inside that workshop I just stood and stared, as men of the 27th ran past, and looked in every hole and crack for hidden Frenchmen or other perils. They were doing that all over the Barracks, and they didn't even glance at the machinery. But I did, and I knew that if the Buddhists of the Indies are right, and there are more lives to come after this one, then by George but I'm going to be an engineer in the next one!

I was so fascinated that I must have been in that machine shop for hours, going from one wonder to the next, convinced that I was looking at the world of the future, which indeed I was, my jolly boys, because everything that I saw at Fragnal became the routine steam world of Queen Victoria in years to come. I was most happy and contented looking at all this, until who should come in but Rowland, leaning on his stick and on Kershaw, who'd been ordered to keep out of the fight, because he was a precious expert that couldn't be risked. So Kershaw had followed along behind us with his sketchbook and pencils in a satchel over his shoulder, and come across Rowland, struggling along under his age and afflictions, and trying to keep up. Rowland looked grim: grey in the face and burdened with pain.

Kershaw didn't look himself, either. He'd been hugely affected by the sights and sounds of battle, even though he'd taken no part himself and had merely walked through the ruins afterwards. But he'd seen blood and dismemberment enough to change him forever. I didn't understand this at the time, but on reflection I supposed that he was a creature who'd run and jumped and battered men with his fists, and thought himself a bounding boy. But he'd never seen the damage done by powder and sharp steel, and now he had, and now he was changed, because actual killing – or even seeing it done – is a thing unlike anything else in life's experience. It can work dreadful effects on men, and so it did to him. He'd always been peculiar and now he was worse. These were my later thoughts, but now Rowland was speaking.

'Ah, Fletcher,' says he, 'there you are. I gather the English traitors have been secured within the Barracks building.'

'Yes,' says I, 'they have.'

'Indeed,' says he, 'But I have spoken to Captain Brady, and ordered that they be moved at once.' He paused, and studied my expression.

'Where are they going?' says I, 'Where will you put them?'

'The Barracks has a gunpowder magazine,' says he, 'I shall put them in there.'

Chapter 40

'Well, Captain Fletcher?' says Rowland, 'Have you nothing to say?' For the moment I hadn't, because I couldn't quite believe what my imagination was telling me. 'So,' says he, 'Nothing for the moment from our representative of the Sea Service?' He leaned against a bench, and detached himself from Kershaw, who was still trying to hold on to him, but was gazing round-eyed at the machine shop. Rowland had got his breath back now, and had more colour in his cheeks. He looked down upon Kershaw and smiled as if upon a pet dog. He just about refrained from patting his head.

'Now then, Mr Kershaw,' says Rowland, 'I think I can safely leave you to your sketching duties, because Captain Fletcher and I have matters to discuss.'

'Yessir, yessir,' says Kershaw, split between gazing with awe at Rowland, and gazing with awe at the machine shop. 'Will you be all right, Sir?' says he.

'Indeed I shall,' says Rowland, and ignored him thereafter. 'Shall we take a walk, Captain Fletcher?' says he.

'Yes,' says I, and out we went into the courtyard which was full of lively activity. The dead who were in one piece were being carried off for burial, while the bits of what were not whole men, were being shovelled into buckets. French muskets were being carried off to be put where the prisoners couldn't get them, should they break loose, and our horses were being brought up to the gates, and fed and watered, while food and drink was being prepared in a field kitchen for the men. Meanwhile other troopers were stacking timber and anything else that would burn, as if preparing for a bonfire. It was all very neat and proper, and Vasily Brady came up to Rowland and saluted.

'Everything is in hand as agreed, Mr Rowland,' says he.

'Good,' says Rowland, 'then for the avoidance of doubt,' he smiled, 'I'd be infinitely obliged, Captain Brady, if you'd repeat what we've agreed,' he turned to me, 'since it would inform Captain Fletcher of those details which were discussed,' he smiled again, 'while he was amusing himself with steam in the workshop.'

Vasily laughed.

'Yes, Sir,' says Vasily, looking at me, 'So! We shall evacuate all the prisoners, and confine them in a little village of wooden houses, outside the Barracks. It's some sort of living quarters for married people, according to the women.'

'Have you spoken to the women?' says I.

'Of course,' says he, 'they are most anxious to be re-united with their husbands.'

'Husbands?' says I, 'what husbands?'

'They are most of them married,' says Vasily, 'married to our English traitors.'

'Good God,' says I.

'Do go on, Captain Brady,' says Rowland, 'Captain Fletcher will confine his religious astonishment until you are finished.'

'Yes, Sir,' says Brady, 'We shall evacuate the women and the prisoners to be guarded inside the wooden houses and left behind as we retreat.'

'And the wounded,' says Rowland.

'Oh yes,' says Vasily, 'those also. Ours and the French. I fear that those of our men who cannot ride, will have to be left behind,' and he shrugged at sad necessity, 'as will some dozen others since we do not have enough fit horses to carry us all on a forced march.' I nodded. That was understandable, and the men of the 27th were soldiers in uniform, whom the Frogs would treat decently as prisoners of war. 'But we shall take the English traitors with us,' says Vasily, 'under strict guard, and for trial in England.' I looked at Rowland.

'You look puzzled, Captain Fletcher,' says he, 'Did you expect anything else?'

'We shall also take five of the French civilians with us,' says Rowland.

'What civilians?' says I.

'Not all those found in civilian clothes here, were Englishmen,' says Rowland. 'Some were French craftsmen being trained up in the art of steam. They are now so proficient as to be a danger to England, since their knowledge would enable the French to reproduce these works,' he waved a hand to encompass the Barracks and all within it, 'and therefore we shall carry them back to England as prisoners.'

'Is that allowed?' says I, 'Can we do that to civilians?'

'Whether or not we are allowed,' says Rowland, 'it is what we shall do.'

'Yes,' says Vasily, 'also, we have taken advantage of the large gunpowder magazine we have found here. It contains nearly fifty barrels of…,' but I interrupted.

'This magazine,' I looked at Rowland, 'Isn't it full of prisoners?' Vasily glanced at Rowland, and they both smiled.

'Yes, Captain,' says Vasily, 'But of course we shall soon remove the prisoners, and then we shall add French powder to the demolition charges we have brought with us, to effect a more complete destruction of the steam machinery,' he smiled. 'Boom!' says he, and he waved hands to mime an explosion. 'We shall place the gunpowder inside the steam workshop and the great engine,' we looked at the magnificent monster and nodded, 'Then we shall surround both with timber, and set fire to it as we leave, allowing the conflagration to ignite the gunpowder,' he paused and pointed. 'See?' says he, 'My men are stacking the timber even now, but we shall move the powder last of all.' Then he smiled, Rowland smiled, and I wondered if my imagination was too fevered.

'Captain Fletcher,' says Rowland, 'Since you performed such heroic feats during the recent action, and must surely be tired and have no duties at present,' I looked at him with suspicion, 'You have my permission to stand down, and get some victuals inside of yourself and perhaps take some sleep.' He pointed to the pots, kettles and other dining gear laid out on trestle tables in the courtyard. 'Your dinner awaits you, Sir!'

So I walked off and left the army to it. There was nothing else for me to do, so I did get some dinner inside myself, and took a nip of rum – a privilege of rank – and some vile tea brewed up in a cauldron, with too much sugar. At least it was wet and the rum helped.

I was indeed tired, and I dozed in a corner sat up against the wall, until Rowland roused me. I looked around. It was dusk: early evening with the sun dipping to the horizon. I looked up at Rowland, and at Kershaw who was standing beside him, grinning and chuckling as if at some joke, the little swab.

'Ah!' says Rowland, 'There you are again, Captain Fletcher. Taking your ease while so much else goes on around you. I should now be most infinitely obliged if you would get up and come with me.' He nodded in a business-like fashion, and Kershaw chuckled again. The little bugger looked fevered; un-naturally excited. So I got up and followed Rowland.

It was like my first meeting him aboard *Neptune* so many months ago, in that he strolled past sentries and guarded doors as if he were King George Himself, and the troopers of the 27th saluted him as he passed. He led on without a word into the Barracks block and down some flights of stairs and a long, dark corridor with candles here and there for light, and with dark arches on either side leading into more cellars, and a right angled turn in the corridor leading to a massive thick door with four troopers outside of it, who throw it open, and went in first with bayonets fixed to clear the way. It was the powder magazine.

That was obvious, because it had many features in common with the powder magazines aboard ship. Thus what we were entering, all deep below ground and made from heavy-squared masonry, was an ante-chamber – quite large – with a big, locked door on the far side of it, set beside a smaller door leading into a lamp-room whereby the magazine proper, which was beyond the locked door, could be illuminated through double-glazed windows by lights burning on the safe side. It was exactly the same with the magazines aboard ship because nobody takes a light into a powder magazine!

But that's not what I noticed first, because the ante-chamber was full of men: a group of miserable, downcast men in civilian clothes. I guessed that two of them were more of the McCloud brothers. They were tall men standing forward of the rest as if they were leaders. They looked just like Alasdair McCloud, who Rowland had shot dead – murdered in my opinion. The others had the look of tradesmen or mechanics and I realised that these were the English traitors, together with those of the Frogs who had learned enough about steam to earn themselves free passage back to England. All these men stood up and blinked at us as we entered, but they kept well back from the fixed bayonets, and none looked fierce or warlike. They were frightened and with every reason to be frightened. But Rowland bustled in all cheerful and charming.

'Stand easy gentlemen,' says he, 'this is merely an inspection and you have nothing to worry about.' Then he gabbled in French saying the same thing, I suppose. He was such a cunning, convincing bastard that they all relaxed and looked in relief. 'Take a good look round, 'Captain Fletcher,' says Rowland, and if you'd remove your shoes with their iron nails, together with any other ironware about your person, I would be grateful if you'd pass through into the powder room while there is still some daylight.

'I know the drill for a powder magazine!' says I, annoyed, and I did as he said: passing my shoes and some other bits and pieces to Kershaw, for want of anyone else. Then I put on a pair of felt slippers from a shelf by one of the doors. There were several pairs of these, for ready use. As I said, it was just like a magazine aboard ship.

'Key!' says Rowland, and one of the troopers handed him a key which he used to unlock the big door. 'Now be so good as to go through,' says he. So I did. There was another door beyond the big one, with copper hinges and fittings because copper strikes no sparks, and set into a timber-built wall. Then I was in among the powder barrels, and the door closed behind me, and there was light from the lamp room, and a light shaft at the far end, which led up to windows at ground level. I looked round. It was all very neat and organised: very French. There were shelves and tables with cartridge boxes, spare staves for powder casks and copper bands to go with them, and coils of slow-match and quick-match, as well as various pyrotechnics. I looked round again and went out as quick as could be. There was nothing more to see and powder magazines give me the horrors, because there's always a few loose grains about and it takes just tiny spark to set them off, and then God help us all. Aboard ship, only the Gunner has the keys to the magazine, and he's always chosen as the steadiest and most sober man aboard, because he's the only man aboard that can kill us all in a thundering ball of fire, and with just one mistake.

As I came out, Rowland closed the two doors and smiled. God how that bugger smiled! And beside him, Kershaw was fairly gibbering to himself about something. I looked at Kershaw and decided that he was one who should never be allowed within a mile of a powder magazine. By George I was right too, and didn't know just how right I was!

'Thank you, Captain Fletcher,' says Rowland, 'Thank you gentlemen,' says he to the rest, and then the same again in French. Then off he went, with Kershaw and me behind him – myself hauling on my shoes – and he led on up stairs and corridors to a room he'd taken over, and which had been an office. It had desks, papers, tables and chairs, and lots of cupboards. Rowland opened one of these, and brought out some candles which he lit from one stood already burning, because it was now dark, and he got out a bottle of something French that turned out to be brandy. 'Sit down, my good fellows,' says he, 'and will you take a glass, Captain?' I nodded, Kershaw muttered, and Rowland poured: One for each of us. Then he sat down and his manner changed entirely. The age fell off him, he fixed me with his eye and all the dominating, self-assured charisma of him focussed hard down on me. Even Kershaw fell silent after one look from Rowland.

'Now then Fletcher,' says he, 'let's get to cases.' I nodded. 'You've seen the magazine?'

'Yes,' says I.

'You've seen the light shaft at the back?'

'Yes.'

'Then that's how it shall be done.' He turned to Kershaw, who flinched as the great man's attention fell upon him.

'Show him!' says Rowland. Kershaw shivered with excitement and got up. He found another cupboard and took out a pair of bottles. They were full of something dark that was not wine, and had fuse-cords sticking out of the neck and wound around them. Kershaw put the bottles on the table, and looked at Rowland as if awaiting orders.

'Sit!' said Rowland, and Kershaw sat. 'Tell him what they are,' says Rowland. Kershaw stuttered out his words as if intoxicated.

'Grenades' he said, 'they's, they's, they's…full of powder and has fuses to be lit.' 'What?' says I.

'Grenades,' says Rowland, 'because Mr Kershaw made them to my orders with materials taken from the magazine on a previous visit. One would be sufficient, but two makes failure impossible,' he looked at Kershaw. 'Isn't that right?'

'Yessir,' says Kershaw.

'So the plan is, Captain Fletcher, to fuse these grenades with slow-match, then drop them down the light shaft and get ourselves well clear before the explosion. You will have noticed that while the light shaft is glazed at the upper end there is no glazing down at magazine level, thus we may pierce the upper glazing, and the grenades will pass right to the magazine floor, with perfect ease.' He smiled. 'And have no fear,' says he, 'that the bottles will smash on landing and therefore fail to explode, because the floor of the magazine is naked soil: very ancient, very dry, and very soft.' Finally he leaned back in satisfaction, and stroked the palms of his hands across the table, as if smoothing a cloth, 'So there you have it, Captain Fletcher,' says he, putting his head on one side in enquiry. 'And now that you have it, what shall you do with it?' I said nothing. I was never so taken aback in all my life, though I shouldn't have been. So I said nothing at all. 'I see,' said Rowland, and looked at Kershaw. 'You may go,' says Rowland, 'but leave the grenades, and be sure to close the door behind you.'

'Yessir.' says Kershaw, and he was gone and the door banged. Rowland watched him go, then quietly got up and snatched opened the door to check that Kershaw wasn't listening. He wasn't. Rowland smiled and shut the door, and came back and sat down. He got himself comfortable and spoke.

'You threw the dagger away, didn't you?' says he, 'You threw it over the side.'

'Yes,' says I, wondering which of my old crew had been his spy.

'But still I have hopes for you.'

'Do you?'

'And do you know why?'

'I don't care,' says I, 'you lying, deceiving bastard. You did murder that Alasdair McCloud, didn't you?

'Huh!' says he, as if it were nothing.

'And you told us that the prisoners – the steam traitors…,'

'Steam traitors?' says he, 'What a gift for words you have, Fletcher. Have you ever considered writing your memoirs?'

'You told us you were going to take them back to England for trial.'

'Of course,' says he, 'What else should I have said in front of witnesses?'

'But really you're planning to murder them!'

'No,' says he, 'I am planning to remove a deadly threat to our nation.'

'Bollocks!' says I, which he ignored completely.

'I shall remove this threat,' says he, 'in a tragic and ever-to-be-regretted accident: an accident involving gunpowder, which devilish substance is known by all the world to be dangerously un-predictable,' he nodded. 'And don't you just know that, Fletcher? You should have seen your face when you came out of that magazine! I've never seen such relief in a man's eyes.' That shut me up for an instant, such is a young man's vanity, but I came back on a fresh tack.

'If you blow that magazine,' says I, 'you'll not just murder those men, you'll destroy the entire Barracks with everyone in it: our men, the French prisoners, the women, the wounded…everyone!'

'Ah?' says he, 'So we turn from the moral to the practical? I congratulate your pragmatism, Fletcher, but I really do assure you that the magazine is so located that the entire blast would avoid the Barracks and everyone in it.'

'Would it?' says I, wondering.

'Yes!' says he, and I thought about that. He saw me hesitate and pressed on. 'Fletcher, why do you think I am telling you this?'

'What do I care?'

'Just listen,' says he, 'because I do not actually need you for this business. The man Kershaw is deranged. He is consumed with lust for revenge upon the McClouds.' He paused as if wondering whether to say more. Then he shrugged, 'And here's another secret for you, since you know so many already. Our Mr Kershaw doesn't know the difference between slow-match and quick-match. He thinks his grenades are fused with the former, allowing ten minutes to get clear when he drops his grenades down the shaft, whereas I gave him the latter, and the grenades will burst in seconds. Thus the business will be carried through with the entire certainty that Kershaw will tell nobody what he has done, and everything left neat and orderly.' He gave a satisfied little smile, as if he'd tidied the papers on his desk. And he wasn't done. 'Just believe me, Fletcher, Mr Kershaw will detonate that magazine, as ordered, on the stroke of midnight. He will do it and I don't need you to do it,' he paused again, as he came to his main point. 'But Kershaw is just a tool. He is a trained ape and I want something better. Do you understand?'

'No,' says I, 'I don't understand. What the hell are you getting at?'

'What I am getting at is you,' says he, and all the charm I'd seen in him before, came glowing out of his face, such that in that moment I liked him again, just as I'd liked him at first. That was Rowland. That was the man that he was. Perhaps he was an actor? Perhaps not? But I do believe that he meant every word of what he said next. 'I want you,' says he, 'I've followed your career. I've met you, I've judged you and I am convinced that you are a man exactly like myself. Thus I brought you on this raid principally to test you, and now I want you as my successor in this profession of mine: the profession that I learned from my own master sixty years ago, and that I want to pass on to you.' He spread his hands in emphasis, 'Look at me! I am old. I haven't much time, and in you I have found the ideal man.' Then: 'What's more,' says he, 'You're not just my equal, Fletcher. It is my fixed opinion that you will be better in my craft than I was myself in my prime, or even my master before me.' He paused and looked at me hard. 'So, Jacob Fletcher,' says he, 'What is your word in this matter?'

'What about getting me out of the Navy?' says I, uttering the first thought that came into my head. 'Isn't that what you promised?' But he just laughed.

'Is that really all that you want, Fletcher? Is that the limit of your desires? To be a tradesman selling cloth? Or sugar? Or kettles? Is that really you? The man of action who will not be bound by convention, or by law, or by anything…if it gets the job done?' he seized my arm and shook it, with his age-spotted hand that had no finger-tips, and he moved so close that his old man's breath whispered in my face, 'I am not the only man in this,' says he, 'a liaison of the great and good stands behind me, won by manoeuvres and politicking over the years and I shall name you formally as my successor. Indeed I have already advised them that you should follow after me. And then! Do you know the power you will wield? Dukes and Princes will fear you! Prime Ministers will kneel to you! You will be able to do anything,' he frowned at that, and carefully corrected himself. 'Anything that is right for our nation,' says he. And with that, he leaned back and was done. He just stared at me, awaiting my response.

And thus was I, Jacob Fletcher, personally tempted by Satan.

Chapter 41

'Such times we live in. The world gone mad. I did not know that an English milord could act like this, and I thank God that he was restrained by another Englishman because this is what the milord proposed...'
(Translated from a letter of September 13th 1796 from General Claud Bernard, at the Montfer Barracks, to Madame Aveline Bernard, the White House, Rue Orbec, La Chapelle Yvon.)

*

Sauvage knelt beside Bernard and shook him. He spoke softly.

'Wake up, my General!'

'What?' said Bernard, and was pleased to be dragged from a dream of shame and defeat until he awoke and remembered that shame and defeat were reality.

'Shhh!' said Sauvage, 'Come and listen.' Bernard sat up. He was in the Barracks lock-up where normally the defaulters were confined, but now it was crammed with the entire, surviving garrison. Men lay side by side in their greatcoats with shakos as pillows and tried to sleep. The big, whitewashed room stank of sweat and stale breath, and men shifted and coughed in the dark. 'Listen,' said Sauvage. Bernard listened and heard Englishmen arguing. There were two of them. They were outside the lock-up door. They were arguing in whispers.

Quietly, Bernard and Sauvage got up and stepped between the men laid on the floor. Then Bernard and Sauvage were at the door, which had an iron-barred grid in the middle, enabling jailors to keep a watch on the prisoners. There was no light inside the lock-up, but the corridor outside was lit with lanterns so Bernard and Sauvage could see everything outside, without themselves being visible to the two men facing each other outside the door, while beyond them stood the guard of English dragoons.

Bernard moved his head from side to side for a better view. There were four dragoons who obviously could not hear what the men outside the door were saying. Bernard looked at these two men. One was a huge figure: a young man in a blue uniform coat. Bernard recognised him as the man who'd stood beside Captain Brady, the officer who'd taken Bernard's surrender. The other was much older. He was tall and dressed in gentleman's clothes: obviously an English milord. The two men faced each other and hissed away in their ugly language, occasionally looking over their shoulders at the dragoons in the most furtive manner. They spoke softly but were in a passion of discord.

'Who are they?' whispered Bernard, 'What are they saying?'

'The big one is Captain Fletcher of the English Navy,' said Sauvage.

'Their damned Navy,' said Bernard. 'It's what we feared.'

'The other one is called Rowland,' said Sauvage. 'I don't know what rank he holds, but he's important. The guards all jumped when he spoke to them.'

'What are they saying?' said Bernard. Sauvage listened, and frowned.

'They're talking about the powder magazine.'

'What?'

'The magazine!'

'What are they saying?'

'I don't know. Let me listen.' Sauvage concentrated hard. He followed the English voices and couldn't believe what he was hearing.

*

So the Devil himself tempted me. It was a powerful temptation, but I didn't go over at the first push. I didn't then, and neither should you youngsters now: not when you're bargaining for something that you want. You must never take the first offer because that's not good business. So, as much as I was flattered by what Rowland had said, and vastly intrigued by what was on offer, I wanted to know exactly what I'd have to pay in order to get it.

'I don't believe you,' says I, 'And I want proof.'

'Proof?' says he, 'Proof of what?' He was taken off guard. He'd been spouting philosophy and expected the same from me. So he didn't know what I was asking. 'What do you mean by proof?' says he. I nodded. That was good. I'd knocked some of the bounce out of him.

'You say we can blow the magazine,' says I, 'and kill only the prisoners in it. But I want proof.'

'Ah!' says he, smiling, as he understood.

'So,' says I, 'let's you and I take a tour of this Barracks, so you can show me just what thickness of stone and bricks lies between the magazine and everything else.' Which is what we did. We went out past Kershaw, who was standing like a good boy well away from the door, and who genuflected as we passed.

'Get back in there,' says Rowland, to Kershaw. 'Guard the grenades and await orders.'

'Yessir,' says Kershaw.

So off we went, with few words exchanged, and I was surprised to find that there was some truth in what Rowland had been saying. Thus our improvised hospital, was on the front, courtyard-side of the Barracks, well away from the underground magazine which was built into ancient cellars that stuck out beneath the back of the building. Likewise the rooms where our troops were sleeping were at the front, and the Barracks was massively built, so maybe – just maybe – the explosion wouldn't kill the wounded and our men. But then we came to the rooms where the women were kept, which were far too close to the back of the building, and as for the French soldiers, they were locked into some sort of prison cell right at the back, so there was no pretending that they wouldn't be pulverised in the explosion.

We stood outside the door leading into the prison. The four guards saluted us, and Rowland dismissed them.

'Stand over there, my good fellows,' says he, pointing to a corner as far away from him and me as possible. 'Captain Fletcher and I have matters to discuss that are confidential, and privy to the King's service, God bless him!'

'God bless him!' says they and stood back, and I looked round. We were in first floor corridor with a nail-studded door leading to the prison. The door had a grill on it, but there were no lights inside and we couldn't see the prisoners. It was all quiet and I supposed they were asleep. I turned to Rowland, lowering my voice to a whisper.

'We're not more than twenty yards from the magazine,' says I, 'and if there's fifty barrels of powder in it and we explode it, we'll kill everyone in there.' I pointed at the prison, 'them and our guards, too.' Rowland responded with a deep sigh, and off we went into the most complicated discussion I ever had in all my life. And I would point out that the whole thing was conducted without the least sign of anger or acrimony from Rowland. He was just too clever for that, and whatever emotion was inside of him he kept it controlled, and just answered me word for word in a soft whisper.

'Fletcher,' says he, 'Men get killed in war. Many men. Those on the enemy's side, and those on our side.'

'That's war,' says I, 'this is murder!'

'No. It is saving our nation from invasion.'

There was much more and I can't remember all of it: just some of the outstanding bits.

'What about Pitt?' says I, 'the Prime Minister? You say that Prime Ministers kneel to you?'

'In effect, yes they do,' says he, which wasn't a straight answer.

'Then what happens,' says I, 'if Pitt finds out you've deliberately murdered dozens of men? Will he back you?' By George, but he blinked at that! I could see it. He said nothing but his eyes told me that he'd be on his own if Pitt found out, as confirmed by the fact that he instantly changed the subject.

'Fletcher,' says he, 'Reflect carefully. Think what I am offering you.'

'I've thought,' says I, 'and I don't like it.'

'Listen, Fletcher. Consider. A few deaths now to prevent thousands later?'

'I'll still not be part of it,' says I, 'And I'll not tell lies to protect you.'

'Are you proposing to betray me?

'I'm certainly not proposing to hang for you!'

'Then beware, Fletcher, because I take no prisoners.'

That was a threat. It was a clear threat and I should have paid more heed. He uttered more later and hinted that those behind him – his liaison of the powerful – would be seriously displeased if I didn't do as he asked. So perhaps I should have listened? Perhaps I should have been warned? But I didn't and I wasn't, and finally I read him the rule book and no mistake.

'Look here Rowland,' says I, 'Just get it into your head that I'm not going to be your bloody successor in your bloody craft, because I don't want it, I don't like it, and I'm bloody-well not going to do it. Do you bloody-well understand that?'

He fell silent and thought hard, and I suppose he came to a great moment inside of himself, though never a flicker of it showed on his face. He just stood back, and leaned on his stick, and panted with exertion, and stared at me a while. Then he shrugged and gave a beaming smile and came up with what sounded like a reasonable suggestion, couched in a reasonable manner.

'Now see here, Fletcher,' says he, 'You have made some good points, but I think you are mistaken,' he nodded as if to a friend, 'You are honestly mistaken, 'says he, 'but I think I can see the way clear of this impasse.'

'Mistaken about what?' says I, because I was nowhere near believing him. He smiled again, and put a hand on my shoulder.

'Come with me,' says he, 'It's better to show rather than tell, and I have the strongest feeling that there is something that will change your mind.' I thought about that and nodded. What harm could it do? He was old and feeble, I was young and strong and I had my sword and pistols. So I followed him and went down flights of stairs, and past guards and down the long corridor towards the underground magazine. He got me to pick up a lantern among those hanging on the walls and was friendly as could be. He stressed the opportunity he was offering, and led my thoughts down an interesting road.

'You'll find that women will admire you,' he said, 'it's the air of mystery that the craft brings,' then he looked me up and down and grinned, 'Though perhaps the women already admire you, Captain Fletcher? I know you've had your successes.'

'Hmmm,' says I, thinking that over as we went past dark arches leading into dark places. By God, I was being stupid. But his words made me think about the women in my life, starting with the most recent: Miss Sophia Maitland. It was a line of thought to occupy the mind of any man, and it occupied mine.

'Here we are,' says he, just before we reached the right-angled turn, leading to the outer door into the magazine. It was a place where we couldn't see the magazine door with its guards, and they couldn't see us. 'This one,' says he. 'It's in here.' It was an arch like the rest and there was utter darkness inside. I raised the lantern. I could see nothing other than stone flags and walls. 'It's further in,' says he, and started to lead the way, but his stick seemed to slip on the stone and he stumbled. 'Never mind!' says he, and smiled, and casually pushed me forward to lead the way. 'Go on,' says he. So in I went and raised the lantern again, and saw absolutely nothing. I was about to say so, when something whisked over my head, tightened with vicious strength around my throat, and I began to choke.

I kicked and struggled with all my might. I tried to get my fingers inside of whatever was crushing my windpipe. But it was too thin and too tight. I couldn't do it. So I rolled and wriggled and fought. But it was no good. I couldn't get free, nor could I shake off the weight on my back.

Well, my jolly boys, if ever you've wondered what it feels like to be hanged, then you've only to ask your Uncle Jacob, because he knows it because he's felt it, and it's appalling as your lungs heave and strain for air and can't get any. Beyond that, I even know what it's like to die, because the consciousness slowly left me and my hands dropped and I ceased to struggle, and everything went black except for angry coloured lights and the image of veins at the back of my eyes. And then there was nothing but black.

*

'What were they saying?' asked Bernard, when the two Englishmen went away.

'God in Heaven,' said Sauvage, 'they were arguing over how much of the Barracks would be destroyed if the magazine blew up!'

'Why should it blow up?'

'The milord wants to blow up the magazine, and the other one says it would kill everyone in the Barracks!'

'Why should they do that? Do they want to kill us all?'

'No! Not all of us. The milord wants to kill the Scottish-English. He's got them in the magazine. He wants to kill them!'

'Why?' said Bernard. 'Because they are traitors?'

'Yes!' the English are here to destroy all our steam works, and they want to kill the Scottish-English, and our trained men, too! That's why they've been put down in the magazine!'

'But that's monstrous,' said Bernard, his traditionalist soul shocked to its roots. To Bernard it was hideous that even the English should do such a thing. 'They can't do that,' he insisted, 'It's against all the laws of war. It's murder!'

'That's what the other one said: Captain Fletcher.'

'Then he's a good man. What did the milord say to that?'

'He said that it doesn't matter how many people they kill, because this would stop our plan for England. It would stop our steam-boats towing ships across La Manche.'

'Do they know about that?'

'Yes! The milord knows. He knows everything.'

'But what about the officer who took my surrender?' said Bernard. 'What was his name? Brady! Captain Brady. He was an honourable man. Does he know about blowing up the magazine?'

'I don't know,' said Sauvage. 'They didn't mention him. But Fletcher is a good man. He argued fiercely against doing it. He said it was murder. He said that over and over again.'

'Did he convince the milord?'

'I don't know,' said Sauvage, 'they went off to talk some more. The argument wasn't ended.' Bernard groaned and forced himself to think. What could be done? Would help arrive in time from Montfer? Would it arrive at all? He

274

looked into the darkness of the prison. There was no way out. No way to break the door. And even if they did break the door, there were four armed guards outside. 'Ah!' said Bernard. 'The guards ... Sauvage!'

'My General?'

'Call the guards! Tell them what's happening. If they are decent men, and their officer is a decent man, we can stop this. Call the guards!'

'Yes, my General!' Sauvage shouted through the grill. He grabbed at the iron grill and shouted.

'Here!' he said, in English, 'Messieurs the English! Over here! Over here! Over here!'

The corporal in charge of the guard heard the noise. He looked at his men. He picked up his carbine and walked over to the door.

'Shut your fucking gob, you fucking Frog!' he said, and smacked the butt of his carbine into Sauvage's fingers.

*

I woke up. Of course I did, or you'd not be reading this. I woke up, laid flat in the dark with pain all round my neck, and I struggled to get clear of the thing that had nearly killed me. It was a waxed cord like a ship's log-line: thin and strong. It was about three feet long with wooden toggles neatly fitted into worked eyes at either end. It was a garrotte. I felt it rather than saw it, and threw it away as if it had been a snake or a hideous spider. I shuddered and shuddered and was sick to the pit of my stomach because it's a nasty, dirty, hideous weapon. An expert garrotter explained it to me in later years. He was a follower of the Thuggee cult in India: the cult that garrotted travellers for the pleasure of their god. This beauty said that once you caught the victim round the neck, there was nothing he could do because his struggles only choked him faster, and all the killer had to do was hang on and it didn't even take much strength. He said that just before we strung him up for a hearty choke on his own behalf; and serve him right, too.

So that's what Rowland had in mind, and explains why a man of his infirmities was confidant of killing a man like me, and had nearly done it too. So I sat up, tried to stand, and put one hand on a dead body, and I shuddered and shuddered again. By God, it was an awful moment.

But then I did get up, and I staggered out from the utter blackness into the relative light of the corridor. There I leaned myself against a wall, and got back some of my strength, and anger filled me up. I was angry at my own stupidity in letting so dangerous a man lead me to my death, and I was angry with him. So I went back into the dark, and dragged him out just to make sure who it was, and yes of course it was Rowland, and yes of course he was dead. I looked down at him, and gave him a mighty kick just to make sure. But he was dead. According the what the doctors have since told me, he'd died from a stopped heart and had shown all the signs of it coming on: pains in the left arm and fighting for breath, such that any extreme of exercise might drop him dead. He was nearly eighty after all, but a master-craftsman when it came to strangling, and I've often wondered how many others he killed like that in his sixty years of service?

He left blood all over my collar where he'd broken the skin, and a fine white scar that I see every day when I shave, so I'll never forget him. And there you have it, my jolly boys. I'd been very, very stupid indeed, and was very, very lucky indeed because Rowland must have died just seconds before I nearly did, and no credit to me that I didn't.

'You bastard!' says I, standing in the corridor. I said that and more to his corpse, which did no good because he couldn't hear. But I realised why he'd wanted to kill me. He'd given up trying to persuade me, and needed me dead to keep his secrets. But he didn't want my body found and questions asked, so he'd brought me here where I'd be blown to atoms when the magazine went up. And he'd spoken so plausibly and I'd followed like an idiot and now I felt sick all over again. Then there was shouting from up above, and footsteps running, and more shouting, and the guards from the magazine came round the corner, and more dragoons came running from upstairs who – to my amazement – were led by a Frenchman: General Bernard, with Vasily Brody astern of him, and lots more dragoons. They were all running fit to bust.

They skidded to a halt by me, and Rowland's body. Bernard the Frenchman saw me and seized my hand, pumping it up and down in a frenzy and smiling, and finally throwing his arms round my neck and kissing me on both cheeks.

'Ugh!' says I and shook him off. He gabbled in French. Vasily translated.

'Monsieur the General thanks you,' says he.

'I can see that,' says I, and Bernard gabbled some more.

'He persuaded the guards to let him out, and to warn me,' says Vasily. 'They didn't listen at first, but he persisted.'

'Very good of him,' says I.

'Fletcher,' says Vasily, 'We must get everyone out of here! Everyone. We are evacuating the whole building and moving everyone out of the Barracks. Rowland is gone mad and is going to explode…,' but he didn't finish. 'Oh,' says he, looking down at Rowland's body.

'No!' says I, 'It's not Rowland you've got to worry about. It's Kershaw. He's under orders to drop bombs down the light shaft at midnight, into the magazine.' I felt for my watch, even though I hadn't got it, because you don't take a Spencer and Perkins gold watch into battle. But Brady had a tough one, fit for campaigning. He looked at it.

'Just past twenty-to-twelve!' says he. 'Twenty minutes to midnight'

'Then get men looking for Kershaw,' says I, 'and get men guarding the outside end of that light shaft. And get everyone out of the bloody building!'

The next minutes could have been mad chaos but Vasily rose to the occasion. So did Bernard. Thus the steam-men were let out of the magazine, and led upstairs and out into the yard. The French soldiers were brought out, so were the French women, and so were the wounded who could none of them walk, and each one had to be carried by at least two fit men, to get them out beyond the courtyard walls, and all this in the dark lit only by lanterns and flaring torches. Meanwhile, men were running everywhere trying to find Kershaw, and we made the nasty discovery that nobody could find the upper end of the magazine light shaft.

'What do you mean, you can't find it?' says Vasily to one of his lieutenants.

'It's all overgrown round the back, Sir,' says the lieutenant. 'The bushes are dense and we can't find the window in the dark.'

'Mon General,' says Vasily to Bernard, and asked him in French if he knew where the window was.

'Non,' says Bernard, and shrugged in deep apology.

'And it's ten minutes to twelve,' says Vasily, 'keep searching!'

'Yes, Sir!' says the lieutenant, and ran off. And that wasn't all we had to worry about, because, even though we heavily outnumbered the French, there were too few of us to get out the wounded, and guard all the prisoners in the dark, at night with so many opportunities for escape. So Vasily had a swift negotiation with General Bernard, in the courtyard, with men and beasts in action all round, and wheels rumbling, and our gun-carriage moving, and the first few of the wounded being carried out, and a large body of French soldiers clumped together, steadily moving towards the courtyard gates. They were scowling at the few dragoons in charge of them, and getting ready to take their chance, while our men cocked their carbines.

'Monsieur le General,' says Vasily to Bernard, and asked a question that ended in the word 'parole'. Bernard stood to attention and saluted.

'Monsieur le Capitaine,' says he, and gave an answer ending in the same word: parole!' Parole was a strict promise under the laws of war not to attempt escape. Vasily and Bernard believed in such things, so they shouted at their men, and soon it was Frogs and Rosbifs working together, carrying out the wounded, and shepherding the women, though these screamed on sight of the steam-men as they were led past, and women were running past the guards and embracing their men. There were tears as our dragoons tried to pull husbands and wives apart, and everyone stared, and the French soldiers roared in anger. As for myself, I'd put up with a lot from Rowland: a lot that I didn't like, and I didn't like what was going on now, especially because the women were all young and remarkably pretty and I'll stand no cruelty to such as them: not on my watch; not on your Uncle Jacob's.

'Belay that!' says I, in a great shout. 'Leave the women alone! Leave 'em alone so long as they get out of the yard.' Everyone looked at me, then the dragoons turned to Vasily who shrugged and nodded, and the women were allowed back into the arms of their English husbands. The Frog soldiers cheered, everyone got back to work, General Bernard beamed, and I stepped back for fear he'd attempt to kiss me again.

Then right in the middle of all this excellent work, and at five minutes to midnight by Vasily's watch, we found Kershaw.

Chapter 42

'Sir! Mr Brady, Sir?' A dragoon was yelling from the right-hand end of the Barracks block, 'We found Kershaw! He's round the back!'

'Good!' says Vasily and turned to his senior lieutenant, 'Be so good as to take command,' says he.

'Yes, Sir!'

'Keep everyone moving. Get them clear and safe.'

'Yes, Sir!'

'And you!' says he to another of them, 'Bring five men and follow me. And bring some torches.'

'Sir!' says he, and we were off; Vasily, me, the dragoons and General Bernard and another French officer who'd joined him and whose name was Sauvage. Round the block we went, with a man with a torch in front, and found ourselves in dense gorse bushes and deep shadows, and ourselves up to our elbows in foliage, and no sight whatsoever of Kershaw.

'Where is he?' says I.

'He is here, Sir,' says a dragoon, 'We saw him running. He's here all right.' And some dozen of us fumbled around, and those with torches held them up and failed to do any good. Then I had an idea. I got into some light, drew my pistols, cocked them, and held them up for all to see. Everyone nodded. Everyone cocked firearms.

'Kershaw!' says I in a great shout, 'You've been tricked. Rowland gave you quick-fuse, not slow-fuse. If you light those grenades you won't have time to run. You'll be killed in the blast.' Silence followed, silence except for the sounds of people and movement from the front of the Barracks.

'Kershaw,' says I, 'You'll be killed. You've been wickedly deceived.' Silence. I tried again. 'Rowland said you are a fool not to know quick-fuse from slow-fuse.' Silence. 'He said you were mad.' Silence. 'He said you were just a trained ape. Not a man at all.'

'He never did,' says a little voice in the dark, hard up against the block. Everyone trained their guns on the sound. It came from remarkably close to where I was standing, and it was Kershaw.

'He did,' says I, 'Rowland said you were a bloody madman, and he wanted you dead.'

'Never!'

'Yes he did, and he said your drawings were useless rubbish.'

"What? He never said that, neither. You're a soddin' liar you are!'

'Kershaw,' says I, 'I've got a letter here, signed by Rowland, saying that your drawings are technically inept and utterly useless.' There was a rustle in the bushes, I held my pistols behind my back, and Kershaw stood up not ten feet from me. He had a dark lantern in one hand, and a bottle-grenade in the other.

'You bleedin' liar,' says he, 'Just you show me that letter!' he opened the shutter of the dark lantern, light spilled out, and he raised his grenade so that the fuse was an inch from the flame. 'You show me that soddin' letter or I'll soddin' blow you up first of 'em all.'

'Here it is,' says I, and levelled my pistols and fired. I don't know if I hit him because all present let fly in a thundering volley and down went Kershaw. Instantly I dropped my pistols and ran forward, just in case he'd lit the fuse and just in case he was about to drop it down the shaft…and, oh, God Almighty the fuse was hissing, and oh, God, Almighty the grenade was rolling right next to the upper end of the hidden light shaft where Kershaw had levered open the window…and the grenade was going in…it was going in, it really was…and I grabbed at it and couldn't hold it, and it slipped and rolled … and oh, God, I missed again…and again…and then I got it and heaved it with all my might, and up it went and burst in the air like a skyrocket. Then everything was quiet other than the ringing in my ears.

Bernard fell upon me like an old grandpa with his favourite child. He threw his arms around me and kissed me, and I hadn't the strength to push him away. Then he chattered so furiously in French, that Vasily joined him in that same language and was chattering too. The other Frog, Sauvage, had more sense and spoke English.

'Monsieur the General, and Monsieur the Capitaine, they say, well done,' says he. All very nice, my jolly boys, but I said nothing. I was in quite an emotional state by then, as perhaps you might understand, since I'd been tempted by the Devil, garrotted, and nearly blown up all in the same night. So I don't remember much more, other than the fact that someone was kind enough to find me some rum, and give me back my pistols all cleaned and loaded, and got me into a quiet room with a bed.

I would have fallen asleep at once, but Vasily Brady appeared. He looked round to check nobody else was there, then stood dithered before speaking.

'Well?' says I, and unconsciously touched my neck where it hurt.

'Ah!' says he, seeing the gesture. 'Fletcher, can we agree how Rowland died?'

'What for?' says I, thick with exhaustion.

'Because we must,' says he.

'Why?' says I, 'the bastard dropped dead trying to strangle me, and that's all there is to it.' Vasily looked round all over again, just to check nobody was listening. 'Oh, get on with it man,' says I.

'Fletcher…,' says he, and sighed and fell silent.

'Oh for God's sake, man,' says I, 'Piss or put it away.'

'Fletcher, I know more of Rowland than you do.'

'Do you now?' says I, because that was a surprise.

'My mother the Countess, and my father Sir Edwin, both know him,' he corrected himself, 'or rather knew him. They knew him in high diplomacy. They knew him very well.'

'So?'

'Knowing their judgement of Rowland, I do promise you, Fletcher, that it would be better for both of us if we agree in our reports, simply that Rowland died of apoplexy.' By then I was very, very tired, and more than anything I wanted him to shut up and go away.

'Write what you damn-well please,' says I, 'and if nobody presses me, I'll say nothing at all.'

'Is that your promise?' says he.

'Yes, damn you.'

'Thank you, Fletcher,' says he, 'and my report of your own behaviour will be exemplary and glowing.'

'Ain't that nice,' says I, 'and now be so good as to bugger off.' So he did, and I fell asleep and stayed asleep until they waked me just before dawn. Then I dressed, got my sword and pistols on board of myself, and found that a decision was waiting for me.

'My men worked through the night,' says Vasily. We were in the courtyard again, with some of his officers, and with the two Frenchmen, Bernard and Sauvage, who were sticking by Vasily under parole. Vasily looked haggard, but so did everyone else. The 27th really had worked to great effect. 'We moved the powder,' says Vasily, 'and we finished stacking the timber,' I looked and saw. All it needed was a light to set it off, and blow everything to the skies when the flames found the gunpowder. 'And we got the prisoners and the women into the wooden village, and the wounded men, too.' Vasily's mouth went down, in an almost French expression, 'We lost five of the wounded. Their stitches parted when we moved them, and they bled. But it was that or leave them, and we thought the danger was real.'

'It was real,' says I, and he nodded.

'Also, two of the married couples have contrived to escape.'

'I see.'

'And now we have a problem,' says Vasily, and all his officers looked at me.

'Have you now?' says I.

'Would you come with me, Captain Fletcher,' says Vasily, all formal

'Of course, Captain Brady,' says I, and we walked out of the courtyard to where the horses were lined up, saddled and equipped. They were tethered in rows with a few men watching over them. Vasily walked forward and patted the neck of the nearest horse.

'The problem is, Captain Fletcher,' says he, 'that the mounts suffered heavily on the march here, and there are now too few to carry away all of my men.'

'Yes,' says I, 'We knew that already.'

'It comes down to arithmetic,' says Vasily. 'If we carry away the ten English steam-men and five of the Frenchmen, we shall be thirty horses short of those needed, and I shall have to leave behind thirty of my men, as well as those of the wounded who cannot ride.'

'So leave the steam-men and the Frenchmen,' says I.

'Ah!' says he, well pleased, 'Is that your opinion?'

'Yes,' says I, and his officers sighed with relief.

'Forgive me if I press you,' says Vasily, 'But you are the sole representative of the Sea Service. Thus your opinion may be sought at some future date.'

'So?' says I, and Vasily looked a little sheepish.

'I had some discussion with the late Mr Rowland,' says he.

'Did you now? And where is he incidentally?'

'We buried him,' says Vasily. 'Him and Kershaw.'

'Good riddance to the pair of them,' says I.

'Quite,' says Vasily, 'But when I spoke with Mr Rowland, it was his opinion that the steam engineers should not be left in France to carry on their work.'

He looked at me for comment, and I looked at him and wondered how deep in Rowland's confidence he'd been. But damn Rowland. He was dead.

'Well it ain't my opinion,' says I and out came a line of argument that had been brewing inside of me for some time. 'It's all rot,' says I, 'all this spying and back-stabbing. What matters in war is a nation's total strength: its iron and coal and 'factories, and its manpower and will. And as for secrets – steam or any other – there ain't no secrets once they've been used in battle, 'cos the other side always sees them and copies them!' I pointed back into the courtyard, 'Burn and blow up those works by all means, but do you think so clever a nation as France won't just build them again? Just as they'll build the canal locks again?' I turned to General Bernard, who'd been kept up with my flow by Sauvage.

'Ain't that so, General?' says I, 'Won't your people just build all this again?' Sauvage translated and Bernard stood up straight and spoke, full of pride in his country. His expression alone gave the answer. But Sauvage confirmed it.

'Monsieur the General, says yes,' says he.

'There you are then,' says I, 'leave the steam traitors to the French. Them and their wives, and certainly don't take French civilians because that just can't be right. Not under the Laws of War,' says I, touching on Vasily's beliefs. His and Bernard's, too.

'Non!' says Bernard, firmly, and that was that.

'I am immensely relieved,' says Vasily, but there was more to come. I could see it.

'Turning again to arithmetic,' says he, 'that means that I still have too few horses to carry away all of my men, and must leave fifteen of them behind.'

'So?' says I, with the nasty feeling I knew what was coming.

'I hope you will understand, Captain Fletcher, that my principal duties were to destroy the Fragnal works, and to bring away the detailed drawings of its machinery.'

'Go on,' says I.

'The destruction of the works is imminent, but it remains my duty to ensure safe delivery of Mr Kershaw's drawings.'

'And so?'

'And so, Captain Fletcher, honour dictates that my men should not be abandoned without a senior officer to stay with them, and to represent them opposite the enemy when they are made prisoners.'

'Honour dictates, does it?' says I, because I'd become so suspicious after dealing with Rowland that I looked into Vasily's pretty face to see if there was anything behind his words. But there wasn't, and General Bernard proved it. He stepped forward, bowed, and spoke in French. Then Sauvage translated.

'Monsieur the General agrees,' says he, 'Monsieur the General commends Captain Brady for his true statement of the situation,' Sauvage turned to me, 'and Monsieur the General promises Captain Fletcher that the General will act before the Revolutionary Authorities to ensure that Captain Fletcher is treated as an honourable enemy.' Then Bernard said something else. Sauvage looked surprised, but Bernard insisted, and Sauvage translated. 'Also, the General warns Captain Brady and Captain Fletcher, that word has been sent to the French garrison at Montfer, and that a relief column is on its way and will soon be here.' Sauvage and Bernard smiled at the way we jumped at those words, because it was a red hot poker up the beam ends.

Vasily gasped, then shouted orders, and after that everything happened at high speed, and all of it, incidentally, without any word from myself that I was going to stay behind. But I did. I stayed as atonement because I was fed up with the whole business: blowing up the locks, blowing up the beautiful engine and workshop, Rowland murdering Alasdair McCloud, and trying to murder me. All that and the sight of those two poor women at the lock-house, throwing their aprons over their faces in grief when Rowland told them that the lock-keeper was dead. That's stuck in my mind for ever.

So I stood beside Bernard and Sauvage, while Vasily and his men fairly jumped on their horses, and one of the lieutenants ran into the courtyard and set fire to the prepared timber stacks, and our men ran from the wooden village where the prisoners and the rest were locked in their houses. Then the fifteen who were to stay behind were chosen by lot, and marched at a miserable double to guard the wooden village.

Finally Vasily took his place at the head of his men, with his officers and trumpeter behind him, and he saluted me and Bernard, and we raised our hats in return. Then off they went with a jingle and a cloud of dust. It was an hour after dawn on Sunday the 11th, with good time for them to reach Lyommeville before noon on the 12th when the Navy would take everyone off the beach and depart for England. Soon they were gone, and I was left in the company of Bernard and Sauvage, and two dragoons who stood behind me as a personal escort. The rest were pacing up and down the wooden village, ready to shoot anyone who tried to break out. Meanwhile, the bonfires in the courtyard flared up, and the flames reached high.

'We should move back, Monsieur the Capitaine,' says Sauvage.

'Yes,' says I, and we did. We walked to the little settlement of wooden houses, and looked back as the flames and grew, until about half an hour after the fires had been started, there came two enormous and separate explosion. First the engine exploded and we saw its huge rocking-beam thrown high into the air. Then the workshop went up. What a bloody tragedy. What waste. We were clear of anything other than noise and a few bits of rubbish that fell among us, but the explosions were huge and it was obvious that if we'd done what Rowland wanted, then the loss of life in the Barracks – English as well as French – would have been dreadful.

After that, Bernard insisted that arrangements should be made for sanitation in the locked houses, which meant empty buckets going in through the windows, and unpleasantly full buckets coming out later for our men to empty. With only fifteen men on guard duty, it was fortunate that everyone knew what Bernard had said, that French troops were on their way, and all the French would soon be free and all the British prisoners. So the French rested easy, not troubling to escape.

Later I had some dinner with Bernard and Sauvage, all prepared by Sauvage himself since the French are good at cooking, and the wooden houses were stocked with food and drink. So we drew corks and got on rather well. Bernard in particular was a decent old stick, and a trained gunner: a technical man.

'You are in the Sea Service of your King, monsieur?' says he, via Sauvage, when we were sitting together after the meal.

'Yes,' says I.

'Then that is good,' says he, 'because in France, the gunners and the seamen always form alliance. We are natural friends. We two, and the engineers of course.'

'Well I'm damned,' says I, 'Do you know, it's exactly the same with us?' It was too, and ever was, and still is.

'Poof!' says Bernard, in contempt, 'What do these soldiers know? And the cavalry with their fancy uniforms?' I laughed aloud. I was astonished. It was like talking to brothers. So I raised my glass.

'Here's to the gunners and the Sea Service!' says I.

'The gunners and the Sea Service!' says Sauvage, while Bernard said the same in French, and it was all very cosy. It was fraternising with the enemy, but it was cosy and I suppose I was indiscreet. I told Sauvage and Bernard all about Lyommeville: how we'd blown the canal, and so on. I think I was apologising more than anything, and they listened and were kind – at least Bernard was – and thus I learned the only French I've ever remembered:

'Fortunes de la Guerre,' says Bernard, when I'd finished describing the ruin of the magnificent locks. 'Fortunes de la Guerre,' says he.

[Note that this is the only place in the Fletcher memoirs where a French expression is written correctly, and this by Fletcher's own command. S.P.]

Afterwards I went round by myself, to check that the men were at their duties and had likewise been fed. But there wasn't much to do because there was a sergeant in charge, who'd drawn up a duty roster to get us through the night.

'D'you suppose them Froggies'll be here in the morning, Sir?' says he.

'I shouldn't be surprised,' says I, 'This is their country after all, and we must be discovered fairly soon. Especially after the big explosions.'

'Yes, Sir,' says he, 'And do you think we'll be kept for long as prisoners?'

'Oh, no,' says I, 'We exchange prisoners regularly with the French. It's in their interest as much as ours.' That's what I told him, for the good of morale. But I didn't know. How could I? So I fell asleep that night thinking about it, and woke up thinking about it. Then I had some breakfast with Bernard and Sauvage, though I thought it best not to get too friendly with them, and went off on my own afterwards.

I looked at the smoking ruins of the Barracks. I looked at the countryside all round. I looked at the birds and trees and flowers. Finally I looked at the road along which Vasily Brody and his men had gone. I did that, and by George the misery of abandonment fell upon me. It was the bright and early morning, yet I was miserable. Even if I were prepared to desert the fifteen dragoons and had the best horse in the world, it was now too late to get to the Lyommeville beach before the Navy cleared off. I was doomed to imprisonment in France, which might be for years. That was assuming of course that the Revolutionary Frogs didn't turn nasty and refuse to accept me as the honourable enemy that General Bernard said I was. I wondered why he'd mentioned that? What did he know about the Revolutionaries that I didn't?

That was a nasty thought.

It weighed me down.

I had nightmares in daytime.

I saw a firing squad.

I was in a pit of despair.

And then something wonderful happened.

Chapter 42

I was sitting on the grass, with my arms round my knees and looking away from the Barracks and everything else. I was looking into the trees because a woodland brings powerful comfort to a man when he's depressed. So I didn't see Bernard and Sauvage approach, and I didn't hear them. I was wallowing in misery.

'Monsieur?' says Sauvage, 'Capitaine Fletcher?' I looked up. I got up. They both had serious looks on their faces. They were both frowning, as if under some sort of burden. I didn't like that. It looked bad.

'Gentlemen?' says I. Bernard nodded, and said something to Sauvage, who translated.

'Will you please come with us, Capitaine?'

'Why?' says I.

'Because we have something to show you.'

Well, my jolly boys you can easily imagine that I didn't like that. Not one little bit, considering what happened the last time someone took me to see something.

'And what might that be?' says I, and dropped my hand on to my sword hilt. They saw that and hesitated, and looked at each other.

'Pah!' says Bernard and rattled off at high speed to Sauvage, and the two of them gave that odd shrug that Frogs give, to express all sorts of things, and then they laughed, and Bernard spoke some more and Sauvage turned to me, and smiled.

'We apologise, Capitaine Fletcher, if we have given you cause to worry, and we assure you that you have nothing to fear and very much to gain,' and Bernard grinned and leaned forward and reached out and pinched my cheek, and said something that was obviously friendly, and looking at the cheerful face of him, I was reassured, so off we went

We went back to the collection of wooden houses, with the dragoons still on guard, and faces looking out of the windows. We went past one bigger building that was a church, and then to another which was some sort of barn. We stopped at the door, which was padlocked, and Bernard produced a key and undid the lock. Sauvage had a go at hauling open one of the two doors, and I joined in and hauled on the other.

'See!' says Sauvage, and waved a hand to bid me look inside. The barn stood against the early morning sun, and what with it being dark inside, I blinked at first, and then fairly staggered back at the most amazing thing I ever saw in all my life.

'Jesus Christ!' says I, and Bernard frowned, being a Catholic, but then he laughed, as I stood forward and stroked and caressed the amazing creation that was inside.

It was a locomotive steam engine. It was the full-sized, enormous, amazing, unbelievable reality that I'd played with back in England as a tiny model. It gleamed and shone, and was painted red, white, and blue, and the smoke stack reared up like a tree trunk, and the wheels were huge, and steely, and yet amazingly light. In fact the entire thing was huge, yet light. It had the look of a gentleman's racing carriage, but made in metal, not leather and wood. It wasn't some lumbering beast like the steam-rollers of later years. It was something of its own, the like of which was never seen before or since, and I gazed at it totally awestruck and I walked round and round, and there was not one direction from which I could look at it and not be amazed.

I could vaguely hear Bernard and Sauvage laughing in pleasure at my reaction. Then Bernard was patting my back and pointing. He was pointing at a brass ladder, whereby the commander of this beast could get up on its back to the levers and wheels that steered and controlled it. So up I went, my jolly boys, and stood at the helm, and gazed past the smoke stack, and out into the light, and all the world beyond. Then Bernard and Sauvage were calling me. I didn't really listen, but they were pointing, into the barn, behind the engine, and I gaped again, because there was a tender, just like the little ones I'd seen before, and a big, iron-wheeled wagon to be towed behind the locomotive for cargo, and both of them full sized, and ready for work.

Then I looked again, and a prickle of excitement began to replace the wonderment as I realised that these machines were indeed ready for work, because the tender was full of coal and its water-barrel was full of water: I checked that myself, because the filling cap on the barrel was exactly the same in full size as I'd seen in the models. So I stood and looked and my heart began to beat.

'Come down, monsieur!' says Sauvage. He'd been saying that for some while, and the pair of them were beckoning me and waving to get my attention. 'Come down, monsieur, we have things to say.' So I got down, and was led out into the light, and listened to what Bernard had to say. He spoke, Sauvage translated, and this is what he said:

'Capitaine Fletcher,' says he, 'First of all, we owe you lives. You found the man with the grenade. You alone found him, and you threw his bomb into the air, which would have exploded the magazine and killed us all.'

'Yes,' says I, because indeed I had, and there was no point being modest.

'And you would permit no miss-treatment of the women!' says Bernard.

'No,' says I, firmly, because I didn't then and I won't now. Not ever.

'And you are a man of honour!'

Well, my jolly boys, you can form your own opinions on that, but I thought it best to say yes. So I did. But there was more.

'You are a man of honour because you argued with milord Rowland who wanted to kill the Scottish-English and all the French.'

'Were you listening?' says I, and Bernard nodded and got very confidential. He put an arm round my shoulders and spoke to me like a father. He was well old enough for that, after all. He spoke quietly but with such feeling that I felt that I understood him through the fog of language, though of course Sauvage was giving it in English.

'I am sick of this whole business,' says Bernard, 'dealing with these Scottish-English traitors, and the constant need to keep them happy. And I am sick of the Revolution and what it does to men,' he leaned close, 'Thus I fear for your position, my boy.'

'What position?' says I.

'The authorities will be furiously angry with what you have done at Lyommeville and here,' he looked towards the ruined Barracks. 'They will be humiliated, so they will seek for scapegoats, and they will seek revenge. And so, my boy, they will seek revenge on you, if they catch you.'

'I see,' says I, recalling my thoughts of firing squads. 'Is that why you said you'd try to make them treat me as a prisoner of war?'

'Yes,' says he, 'But Sauvage and I have discussed the matter, and we think they won't listen to us. Do you understand?'

'Yes,' says I.

'So,' says Bernard, 'You must be on the beach at Lyommeville before noon today, yes?'

'Yes,' says I.

'And it is now about eight o'clock, and four hours before noon, yes?

289

'Yes.' Bernard smiled again.

'Listen, my boy, there is a good road from here to the canal, then another along the canal to Lyommeville, and the distance is one hundred kilometres.'

'Is it?' says I, because I didn't know a kilometre from a pound of tripe. But Bernard pointed at the locomotive.

'That machine, with its tender and wagon fully loaded, can move at over thirty kilometres per hour.'

'What's that in miles per hour?' says I.

'It doesn't matter,' says he, 'all that matters is that you can reach Lyommeville in about three hours, in time to be rescued by your Navy.' I could barely believe it. It was resurrection, it was salvation. It was joy and delight.

'We ask only one thing,' says Bernard.

'Yes?' says I.

'We ask that, should you be caught, then this conversation never happened, and you found the steam machine by yourself.'

'Of course,' says I, 'So how did it get here?'

'We put it here when we knew you were coming.' Bernard laughed, 'So you English could not find it!'

Then Bernard did the kissing on both cheeks again, and he shook my hand, and Sauvage just shook my hand.

'Good luck, monsieur,' says Sauvage, and Bernard said the same in French.

'Now we must be gone,' said Bernard, 'So remember your promise,' he looked at the engine. 'We had nothing to do with this.'

'You have my word,' says I.

'The word of an English Gentleman,' says Bernard, which made me blush. Then off they went and that was that. They went into the little house where we'd dined together, and closed the door and didn't come out again, and bless them both for two of the best friends I ever had. But then I was running and shouting, and getting my fifteen dragoons together, and using their brute strength to haul the machine out into the light, as they gawped and damned themselves in amazement, all round-eyed with surprise.

'Are we going in it?' says the sergeant.

'Yes,' says I, 'Now clap a hitch on your jaw and heave.'

We got it out, I climbed aboard, and then, thinking of the little model engines, I realised that the first job was to get a fire going, to bring the beast alive. Then I looked at the controls, which were not at all the same as in the model, and pondered a moment, before inspiration struck.

'Sergeant!' says I.

'Sir?'

'Go and find either or both of the McCloud brothers. They're in with the English prisoners. Bring 'em here, and tell 'em they've got nothing to worry about because I'm going to let them stay in France if that's what they want.'

'Sir!' says he, and off he went, and I lit a fire of small sticks in the furnace, and it was blazing nicely and I was shovelling small bits of coal over it, when the sergeant came back with two tall men, and dragoons prodding them with bayonets.

'None of that!' says I, and the dragoons fell back. I got down from the engine and looked at the McClouds. 'What are your names?' says I.

'James McCloud,' says one.

'Duncan McCloud,' says the other, looking fearful and suspicious, the pair of them, and I had the weary task of convincing them that I really was going to let them go, once they'd given me enough advice to get their machine running. They cheered up after that, and I think they were pleased to see the machine run, and I certainly wouldn't have done it without them.

'No, not like that, like this!' says they.

'Let it half-way open, and watch the regulator.'

'Gently! Gently! Ease it forward.'

'Swing the steering wheel hard round, and then the other way.'

'Don't let the safety valve get caught by the flywheel.'

It was all tremendously fascinating, but it took a long time to get the machine fired up, so I set the dragoons foraging for food and drink for the journey, even if it would be just a miraculous three hours. Also we man-handled the machine on to the branch road to the canal, with the tender and wagon behind, coupled up ready to go. That turned out to be the saving of us, because just as we got the machine fully steamed up, there came the distinct sound of horses approaching.

'Sir!' says the sergeant, 'Look!'

'Damnation!' says I. It was Bernard's relief column, come at last from Montfer. It was a substantial troop of cavalry coming from the opposite direction from the branch road. They were moving at a fair trot, with hoofs pounding, and some officer at the front waving a sword. 'Right!' says I, 'everyone aboard,' I looked at the two McCloud brothers. 'Last chance,' says I, 'Are you staying here, or coming with us?' They didn't even hesitate.

'We're French citizens now,' says the elder, 'We stay.'

'Well, bugger the pair of you then,' says I, because nobody likes a traitor.

Bernard certainly didn't, and neither did I. So I threw some levers, and left them standing, as the machine lurched forward, hissing and clanking, and gathering way, dropping water and ashes, while the tender and wagon clashed their couplings and the fifteen dragoons cheered in the wagon. 'Never mind bloody cheering!' says I, 'load ball cartridge, and stand by to repel boarders!'

'Yes, Sir!' says they and those that weren't already loaded, bit cartridge and rammed home.

Then it got nasty. The horsemen had seen the locomotive engine, and the smoke that it threw up. A bugle sounded, and they cantered. Another bugle call and they yelled out some sort of war-cry, and charged. The engine wasn't up to full speed, and they easily got alongside of us, and there was a blazing exchange of fire: pistols on their side, and carbines on ours, and most of it missing because everyone was bouncing up and down on bumpy grass, and couldn't take aim. But one of our men was shot clean dead, I got a bullet through my hat, three horses fell back wounded, and then the French drew swords and came on again.

They were hussars, with curved swords only good for slashing, while my dragoons were in a wagon with sides reaching up to a man's chest, giving protection against sword strokes, and the horsemen couldn't get close, not with the iron wagon-wheels sticking out on either side. Nor could they get a good cut at me, because the huge drive-wheels were on either side my station at the machine's controls. Indeed, not only could they not reach me but they had to take care not to get caught in the revolving spokes of the wheels. Worse still for them, the greater reach of the dragoons with carbine and bayonet, and the simpler motion of thrusting, gave advantage to our side, and the French fell back, giving my men time to reload. Then it really did become deadly for the horsemen to come near us, especially when we got on to the flat of the branch road and rolled along smoothly, because the dragoons could take proper aim. So they emptied some saddles and the horsemen dropped back still further till there was little they could do than follow, while the dragoons kept up steady fire astern of us, and cheered whenever someone got hit.

So I pressed the dragoon sergeant into service as a stoker, and concentrated on steering, and it was wind in the hair, water in the eyes, and all the beauty of steam under way, and the most wonderful exhilaration and excitement. I was no expert steam pilot, but what with my experience of the model and the McCloud's instruction I managed, and I forced the machine into its best top speed in my determination to reach Lyommeville before the Navy left. I don't know what speed it was, except that it wasn't fast enough to leave a galloping horse behind, but horses get tired and steam engines don't. So once we got on to the long road beside the canal, the cavalry troupe was left ever-further behind, and troubled us no more.

So we steamed along the canal side, and passed the lock house and the burned out steam-boat. We proceeded down the road to Lyommeville through the most empty parts of France, and those few people we met jumped clear and stared in amazement as we passed. The dragoons sat down in the wagon, with carbines between their knees. Food and drink was brought out, and the dragoons got up and pointed when we went by the bodies of horses that the 27th had ruined and shot. There were quite a few of those, and my sergeant-stoker didn't like it, and shook his head. But the miles flashed past and we thought we were safe home, and nothing more to worry about. Then just outside Lyommeville, the engine failed us.

I had driven it too hard. There's no doubt of that, because I've learned since that it had never been on so long a run as we'd just made. Or perhaps it had flaws of design? It was the first of its kind in all the world, so that was a possibility. But it began to rattle and shake, and steam began escaping from the riveted plates over the long, tubular bow. I told the sergeant to stop stoking, and then there was a great clanging of metal, as something broke inside, and I saw the safety valve drop down, and stick. It was not such a design as I ever saw in later years, and I suppose the McCloud brothers are culpable for that. But stuck it was, and I couldn't knock it free, and that was very bad.

'All hands stand by to jump!' says I, and clapped on the brake, and the dragoons all stood up in alarm. The brake didn't quite work, because the engine was still driving the wheels, and wouldn't answer the controls when I tried to stop it, so the brake merely slewed the locomotive round to one side with a great slither. Steam hissed out, still worse. The whole body of the engine shook. But the scraping and sliding, slowed us right down, and it was time to abandon ship. 'Follow me, men!' says I. So I jumped, we all jumped and we rolled, and got up. 'With me, lads!' says I and ran as far away from the engine as I could, and just before the boiler burst with a huge steam-cloud explosion that ripped the whole machine apart and laid it in ruins, which included the mangled remains of the dragoon who'd been shot.

It was a sad sight. But we had no time to stare. We had to press on and march – on foot – to Lyommeville, and past the horrible ruins of the lock staircase, and through the washed-out town, challenged by those of our sentries who were still on guard. It was a fine, cheerful sight to see the red coats, which proved that the Army was still in command of the town, and the Navy not yet left. So the sergeant formed up his men and they marched in step, with a bit of swagger and with carbines on their shoulders.

I soon left them to it, because I was seized upon by the office in command of the town: the same Brigadier General Lavery, whom I'd met on the beach when we landed. He knew all about where I'd been and what I'd done, because Vasily Brody and the 27th had arrived a few hours before, and Vasily had made a report with tremendous praise for myself. So thank you, Vasily. Consequently, while Lavery didn't quite turn out the band to play *See the Conquering Hero Comes*! I was greeted most warmly, and I got several glasses of wine in exchange for a lot of questions, with everything taken down in writing by Lavery's secretary. Both then, and later when the Navy wanted a written report of my actions, I took Vasily Brady's advice and never mentioned what Rowland was doing when he died. I did this partly because Vasily had spoken very well of me, but mainly because I didn't want the powerful men behind Rowland to know that he'd wanted me dead, in case they sent someone round to finish the job.

Then finally and with beaming smiles, I was given a horse so I could ride beside the General, whose duty it was to be last man off the beach as we withdrew, which manoeuvre was carried out neatly and nicely, in Navy style. The Coldstream Guards were taken off, the guns were taken off, the horses were taken off, and out to our squadron laid close insure. Finally, at precisely twelve noon, Brigadier Lavery was the last man off and I was the one before him. He was taken to the flagship, where a boat was provided to take me back to *Euphonides*.

And that was my part in The Great Raid, as it came to be known. Going aboard *Euphonides* was a joy. The tars gave three rousing cheers, Mr O'Flaherty was genuinely delighted, and the officers were pleased to see me including even Mr Pyne the First Lieutenant, because despite all the supposed secrecy, everyone knew what we'd been doing at Fragnal, everyone believed that we had saved England from invasion, and my adventures with bottle-grenades, were known throughout the Fleet.

It was a good end to a bad business, though it took me some days, and a lot of rest for these events to settle in my mind. The routine aboard *Euphonides* helped enormously: the steady succession of watches, the homely striking of the ship's bell, the feel of a magnificent ship under my feet, and the company of a fine body of men. I had good time to think, because we had foul weather and were some days getting back to Portsmouth, and in all that time I had little to do, because so great a lord as the Captain of a Royal Navy frigate, has no need to navigate his ship. All such is done by his minions, though I always took my noon observation and calculated ship's position for the pleasure of it.

By the time we anchored at Spithead, I was clear in my mind both of the past and the future. With Rowland gone I had no patron to get me out of the Navy. But if so, then the worst that could happen to me was to continue as Captain of the finest ship in the fleet, and that would do very nicely for the moment.

The one thing that I did not want, was to have anything more to do with such underhand, murdering, lying, back-stabbing association with spies and agents, as was practised by Rowland, and it was my fixed determination never, ever to do such work again. So that door was firmly closed.

Epilogue

(Transcript of a letter of Friday 25th November 1796 from the Duke of York, Commander in Chief of the British Army and second son of the King, to the Prime Minister, Mr William Pitt. No addresses appear on the letter.)

Dear Pitt,

I send this in advance, while my staff amass full documentation:
Agents of our ally, King Humboldo of Milan, have intercepted a message from Bonaparte to General Bernard. The message proves that Bonaparte –dismayed by The Great Raid –has abandoned further plans for machinations with steam. He heaps praise upon Bernard for his efforts and –incredibly in my view - agrees with an earlier report byBernard stressing the intolerable dishonour to France in making use of traitors. All such have therefore been dismissed by Bonaparte, with pensions to keep them silent. Thus these creatures are doubly fortunate in having escaped both Britannia's wrath and Bonaparte's.

Note that Bonaparte does not give up his plans for England but merely discards steam, while seeking other ways to leap the Channel. Given that, and the calamity of our losing Rowland, I am pleased to say that before his death Rowland advised me that his successor should be Captain Jacob Fletcher, whom he praises as a ruthless, ingenious and formidable young man. I concur, and recommend that in future, whenever we might wish for Rowland we should turn toFletcher.

I am, Sir, etc, etc,
York.